SHAY ELLIOTT
and Collected Short Stories

SHAY ELLIOTT
and Collected Short Stories

by
John Flanagan

authorHOUSE®

AuthorHouse™ LLC
1663 Liberty Drive
Bloomington, IN 47403
www.authorhouse.com
Phone: 1-800-839-8640

Certain characters in this work are historical figures, and certain
events portrayed did take place. However, this is a work of fiction.
All of the other characters, names, and events as well as all places,
incidents, organizations, and dialogue in this novel are either the
products of the author's imagination or are used fictitiously.

Published by AuthorHouse 04/24/2014

ISBN: 978-1-4969-0797-4 (sc)
ISBN: 978-1-4969-0759-2 (e)

Library of Congress Control Number: 2014910061

CONTENTS

To my dearest wife Hong Ren.

THE ALTAR BOY

by

JOHN FLANAGAN

"Now Son, make sure you practice the Latin on your way down to the Church. And look, you haven't finished polishing your shoes yet, and remember," said my mother with a final admonishment, "don't smile, you're on the altar of God."

I sat on the chair in my stocking feet, spit on my shoes and as I brushed them into a semblance of a shine I wondered why I let myself be talked into joining the Altar Society of the Pro-Cathedral in Marlborough Street. Dublin. The trouble started when Father Thackaberry came to my school to ask for volunteers to assist at the Mass and I put my hand up. I thought I'd get time off school to learn the Latin but found out too late I had to go to the Church on my own time. Most of my friends were already assisting at the Mass but until I learned the Latin I would be relegated to the role of candle bearer.

I left home at 7:30 P.M. to walk the short distance to the Pro-Cathedral, Dublin. An icy drizzle was coming down on this dark midwinter's night, drawing the tenements near and drenching the empty dismal Dublin streets. I pulled my collar up around my chin as the rain poured down my face. Everyone else was at home, cosy and comfortable around a warm fire. Well, the lucky ones at least.

It is unusually quiet in Parnell Street, apart from the wind and rain. The street traders deserted stalls were still out, the fruit, vegetables and fish under tarpaulin covers. The traders are all in there, in the snug of the Blue Lion pub or down at The Shakespeare pub seeking respite from the weather and the hard times. The sound of boisterous singing drifted out from the pub. At the age of 14 years I couldn't imagine how they could find pleasure in drinking for hours on end. I once heard a trader telling my mother that the reason she drank was to make the company of some, who would remain anonymous, more bearable. The world's worst bore after a drink, it would appear, could be made omniscient.

I turned left into Marlborough Street. A salubrious name of an English Duke for a ramshackle street with tottering Georgian tenements, pubs and pawnbrokers galore. Ahead of me is the protestant chapel. Rumour has it that if you ran around that pagan edifice three times you'd see the devil. At one time I ran around it twice and then went straight home, I saw no sense in tempting Providence. Suddenly I remembered the Latin and recited the little I knew;

> Ad deum qui laetificate juventutem maem
> quia tu es deus fortitudo mea quare me repulisti
> et quare tristas incedo dum affligate me inimicus
> et . . , et . . ,

I had forgotten again. I hadn't a bent for foreign languages. I crossed Cathal Brugha Street. Before me, under the enamelled, blue awning of Lyons Tea, sat the huddled, shapeless figures of the two winos, Jack the Boxer and Malachi the Poet. They were laughing hysterically as I passed them and when they raised their red-glazed eyes to look at me, I quickened my pace. They were in the throes of a delirium that made them impervious to the chilling rain and cold. Their emaciated faces were ablaze from the raging fire of the alcohol. Empty Red Biddy bottles lay scattered about their feet, drained of the magic elixir that had woven kaleidoscopes of wondrous images, until reality was suspended and happiness, however illusory, embraced them for a few fleeting moments. Jack had been a Garda Siochana and a heavyweight boxing contender. He was massively built with a great shock of sleek black hair. He was handsomely imposing in the way some men of the West are, being as many are descended from Spanish sailors washed ashore in Galway after the carnage of the Spanish Armada in 1588. It was said he was a dab hand at the Irish dancing and the floor would tremble when he got going in the Siege of Ennis. Great things were expected of him in the ring until the drink, an opponent he would never defeat, gained the upper hand and smote him down. Malachi had had his poems published in a national newspaper. He was thin and frail with sparse fair hair and a long delicate face. He had been brutalized since childhood by a drunken lout of a father. To add to his woes he was an epileptic but Jack seemed to know how to help him when he had a seizure. Malachi clung tenaciously to life and to his sanity by his fine intelligence and his love of poetry. And as timorous men seek strong friends, Malachi was drawn to Jack to lessen the burden of his private hell. I left the two winos as I found them, dispossessed orphans of the storm, unwitting players strutting their hour on the stage in the role of the damned. Fate, which we are taught is

JOHN FLANAGAN

the fulfilment of God's will, could as easily have cast them in the role of a King or a Merchant Prince with the most benign indifference. Tomorrow the grinning face of the piper will wake them, and the frenzied laughter of this night will be paid for in full.

Malachi once stopped me in the street and, quietly sober, told me that but for him, I wouldn't exist. He said his life negated mine and I was merely an image on the periphery of his vision, and if he had not been born to see me I wouldn't be here. He said our identity needed to be verified by others, because it was impossible to prove our existence to ourselves alone. It was all over my head but Malachi was a poet, so you had to make allowance.

I went up the steps of the Pro-Cathedral, went in and looked at the clock above the door. I had time to get confession before I got ready to assist at Benediction. In the pervasive silence I walked tiptoe past a row of old women wrapped in black shawls, all intently praying, some holding rosary beads. A few eyebrows rose with faint smiles of recognition as I was well known to the Parnell Street traders. I used to steal their apples and oranges, but when they offered me fruit without the asking, their generous hearts refined my callous instincts and I've been straight ever since. I genuflected, went over to my right and sat on a long seat outside the confessional. Before me a statue of the Blessed Virgin appeared to levitate over a pyre of penny candles. I looked up at the name over the confessional. A priest I don't know and I'm glad, I don't like confessing to the ones who know me.

Four penitents on my side, five opposite, all black-shawled street traders. Eyes staring into space, the lined sallow faces translucent in the dim light. Where do they go? To what lofty realm do their supplications and hopes soar and finally rest? Meditating on their transgressions against

4

the decrees of God and His Church. From this prelude of misery and despair they will leave the Church re-born in a state of grace, metamorphosed from sinner to divine, shining in the light of God's love. It's almost worth sinning. You'd miss a lot by being holy all the time.

Two to go, sliding sideways on this hard wooden bench, highly polished by countless generations of Dublin bottoms sliding to redemption. The door of the confessional opened, one out, one in. A quiet thankyou for the door held open. Now an indiscreet penitent inside the confession box is talking above the normal whisper. He is hard of hearing so he talks louder and I can hear everything he has been up. I feign piety and cover my face with my hands as if in prayer but it's only to stop myself smiling. My smile vanished as I saw an old woman sliding wearily on the seat opposite. I recognized Mrs. Mulvey, one of the Parnell Street traders. Emaciated and worn out, a black shawl covered her inclined head. If God ever visited crosses on anyone in this life He heaped them to excess on that unfortunate woman. She sold fish and had her stall near the Blue Lion pub in the snug of which she spent most of the day. She had steady customers who would take the fish, wrap it themselves and go in and pay her in the pub. She often sold a whole box of mackerel without leaving the Blue Lion. She raised 16 children in a two pair back in a tenement house in Gardiner Street. I never saw her looking so sad and unhappy as she did at that moment. She edged sideways again towards the confessional and came to rest in the lamplight that filtered in through the stained glass windows. The light illuminated her hands, fingers entwined. A rosary passed between a knurled finger and a thumb. Her hands like her face were of a deathly pallor, a wax-like patina of marble.

JOHN FLANAGAN

I went into the confessional and knelt down. A crucifix appeared out of the darkness as my eyes became accustomed to the gloom. A small wire mesh in front of a sliding panel. The panel slid across. The profile of an old head, white, weary and bowed. I whispered through the wire mesh.

"Bless me Father for I have sinned. It's a week since my last confession. I cursed and committed . . , eh, unholy actions."

"You must try to mend your ways, my son, and keep from bad influences. Remember the devil is always lying in wait. You must fight the forces of evil. How old are you, my son?"

"I'm fourteen, Father."

"Why were you cursing, my son?"

"I don't mean to Father; it just comes out all of a sudden."

"It's the devil getting hold of you. And what about the unholy acts?"

"I . . . I . . . eh . . ."

"Don't be shy in front of God, my son."

"I . . . eh . . . I kissed a girl Father."

"Why, my son?"

"I don't know, Father."

"Is there anything else?"

"No, Father."

"It's the devils work, no doubt about it. You are young and at the crossroads of your life. Seek recourse in the saints. Pray to Saint Jude, the saint of Hopeless Cases. He will come to your aid but only if you are holy and contrite in your heart. You must never see that girl again, for she will corrupt your soul for all eternity."

"Yes, Father."

"For your penance say three decades of the rosary and offer ten Hail Marys to Saint Jude. Now say the Act of Contrition."

6

I recited the final prayer for him. He leaned towards me before he closed over the panel.

"God bless you, my son. Remember me in your prayers."

I left the confessional and went over by the statue of Archbishop Murray and knelt down in the semi-darkness. The damp flagstones made my knees numb as I said my penance. I always kneel on the cold flagstones instead of the pews as someone told me I'd get more indulgences that way. Three decades of the rosary, I'll be here all night just for kissing Una. I lost count of the Hail Marys. When some altar boys passed me on the way to the vestry I cut my contrition short and followed them down the narrow steps to the changing room. A babble of excited chatter filled the room as Charlie the Sacristan handed me a black soutane and a white surplice. I put the soutane on and quickly buttoned it down. The surplice was crisp and starchy. I peeled the folds apart and pulled it over my head. Charlie asked me to recite the Latin but I was so nervous I couldn't remember it. He was very annoyed with me and said he wasn't sure I wanted to be an altar boy. My head was just too full of worldly affairs, Una for instance. After last minute instructions four of us went up to the vestry and picked up the Benediction candles. Charlie lit the candles while Father Thackaberry waited for us to precede him to the altar. I felt a tinge of nervousness as I went out to make my debut as a candle bearer in the Pro-Cathedral.

Charlie opened the door and our tiny procession wound its way through a packed congregation to the high altar. I was alright until I saw the holes in the socks of Noel Styles, the candle bearer in front of me. I had to suppress a smile that now threatened to spread across my face. You'd think his mother would darn the holes in his socks if he was going to peregrinate on the altar of God. We went up on the steps of the altar and took up our positions. The congregation stood and sang.

> O salutaris hostia
> quae coeli panis ostium
> bella premunt hostilia
> da robur fer auxilium.
> Amen.

Father Thackaberry opened the tabernacle, enthroned the Blessed Sacrament and began the reading. We turned and faced the congregation. It was Friday night, the nave, transepts and aisles were filled to capacity.

A priest, a big culchie with a rotund suety face, climbed awkwardly up to the pulpit. He rubbed his hands together and smiled benignly over a sea of wan faces. In a subdued voice the priest began his sermon by reminding the congregation of the timely remittance of their pledged dues. Punctuating his soothing tones with reassuring nods and smiles he expressed his regret that henceforth the names of recalcitrant payers of dues would be printed in the Church newsletter and read out in public. The fear was palpable in the many who stared at him open mouthed. A deathly silence and gasps of disbelief now fell over an already subdued congregation. The priest's thick country accent went up a few octaves as he warmed to his theme and in no time he had stopped smiling and was bellowing like a man possessed. With eyes bulging the priest directed his fiery rhetoric at the nave of the Church wherein sat societies destitute, all the street traders among them, cringing with guilt under the onslaught. In a fit of anger he thumped the pulpit with his huge fists. With a pointed forefinger he described an arc over the heads of the petrified congregation and expounded on the wages of sin and the hellfire to come. If he had an ounce of sense in his thick culchie head he'd know the largest part of his congregation was already living in hell, in rat-infested tenements with families of up to 16 living in two rooms. The jowls under his chin undulated like a turkey's wattle each time he moved his head. His suety face by this time was scarlet, as if scorched by the very flames he alluded to.

My wandering eyes fell on Una. She was looking straight at me, and smiling and whispering to two other girls. She was probably telling them about us, as if she wasn't the one who started it all. I couldn't take my eyes off her. She was wearing her red beret, the one she had on when she asked me to be her boyfriend. I said we were too young. She said Romeo's Juliet was also only 14 when she fell in love and how could I counter that even if I wanted to.

The incense rose in small grey clouds from the thurible, filling the Pro-Cathedral with its sickly sweet aroma. Father Thackaberry elevated the Host. We inclined our heads forward for a moment in adulation. The congregation rose to its feet and sang the second hymn.

> Tantum ergo sacramentum
> veneremur cernui
> et antiquum documentum
> novo cedat ritui
> prestat fides supplementum
> sensuum defectui. Amen.

I could never see Una or talk to her again under pain of mortal sin. Henceforth I would walk in the light of God's love and cast out Satan. From the pews she smiled at me again with those dark lustrous eyes that would lead a saint astray and already I feel my resolve weakening. O Saint Jude, Saint of Hopeless Cases, pray for me.

The careworn faces of the women at the altar rail, their beauty decimated by squalor and abusive husbands. They are nature's sweet bounty, orchids that can somehow survive even the compost heap of the Dublin tenements. Mrs Mulvey is among them and I was delighted to see her face lightened briefly by the euphoria of absolution. The Divine Praises begin.

> Blessed be God
> Blessed be His Holy Name
> Blessed be His Most Sacred Heart
> Blessed be the Most Holy Sacrament of the altar.

I think I'm going to have trouble with Una. I wish she wasn't so pretty. It's a test of faith. What am I going to do when she says hello? Saint Jude, help me not to think of her anymore. Father I am not worthy I should enter under your roof. Forgive me my trespasses. If I can't be holy and chaste here in the shadow of the tabernacle, what hope have I got on the outside. But I must try. Benediction was over. I left the altar with the other candle bearers as the last hymn was being sung.

> Adoremus in aeternum
> laudate eum omnes populi
> quoniam confirmeta est supernos
> misericordia ejus, et veritas domini
> manet in aeternum.
> Amen.

Inside the vestry again, we were all talkative and jubilant, and Father Thackaberry smiled indulgently at us all. I went down to the changing room where I carefully put away my soutane and surplice. By the time I had finished all the other altar boys had left. All the garments were strewn around the room. Would I become careless in time, how could that be possible? Something so full of infinite meaning as the Mass and Benediction could never be staled by custom or repetition. But they were like me once, starting, awed and in wonder, reverential. No it would not happen to me. I looked at the clock. 9:00 P.M. A desultory chime of a pendulum striking the hour, echoed eerily through the damp gothic cell beneath the Pro-Cathedral. I put out the light and walked up the stairs. The Church was empty. A bolt slammed noisily into place as Charlie, the sacristan, locked up for the night. I knelt for a moment in the last pew and fervently joined my hands. I will go forward in Your light. This embracing love of God that elevates and lightens the soul. Tomorrow I will talk to Father Thackaberry about some things that have bothered me of late. Maybe he can explain to me why God is so angry and unforgiving of human frailty since, Him being God, He knows in advance how everyone is going to behave? I watched as Charlie walked up the steps of the altar and extinguished the candles. Thin wisps of white smoke spiral upwards as he moved from one candle to another. I blessed myself, genuflected and went out into the cold night air.

The storm had passed and the rain had stopped. The air, washed clean, was fresh and invigorating. Above me a galaxy of brilliant stars shone like finely cut diamonds against the purple velvet of the night sky. Suddenly a girl's voice rang out in the clear air.

"Give me my Romeo, and, when he shall die
take him, and cut him out in little stars,
and he will make the face of heaven so fine,
that all the world will be in love with night
and pay no worship to the garish sun."

It was Una, and I was not surprised, as she was a member of her school drama society. She had a better memory for Shakespeare than I had for Latin. She had been waiting for me, sitting on her bicycle. My confessor's words were ringing in my ears. You must never see or speak to her again under pain of mortal sin. Even so I couldn't suppress how good I felt at seeing her. I conceded a weak smile, having regard for the state of grace I was in.

"Hello Una," I said, "what are you doing out here in the cold?" As if I didn't know, I thought to myself.

"Ah sure," she said, "I thought it would be nice to walk with you."

Those eyes in the dark, inviting and mischievous. I walked along the edge of the footpath as she cycled on the road with her hand on my shoulder. She was cheerful and talkative. At Lyons Tea the twisted forms of Jack and Malachi kicked and moaned as they tried to sleep. Their atonement has begun.

"God help them," said Una, looking at them with a mixture of fear and pity.

"He will," I said in my innocence.

At Cathal Brugha Street I said I would walk her home as it was getting late. But she said no, she would be home in minutes on her bicycle. We stopped under a lamplight. Her eyes probed mine.

"Do you want to see me again?" She asked.

"Sure Una," I said in a holier-than-thou manner and I made a move to extricate myself from her. Still seated on her bicycle she tightened her arm around my shoulder and pulled me closer to her. She brazenly stuck her button of a nose under mine.

"Kiss me," she demanded, with all the vampish arrogance of Circe enticing a subdued Ulysses. She smiled triumphantly when she saw my moment's hesitation. I tried to give her a quick peck but she would have none of it and locked me to her lips. There. It was done. And gone was my state of grace. I stood on the footpath and watched as my sorceress cycled away. The old and worn Georgian tenements seemed to cringe back as she sped through them, exuberant in her joy of well-being. When she was almost out of sight she turned and waved to me with a smile lighting up her lovely face. And I know, as sure as the sun will rise tomorrow, I will soon be back in the confession box again.

THE END

THE ARYAN AGENDA

by

JOHN FLANAGAN

IN THE FLAT EURE ET Loire region, in Normandy, France, close to the market town of Ivry la Bataille, retired Army Captain Marc Claudel was pottering about in the garden shed of his cottage. His wife Solonge had left him alone since early morning; he had a lot on his mind and needed some time to think. She knew he had received a telephone call from the Surete Headquarters in Paris and she felt uneasy, hoping another dangerous assignment was not imminent.

Claudel had retired from the Army some years before, having spent much of his career with Military Intelligence at the Ecole Militaire in Paris. Later he was sequestered to work with the Surete in matters involving national security. They still called on him although he had officially hung up his hat. One local police officer, Inspector Oliver Brunet stationed at the nearby town of Evreux provided back-up and assisted Claudel in his role as a special investigator for the French government. Sologne knew of the double life of her husband. He made light of the dangers involved in his work and would often catch her off guard with jokes and mischief when he saw her taking life too seriously. When he did so he reminded her of her father, Umar, who, despite his reputation for ruthlessness in the boardroom, was a childish prankster in the family home in Damascus in Syria. Claudel and his wife were avid botanists. They grew prize roses, attended flower shows and generally led quiet unobtrusive lives.

Claudel finally emerged from the shed and prepared to keep an 11:00 AM appointment in Paris. Two days earlier Chief inspector Andre Prejean of the Surete had telephoned and asked him to come to his office. As usual Prejean had given no hint as to the reason for the request. He had sounded terse and abrupt which was unusual for the two men had become good friends in the course of many cases they worked on over the years. When he was ready to leave he kissed Solonge goodbye and went out to his car. She walked out to the gate of the cottage and waved as he sped away.

The drive to Paris was enjoyable on the pleasant June morning. When he reached Versailles, the Friday build-up of traffic entering and leaving Paris had already begun. He crossed the Bois de Boulogne and was soon turning right onto Rue Grande Armee. Within a half hour he parked the car in Rue Saint Roch and walked across the Rue de Rivoli to the Jardin des Tuileries. When he entered the gardens he saw Chief Inspector Prejean in the distance and wondered why they should be meeting here instead of his office. When he reached him they shook hands and sat down on a nearby seat. Neither man spoke for a few seconds. The gardens were ablaze with color and light, the exotic flowers and plants blossoming in an early summer; spray from water sprinklers made dancing beads of light in the brilliant sunshine. Children were everywhere frolicking about, yelling excitedly. It was a relaxing scene, light years away from the thoughts that filled the minds of both men. Claudel didn't know what was coming as he looked sideways at the Chief Inspector, only that it was serious enough to etch a furrowed crease into his brow. Prejean turned to him.

"Marc, did I ever tell you how much I love France ?"

"Many times Andre."

"You know the very thought of France makes me emotional. I can't bear to be away from her for very long. Last year my family forced me to take them to Spain for a vacation. I felt like a child who had been torn away from its mother, miserable all the time. When I got back on French soil I was so happy I wanted to kiss the ground."

"What's on your mind Andre?"

"Look at those kids. Happy and carefree. How could they begin to understand the sacrifices of French lives so they can laugh and play like that?"

"Not just the kids Andre, all of us owe something."

"Freedom is like those long stemmed tulips over there, delicate and fragile. They'd wither without the watchful eye of the gardener." He paused for a moment and turned to Claudel. "You haven't the faintest idea why I asked you to meet me, have you Marc?" "I can only suppose it's something very serious."

"Let's walk awhile shall we? It's such a treat to get out of the office on such a beautiful day."

They strolled and stopped occasionally to savor the floral fragrances on the warm air. As they passed a bench seat Claudel touched Prejean on the arm.

"Andre, let's sit here for a moment."

"Of course," Prejean smiled, "are you tired already from our little walk? You are getting soft since you retired, my friend. That lovely wife of yours is feeding you too well . . . ," He stopped smiling when he turned and looked at Claudel's grave face.

"Andre," said Claudel slowly, "Do you know we are being followed?"

"What?"

"Don't look around. Just past my shoulder you'll see some people around an ice cream vendor. There's one guy there, off to the side. He's wearing a blue denim jacket. See him?"

"Yes, he just sat down."

"Do you know him?"

"No, no . . , but he could be connected to the reason I asked you to come to Paris."

"He looks like a nasty piece of work. Do you have a cell phone?"

Prejean patted his suit jacket and nodded his head.

"Call your office. Have a couple of your men come and pick him up. Tell them to be careful."

After Prejean made the telephone call, they resumed strolling about the gardens for the next twenty minutes. On reaching the end of the garden path they turned and retraced their steps slowly. Thirty metres away the man in the denim jacket stopped in his tracks and quickly brought a newspaper up to his face. As if something clicked in his mind he lowered the newspaper and looked about him. Two plain clothes police officers were closing in on him. He dropped the newspaper and made a run for it. After a brief chase and a struggle the officers were handcuffing him when Prejean and Claudel arrived.

"Good work," said Prejean to the officers. "Take him to headquarters. I'll join you there later."

Henry Wilkins was sitting at a table in a room on the second floor of headquarters building of Surete National de France. A background check had revealed that he was English, a window cleaner by trade. A telephone call to

Scotland Yard unearthed a record of several prison terms for offences ranging from burglary to soccer hooliganism and one for wife beating. Details were not forthcoming about how Wilkins had ended up in France with a French passport. When Prejean and Claudel entered the room and confronted him he scowled and chewed on a thumbnail. Wilkins' French was redolent with a thick cockney accent.

"Why was I nicked? You got no right to pick me up like that. I was minding me own business, not bothering nobody. I'm a French citizen I am, I got me rights."

"Relax, take it easy. You're free to go." said Prejean.

Wilkins stared at him suspiciously.

"Say, what is this? You mean I can just walk out of 'ere?"

"That's right. Now you better go before I change my mind."

Wilkins got noisily to his feet, pushing the chair back behind him. His thin lips broke into a humourless grin which changed just as suddenly when Prejean took a menacing step towards him. Wilkins hurried out of the room. Prejean returned to his office with Claudel.

"Well Andre, maybe now you'll tell me what's going on. Why is a lowlife like that following you around?"

"Have a seat Marc." They sat down facing each other. "Have you heard of the Aryans?"

"Of course. Right-wing fascists weren't they? They created quite a stir in the 60's and 70's. But they've been out of the news . . ."

"But by no means have they disappeared. As a matter of fact, they are more dangerous now than ever. Do you remember how it was before? Gangs running riot in London and Berlin, here in Paris."

"Just how strong are they now?"

"The Aryans are especially strong in the United States, Canada, Europe. Just about anywhere there are large concentrations of minorities. When the Aryans first went public, they were seen as a lunatic fringe, and the public was contemptuous of them. Then the skinheads were invented, a gang of social misfits somewhat like our Henry there. When they started marching behind swastika banners the French public became outraged and the Aryans went to ground. We hoped it was the end of them but . . ." Prejean shook his head, "a link was discovered between certain of our present government ministers, right wing newspaper owners, some wealthy businessmen and the Aryans. They have learned from mistakes of the past, they will be smarter this time in smoothing over public fears about their aims and agendas. Some of the oldest families in France have become members of the group. Right under my very nose and I didn't know a thing about it . . ."

"How did you find out?" asked Claudel.

"Purely by accident. One of my men was at a wedding party. There was a lot of drink flowing and he overheard some loose talk. By the end of the day he was able to piece together what I've just told you. The drunk he was talking to was suddenly bundled out of the hotel by two heavies in business suits." Prejean got up from the desk and walked to the window. He looked down at the street below. "That agent was one of the best . . ."

"Was?" queried Claudel.

Prejean sat back down at his desk and nodded his head.

"Two weeks ago he was found dead in his car. He had a bullet in his head from his own gun . . ."

"Did he . . ?"

"Suicide? Not a chance. He had a happy home life, nice wife, his kids adored him and he'd just been promoted. No, he was executed by an expert who made it look like suicide. I guess you must know by now Marc, this is the reason I sent for you. I want you to take over this investigation."

Claudel nodded.

"Where does Wilkins come into this, why was he following you?"

"Since I've re-opened the file on the Aryans activities . . . it's, well, by putting Wilkins on me they're letting me know they can get to me, anytime they want . . ."

"Correct me if I'm wrong but you have the entire gendarmerie of Paris at your disposal. Why not bring in some of the leaders, question them?"

"On what grounds? The law protects them. Not one racist incident has been connected to the Aryans over the past five years."

There was a knock on the door. Prejean's secretary entered carrying a tray with coffee and biscuits. She put the tray on the table and left. Prejean poured the coffee and handed a cup to Claudel and took one himself.

"What do they want to accomplish in France?" asked Claudel.

"The same as in every other country, political clout. Marc, we've been friends for some years now . . , you know that I am a Jew?"

"Of course. Is that the reason they're targeting you?"

"It's one of the reasons." He went to a filing cabinet and took out a manila folder. He handed it to Claudel.

"That's the latest incident we've had. As you see it's out in your neck of the woods, in the village of Dreux. Three nights ago the home of an Algerian family was razed to the ground. They owned a small filling station and lived over the garage. The petrol pumps were set on fire. There was an explosion and the whole garage collapsed. It was a miracle the parents escaped with just minor injuries. The two children fared worse but they'll pull through alright. They are all in a hospital in Evreux."

"I remember seeing a report of it in the local news."

"If we could prove this is the work of the Aryans I could start making some arrests. Marc, I'm not happy about having to ask your help in this matter. Just be careful. You know men like Henry Wilkins are as sadistic and insane as the Gestapo were, that's who they fashion themselves on . . ."

"When do you want me to start?"

"Right away," they shook hands, "I'd like you to begin with the bombing in Dreux. You'll be working again with Inspector Brunet of Evreux. I'll send him all the information we've come up with. We'll be pulling rank on the Evreux police and taking over the investigation. It's too big for them to handle with their limited resources."

After dinner that night Claudel and his wife sat on the sofa and watched television. She attributed his unusual quietness to the fatigue of travelling to Paris and back, she dared not assume anything worse. His head was on her lap with his feet stretched out over the arm of the sofa. She ran her fingers slowly through his hair.

"Something is on your mind, do you want to tell me?" She said.

"Do you recall that news report about the fire in Dreux, a garage was burned down . . . ?"

"Why yes, I remember that . . ," she suddenly went tense, "was that why you went to Paris?"

He nodded.

"I'll be working with Inspector Brunet again."

"Why you, can't they get someone else?"

He sat up and turned to face her. He said nothing for a few moments. He took her hands in his.

"They believe the house was burned down by a racist group called the Aryans. They're dangerous people. My dear, until this clears up . . ."

"Don't say it; please don't say it . . , not again . . ."

"I must. I want you to stay with your parents for a while."

She withdrew her hands from his. Her mouth closed tight as tears filled her eyes. He moved closer and embraced her.

"Don't send me away," she pleaded, "this is my home, and my place is with you. How can you send me away from you?"

"These people already know I'm involved in the investigation. They are very resourceful, I'm sure they know where we live. They may attack us here in the house."

She buried her face in her hands, fighting back the tears.

"When do you want me to go?"

"Right away . . ."

She drew back from him, resigned, drying her eyes.

"For how long?"

"I don't know. I'll call you every day . . ."

"I'll go. It will be so lonely there without you."

Early the following morning Claudel watched as the Boeing 747 aircraft lifted from the runway at Charles de Gaulle airport in Paris. She would be in Damascus in a few hours in the safety of her parent's home. He went to a telephone booth in the airport lounge and put a call through to Inspector Brunet.

Two days later Claudel and the Inspector were sifting through the wreckage of the burnt out filling station in the village of Dreux. Claudel was exasperated. Around the clock probing by experts had given him nothing to work on. Inspector Brunet was muttering aloud as he kicked over a pile of rubble.

"The owner and his family are French citizens. They are also devout Muslims. They go to their mosque every Friday and give to charity. They pay their taxes and get along well with their neighbours. What madness is this . . . ?"

Claudel was brusque and tight lipped as he looked about him.

"Are your men finished here?"

"Just about." The Inspector called out to one of the detectives probing the site. "How are we doing Gerard?"

"We've gone about as far as we can go here Inspector. We can wrap it up today."

"We haven't much to go on," the Inspector said to Claudel "two men on a motorcycle were seen speeding through the village at two o'clock in the morning. That's all there is . . ."

That evening Claudel and the Inspector sat over coffee in the foyer of the Hotel de la Gare in Evreux. The foyer was dimly lit with recessed cubicles that accorded just the degree of privacy the two men needed. The Inspector was glad the investigation enabled him not only the chance to work with Claudel but it was one of those rare occasions when he could forego his uniform and wear plain clothes. He was smartly dressed in a double-breasted suit and a pearl tiepin gave him a dapper, if dated look. Claudel appeared dour by comparison in his casual attire. The Inspector coughed and cleared his throat.

"Monsieur Claudel, do you remember the case we worked on about a year ago. All those precious paintings buried in a field out in Saint Andre?"

"How can I forget that? It got pretty risky at times."

"But you know, even though it was dangerous I wasn't really scared. What really scares me are these Aryans. Wanting to kill people because of their race or the color of their skin."

"They are fascists, it's what they do."

"Have you a plan Monsieur?"

"No, not really. There's nothing for it but for me to jump into the lion's mouth. The chief told me you had the name of a member of the Aryans."

"Ah yes," said the Inspector, digging into his pocket and bringing out a notebook, "his name is Seamus Lowry."

"What . . ?" said Claudel suddenly.

"Pardon Monsieur?"

"Oh it's nothing. I used to know someone of the same name. Please go on . . ."

"Seamus Lowry. Semi-retired, he's a Professor Emeritus at the Sorbonne . . ."

"It can't be, it can't be him. Not Professor Lowry. There must be some mistake."

"Do you know this man?"

"I know him very well. I was one of his pupils for many years. Are you sure about this? It's over 20 years since I went to the University but I remember him so well."

"And you had no idea of his political leaning?"

"Inspector, I'm telling you, it's not possible that the man whose classes I attended could be part of the Aryans. He would be about 60 years old now. He was kind, witty, a lovable rogue with a mischievous sense of humour. He came all the way from Connemara in Ireland with a rich Irish brogue. When he spoke French with that accent of his he made music of the language. The students loved him. He taught History and Anthropology, always as I remember, to full classrooms."

Inspector Brunet finished off his coffee and put the cup down thoughtfully.

"Well Monsieur, all I can say is someone must have got to him. This man is now writing propaganda for the Aryans. I got this from the chief himself; Professor Seamus Lowry is a member of the Aryan Guard."

Claudel drove to the Sorbonne University in Paris the following day. He had been able to find out that Professor Lowry was scheduled to give a lecture in the afternoon.

When he arrived at the university the hallowed old halls and campus brought back memories of his student years when he seemed to be perpetually hungry. He had a room in those days with a slanted floor and a tiny skylight over a butchers shop in the Rue des Ecoles. He remembered the earnest shining faces of his fellow students huddled over cups of coffee discussing Sartre and existentialism; the trilling laughter of the women resounding through the narrow streets.

He ascended a staircase leading to the lecture hall. When he pushed open the door the packed hall was in semi-darkness as he sat down behind the students. Professor Lowry was standing at a podium a few feet back from the front of the stage, his head inclined over material he was reading. Claudel looked at his watch. The lecture should soon be coming to an end soon. The Professor had not changed greatly since he saw him last, all those years ago. He had less hair, he wore glasses now and seemed less tall than he remembered him but the intervening years had not exacted a great toll on his appearance. Claudel sensed the same convivial atmosphere that permeated the hall in his own student years. Lowry raised his head and coughed a little. He smiled as an immediate silence fell over the hall.

"And so, to conclude this series on the Neanderthal Man," he turned to a blackboard at the rear of the stage filled with sketches and dates. As he talked he moved slowly and deliberately, emphasizing important points by raising his voice.

"Early man's remarkable will for self-preservation saw him adapt through great environmental changes. After the third interglacial period when all of Europe was once more covered in ice, Neanderthal Man retreated to the caves and took to wearing the hides of animals he killed. By all accounts he continued to thrive in Western Europe up to about 40,000 years ago."

A hand went up in the audience. Lowry peered into the left wing of the stage and shouted.

"Gaston, can we have some lights please?"

The hall's lights were turned on.

"That's better, thank you Gaston. We have a question from someone?" The hand went up again. "Yes Therese?"

"Professor, did the Neanderthal man have the same savage instincts as Homo Sapiens?"

"Of course. Without those instincts man could not have survived as a species."

"It's all so gruesome. The history of man is all savagery and killing and survival of the fittest. It makes my blood curdle. What is the point of it all? I mean, if I could see a reason maybe I could understand. It's just unending savagery and chaos without respite, why?"

"I don't know, my child. It just is. Perhaps the mystics could give an answer as to why but in anthropology all we can concern ourselves about is, what is. Therese, I know this is serious subject matter but would you please unfurl your brow, unburden your countenance and be less solemn."

A titter ran about the hall. The young woman smiled broadly and sat down.

"But take heart Therese, the Neanderthal Man left us more than a grim legacy of survival. Let me explain. In order to survive as a species, from wild animals and each other, early man developed strong canine teeth. He bared his teeth to scare his enemies and also to disguise his own fear. Much the same way a lion's mane swells up or a cobra puffs up when faced with danger. That baring of the canines in early man is known in modern man as . . , a smile."

To emphasize his point Lowry smiled theatrically, bared his teeth and glared wide-eyed about him. Laughter rippled through the hall. A hand shot up. Lowry pointed to a student.

"Yes Alain?"

"Whose theory Professor?"

"Whose theory? Why I guess it's my own. Call it the Lowrian theory."

More laughter came from the class. A voice rang out.

"You're kidding Professor, right?"

"Well not entirely. Let's go into it. Consider a smile, its function, anyone?"

The hall was silent for a few moments. Another hand went up.

"Yes Gilbert?"

"A smile is a friendly gesture, you're telling someone you like them, or love them."

"Is it really that simple Gilbert? Christ and Shakespeare's Othello were betrayed by a smile. A smile doesn't always reflect the thought behind it. Take the smile of Othello's nemesis Iago. Iago's smile was a façade to hide his villain's heart. An adversary can be inveigled into acquiescence if he misinterprets, as Othello did, the smile of Iago. And just as all conversation is persuasion, a smile can be an instrument to aid in the imposition of one's will over another. A smile above all, is disarming."

Another hand went up.

"Susanne?"

"But people don't always show their teeth when they smile."

"That's a yellow smile, half-hearted and weak, and only to be indulged in by those of you who left your teeth at home in a glass."

More laughter filled the hall as several hands went up.

"Sophie?"

"You make the reason for smiling sound so heartless, so cold. When I'm with my friends and I smile, I'd hate to think I'm just trying to impose my will on theirs. I'd rather believe I'm just happy in their company."

"Sophie, the will is always paramount. But it doesn't mean you don't love your friends because your will is asserting itself."

"But Professor, what about a helpless infant, what does it know about imposing its will on others. Yet it smiles all the time."

"A helpless infant? Just think about it. When an infant looks up at two doting parents and smiles, just smiles, they can be reduced to tears, made helpless with wonder. Are there many things on earth that can move us like a smiling infant? It comes into the world with all its sensory motors running, not even aware of its own powers. With a mere smile an infant makes of us an involuntary extension of its will. We are moved as if by divine decree to tender to its needs. A helpless infant Sophie? I think not," he looked at his watch, "well that's it, that's all we have time for today. Now I want all of you to smile and negate each other as potential adversaries. Go on home, attend to your studies, do something useful."

The students broke out in applause and laughter as Lowry returned to the podium. The lecture hall gradually emptied. He was filling his briefcase with papers when he looked up and saw Claudel sitting at the back. His eyes narrowed as he sought to identify Claudel as he joined him at the podium. Lowry flinched slightly in recognition.

"Professor Lowry, my name is . . ,"

"There's no need to introduce yourself, I know who you are. Sort of an agent-in-waiting for the Surete aren't you?

I suppose I should feel honoured. However I didn't quite expect to find you in one of my classes."

"The Aryan Guard is not listed in the telephone book."

Lowry grimaced. He looked about to see if they might be overheard.

"We can't talk here," he snapped the briefcase shut and turned to Claudel. "You were a student of mine at one time, weren't you?"

"That's right. I came here Professor hoping that some kind of a terrible mistake had been made. My memory of you won't allow me to connect you to fascist despots."

"There's a café not far from here. We can talk there."

They left the university and walked to a café on Rue Sufflot. Here they sat at a sidewalk table and Lowry ordered two coffees.

"I remember you," said Lowry as they sat down. "you were a good student if a little on the serious side. You were never very active in the social life of the university."

"I couldn't afford to be. I went from classes straight to the Hotel Excelsior and washed dishes half the night. Professor, I'm sorry but I have to ask you some questions. If you prefer you could meet me with your lawyer and we could talk at the Surete headquarters."

The Professor waved his hand.

"No, no, let's get it over with. Just going into a police station gives me goose pimples."

"Would you mind telling me how long you have been a member of the Aryans?"

"About a year . . ."

"Forgive me for asking, what brought this on, did you rediscover Nietzsche?"

"You are being facetious. Nietzsche could have been a saviour to mankind if intelligent men had listened."

"But Professor, there's the problem as I see it. Intelligent men did listen. All the intelligentsia of Germany listened, the German nobles listened, the German Catholic Church listened. Let's not forget the jack-booted officers of the Gestapo, they were intelligent men, they listened. Do you really want the world to return to the insanity of the Third Reich?"

Lowry looked away from Claudel and thought for some time.

"Plato," he said finally, "summed up our human plight very succinctly don't you think? Might is right. In the affairs of man power alone holds dominion. That's a basic law that man ignores at his own peril. The big fish eat the little fish, brute force and strength is the final arbiter from which all values and ultimately all morality evolve . . ."

"I always thought there was more to man than brute force . . ."

"I suppose next you'll tell me man is made in the image of God. Man is the most ferocious beast of prey ever to set foot on earth, there's nothing God-like about him."

Claudel shook his head and took a drink of coffee.

"You used to receive the sacraments every morning before you began your classes, you used to pray for your students . . . ."

"I was so naïve then it's embarrassing to remember. I wasted my time and my life."

"Nevertheless, you were a happy man back then."

"I was happy like the village idiot is happy. I have nothing but contempt now for all religions. Yes, I once worshipped God, which was my weakness. But I caught on, as the saying goes."

"What caused this . . . volte-face. Was there some . . . defining moment. I remember the kind of man you used to be, I would truly like to know?"

Lowry's tense expression relaxed for a moment as he sipped the coffee. He was a little condescending with Claudel with a slight touch of arrogance to his voice.

"A defining moment"? he said, "I suppose when I read again the Summa Theologica and the Summa Contra Gentiles of Saint Thomas Aquinas. He was canonized as a Saint after his death in 1274. Even with his extensive doctrines on reason and faith, what do you think he did with all his knowledge and his wonderful mind? He subordinated all human endeavours to the emphatic dogma of the Catholic Church."

Lowry leaned forward as if to emphasize his point.

"He set the stage for the brutal excesses of the Catholic Church during the reign of King Ferdinand and Queen Isabella in what we know today as the Spanish Inquisition." He stopped talking abruptly and looked quizzically at Claudel. "are you sure you want me to go on, I'm probably boring you to death?"

"I'm listening Professor . . ."

"Well, in the year 1483 along came this man of God with a penchant for mayhem by the name of Tomas de Torquemada. He was the first Inquisitor General appointed by the Spanish Court. Well, sure all hell broke loose if you'll excuse my choice of words. There followed under Torquemada and the Spanish Inquisition the most hideous chapter in the long history of the Roman Catholic Church. Beneath the altar of God that housed the Blessed Eucharist, subterranean chambers of horrors designed specifically for torture became an integral part of the new cathedrals of Europe. Rivers of blood flowed in the name of Christ. Unspeakable cruelties were inflicted by cowled monks on suspected deviants from the one true Church. Public burnings at the stake and garrotting of dissenters was common practice".

"Ahh," Lowry waved a hand in the air, "I'm well rid of all that superstition and idol worshipping. Religion came to invoke in me the spectre of the three witches of Shakespeare's Mc Beth stirring a cauldron, muttering incantations and calling on the powers of darkness. Tell me, how big a leap is it from that to clouds of incense rising from a thurible or lighting penny candles at the feet of plaster cast images of the saints?"

"So the catholic religion doesn't work for you, does that make it wrong for everyone. What arrogance. There are millions who find help and answers in the catholic faith. Should they throw love of God and the Church aside just because you are no longer a believer?"

"They can believe whatever they like, that's their business. But I'm telling you it's all sham, there's not an iota of truth in any of it."

"Truth? An influential man like you shouldn't bandy that word about too often. When you speak you are saying what you alone think, it does not follow that you are expressing an inviolate truth. It's only what you think it to be. Every man is entitled to his opinion surely."

"Ahh, I should have stayed in Ireland but I got out of it, for the same reason as James Joyce. At one time all I wanted to do was dispel religious illusions in the same way Saint Patrick got rid of the snakes."

"A tall order Professor, half of mankind's happiness depends on illusions. Is truth really worth serving if it's to the detriment of happiness? But let's continue, you lost God and found the Aryans in one fell swoop."

"I never lost God; I just lost my belief in His infallibility . . ."

"Professor if you've arrived at a point in your life where you've figured everything out about God, the world, your place in it. Why don't you enlighten me a little, what are we all about . . . ?

"Better be careful, I could win you over to my side . . ."

"God and choices . . . , start with that. Indulge me . . . , humour me. Aren't we free to make choices, to choose good over evil . . ."

Lowry threw his head back and laughed out loud.

"Ah, what a lost little soul you are. Free will is it? Listen me bucko, get it into your head there's no such thing as free will. And even if there was it wouldn't matter and I'll tell you why. God is God, right? The Almighty, the Creator of all things, the Father, the Son and the Holy Ghost, Sacred, Holy, All seeing, All knowing. That being so, God knew how each person would use the free will he or she was given, after all, He is God. Look now; let me explain this so a 10 year old would understand," Claudel could not control an involuntary smile that briefly crossed his face. He felt for a moment he was a student again in one of Lowry's classrooms. "God gave, say, Hitler," Lowry continued, "a free will and being God He knew Hitler would commit atrocities, become an insane butcher before He breathed air into him and gave him life . . . My point is, if God already knows the choices we are going to make, where is the freedom of choice?"

"So you hold God responsible for all the evil in the world, for man's inhumanity to man?"

"Don't you mean God's inhumanity to man. You have to ask yourself what kind of a God would allow Man, His creation, to suffer such ignominy, such heinous brutality from wars and genocide and other natural disasters. Don't you realise the significance of that . . . ?"

"I have to admit I've never given it much thought Professor, I just . . ."

"It all comes down to power, just power . . ."

"Power . . . ? You've lost me."

"Power; between good and evil."

"Oh, so you believe in God . . . ?"

"Sure I do, but l just don't believe in a powerful God, and l do believe in Satan . . . , evil does exist in the world."

"Maybe there's hope for you after all . . ."

"Be that as it may I think what God lacks is power, good old fashioned power. You'd agree with me I'm sure that the world has known wars and rumours of wars since time began. Compared to what Satan has been up to in this world God seems a wimp by comparison, as if His hands were tied behind His back. He's a powerless Captain running His ship up on the rocks."

A waiter came to the table and asked them if more coffee was required. Lowry looked at Claudel and raised his eyebrows.

"Well now, all that talking has given me a fierce thirst. How about yourself, would you like anything stronger than coffee."

"l have a long drive ahead of me . . . ," said Claudel, looking at his watch. He shrugged his shoulders and nodded. "sure, why not?, I'll have a whiskey . . ."

"Two whiskeys Antoine please, make mine a double."

Lowry's facial muscles relaxed and he eased back into the chair as he looked at Claudel. They sat in contemplative silence until the waiter returned and set down the whiskeys before them. Without a word Lowry took his glass and half emptied it. Claudel sipped his and put the glass down.

"You know," Said Lowry, "I've been searching for God my whole adult life and I felt like an ineffectual Don Quixote tilting at windmills. All of a sudden l saw life as a giant cosmic lie, a riddle l would never solve where doubt could even be thrown on the reality of existence. The philosopher Rene

Descartes had created only confusion by his dictum 'I think therefore I am'. Since Man is subject to the continuum of time and space, time and matter being in a state of constant flux, a millionth part of one single second cannot halt its progress, cannot stop for the briefest time so we may say, behold existence. If the present becomes the past at the moment of its definition how can the reality of existence be proven? I saw the spinning out of our little lives as fireflies on a midsummer night, flickering for a moment in the limitless infinity of time, a brief hiatus in the interminable void of all that was and the eternity of what has yet to be. Ah well . . ." The Professor held up his glass and swirled its contents around. He said to Claudel in a more mellowed voice. "That's a grand drop of whiskey and I talk too much . . . , I'm sorry for ranting on."

"Professor I think perhaps . . . , you should get along home, get some food in your stomach. Your wife will be worried about you. I'll call you tomorrow . . ."

"Home, wife is it? I live in a one bed-roomed apartment with a one-eyed cat called Günter and he has a bad attitude."

"If I remember correctly, when I was one of your students you were married at the time."

Lowry picked up the glass and finished his drink.

"Sophie passed on . . . , she's been gone three years now."

"I'm sorry to hear that . . ."

"She was always in delicate health, it was her heart you know."

"Oh, did you have any children . . . ?"

"No, no we had no children. I've not one solitary soul to keep me company since Sophie passed on, just me and a one-eyed cat. And I'll tell you something else, that cat blamed me for Sophie not coming back."

Claudel raised his glass and finished his drink. He took out his wallet, left some money on the table and stood up.

"That will cover the drinks Professor. Look, maybe something you wrote was taken out of context. I think there's been a mistake made linking you to the Aryans . . ."

Lowry's shoulders collapsed. He stared mutely at the whiskey glass he grasped in his hands. Minutes before he was waxing eloquently; now he struggled to express himself.

"No, no . . . It's all true, all of it. It's too late to turn back now."

"What were you thinking of, were you coerced into joining the Aryans . . . , did they have some kind of a hold over you?"

"No, nothing like that."

Lowry's shoulders sagged as he buried his face in his hands. After a few moments he sat up straight.

"Professor I'm talking to you now as a friend, but I also happen to be a law officer. Give me something to work with; I want to help you . . ."

"That's all I need at this point in my life, become an informer. That word, informer, has a particularly onerous meaning in Ireland stemming all the way from The Troubles. I better shut up, my mind is starting to wander. Anyway, about these Aryans, no there's no mistake, no mistake, I belong to them body and soul."

"Why . . . ?"

"Because, because of a lot of things. Because I don't know who I am. I don't know what I am. I don't have a life . . . At first I believed I was debating politics and philosophy when I got an invitation to an Aryan Brotherhood meeting. There were people there from all levels of society. They started chatting together, had some drinks together, full of bonhomie. What a buzz, there were well known public speakers there. When the discussion got around to Martin Heidegger and Nietzsche's Man and Superman, I felt a spark ignite inside of me; I suddenly became alive for the first time since Sophie died. I was invited to regular get-togethers and meetings. And then, how can I explain it? It was like reading Nietzsche for the first time. His ideas became like magnets; I couldn't refute them. It was all there, the road to a better, happier mankind. His ideas fuelled me, filled the empty vacuum that was my life . . ."

"A better, happier mankind? Please tell me you're kidding me. Nietzsche advocated nothing but brute force and racial intolerance in a Godless universe. What have they done to you? You must know the ripple effect of everything you write for that fascist rabble. It's the half-witted you inspire the most, men like Henry Wilkins. They serve the same purpose as Hitler's Gestapo, killing and beating up weak and defenceless people."

Claudel stood up. His face was flushed as he looked at his watch.

"I better leave you Professor because I feel myself getting angry . . . , there's an Algerian family in a hospital in Evreux I'm going to visit, two of your Aryan friends bombed them out of their home . . ."

Lowry's face blanched.

"I didn't know . . . ."

"Go and see the result of your ideas and the pamphlets you write, in that hospital. The doctors are still removing splinters of glass from the boy, and the girl has a skull fracture. I've sent some hard men to prison in my time, but when I think of it, they were saints compared to you, dupe that you may have been to your fascist masters. A family was bombed out of their home; you justify it by quoting some philosophical imperative of Neitzsche. In another time, another place you would be goose-stepping with the Gestapo along the Marienstrasse."

Claudel left the café with Lowry slumped in his chair. He walked for hours through the streets until the anger within him abated. Finally he went to his car and drove home. When he opened the door of the cottage he saw the light flashing on his answering machine. He pressed the button. It was Lowry's voice.

"South of Pacy sur Eure on route 141 there is a village called Le Plessis-hebert. There is a Bar called L' Estaminet. If you want my help be there precisely at 2 o'clock tomorrow afternoon."

The following day Claudel braked slowly as he approached the sign that read Le Plessis-hebert. Just before the village he saw the L'Estaminet Bar huddled in a glade of trees. It was a small one-storied granite building that looked as if sometime in the distant past it might have served as a meeting house or a small Church. A small Cessna aircraft droning overhead broke the silence of the pastoral landscape. One car, a red Volvo, was parked in the gravel driveway leading to the Bar. When Claudel pushed through the door a woman who had been seated and reading a newspaper went to the bar and began filling two glasses with cognac. She nodded towards Lowry to indicate he had ordered the drinks. The interior of L'Estaminet was similar to the décor of many Bars in the agrarian province of Eure et Loir. It was dark and uninviting with the lighting reduced to conserve on overheads. Lowry was seated at the back near a bagatelle table. Claudel picked up the glasses and brought them to the table. Neither man proffered a hand in greeting.

"Perhaps you would like something stronger?" said Lowry

"Thanks, this is fine," Claudel put the glasses of wine on the table and sat down. "why did you travel this distance from Paris? I could have picked you up."

"In this flat countryside I can see if I'm being followed. Now before we begin I want to make something clear. Keep your remarks and insults to yourself from here on out."

"Make your point."

"The point is you brought me to my senses. I don't feel like thanking you right now though I probably should."

"Professor, no one could connect to students in a classroom the way you do, and condone the brutality of those thugs."

Lowry shook his head slowly.

"Yesterday you verbally knocked the hell out of me, and now you make me want to cry . . ."

He picked up his wine glass and sipped slowly from it.

"Have you any idea what you're up against with these Aryans, how powerful they are?"

"We have records of racial attacks, even murders where race or religion was the obvious motive but beyond that . . . ."

"They've been around for over 40 years. The founders were French army and navy officers who rebelled against de Gaulle after he gave independence to Algeria in 1962. They allied themselves to fascists groups in Germany and Britain. Today in France the Aryans are controlled by politicians, wealthy businessmen and a few aristocrats. The membership is made up mostly of professional middle-classes, doctors, lawyers, land-owners. Well known sitting government ministers operate behind the scenes. Things are very different now since they are preparing to go public. There are no boot boys or skinheads anymore. This time round they've hired mercenaries to do their dirty work. The front man is a Paris dentist by the name of Jacques Malin. Below him are the mercenaries and other misfits like Henry Wilkins. They have their own hierarchy and identify themselves only with Malin. Malins personal henchman is Ewe Bauer, a German national. He's a fat little man with bulging eyes and tiny hands and feet. Malin treats him like dirt and the little fellow wallows in it."

"And the leaders?"

"They are known as the 'Group of 12'. When the climate is right they will go public and form an ultra-right political party. What you have to understand is the Aryans appeal to the psyche of the French bourgeoisie especially. The bourgeoisie and aristocrats ardently hoped for a German victory in the Second World War; for class preservation, social prestige and so forth. Well in the last 80 years the French ruling classes have lost their vast fortunes and seen the Empire turn to dust, culminating in the loss of Algeria. Many of them see the Aryan Brotherhood as Messiahs, leading France back to glory."

"I predict," said Claudel, "the Aryans will bring more devastation to France than the Germans could ever accomplish."

Lowry took a sip from the glass. He looked at it for a few moments and swallowed the remainder.

"I don't normally tipple at this hour of the day . . . ."

"Let me get you a cup of coffee Professor, it's a tiring enough drive back to Paris."

"Oh I'll be alright. Now where was I? Oh yes, well these new statesmen of the far right have great changes in mind if they come to power, and they surely will come to power this time."

Claudel took a drink from his glass.

"They'll begin," said Lowry, "by blaming the immigrants for everything from social unrest to economic instability. Anarchy will result. Then their moment will have arrived. Also there's something really big in the works that they wouldn't let me be privy to . . . , I guess they consider me a security risk after all . . . ."

Claudel made a signal to the woman at the bar and a coffee machine gurgled to life. When it stopped she filled two cups and brought them to the table. Outside the sound of the aircraft could be heard over the quiet countryside.

"What can you tell me about Malin?"

"He doesn't practice dentistry anymore. He owns a mansion in Saint Germain en Laye on 200 acres of land. He has a stable with his own racehorses, a Lamborghini, two Rolls Royces. I've never heard anyone speak with such fiery oratory as Malin. At an Aryan rally a thousand French flags would flutter over a delirious crowd after the playing of the 'Marseille'. It was usually a prelude to racial violence. You'd have to meet Malin to understand his charisma. He has the mad black eyes of Rasputin."

"The bombing in Dreux, was it the work of the Aryans?"

"It was the handiwork of Henry Wilkins and Ewe Bauer . . . ." His voice trailed off. He held Claudel's look for a few moments. "there's something else . . ."

"What . . . ?"

"I've something to tell you. You're not going to like it."

"What are you talking about?"

"They know you sent your wife to Syria . . ."

Claudel leaped to his feet.

"Why didn't you tell me . . . . ?"

"Because I just found out myself this morning. Sit down. You're making me nervous."

"I've got to get to a telephone. I must call Damascus . . ."

"Sit down, please . . ."

Claudel reluctantly sat back down.

"Now listen to me." Said Lowry, "your wife is in danger, but not in immediate danger, and before you fly off the handle again, hear me out. They sent a Norwegian named Rolf Gustafson to the Hotel Marhaban. It's on the airport road going into Damascus. He is to wait there for further instructions. Rolf Gustafson is an assassin."

When Claudel stood up again Lowry knew he could detain him no longer. They shook hands.

"Professor, thank you."

"No, thank you for giving me back my self-respect. What's she like this wife of yours?"

"She has a smile that would light up this room. She sews, she makes bread with her own hands. You will meet her when all this is over. I've got to go now, will you be all right?"

"I'll be fine. Call me later. Go now . . ."

"Goodbye Professor."

"Goodbye my friend."

Claudel left the L'Estaminet Bar and drove to the village centre. He found a telephone booth and dialed the number of his wife's parent's house in Damascus. It rang for some time before it was picked up by Solonges' father. Umar Peera greeted Claudel in the loud friendly manner that was his way. He loved the quiet Frenchman and was always glad for a chance to speak with him. After a few moments his whole demeanour changed. His face became a graven mask as he listened to Claudel.

"All right, all right. I want you to leave this to me. Yes, she is here. She's in her room. I'll put you through to her."

Solonge let out a joyous cry on hearing his voice.

"My dear, I've been so concerned about you. I can't sleep. It's wonderful to see Maman and Papa but I want to come home."

"Soon I promise you."

"When will the investigation be finished, is it dangerous?"

"Not at all. It's very routine."

"Did you remember to water the flowers?"

"Yes, I . . . did."

"And the house plants. And be sure to put the milk back in the fridge when you use it."

"I will."

"Do you miss me?"

"You know I do."

"Say something nice."

"I love you."

"That's better."

"My dear, I want you to promise me you will do exactly as your father tells you."

"Of course I will."

"We will be together very soon, you'll see."

On his return journey to Paris from Le Plessis-hebert Lowry checked his rear view mirror every few kilometres. He felt greatly relieved having unburdened himself to the Surete agent. He reasoned it had to be a form of senility that caused him in his advanced years to become a member of the Aryan Guard. Why had he allowed himself to be carried away by the insidious reasoning of Nietzsche which, when coupled to Malin's rantings had caused him to almost lose his sense of reason? He had agonized through a sleepless night until he saw with the clarity of a revelation that he had been de-humanized by Nietzsche in his search for the truth. He had re-read the four parts of 'Thus spoke Zarathustra' and came to the conclusion that the little Prussian had become mentally unbalanced long before his ignominious end. Nietzsche condemned compassion, exalted cruelty as a virtue and saw peace as a prelude to war. Cutting ties with the Aryan Brotherhood was one of the better decisions of his life. He checked the rear view mirror again as he picked up the N12 going East to Paris.

When he had left the Bar in Le Plessis-hebert Lowry failed to notice the small Cessna aircraft circling above him at 1200 feet. The pilot tracked the Red Volvo, vivid in the flat deserted countryside, as far as Aigleville. From here he veered East. He held this course before he nosed the Cessna down and landed on an airstrip in a private estate in Saint Germain en Laye on the outskirts of Paris. As he taxied to a halt on the runway a Rolls Royce drew up alongside. A liveried chauffeur went from the car to the aircraft. He exchanged some words with the pilot, then ran back to the car and spoke to a passenger in the rear seat. He then drove to a chateau on the estate and let his passenger out.

Lowry had entered Paris through Point Saint Cloud, crossed Bois de Boulogne and immersed himself in the heavy traffic along the Avenue de Champs Elysees. As a precaution he had taken several detours before turning into Rue Royer Collard where he had his apartment. He pulled into his parking space and looked around before getting out of the car. On entering the building he was surprised to see the lights were out in the office of the concierge, Madame L'Estrange. Normally she sat and knitted in her tiny cubicle watching the comings and goings of the tenants. She was a loud disputatious woman whose character and temperament seemed to have been formed by the requirements of her profession. She had a voice so shrill it could carry all the way to the fourth floor of the apartment building. He went to the elevator in the foyer, pushed the button and waited. The office door opened behind him. He turned around to see the barrel of a gun pointing at him. His aging reflexes failed him as he made a run for the door leading to the street. The gun roared twice as he pulled open the door. He was struggling to stay upright when he gripped his chest and collapsed out onto the pavement. He was dead by the time an ambulance was called.

When Umar Peera put the telephone down after speaking with Claudel he began issuing instructions to his household. He was a man used to being obeyed though he never overtly imposed his authority on his household, least of all his servants. In business he was a different man. In the close confines of a boardroom he could terrify colleagues with his booming voice and pounding fists. In his house he was treated almost deferentially by a staff who had never even heard him raise his voice. When his wife realized something serious was happening she took over from him and prepared for a quick departure from Damascus. Umar Peera was on the telephone again, calling one of his three brothers in Halab in Northern Syria.

Three cars filled with men and weapons sped through the night towards the Hotel Marhaban. Nearing the hotel they pulled off the road and parked. They turned off the engines and waited.

From the edge of the runway Umar Peera waved to his wife and daughter in the light aircraft. The engines were revving as the pilot talked to the control tower. The aircraft moved forward and began its ascent. When it had become a point of light in the night sky Umar Peera turned quickly and stepped into a waiting car. He was taken to the three cars parked near the Hotel Marhaban. He rolled down the car window and nodded to one of the drivers. The twelve men in the cars got out and walked into the kitchen at the rear of the hotel. The kitchen staff of the small hotel had been bribed earlier and had vanished from view.

Rolf Gustafson was stretched out on the bed when the door was suddenly smashed in. Before he had time to re-act he was pinned down; duct tape across his mouth stifled his attempt to scream. His eyes bulged in disbelief as he was quickly bundled out of the hotel and into one of the waiting cars. He was taken to a warehouse owned by Umar Peera. Gustafson trembled in fear as he was pushed on to a chair in one of the offices. Ten men stood about the room. It was like a nightmare. From the comfort of his hotel to this, this, madness. Only a short time ago Malin had promoted him when his talent for marksmanship came to light. He had already killed three men with impunity and took pride in being a hard-core killer in the cause of the New Order. He had done well with his life. He had a new Ferrari, all paid for. He wore designer clothes and the most beautiful women were his for the asking. He was one of the elite, Malin had told him so. His illusion of his toughness now vanished as Umar Peera entered the room, picked up a chair and spun it around. He sat facing Gustafson with his arms folded over the backrest. A debilitating nausea overcame Gustafson when Umar Peera picked up the metal gun-case and unsnapped the locks. He opened the cover and un-ended the contents. A detachable rifle stock, a barrel with a telescopic sight and a clip of ammunition crashed noisily to the floor. Gustafson stared dumbly at the floor, his eyes glazing over. There it was, his pride and joy, the possession of which distinguished him from other mercenaries of the Aryans Brotherhood. He had never shared with any human being the intrinsic involvement he shared with his rifle. He spent hours in its care until the rifled barrel shone like a mirror. Yet there it was in an ignominious heap on the floor. His chest heaved from the effort to breathe. Umar Peera reached down and picked up a magazine clip. He eased a round from it. Fingering the round he closed his eyes briefly then gave his full attention to Gustafson. He reached forward and pulled the duct tape from the assassin's mouth. He moved the strewn rifle parts with his foot.

"How did you get these through the airport customs?"

"Please . . . , I wasn't . . ."

"Answer my question."

47

"My ticket was booked through to Kenya. I had papers to say I was going on to join a safari."

"Do you know who I am?"

"No sir, I . . . ."

"It was my daughter you came here to kill."

Gustafson's shoulders fell as he groaned.

"Please sir, I beg you . . . ."

"Do you see the men in this room?" Umar Peera indicated with his hand as he spoke and pointed to two older men. "That is Ahmed, that is Hassan, they are my brothers. God has blessed them with these sons. That is Barrak, that is Fetir, Yusif, Salim, Mohammed, Ali, Riad and Akbar. My brother's sons are my sons. God has blessed me with just one child, my daughter Solonge. Coming from the West you would have no idea of the closeness of family life in Syria. You couldn't begin to understand what my daughter means to all of us. She is the only girl you see. I must tell you, my nephews had a heated argument about you; in fact they almost came to blows. Each one of them wants to be your executioner."

He held up the round of ammunition to Gustafson.

"You came here to take my daughter's life with this, to leave her in a pool of blood somewhere . . . , now, what I want from you is a name, who sent you here . . . ?

"It . . . , it was Malin, Jacques Malin. Please . . ."

Umar Peera stood up and nodded to the men in the room. Gustafson was taken away screaming, pleading for his life. Umar Peera waited until he heard a gunshot in the distance. He picked up the telephone in the warehouse office. In the cottage in Ivry la Bataille Claudel grabbed at the telephone when it rang.

"Hello."

"Marc, it's me . . . ."

"Where is she? Is she alright?"

"Marc calm yourself, she is safe."

"Thank God, where is she now?"

"She's in my brother's house in Halab. Until I hear from you the house will be an armed fort. There's absolutely no need for concern from this end."

"What about Gustafson?"

"He was sent by someone called Jacques Malin."

"Where is Gustafson now?"

"It's the law of the land here. Mad dogs are put to sleep."

When he learned of Lowry's murder Claudel stayed in his cottage for two days, sickened by the news. He had just finished a bottle of Scotch whiskey and decided to call it quits. His penchant for whiskey was the only secret he kept from his wife. He hid bottles in the cellar and only drank on those occasions when she was away for an extended period of time, which wasn't very often. But he knew he was fooling himself believing she was unaware of it. At any rate she never mentioned it so he just drank when the opportunity arose. He thought again of Lowry. At the eleventh hour his old Professor had turned his life around and made amends for misplaced loyalties and bad judgement. He had been one of those academics who for all their learning, could still manage to be childishly naïve for the greater part of their lives. Claudel reached for the telephone and dialled a number. For the next half hour he talked with Inspector Brunet. He then drove to Lowry's apartment in Paris, picked up Günter the one-eyed cat and brought it back to his cottage in Ivry la Bataille.

At 10:00 A.M. the following morning Claudel drove to the Foret d'Evreux, a short drive from the town of Evreux. As he expected the punctilious Inspector Brunet was waiting at the prearranged place. They sat on a bench overlooking a small pond.

"Try not to worry Monsieur," said the Inspector, "from what you tell me your wife is in good hands. Have you decided on your next move?"

"To tell you the truth Inspector, I'm a little shell-shocked right now."

"It's understandable under the circumstances."

"Do you remember the Englishman I told you about, the one we questioned in Paris?"

"Of course, Henry Wilkins." Said the Inspector.

"That's him. We brought him back in for questioning with the same result, couldn't get a thing out of him. What we have to do is to make him feel threatened."

"I wish I could do more to help . . . ."

"What else have we got on Wilkins background?"

"Quite a bit," the Inspector took out a notebook and read from it. "he's a nasty piece of work. He's been in and out of prison since he was 16 years old. Aged 32, divorced, hmm, assaulted his wife, put her in hospital. And here's something we didn't have on our files . . . , there's an outstanding warrant in England for assault with a deadly weapon."

Claudel turned suddenly to the Inspector.

"A warrant? Why that's it, that's the break we need. Can you contact Scotland Yard?"

"Right away Monsieur."

"Good, because we're going to need their help."

Two plain-clothes detectives attached to New Scotland Yard boarded an aircraft at London's Heathrow airport at 9:55 A.M. A little over an hour later they were met at Charles de Gaulle airport in Paris and taken to Surete Headquarters. Detectives Len Bruton and Sidney Cox spent the rest of the day being briefed on the activities of the Aryans Guard. That evening Wilkins was arrested in the apartment of his girlfriend and brought to the Surete. When he was shown a seat Wilkins sneered as he sat down. He took out a cigarette, lit it and began casually blowing smoke rings in the air. The sneer changed to shock when the two English detectives entered the room with Claudel. He sat bolt upright in his chair as the detectives sat down.

"Ello 'Enery," said Bruton, "so this is where you've been 'iding all these years, gay Paree no less."

"I 'ardly recognize you old chap," said Cox, "without your 'tash and beard. A proper twit you look 'Enery I must say."

Wilkins pulled nervously on the cigarette.

"I want to use a telephone."

"You're coming back to London wi' us 'Enery," said Bruton.

"You can't do that. I'm a French citizen now. You've got no jurisdiction over me."

"Cor, listen to 'im," said Cox, "that's very good that is. Now that would be all very well 'Enery, but the fact is you are a fugitive from British justice."

"I want to talk to my solicitor . . . ."

"'d'e can't 'elp you now 'Enery. You remember the Manchester United game against Liverpool at Old Trafford, the one when you beaned a Liverpool supporter with a crowbar . . . ? well, that's why we're 'ere . . ."

Wilkins nervously stubbed out the cigarette.

"Come off it, you're lying . . . ."

"Would I lie to you 'Enery, me old flower?" Cox took a folded paper from his coat pocket. "This is an extradition warrant for your arrest."

Wilkins jumped to his feet in panic.

"No, you can't, you can't do that to me . . . ."

"'Enery, our French friends need certain information about Mister Malin and the Aryan lot. You 'elp 'em and I'll 'elp you, I'll put in a good word for you back 'ome. 'ow does that sound?"

"ow much do you think my life would be worth if I did that?"

"'Ow much do you think it's worth right now? All right 'Enery, if that's the way you want it."

He made a move towards Higgins.

"I'm not leaving 'ere until I see a solicitor. I'm a French citizen . . . ."

"Now we can do this two ways. You can come peacefully or we can sedate you and dump you in a diplomatic bag. Either way, you're coming back to London wi' us."

Wilkins slumped back in the chair. His hands shook as he lit another cigarette.

"What do you want to know?"

"Who killed Professor Lowry?" Asked Claudel.

When Wilkins maintained a sullen silence Cox turned to Bruton.

"Detective Bruton, will you explain to our 'Enery I can arrange to have 'im put in with some black cell mates in 'olloway Prison. Do you think 'e knows what they do to Aryans in 'olloway?"

"Strewth 'Enery, you don't want to go down that road." Said Bruton.

"If I tell you I'm dead. You don't know these people . . ."

"Who killed Professor Lowry?" Repeated Claudel.

"It was Ewe Bauer . . . ."

"Who bombed the house in Dreux?"

"It was Bauer . . . , and me."

"Will you put it all in writing 'Enery? Asked Cox.

Wilkins nodded dumbly.

"Good. There's paper and a pen over at that desk. I want to know everything about the Aryans."

Claudel left Evreux and was speeding along route N 13 to Saint Germain en Laye. He checked the time. It was just after 11:00 P.M., late for visiting. But after the death of Lowry and arrest of Wilkins he had to get to Malin before he went into hiding. The traffic was relatively free and forty five minutes later he turned off the main road. After a few kilometres he stopped before the massive gates of Malin's estate. A security guard came out and spoke to him through the iron barred gates. He said he would have to telephone the chateau for permission to open the gate because of the lateness of the hour. Claudel identified himself and quietly told the guard to open the gate or he would be arrested for obstructing him. The flustered guard opened the gates and waved Claudel through. When he closed the gates over he ran to the hut and made a telephone call.

The heavily wooded estate was brilliantly flood lit as Claudel began his drive. He passed the ruins of a 16th century church choked to the belfry of the steeple in rampant ivy and creepers. At the rear of the church a glade of elm trees encircled a derelict graveyard. Desecrated by weather and time, buffeted by raging storms the ancient engraved tombstones and crosses were arrested in mid-collapse by a stranglehold of tangled weeds, undergrowth, hawthorn and briars. The drive wound its way through paralleled rows of Linden trees until it stopped at a clearing. A two-storied cut stone chateau loomed up before him, the parking areas filled with taxis and limousines, many of them with chauffeurs. Claudel parked the car, went over to the house and pressed the doorbell. Ewe Bauer opened the door. Claudel immediately recognized him from Lowry's description. Bauer avoided eye contact with Claudel as he quietly, almost meekly walked ahead of him. He finally entered a room, beckoned to an armchair and left. Claudel remained standing.

A recording of a baroque sonata of Bach was softly playing as he looked about a capacious living room. The cream colored sofas and armchairs, the gold and white of the Fleur des Lys wallpaper and the glittering chandelier filled the room with a profusion of light. A painting of the coronation of Emperor Napoleon Bonaparte hung over a massive fireplace of black Italian marble. Between two windows bronze busts of Cesare Borgia and Niccolo Machiavelli were mounted on four-foot marble columns. An ancient Celtic harp stood beside a Steinway grand piano. All this elegance, mused Claudel, some of it redolent of all that was finest in French culture, lacked a human touch. In this setting, every object and artefact had the cold remoteness of a museum. Claudel's attention was drawn to an array of champagne bottles and half-filled glasses and used ash trays about the room. The rich aroma of fine Cuban cigars still hung on the air. He guessed that the security guard at the gate had warned them he was coming.

A door opened and Jacques Malin came in wearing a tuxedo. He went directly to an aquarium, picked up a spoon and proceeded to feed the fish as if Claudel was not present. He was a tall gaunt man sparsely built with a long thin face. His lips were thin and wide and oddly pursed as if he was always about to speak. His small eyes were set close under arched brows. In the throes of a passionate speech his eyes would blaze until he looked demoniacal. Claudel had to suppress an urge to arrest the dentist the moment he saw him but he felt there was bigger game to be had if he bided his time. Without looking up Malin spoke to Claudel.

"Do you make a habit of forcing your way into people's homes without being invited? It must be pressing business Monsieur Claudel . . ."

"It seems I did come at a bad time, apart from the lateness of the hour. I hope I was not the reason for the sudden departure of your guests?"

The spoon slipped from Malin's fingers and pirouetted to the bottom of the aquarium stirring up a cloud of sand. The startled fish darted about the cones and shells.

"State your business Monsieur."

"Certainly, but I think your friends will be interested in why I'm here. Why don't you invite them back in . . . ?"

Just as Claudel had suspected, as the chauffeured driven limousines and taxis were still parked outside, the guests could not have gone very far. A door opened behind him. Twelve men, all formally dressed in tuxedos filed slowly into the room. Claudel could only look on in disbelief when Jacques Perrieux the Minister for Justice passed by him. He found himself facing men distinguished in public and military life. He recognized all but five of the twelve. The most familiar was Army General Lucien Thierry. Captain Raul Janeau like the General had served with him in the Ecole Militaire. Sebastien Bonnet, Jules Sautier and Yves Gagnon were Cabinet Ministers. Jean Claude Decour was an older respected member of the Senate. Illustrious men, greatly admired, whose private lives were part of the public domain. Claudel knew first hand from his time in army Intelligence that the General and Captain Janeau had unblemished records. The Senators were known to give of their time and energies to civic programs concerning homelessness and juvenile delinquency, exemplary citizens both. Jules Sautier was wearing the red ribbon and medal of the Legion of Honour for distinguished service. They were all men of valour, of good families, known for their loyalty and devotion to France. Malin had left the aquarium and was standing at a table pouring himself a drink. Four men left the table and huddled about him, becoming engaged in a hushed debate. General Theirry and Captain Janeau joined them. Standing alone under the vast canvas of Napoleon, Claudel was faced with a dilemma he had not foreseen. After the death of Lowry he had come to the chateau for a confrontation with Malin and suddenly found himself face to face with eminent leaders of the French government. It looked as if he had bagged far bigger game then he would have thought possible. The Justice Minister was looking at him with some apprehension but obviously didn't want to talk with him. When Claudel stared back at him the Minister quickly dropped his eyes and turned away. Several of the seated guests looked at each other in a furtive way that convinced Claudel his worse suspicions were realized. There were just too many questions that begged answers. How could Malin be involved in murder and arson without the knowledge, the consent of these resourceful men? Perhaps he had reacted too quickly to their public image, to the charisma they exuded as highly visible public officials.

"I am Doctor Martin Gervais," said one of the men. He unwrapped a cigar as he spoke, "Surete agent Marc Claudel, I've heard a lot about you these past few days. Perhaps you would tell us the reason for your visit. I presume you have a warrant to come barging into this private residence. Or do you believe Monsieur Claudel that you can act with impunity, as you please?"

"No Doctor, I don't have a warrant but I have the authority to act in the interest of the State"

"Why don't we sit down and make ourselves comfortable." Said Gervais pointing to the long dining table. Claudel left the fireplace and sat opposite Gervais. Other men in the room joined them after some hesitance. "we are a group of citizens bound together by one common goal," continued

Gervais, "that France should fulfil its rightful destiny in the world . . ."

"Why the veil of secrecy to hide such a noble cause," said Claudel, "why not publicize it to all and sundry, let your fellow citizens rejoice in your efforts . . . ?"

A hushed silence fell over the assembly as they looked at each other uneasily.

"Monsieur" Said Gervais, "you cannot be blind to the disasters that are befalling France and it's all of our own making. The world population now stands at over 6½ billion people. In another 50 years the land mass on earth will be so densely populated there won't be enough arable land to grow a head of cabbage."

"That's a global problem, France cannot solve that alone . . ."

"At this moment in time France cannot put its own house in order, never mind the problems of the world. There's never been a time in the history of France when strong leadership was more needed. Look at the inane policies of certain liberals in this present government. The rest of Europe laughs as we try to flex muscles we haven't got. How can we stand aside and allow France to degenerate into a welfare state? Do you know there are three million North Africans in France, a great deal of them on welfare? Our coffers are empty because of this haemorrhaging of our resources. Because of it we have had to postpone or cancel our space programs, our nuclear research programs."

"Isn't that the legacy of colonialism?" said Claudel, "it was France who invaded North Africa. We almost succeeded in destroying the languages and culture of every country we colonized. We plundered land and natural resources, we filled our museums with their treasures. Wouldn't you say by that reckoning we owe them at least a welfare cheque?"

"Be realistic . . . If we had not colonized those countries Britain, Germany or Belgium would have . . . ."

"But we did, that's what matters. And whether mistakes were made or not they were decisions made by the government in our name. Our government still has a mandate from the people. May I remind you we live in a democracy . . . ?"

Malin got up from his seat and sat beside Gervais at the table. They exchanged glances for a moment before turning to Claudel.

"I suspect you are a bleeding heart liberal, Detective." Said Malin.

"I've been called worse in my time."

Gervais leaned forward in his seat and joined his hands on the table.

"Do you really think being a democracy serves the best interests of France or any other country for that matter?" Said Malin, forcefully. "Democracy and Liberalism are but other names for communism, it serves only the will of the working class. Hasn't the lessons of China and Russia taught you anything? Lenin and Mao Tse-Tung began their revolutions by obliterating the ruling classes and aristocracies and with them all their intelligence and creativity. During the Cultural Revolution in China you could be imprisoned for owning a typewriter. And for what? Four decades after the Revolution and China is now flirting with Capitalism. Oh, we need the masses to fight our wars, of course, to wash our windows, to till our fields, to build our roads and factories but what other useful function do workers as a class serve? They breed with their own kind, propagating France ad nauseam with inferior genes. Civilized society as we know it in France is imploding upon itself. Great art and music and literature are disappearing from French culture. Why has there not been another Gauguin, Manet or Cezanne from all the artists we have today, or a Debussy or Berlioz to set fire to the world of music?"

"I can't answer that. Two million soldiers lost their lives in two world wars and you have only contempt for the supreme sacrifice they made for France. Your freedom was earned for you" continued Claudel, "by braver men than you; braver than anyone in this room."

"You shouldn't let your emotions run away with you . . ."

"And you should not let your prejudice affect your reason. It's not leaders that make France great, it's the character and mettle of the average French citizen you hold in such contempt. France will once more be a beacon of light to the world, I have no doubt about that."

"You misjudge us surely Monsieur" Said Gervais, cutting across Malin who was about to speak. "and everything we stand for. I'm certain also that France will regain her status and prestige in the world. That's our sacred mission. Our most imperative need at this moment is to restore those qualities in men and women that once made France great . . ."

"I'm not following you . . ."

"With the help of science; I'm talking about the science of eugenics?"

"Eugenics?"

"Desperate measures are called for," said Malin aggressively, "look at the recent history of France. In 1962, de Gaulle ran out of Algeria with his tail between his legs? France's has been on a downward spiral since that time."

The more he talked the more heated Malin became. Everyone in the room closed in around the long table to listen to the conversation.

"France will survive without you and without resorting to eugenics . . ." Said Claudel.

"Survive . . . ?" Said Malin, "Beggars on the street survive, dogs survive, is that to be the destiny of France . . . No, no . . . , our stratagem, our agenda is the sole hope for France. The time for talk and discussion is over. If we continue as we are going we will be like Britain, a decayed welfare state with almost ten million unemployed."

Doctor Gervais turned to Malin. He patted his arm and briefly smiled as if to mollify the increasingly volatile Malin.

"Look," said Gervais, "why don't we put all our differences aside and join us, you could help us make France great again?"

"You are asking me to become a member of the Aryan Brotherhood?"

"Of course. We have great need for men of your calibre."

"Why don't you explain to me your panacea for the ills of France?"

"Oh it's not just my ideas. Everyone in this room agrees to what had to be done . . ."

Many of the men in the room were looking at each other nervously. One of them, Sebastien Bonnet was visibly agitated. He stood up and took a step towards Gervais.

"Don't," He said. He took a handkerchief from his pocket and nervously wiped his forehead. "D-Doctor Gervais," he stammered, "d-don't say anything, you've said too much already . . . , we're not ready yet. This could ruin everything for us . . ."

"It's alright Sebastien, it's alright . . ." Said Gervais.

Malin stood up suddenly. His face grimaced as he faced the Minister.

"Be quiet, just be quiet and let us handle it . . ."

"Don't you know who he is? Everything we've worked for, he could destroy us all . . ."

"What does it matter what we tell him." Said Malin, "the Minister of Justice is one of us, he can see to it this

Detective takes a permanent retirement from the Surete." Malin turned to where Jacques Perrieux, the Minister of Justice was sitting. "and phuff . . . , just like that the Detective is no longer a problem."

Jacques Perrieux had become rigid in his seat. He stared silently at the floor as if oblivious to all around him. His normally serene face was twisted in a grimace of despair. Claudel ignored Malin.

"You were saying . . . ?" He said to Gervais.

"What I have to say may not go down too well with you but the fact is only the science of genetic engineering will bring back France from the brink of the abyss she now faces." Claudel was about to interrupt Gervais when the Doctor put up his hand. "Since you asked me the questions please do let me finish. Now, the first phase of our overall plan is to complete what we have already begun to build; frozen embryos clinics, sperm bank clinics, fertility clinics in new hospitals specializing in the field of eugenics. It's a daunting undertaking that will require the best minds French science has to offer. We will ascertain the intelligence quotients of the female candidates, their breeding, their eligibility to foster a superior race of French children . . . , with the embryos of famous, gifted men there's . . ."

"Just how far along are you with this project?"

"The clinics and hospitals are nearing completion in Marseilles . . ."

"How can that be? I've been a soldier and a government agent for over 20 years and I've heard nothing about this . . ."

"You're not supposed to know anything," said Gervais. "this project will remain secret to society at large until the moment we launch it. Inspector, look around you at the men in this room. They are from every level of government. They control the media, the army, the police, they will use every means at their disposal to implement our agenda."

"It sounds like you've been planning this for a long time." Said Claudel.

"Of course, and it will cost billions of Euros by the time we are finished the project. But fortunately for us several well-known philanthropists opened their purse strings."

"Tell me Doctor," said Claudel, "do you really believe you're going to get away with this?"

Gervais had turned sideways and was whispering to Malin. A grin, bordering on contempt began to slowly spread across the face of Malin. It was the Aryan's orator who turned to face Claudel.

"We will coordinate the power of the media in every village and town in France and explain our agenda. We have the finest intellectuals ready to acquaint them with the New Order . . ."

"Take me past all that if you would. Tell me what happens when vast numbers of citizens don't want any part of your sperm banks or race purification or genetic improvements."

"Creating a French Master Race is for the general good of all. Harsh measures would be used against non-compliant citizens."

"What you are saying is, you would kill anyone who opposes you . . . ?"

"We're talking about the very existence of France, France that today has become the laughing stock of Europe. A France that has poisonous bacteria running through her veins, she is dying, if to make her well again some lives must be lost . . . ," he gave a Gallic shrug of his shoulders, "so be it."

"If I remember correctly over one million people died including 15 thousand children within a few years of Hitler's experiments with eugenics . . . , is that your idea of success?"

Malin now looked as if he was about to lose his famed temper.

"I think we are wasting our time talking to you." Said Malin, "You're a run of the mill detective, how could you be expected to know the importance of what we are doing . . . ,"

"And you . . . ," Said Claudel, "what talent do you have, I mean beside pulling teeth and inflaming mobs to riot in the streets?"

Malin leaped up and was about to shout a rejoinder at Claudel when Gervais pulled him back down to his chair. Reluctantly Malin, still fuming sat down quietly.

"I will sum up our program in as few words as possible." Said Gervais. "In one year from now our final plans will be ready. We will launch a new conservative political party called the Reform Party of France. With the financial resources at our disposal we will get elected, we've done our homework. A new French constitution will be drawn up and under it non-compliance with the program of genetic engineering will be regarded as treason and will be punishable by death."

Gervais paused as if to allow the impact of what he had said to sink in. As he looked around the table at the august body of renowned Ministers, philanthropists, and military men Claudel was filled with a sense of incredulity that they could commit themselves to what amounted to genocide and ethnic cleansing in France.

"Don't look so shocked," continued Gervais, "how else can we enforce this colossal undertaking."

"So it has come to this . . . ," Said Claudel, "A Third Reich renaissance in France . . . ,"

"We had hoped you would join us in what we have to do. But whatever your opinion the Aryan Agenda will go forward . . ."

"And the logistics . . . , how . . . ?"

"You want to know about logistics? We will have trained doctors and nurses, thousands of them, ready to implement our plans when the time comes. To begin with, the sick and the elderly will be picked up from hospitals, from old people's homes and clinics in every town in France. They will be loaded onto special trains and taken to a sparsely populated region in Gueret in Limousin. To allay fear or suspicion patients will be told they are being moved to improved facilities with more scenic aspects and purer air. At the end of their journey they will be humanely demised by lethal injections and carbon monoxide. Bodies will be moved to a site where they will be incinerated. They will be the first steps to a new France, a new beginning. Listen to me . . . ," said Gervais, spreading open his arms as if appealing to Claudel to be reasonable. "Do you imagine for one moment we are the first to advocate the science of eugenics to alter the behaviour of man? Winston Churchill, HG Wells, George Bernard Shaw and American President Theodore Roosevelt all advocated the use of genetic engineering."

"Yes . . . , but they never went through with it."

"Monsieur I am a doctor. I took the Hippocratic Oath. I save life not destroy it . . ."

"I don't understand you," said Claudel, "there's death and destruction of life in everything you and your friends here are planning . . ."

"You don't seem to . . ."

"You say they are the first steps of the Aryan agenda, what else is coming?"

"All illegal immigrants, regardless of their resident status will be repatriated to their country of origin. We are already building stockades in Marseille to hold illegal non-Aryan immigrants. When we accomplish what we are setting out to do, civilized society as we know it will be changed forever. We will have two distinct classes to distinguish French society. The ruling classes will be of racially pure Aryan stock. The working classes will be culled to eliminate criminal and degenerate elements, the elderly, the incurably ill. Common labourers will be kept docile and subservient with medications for the duration of their lives; they will be implanted with tracking devices to prevent escape. Any sign of dissent or rebellion among workers will be ruthlessly stamped out. Our catholic bishops and religious will officiate in Trade Unions to assuage uneasiness in the ranks. In this matter of the workers; religion will play a vital role. Karl Marks got it right; religion is an opiate of the masses. And the Church got it right; it knows only too well how a religious faith quells the intemperate soul. The altruism of Church doctrine has turned Frenchmen and women to milksops. We will encourage religion among the workers; a belief in a benevolent God, historically it has worked wonders for the Church to keep its flock meek and subjective. It's strong backs we need, not strong minds. And if the workers propagate and multiply too much we'll spread viruses and contagion among them and decimate their numbers."

"Ethnic cleansing in France. And slavery to boot . . ."

Claudel stood up from the table. He had found out much more than he needed to know and that caused him some concern. He knew Malin and Gervais had no intention of letting his leave the chateau alive. He picked up a spoon and tapped lightly on a wineglass. An immediate silence fell over the room.

"Gentlemen, thank you for enlightening me about your agenda for the future of France. Leaving that aside, I came here to arrest Monsieur Malin and Monsieur Bauer for the murder of Professor Seamus Lowry . . . , among other charges."

An audible gasp came from some of the men around him.

"These are very serious charges," said Dr. Gervais urbanely as he lit his cigar, "I speak for all of us when I say no one has the faintest notion of what you're talking about. Such preposterous nonsense . . . , what proof do you have, when did this happen . . . ?"

Claudel ignored the question and the speaker. He was looking at General Thierry.

"General, your presence here disturbs me most of all knowing your reputation. Tell me and I'll believe you . . . , that you didn't know Malin had Professor Lowry killed and that he sent an assassin to Damascus to kill my wife."

General Thierry was a massively built man for his 62 years. A third generation officer, the General was renowned for his devotion to his command. When Claudel questioned him he held his gaze for a few moments before looking at Malin.

"Monsieur," said Senator Decour, "why do you level these charges against Jacques . . . ?"

"Just a few hours ago Henry Wilkins made a written confession about Malin and the murder of Professor Lowry. He was still writing when I left . . ."

No one except Claudel and the General, who was next to him, saw the sudden move of Malin as he reached into his pocket and pulled out a revolver. As Malin lunged towards Claudel the General leapt to his feet and grappled with him. The seated men stood up and backed away as Claudel rushed forward to help the General. The gun suddenly exploded. Malin clutched at his chest, fell to the floor and lay still. Dr. Gervais knelt down and took Malin's pulse. After a while he stood up and faced the General.

"He's dead. Give me that gun."

"Stand back. Unless you want to join him . . . ," growled the General. He turned to Claudel, "you guessed right. Everyone in this room knew what was going on from the start. We condoned it by saying nothing. We fooled ourselves that it was all for the glory of France. We're all murderers . . ."

"Shut your mouth, you fool," shouted Dr Gervais.

A shot rang out. Ewe Bauer rushed into the room shooting wildly at Claudel. The General collapsed to the floor fatally wounded. He reached for the revolver he had dropped, turned slowly and fired. Bauer pitched forward on the floor. Both men were dead. Claudel picked up the telephone and dialled a number. The men in the room looked dazed and crowded around Dr. Gervais as if for guidance. The doctor was staring vacantly in front of him as a stunned silence enveloped the room. The group had left the table and were standing facing Claudel in a semi-circle as others sat down in numbed silence not wanting or daring to speak, aware of the wide-ranging powers of Claudel.

Thirty minutes later the chateau was ringed with the flashing lights of police cars. The leaders of the Aryan Guard were arrested and were being taken away. One older man remained sitting in an armchair as a police officer stood over him. He was wiping his forehead with a handkerchief and seemed distressed and was breathing with some difficulty. The officer standing beside him nodded to Claudel and took him aside.

"This old gent isn't feeling good; I thought I'd stay with him until he recovers a bit . . ."

"Ok officer, you go ahead. I'll stay with him and bring him in when he feel better"

After the police had departed Claudel went to the drinks salver and poured out two drinks. He handed the older man a Cognac. After he took a drink he stopped gasping for air and seemed more comfortable. He held the glass up to the light, took another sip and swallowed.

"Wonderful" He said, "I think it might be Maison Brillet, is it?"

"I just enjoy the taste, I'm certainly not a connoisseur," Claudel returned to the drinks salver, picked up a bottle and looked at the label. He returned and sat down beside the older man. "right on the nose."

"My name is Ernst Muller, I'm a German, I'm also a eugenicist. You're very kind Sir, I'm feeling much better now, thank you. Well . . . ," he pulled open his tuxedo necktie and undid the top buttons of his shirt, "ahh, that's better, society and it's mores. I'll feel better when I'm out of this monkey suit . . ."

A fleeting smile brushed across the aged furrows and lines on a face filled at once with immense sadness, but also with infinite resolve. It was his eyes that most impressed Claudel; they were eyes that had plumbed the dark depths of the soul without wavering in his belief of its inviolate worth. Claudel judged Muller to be about 80 years old, a spry 80.

"Well Doctor," Said Claudel, "I'm glad you're feeling better." He made a slow sweeping movement with his arm, indicating the works of art about the sumptuous room. "this is quite a show, I've never seen anything like it outside the Louvre."

"Yes," Said Muller, "It's heart lifting to see such fine pieces. Very beautiful indeed."

"I'm sorry to have to tell you but . . . , when we are finished you will be taken to Police headquarters. Formal charges will be made against you regarding the Aryan Brotherhood. Before that, do you mind if I ask you some personal questions, off the record, please tell me to mind my own business if you wish."

"No, no, please go ahead, it's alright . . ."

Claudel paused for a few moments as if to consider what he had to say.

"Why are you involved with men like Dr. Gervais and Malin, considering the agenda they have . . . ?"

"Ah well, first I must tell you I never knew that Malin was a murderer, I just heard about those terrible things tonight. And secondly, I was invited to join the Aryans because I was a eugenicist; I wanted to join other scientists in my field. I am little known because I never give interviews and try to remain in the background to get on with my work. But I am very well qualified, let me not be found guilty of false modesty about my work. And I was able to influence my colleagues, the scientists, that is. But Malin and his cohorts seem to have a special mission of their own and they were running the show . . . , we did not have a happy relationship."

"What do you think . . . ," asked Claudel, "can a genetically engineered Master Race be produced, and by contrast can workers be induced by genetics to rejoice in their servility . . . ?"

"Oh yes, very likely. If the will and the means are there and good men run away and hide, of course, anything is possible. It would take a lifetime to accomplish of course. The pain and suffering of the innocent would end for the most part in madness and suicide. What would be the sense of living if life was so obtained? In the not too distant past a similar insanity poisoned the psyche of the German government. History is filled with such atrocities . . ."

"Doctor, why did you stay with the Aryans . . . , if you knew the plans they had"?

"My fellow scientists and I used genetic engineering only for positive and humane reasons. Our labs and offices were set apart in a different building. There were four of us.

JOHN FLANAGAN

We worked on finding cures for diseases and for hereditary illnesses, for research. We intended to quit en bloc when we heard Malin and Gervais planned this Master Race madness . . ."

Muller took a drink and eased back on to the headrest of the armchair.

"As a scientist I would say, I am driven. Before I die I would like to be able to explore the dark, troubled side of man and alleviate and heal that if possible. But the soul is intangible . . . , like the mind." Muller undid his shirt sleeve button and pushed his jacket and shirt sleeve up to his elbow. He pointed to a series of faded barely visible numbers on his forearm. "I was 14 years old when I got that in Auschwitz concentration camp. The rest of my family of seven were gassed or shot. I was the sole survivor." He pushed down the sleeves and rebuttoned the shirt. After some moments he placed the unfinished drink on a nearby table. "thank you for that but it's too late for me to drink any more."

By this time Claudel found himself intrigued by Muller.

"And now," Said Muller, pushing forward in his seat, "I'm getting tired. Do you mind if we get along to Police Headquarters . . . ?"

Claudel stood up and helped Muller to his feet.

"Doctor, there will be no need for you to go to Police Headquarters tonight . . ."

"Oh, when . . . ?"

"You don't have to go at all. Tell me, how are you getting home . . . ?"

"The way I came, by taxi, I'm too old to drive now . . ."

"There's a police car outside, come with me, I'll have him take you home."

Claudel accompanied Muller out to the police car. As they were parting Muller shook his hand.

"There's one more thing if I could ask you." Said Muller, "the other three scientists that were arrested, please believe me when I tell you they knew nothing about this Aryan agenda . . ."

"I'll have your colleagues released immediately."

"I don't know how to thank you."

"Goodnight Doctor. I hope you find the answers you are still looking for."

He watched as Muller was driven out of the estate. He turned quickly on his heels and went back into the chateau. He reached for the telephone and called Damascus. The sonorous voice of Umar Peera came on the line.

"Hello, who is it?"

"Umar, its Marc . . . ."

"Marc, are you alright?"

"Good news Umar. It's all over. The danger is past."

"Ah, say no more. I will put your wife on the 'phone . . . ."

The low clouds over the village of Ivry la Bataille were darkening as Claudel and Solonge strolled in the fields at the back of the cottage. The three dogs were yelping ahead of them, exulting in the freedom of the countryside. Even Horace, the staid and proper English pointer showed a rare excitability in leaping after gadflies. They reached a well-worn path that led to a wooded copse on top of a nearby hill. Here the hedgerows towered above them, screening out everything but the ever darkening clouds overhead. It had been a difficult year for the farmers due to an unexpected drought. The parched earth was caked underfoot, the hedgerows covered in a dry dust. But all that was about to change and catch Claudel and his wife unprepared in what was intended to be an after dinner stroll. It was when the dogs came to heel without being called, when the forest grew ominously silent, and the bulging clouds seemed to brush the treetops that Claudel realized too late the walk had been a mistake. They had ignored an early warning when the sky to the East over Paris had turned dark, erupting with lightning streaks and rolls of distant thunder. Solonge moved closer to Claudel. Overhead the fast moving clouds seemed low enough to touch. The first drops of rain patted the caked earth as Claudel and Solonge clasped hands. Grinning broadly they turned to each other and yelled.

"Run."

Down the hill they bolted with the dogs already out of sight. The first drops of rain was the overture, the fine tuning of instruments in the firmament orchestra, the following soft drizzle the opening chords of the movement. Progressing to brass and percussions, deafening peals of thunder rolled across the sky. Jagged lightening streaked above the runners as the black voluminous clouds unleashed a deluge on the hungry earth. Raging winds filled the air with flying debris as Claudel raced Solonge the few final meters to the cottage where the dogs were anxiously waiting for them. They pushed through the door and slammed it behind them.

Sitting on a matt before the fire Günter the cat raised his head to greet them. He blinked his one good eye and went back to sleep.

THE END

WHO IS GABRIELLE?

by by

JOHN FLANAGAN

MARC CLAUDEL AWOKE DREARILY FROM a deep sleep and reached over to his wife Solonge. As his hand searched the empty space he was not surprised to find her gone. He picked up the bedside clock and stared dumbly at it. It was the ungodly hour of 5:00 A.M. on Friday morning. In a few moments the aroma of freshly baked soda bread set his saliva flowing. What a woman, he mused. When they had married she put all thoughts of pursuing her career as a botanist aside and insisted on staying at home, to look after him, as she so quaintly put it.

They had met in Paris not long after she arrived there from her home in Damascus in Syria. After marrying they moved to his cottage in Ivry la Bataille, a market town 80 kilometers West of Paris. She had devoted herself to married life with fervour and turned the spartan country cottage into a home from which he seldom wished to venture. The daughter of wealthy parents, she would curl up in an armchair and darn the holes in his socks. She had knitted him a cardigan to which he had become so attached

73

he lived in it most of the time. His work as a special agent for the Surete Nationale Francaise was sometimes dangerous and always stressful. She had made it all bearable since entering his life, calming his worst moments with her quiet fortitude.

Solonge came into the bedroom carrying a tray with eggs and coffee and soda bread. She laid the tray aside for a moment and propped up the pillows behind his back. The early morning sluggishness left him as she placed the tray on his lap and sat facing him at the end of the bed. Her forehead was creased in a frown as if she was beset by some insoluble problem. He laughed quietly, shaking his head.

"How long have we been married ?" he said.

"Oh, mm .., it's two years and three months, but why ?"

"In other words long enough for me to know when I'm being set up. What's all this attention going to cost me .. ?"

Solonge colored slightly and smiled.

"Am I so obvious ?"

He put the tray aside and pulled her close to him.

"You must be the only woman in France who blushes. Now tell me, what intrigue is stirring in that mind of yours?"

"I know you will not agree . . ."

"I'm waiting . . ."

"It's .., It's my Uncle Daoud and his family. This weekend there is a party for his daughter and . . ."

"Are you going .. ?"

"Yes but they invited us both."

"Oh . . ."

"It would mean so much if you come also."

"Well I . . ."

"I know how much you hate parties but it's really just a family get-together and . . ."

"Solonge . . ."

"You see they are looking forward so much to seeing you. They haven't seen you for over a year."

"Alright, I was just kidding you. Of course I'll go. Now can you please throw the newspaper in to me while I have my breakfast."

Solonge beamed as she hugged Claudel and left the room. She went out to the front porch and picked up the 'Le Monde' newspaper. She returned and gave the newspaper to Claudel, kissed him and was about to leave when an exclamation from him pulled her up short.

"Marc, what is it?"

Claudel had been reading the newspaper. He suddenly threw it aside, got out of bed and donned a bathrobe.

"I must get to Evreux immediately."

Solonge picked up the newspaper and scanned the front page. Her eyes fell on a report in the bottom left column of the front-page with the heading 'BODY OF WOMAN TAKEN FROM SEINE AT PONT D'ISSY IN PARIS. POLICE OFFICER QUESTIONED.' The dead woman's name was Gabrielle Villon. The officer referred to was Inspector Olivier Brunet stationed at Evreux; the same officer with whom her husband had worked with on several investigations.

The compact single story house of Inspector Oliver Brunet was set back from the main road at Gauville la Compagne, North-West of Evreux. The house was secluded and dwarfed by a circle of fir trees. Not every house on the road boasted the coveted fir trees. When Inspector Brunet had bought the house the trees were the deciding factor even though he could hardly afford the purchase of the house on his Inspectors salary. The encircling firs stood like friendly sentinels guarding his home and family, their foliage forming a cooling shade in the heat of summer and lessened the effect of buffeting winter winds.

If Inspector Brunet could never be described as portentous he could in all fairness be described as a little strait-laced, an abstemious man inclined to be frugal but without being mean. His enjoyment of the house knew no bounds. To make ends meet, his wife Lucille took in foreign exchange students during the summer. Madame Brunet was a rotund dour woman inclined to be argumentative and bossy. Of Flemish farming stock Madame Brunet was not always aware of her brusqueness of manner; she had been raised on a farm in a family that wasted little time cultivating the social graces. With regard to this nonsense in the Le Monde newspaper, this murder her husband was supposedly involved in, she was convinced beyond all doubt of his innocence. This was not out of any laudatory sense of marital fidelity but because she found it impossible to believe any woman in her right mind could be attracted romantically to her husband. The stars in their courses would more likely change orbit than for Madame Brunet to deviate from her entrenched sense of pious rectitude. All men were selfish oafs who couldn't cope with life without the guiding hand of a strong woman. Her attitude towards her husband's foibles was deceptively simple. It was expected of her by the Church, of which she was a weekly communicant, to love her husband. If love was commensurate with duty, she did her duty and that was the end of it.

Claudel turned right off the main road and parked the car beneath the towering firs. When he rang the doorbell Madame Brunet opened the door and bid him enter. He had telephoned earlier and though not moved by the prospect of his visit she had assumed an effected cordiality. She led Claudel to a living room, muttered something about her husband and left. After a few minutes Inspector Brunet joined him. They shook hands warmly and sat down. Claudel was greatly surprised by the unkempt appearance of the usually fastidious Inspector who was now sporting a few days growth of beard. His normally clear eyes were reddish and vein-streaked. Perhaps the most immediate change he saw was the unlit cigarette quivering between his fingers. He had never seen the Inspector smoke before. The Inspector took a box of matches from his pocket and with much fumbling and shaking betrayed the fact that he was not an inveterate smoker. He held the cigarette poised between his index finger and thumb much as a music conductor might hold a baton, or a duellist a foil. Each time he inhaled he coughed. He was coughing fitfully now as he reached for a bottle of wine and filled a glass. He held the bottle up to Claudel who shook his head. He put the bottle down with a sigh.

"I knew you'd refuse, that's why I didn't pour you one."

"Inspector . . ," began Claudel.

"Not for much longer." Said the Inspector gruffly.

"I came to see if there is anything I can do."

Inspector Brunet made a gesture of despair and rubbed his red eyes.

"Forgive my rudeness Monsieur Claudel. If I have an odd way of showing it, I'm very glad to see you. Can I offer you coffee?"

"No thanks. I just want you to tell me how I can help."

The Inspector picked up his glass of Beaujolais wine and stared into its ruby depths.

"Do you believe in the law of retribution Monsieur?"

Claudel smiled.

"To tell you the truth, I've never given it much thought . . ."

"I'm in trouble now because I forgot all about the divine law of retribution."

The Inspector, having imbibed too much wine was struggling to articulate his scattered thoughts. He was about to refill his empty glass when he looked at Claudel and changed his mind.

"Inspector," Said Claudel, "you don't have to tell me you had nothing to do with this drowning, but why did they question you?"

"Because I was .. , eh, involved with . . ."

"You mean . . ?"

"Just so .. , I have known . . . , Gabrielle for oh .. , about three months . . ."

"Sure, but that's no reason to suspend you from duty."

"Well the Mayor of Evreux seems to think otherwise. He's gloating over my misfortune. Everything is so parochial around here, out in the country. The Mayor doesn't like me because I'm a Parisian. But besides that he knows I'm one of the last people to see Gabrielle alive."

"When was that?"

"You know I've lost all account of time. What day is this?"

"It's Friday."

"Friday? Let me see, I was out at her house on Wednesday last. She lives .. , or rather lived in Prey. She was a married woman. I know you must think I'm a louse . . . , but I just couldn't help myself. Her husband is an executive with Astro Chemicals. His job took him abroad, sometimes for weeks at a time. After I met Gabrielle I was out at his house regularly when he was away. Always after dark, like some shameless lecher."

"Did they have any children?"

"No, neither of them wanted children. As God is my judge I can't explain the madness that overcame me. She was so beautiful, I lost all sense of reason . . ."

"The important thing now is to get your name cleared of this murder."

"You don't understand Monsieur; my whole life has been turned upside down; my family's name and reputation is ruined. Worst of all has been the pain I caused to her husband Gilbert Villon. What a damn hypocrite I am, do you know I'm a guild leader in my Church?"

The Inspector poured himself another glass of wine, took a drink and put the glass down. He sat back in his chair and shook his head, looking at Claudel with a wry smile.

"Monsieur has anyone ever fully explained that spell a woman can put on a man?"

Claudel shook his head, glad for even a momentary respite from the Inspector's gloomy disposition.

"Some of the poets have come close but it's still shrouded in mystery. I'm inclined to think it's better that way . . ."

"Gabrielle seemed to like older men for some reason. I don't know why, she was so exotic, such a joy to be with . . . , she could have had any man she wanted just by snapping her fingers."

"Did you meet her husband?"

"Gilbert? Please don't remind me. One of the nicest men I ever met, a born gentleman. One day I went to the house to meet Gabrielle thinking she was alone only to find he had cut short a trip and he was there. I was able to make a convincing pretext for being there because I was in my police uniform. He invited me in. When he discovered I played chess he invited me to stay for supper. There I was enjoying his hospitality, eating his food and making eyes at his wife behind his back. I felt like something vile that should be trodden underfoot yet I was powerless to stop myself. Can you believe it? Every time I left her arms I'd go to Church and pray for the moral strength to end the affair . . . , but I always went back to her."

"Inspector . . ."

"It's all right Monsieur, I'm trying to understand my own state of mind. The affair was well over before she died. I saw her with another man you see. I was insane with jealousy but what could I do? I was the mad Lothario bringing chaos to other people's lives. It brought home to me how her husband must have felt. During one game of chess he told me he knew Gabrielle and I were having an affair. She had brought other men into his home and flaunted them before him . . ," the Inspector stood up and paced about the room. "excuse me Monsieur Claudel, I didn't mean to be vulgar . . ."

"My friend, are you forgetting I spent 20 years in the army."

"At first I felt nothing but contempt for him. He was a cuckold and deserved what he got. But what he said cut right through me. You can't imagine how sick and wounded he was while presenting a dignified countenance to the world at large. You see he loved his wife so much he endured all the slander and mockery from me and others like me rather than lose her. This was a proud and successful man brought to his knees . . . Gabrielle destroyed him . . ."

He stopped talking and sat back down, looking at the cigarette as if wondering where it came from. His wife came into the room and asked Claudel if he would like coffee. When he declined she left, not even having looked at her husband. Claudel remained with the Inspector for another hour, quietly listening to his plethora of woes.

Later that afternoon Claudel drove to the village of Prey, 16 kilometers South of the town of Evreux. Gilbert Villon lived in a quiet estate of manicured lawns and hedgerows. Each house was fronted by white picket fencing. The estate was horseshoe shaped with flowerbeds and a water fountain at its centre. The Residents Association employed a part-time gardener to tend the landscaping in the exclusive cul de sac. The house of Gilbert Villon was at the center of the curve of the horseshoe. Claudel pulled the car alongside the pavement and turned off the engine. He pushed the fence door open and went to the house. When he pressed the doorbell Gilbert Villon greeted him cordially after he introduced himself. He was tall, inclined to corpulence with a neatly trimmed beard and mustache. Villon had begun his career as an academic. After graduating with honours from the Sorbonne University in Paris he taught languages and literature in a private school in Paris. Before long the substantially greater rewards of commerce tempted him and he joined the Astro group of companies. He was a quiet reflective man with exacting personal standards, the sort who would not have many close friends but made an ideal neighbour. There was an aloofness to his manner that was not intentional but which, given his intellectual prowess persuaded his peers in Astro Chemicals to treat him with caution and respect. He was slow to anger but he could be devastating when provoked, often unleashing a stream of vitriolic abuse at overly ambitious young-bloods in the Company. On the other hand the elderly cleaning woman who made his coffee every day could make him emotional by brushing a piece of lint from his suit or by simply handing him his coat and scarf. His income would have allowed him to live on a grander scale but his wife had chosen the house in Prey in happier times and he had grown used to it. After they shook hands Claudel followed Villon into the living room. "Would you like coffee, a drink perhaps?" Villon was holding a half-filled brandy glass in his hand.

"Well, perhaps a small whiskey if it's not too much trouble Monsieur, thank you. I just have a few questions if you don't mind. Allow me to convey my condolence on the death of your wife."

"Thank you. I'll be glad to help in any way I can." Villon went to a drinks cabinet and poured a whiskey which he handed to Claudel.

When they were seated Villon continued.

"I've told the police everything I know . . , such as it is."

"Yes, I've read your statement. About Inspector Brunet, I'd like to reassure you . . ."

"I don't believe for a moment he had anything to do with Gabrielle's death."

"I'm glad to hear it. And I hope you will forgive me if some of my questions may seem . . , indelicate."

"No need to apologize Monsieur, it was no secret my wife had many lovers in the eight years we were married. In the end Gabrielle didn't even try to be discreet, she knew I wouldn't, I couldn't leave her."

Villon leaned back in the sofa and rubbed his eyes. He shook his head and refocused on Claudel.

"You must think I'm a spineless cretin," he said.

"I think nothing of the kind Monsieur. You loved your wife, that much is very obvious. Don't reproach yourself too much, you have your own life to get on with. Can you tell me, is there anyone you know who might have, well, wanted to harm your wife?"

Villon gave a short bitter laugh.

"You mean jealous lovers? Of course, there have been many. But someone who would want to kill her? I don't know . . ."

"What will you do now Monsieur? Have you any plans?" asked Claudel.

"I haven't decided yet. I'll probably sell the house and go back to Paris, start teaching again."

"Do you think I could see your wife's wardrobe, your bedroom?"

"Of course, follow me."

Claudel finished his drink and followed Villon along a corridor and opened a bedroom door. The room exuded an aura of pristine cleanliness. A luxurious white carpet covered the floor. The brass rail bed was draped with a white embroidered eiderdown. All the furnishings were white as were the lace curtains and drapes. Cut glass mirrors etched with cherubs and roses covered the sliding panels of the wardrobe.

"I put the carpet down myself," said Villon, "I wallpapered the room and painted it. I wanted to use warmer shades but she wouldn't hear of it. As usual she got her way. If I objected she'd throw a tantrum and threaten to leave me, even over the color of paint. White was her favourite color, there's something for you to grapple with."

He went to the wardrobe and slid the panels aside to reveal expensive designer coats and dresses. The shelf above them contained rows of unopened boxes of dress shoes. On the dressing table there was jewellery boxes filled with an assortment of gold necklaces, earrings and bracelets. Villon picked some of them up.

"Much of the money I made I spent on Gabrielle and none of it mattered. I could not keep her home. Ironic isn't it, I was just making her more attractive for her lovers."

"Did your wife normally wear jewellery when she went out?"

"Always. She had impeccable dress sense. Everything was ensemble . . ."

"Monsieur can you remember the jewellery she wore the night she died?"

"I remember it very well. She wore a pearl necklace with matching earrings and bracelet. She had on a burgundy dress with white belt and buttons. She was so beautiful it hurt me to look at her, I begged her not to go out."

"The reason I ask is that there were no such items of jewellery when the body was taken from the Seine."

"Could she have been killed for the jewellery?" asked Villon.

"At this point nothing is being ruled out. But I'm sure this investigation won't take much longer."

"Oh . . ."

"For one thing the autopsy report showed tiny fragments of skin beneath the fingernails of her right hand. It looks like she tore at someone before she died."

Villon picked up a piece of paper with a number written on it. He handed it to Claudel.

"I found this telephone number in one of her pockets. The police missed it when they were here . . ."

"Thank you Monsieur, you've been a big help," said Claudel as he prepared to leave. At the door they shook hands. "I wish there was something I could say to relieve your distress."

"It helped to talk about her. I wish I knew why it all had to happen. I treated Gabrielle like a princess, trying to anticipate her needs, her whims. All to no avail."

Late the following night Claudel sat at the bar in Marsal's Bistro in the village of Damville. In the tiny smoke filled space the din from a jazz quartet was deafening. The three barmaids were in constant demand, rushing back and forth between the bar and the noisy clientele. An older couple behind the bar filled the orders for drinks and food. After several attempts Claudel caught the man's eye and ordered a whiskey. While he was paying for the drink he leaned forward and spoke quietly to the older man.

"Monsieur Jacques Marsal ?"

"Yes."

"Monsieur forgive me for not telephoning you first," Said Claudel, discreetly showing his identification, "I'd like to talk to you about Madame Gabrielle Villon."

Marsal had picked up a tray of empty glasses. Minute tremors from his hands made them shake as he put them into the bar sink. He looked about him nervously.

"Are you the owner of the Bar?" asked Claudel.

Marsal nodded his head.

"If I come by at about 10 'O'clock in the morning, would that be more convenient for you?"

"Better leave it 'till eleven, it's going to be a late night.'

Claudel finished his drink and left the bar. When he reached the street he turned around to see Marsal and a woman peering at him through the glass-paneled door. They watched him as he walked away from the Bistro and disappeared into the darkness.

At exactly 11:00 A.M. the following morning Claudel returned to the Bistro and sat at a table out on the sidewalk. The woman he had seen the night before came out from the bar. He ordered a coffee and a croissant. She smiled briefly and made a comment about the weather. He could sense the intense curiosity his presence caused. She wanted to question him but thought better of it. She left and after a few minutes brought back the coffee and croissant.

"My husband is expecting you, he'll be out in a moment. Will there be anything else?"

"No Madame that will be all. Thank you."

The bistro owner joined him, extending his hand. As they shook hands he nodded towards the woman who had served Claudel.

"My wife," he said as they sat down, "my wife Lizzi. It was too noisy for much formality last night Monsieur."

"About Madame Villon . . . ," Said Claudel, "Your name and telephone number was in her house."

As her husband and his visitor got deeper into conversation she ventured closer to where they were seated. Marsel stood up.

"Let's take a walk," he said to Claudel.

They walked a hundred meters to the 'Le Chasseur' Bar. Marsal and the 'Le Chasseur' Bar owner were friends and founder members of the Damville Hunting and Fishing Club. The two owners called into each other's Bars with the aplomb of potentates visiting each other's kingdoms. When they reached 'Le Chasseur' Marsal tapped on the door and waited. In a few minutes the bleary eyed owner with a half smoked Gauloise cigarette hanging onto his lower lip came out and unlocked the door. Muttering greetings he shook both men's hands, put on the Bar lights and went back upstairs whence he came. Marsal relocked the door and went behind the bar. He offered Claudel a drink which he refused pleading the early hour of the day. He poured himself an aperitif and joined Claudel at a table which looked out on to the village square. The silence inside the Bar was strangely remote from the market day traffic building up beyond the plate glass window of the shop front. Marsal was a finely built man who looked much younger than his 53 years. He had aged well, the brunt of his advancing years being borne by the curving forward of his shoulders but even this was not pronounced. He wore a worn panama hat in deference to a bald spot at the top of his head. Earlier in his life he had sported a clipped mustache which he shaved when it turned grey.

"Monsieur Marsal," Began Claudel, "it would be very much in your own interest to tell me everything you know. When was the last time you saw the deceased Madame Villon?"

"The last time? That would be Thursday, yes last Thursday. We had dinner in Point Saint Cloud, in a quiet out of the way place so as not to be seen. She went home early. She said she wanted to do her hair but I knew it wasn't for that. I had the feeling for some time that there was someone else. She got tired of me just at the time I was getting deeply involved with her."

"Where were you last Saturday night?"

"Working in the Bistro, Saturday is our biggest night."

"All night?"

"Yes, of course. There are many people who can vouch for me. I was working the Bar all afternoon through until 2:00 A.M. in the morning. I went straight to bed after that. I live over the Bar. Can I ask you a question Inspector, did Gabrielle jump from the bridge or was she pushed?"

"We have to wait for the full autopsy report."

"I was going to ask her to marry me. I didn't even think how I was supposed to support her if she said yes. How could I compete with her husband, that lavish style she was so used to? Imagine Gabrielle living over a Bar even if she agreed to marry me. And what was I supposed to do with my wife? She would never give me a divorce. Are you quite sure I can't get you a drink?"

"Well ok, make it a small whiskey."

"Good. Excuse me a moment."

Marsal went behind the bar, got another aperitif for himself and poured a whiskey. He rejoined Claudel at the table. As he drank he became increasingly verbose.

"When Gabrielle told me she loved me I couldn't think of anything else in life. Look at me. What do you see? I'm 53 years old, well past it by any standard and this beautiful young woman walks into my life. I never knew what love was until I met her. I don't suppose this makes any sense to you?"

87

"I'm not a moralist in any way but since you've asked me, no, fooling around with another man's wife doesn't make any sense to me at all. My sympathy lies with the husband of the deceased woman."

"Of course. I'm not really very proud of myself. But if you had known her . . ."

"I don't wish to hear any more Monsieur if you don't mind. I came here to establish your movements of last Saturday night. I will detain you no longer."

What perplexed the usually urbane Claudel was the fact that Marsal, like Inspector Brunet, seemed a serious responsible man with substance to his character. Both decent men. Even allowing for the frailty of human nature, both men had known that Gilbert Villon was already broken in mind and spirit by his wife's betrayals. Did they really expect to achieve personal happiness by crushing the life out of Gabrielle's shattered husband? At what point, he wondered, did the allure and beauty of Gabrielle become so irresistible that she made them heedless to any sense of common humanity? They further humiliated an already broken man. Estranging Villon's wife's affections was a disingenuous form of murder. He was reminded of the lament of Shakespeare's Othello;

> I would rather be a toad
> And live upon the vapours of a dungeon
> Than keep a corner of the thing I love
> For others uses.

The coffee and croissant Marsal had for breakfast scarcely inhibited the effect of the aperitifs and at this moment he was feeling a little tipsy. He was a quiet affable man who had never raised his voice to his acrimonious wife in 32 years of married life. Marsal would always contend, even to Gabrielle, that he loved his wife even though they had grown apart over the years. A past of shared memories was the catalyst binding each to the other. They had grown used to, accustomed to each other and for Marsal, who feared loneliness above all else, this constituted love. In his wife's commanding presence he felt futile and insignificant as if he played only a minor part in what was his life. Often when his wife or clients in the Bistro looked at him in that way in which one could be looked at without being seen he wanted to shout out that there was more to him than they saw in a fleeting glance. He shook his head dolefully as the drink's euphoric effect regressed to one of depression.

"Monsieur," said Claudel, "I'd like to have a few words with your wife, just a formality. I won't keep her long."

"I see. Well of course. Eh . . , may I ask you, unless it's necessary, not to mention about Gabrielle and me? You go ahead. I'll telephone her and tell her you are coming."

Claudel nodded curtly. He left the 'Le Chasseur' Bar and walked back to Marsal's Bistro. He went inside and sat down and waited, and waited. He looked at his watch several times as 20 minutes passed. At last Madame Eliza Marsal came out from the Bistro. There was a noticeable change in the appearance of Madame Marsal, known locally as Lizzi. She had changed her dress, retouched her eyebrows and hair and he detected a perfume she had not worn earlier. Lizzi was petite in stature with short hair dyed with henna. She had thin lips and a long aquiline nose, a nose that dipped into everyone's affairs. Gossip mongering was a way of life, a vocation for Lizzi. Over the years she had become privy to the private lives and secrets of the village of Damville at large. This divining of family skeletons gave Lizzi moments of ecstatic bliss and compensated to some degree for the drudgery of her life. She had also inveigled her way into the Cure's confidence and sometimes assisted him at the Sunday mass. Many parishioners shifted uneasily in their seats beholding the two repositories of the darkest secrets of the village in such close proximity to the altar of God.

She led Claudel to an office at the rear of the Bistro. It was a tiny boarded-in space just large enough to accommodate a desk and two chairs. Her husband had just told her the police were questioning people about the drowning of a local woman. She gushed at the prospect of being grilled by the police, she might even get her photograph in the newspaper.

"Madame," said Claudel, "This will only take a few minutes . . ."

"Oh don't be concerned about that, I have all the time in the world."

"Thank you Madame."

"Please call me Lizzi."

"Certainly eh . . , Lizzi. Well I really just want you to verify something for me . . ."

"You live locally don't you? I could swear I've seen you before."

"Why yes . . ."

"Where?"

"Not far . . , Ivry La Bataille."

"I knew it . . ."

"Madame eh, Lizzi, I want to ask you if your husband left here at any time between the hours of 8 '0'clock on last Saturday night and 2 '0'clock on Sunday morning?"

"Jacques. Why on earth do you want to know anything about him?"

"I'm questioning a lot of people, it's just routine. I'm sure you understand."

"Of course Monsieur. It's just so funny to think of him being suspected of anything. But to answer your question he was here all day Saturday and Sunday, day and night. Eh . . , Monsieur, this is all in confidence is it not?"

"Of course . . ."

"To tell you the truth Jacques has been acting a little strange of late. I don't know what's got into him. Only recently he bought himself a new suit. He started to use after shave lotion and he stinks to high heaven. He's discovered art, he gets all dressed up and goes off to visit art galleries in Paris, sometimes for the whole day. The poor thing, I think he's turning senile if you ask me. He doesn't listen to me anymore and who knows what's best for him more than I do?"

Claudel had to make an effort to listen to the further ramblings of Lizzi. Her words issued in a spontaneous flow and seemed to function independently of conscious thought. When he finally took leave of her he breathed a deep sigh of relief.

A telephone number from Gabrielle's diary led Claudel to the gamekeeper's lodge in the former chateau of the Viscount Yves Marie de Rocquefort, now the property of the Bank of France. The lands and fortune of the family had been squandered by the present Viscount through a combination of gambling and ill-advised investments. The bank, anxious to assuage public concern over the acquisition was persuaded by the French Historical Society to open the chateau to the public. The bank hired the penniless Viscount as a curator, giving him free use of the gatekeepers' lodge in which he now lived. The Viscount de Rocquefort lived modestly considering his recent lifestyle. Now in his 57th year, the Viscount, as a result of losing his fortune, had become embittered and reclusive. In a life chiefly devoted to bacchanalian revelry he had already been married and divorced four times. The one extravagance he allowed himself was keeping Catherine the maid who had worked for him in the chateau. She was an attractive woman in her mid-thirties with a cherubic roundness to her face. She was full figured and a large pair of horn-rimmed glasses enhanced her sensuous appearance. Rumors abounded in the village about the Viscount and Catherine. Her detractors said she had aspirations above her station, that she was intent on becoming the fifth Viscountess de Rocquefort. In actual fact Catherine Giroux was a shy and impressionable country girl who was dazzled by the grandeur of the chateau when she first went to work there. When the Viscount was divorced by his last wife, creating a further drain on his meager finances, the entire housekeeping staff was dismissed with the exception of Catherine. Being of a simple mien it had not occurred to her that her savings may have been the reason for the Viscounts' sudden interest in her or his subsequent amorous overtures. When she finally succumbed to his pervasive influence she parted without resentment with all her savings. But that was all in the past. Tonight she was ecstatically happy. The previous weekend the Viscount had given her a gift unlike anything she had ever possessed. She let her simple heart hope that the Viscount had at last grown to love her.

Claudel had left a message on the telephone answering machine at the Lodge to say he would be calling to see the Viscount. All of his previous calls had gone unanswered. When he rang the doorbell of the Lodge Catherine opened the door. She curtsied and led him to a sitting room in the rear of the ivy-covered building. The Viscount was writing at a desk. After announcing Claudel, Catherine left, closing the door behind her. The Viscount continued writing, ignoring Claudel's presence. Finally with a sullen face he threw down the pen and waved Claudel to an armchair. The room was in semi darkness, illuminated only by the desk lamp that highlighted the Viscount's large hands in a circle of white light. When he had sat down Claudel peered through the gloom to try to determine the features and appearance of the Viscount. In the restricted light he could make out only his outline, the mass of his physique. As his eyes grew accustomed to the gloom the face assumed detail and dimension. He saw a wide clamped mouth inverted in a scowl, a large nose and small eyes under arched eyebrows set closely together. The wide forehead, like the back of his hands was peppered with red blotches. He was dressed in the country tweeds of the well-to-do landowner complete with chequered shirt and pinned necktie. Large silver trophies and medals regaled the walls. To his left Claudel could make out photographs of gymkhanas, horsemen riding to hounds, prizes being awarded.

The Viscount's eyes were glinting defiantly at Claudel, like an animal in its lair staring down an intruder. He had picked up a pen and was tapping impatiently on the desk.

"Well," he said roughly, "since you barged your way in here, get on with it . . ."

"Monsieur," began Claudel.

"Don't you fellows have anything better to do than bothering law abiding citizens?"

"I assure you Monsieur, I wouldn't be here if it wasn't an important matter."

"Very well. What is it?"

"I'm making enquiries into the death of Madame Gabrielle Villon."

The Viscount stopped tapping on the desk.

"What's that got to do with me . . ? I can't say I can place the name."

"I see. It's just that your telephone number was in her diary..."

"I know lots of people on a casual basis, is there a law against that?"

The Viscount was confident in his arrogance, self-assured in handling a common detective. Claudel was nonplussed. The Viscount was like many he encountered who mistook his natural diplomacy and courtesy as weakness of character. Claudel was trying to make allowance for the ignominious fall of a once great family but the Viscount was exhausting his patience. He was proving to be a self-serving misanthrope and if this was the game he wanted to play then he would oblige him.

"Monsieur," Said Claudel, "I have a cell phone in my pocket. Unless you give me your full cooperation I will have a warrant issued for your arrest. You will be taken to Evreux police station in handcuffs. If you think it's an empty threat just try me."

Perhaps it was the resolve in Claudel's voice or the fear of being incarcerated in a prison cell that brought the Viscount up short. His head slumped over his hands.

"I didn't know she was going to jump from the bridge..."

"You were with her.., on the bridge?"

"I didn't see her jump..."

"According to the autopsy report she had a bruise on her face, her lip had been split by a blow."

"I don't know anything about that. She probably met someone after I left her. Who knows with a woman like that. Look, I took her to dinner and then we went to a nightclub." He leaned forward over the desk and clasped his hands together, raising his voice in a renewed attempt to intimidate Claudel. "I'll have your job over this," he said, "you come in here threatening me with arrest over a.., a tramp."

"She was a man's wife, a man who loved her. She didn't deserve to die like that . . ."

"Sooner or later someone would have done her in. She was almost asking for it. If you ask me the answer to her problem was on a psychiatrist's couch. Too easy she was, no sense of the hunt with her if you take my meaning."

"So you left her on Pont d'Issy, looking down at the water."

"That's right . . ."

"After you hit her . . ."

"Now look here, I've been more than cooperative with you. Go back and file your report or whatever it is you people do. If you have anymore questions you can talk to my lawyer."

"Your housekeeper . . ."

"Catherine, what about her?"

"Please call her in here."

"What in hell's name do you want with her?"

"Get her in here or I'll have her brought to Evreux for questioning."

Muttering obscenities the Viscount went to the door and called to his housekeeper. He sat down again as Catherine appeared at the door.

"Come in. This is a police officer. He wants to ask you some questions."

Claudel stood up when Catherine entered the room. He sensed immediately her reticence and smiled in an effort to make her feel comfortable and his own presence less imposing. Catherine had been concerned about Claudel's visit. There was an aura of authority he carried with him which for reasons unknown to herself made her apprehensive. Sensing the charged atmosphere between the two men she became outwardly nervous.

"Mademoiselle," said Claudel, "I have the unhappy chore of investigating the death by drowning of Madame Gabrielle Villon. Did you know her by any chance?"

"Why no Monsieur, I never met her. But I heard about the drowning. It was on the news . . ."

"Thank you Mademoiselle. There's another question I must ask you. Something caught my attention when you answered the door for me. I'm sure it's no more than a coincidence but . . , you are wearing exactly the same type of jewellery Madame Villon was wearing the day she drowned."

Catherine's face blanched. Her lips quivered slightly.

"What are you saying Monsieur. I don't understand . . ."

"Mademoiselle, how did you come by the jewellery?"

"Yves . . ."

"Keep your stupid mouth shut . . ," the Viscount shouted at her.

An uncharacteristic edge crept into Catherine's voice as she pointed to the Viscount.

"He gave me the jewellery when he returned from Paris on Sunday night."

"Mademoiselle, I'd like to get a statement from you later but for the moment I have no more questions. Please leave the jewellery until my investigation is complete."

With swift movements Catherine removed the necklace, earrings and bracelet and laid them on a table.

"Can I get them back?"

"Mademoiselle, I'm sorry, I just don't know. In all likelihood they will be returned to Gilbert Villon, the husband of the deceased woman. It's also very likely the Viscount will be charged with stealing the jewellery. It will be decided in Court."

The timorous demeanour that characterized Catherine's personality vanished as she faced the Viscount. She walked over to his desk and stood in front of him.

"You, you vermin." She screamed at him, "Did you steal her jewellery before she died?"

The Viscount was in the act of standing up and yelling obscenities at Catherine when she gripped a heavy wooden bookend from the desk and threw it at him. The bookend caught the Viscount in midriff, causing him to jettison backwards and fall to the floor. Books, an ashtray, the desklamp and other objects were thrown at him by the maid. In a state of rising fury Catherine picked up a fire iron and proceeded to lash out at everything within reach. Bottles of wine and whiskey, decanters and glasses, flower vases exploded as she swung indiscriminately with the fire iron. Next she smashed mirrors and the stained glass panels of bookcases. She was shaking from her exertions when she turned her attention to the fallen Viscount, still laid out on the floor. Her eyes glinted with murderous intent as she moved towards him. Claudel moved swiftly and pulled the fire iron from her hands. She shuddered involuntarily and let Claudel lead her to a chair. Her face twisted into a sneer as her anger subsided. Brushing Claudel's restraining hand aside the housekeeper stood up. She spoke to Claudel as she looked at the Viscount who had covered his head with his arms.

"When he arrived back here after being to Paris he had blood on his face. He said he fell and cut himself . . , that's why he has the room so dark . . ."

She reached out and turned on four switches by the door. With the room drenched in dazzling light Claudel helped the Viscount to his feet. He saw three livid weals run down the Viscount's left cheekbone. "Mademoiselle," said Claudel, "I'll need a statement from you, about the jewellery."

"I will call to the Station tomorrow Monsieur . . ."

"Goodnight Mademoiselle."

"Goodnight Monsieur."

The Viscount opened a cabinet drawer and took out a bottle of brandy. He poured himself a drink and sat down. His hand shook as he emptied the glass.

"This is the thanks I get for treating her so well."

"I think you've got a lot more to worry about than a jealous housekeeper."

"So what do you think you have with those trinkets? Gabrielle gave them to me in the hotel. I gave her a story about being broke, which wasn't too far from the truth. She gave me that jewellery of her own free will."

"Was that before or after you hit her?"

"I didn't say I hit her . . ."

"The autopsy report on Madame Villon showed fragments of skin tissue under the fingernails of her right hand. It's my guess she was trying to defend herself when you hit her."

"I want to see my lawyer . . ."

"By all means Monsieur, even the rights of thieves and women beaters are protected under the law. I am placing you under arrest for complicity in the death of Gabrielle Villon."

The funeral of Madame Gabrielle Villon took place in the cemetery on Rue Saint Louis in Evreux. It was a warm bright morning under a cloudless azure sky. The fresh pleasantness of the morning was at variance with the somber procession of two mourners following the coffin bearers. They halted by an open grave around which four gravediggers waited, leaning on shovels. The coffin was lowered into the grave to a homily orated by a Cure from Evreux. The ceremony was brief. When it was over the Cure departed. Claudel shook hands with and said goodbye to Gilbert Villon. Villon was inconsolable, holding himself responsible for the tragedy that took his wife from him.

Claudel sat on a bench seat in the cemetery and watched from a distance as the gravediggers threw the last shovelfuls of earth on the grave. When finished they patted the surface earth smooth, straightened up slowly as cigarettes were handed around. An animated discussion began but when Claudel was seen their voices became hushed and then fell away. Picking up the accoutrements of their profession they made their way to the cemetery exit. Claudel walked over and looked down at the soft mound of earth, all that remained of a beautiful young woman.

Later that night Claudel drove to Paris and parked on the Boulevard de Clichy. He walked the short distance to the Rue Pigalle and stood on the pavement outside the 'Daughters of Isis' nightclub. When he passed the doorman he was greeted by a shining faced Nubian beauty in a red sequined dress. She ushered him down a stone stairway at the end of which she held a door open. The club was filled to over-flowing as he picked his way in semi-darkness through tightly packed tables to a back wall. Stone arches under a low ceiling gave the club the appearance of a medieval dungeon. Three musicians, crowded on a tiny stage played a strident rhythm on strings and percussions. He found himself gasping for air while waiting to be seated. As every table was taken he was forced to barter with the shining Nubian. She would bring a table especially for him, of course it would cost extra but for a gentleman like himself that should not prove a hindrance. Think of what he would miss, and she would dedicate the first dance to him. Claudel found himself smiling without intending to. It sounded like a well-rehearsed monologue but he conceded because he wanted to be here. Two waiters brought a table. He sat down and ordered a whiskey and was brought what looked like a glass of colored water. He took a sip, winced, and put the glass down. Grey and purple smoke, the exhaled residue of hashish, Gauloise cigarettes and cheap cigars rose like incense to the blackened timbers of the ceiling and hung there like floating diaphanous veils in the still air. A ceiling fan churned ineffectively through the mire. Above him a revolving spotlight threw shafts of blue beams across the room. A light tap on his shoulder made him look up. The shining Nubian was standing over him, smiling broadly. She was now wearing a costume adorned with several layers of the sheerest of silk. She had bangles on her bare feet and gold bracelets on her wrists. She laughed as he held her gaze and then ran to the centre of the dance floor to begin a dance that belonged to antiquity, the Veils of Salome. Beginning with slow gyrations of her hips her movements became erotic and sensuous with the increasing tempo of the music, her arms and legs rippling beneath the shifting veils. Hands shot out of the darkness to stuff banknotes into the folds of her costume. The clientele, mostly Middle Eastern and African men in varying degrees of inebriation whistled and applauded loudly throughout the dance. A contingent of American tourists stared dumb-faced as the dance progressed and the Nubian's veils floated to the floor. Finally with very little left to hide she ran modestly from the dance floor.

Claudel took another sip of the tasteless concoction and thought again of Gabrielle. Who was Gabrielle? Was it this den of inequity that precipitated her fall from grace and closed each door behind her so she could never look back? What obsession was it that caused her to take her own life when she had an adoring husband and all the trappings of the good life. From what he had learned since her death she had been an intelligent, well-educated daughter of middle class parents. She had been a member of a school of ballet where she was remembered as a talented dancer with an exuberant personality. She went to work for the Astro Group where she met and married Gilbert Villon. After that, details became sketchy. Bernice Breugnol, a friend from her school of ballet days who had kept in touch with Gabrielle had her own ideas. Gilbert, she said was adoring and conciliatory to a fault, he treated Gabrielle too much like a princess, forever fawning over her. For two years the marriage proved idyllic. It was about that time when Gabrielle told Bernice she felt suffocated by Gilbert's generosity, that she felt trapped, almost claustrophobic in his presence. She couldn't point to a single fault of Gilbert's that caused these feelings of resentment. She called him a great man and meant it sincerely but she no longer loved him. She didn't want to feel possessed by Gilbert however magnanimous his nature. He would condemn her to a life of custom and repetition where she would never be free to wonder what tomorrow or next year or the next 20 years would bring. She had to fly from her gilded cage because life had no meaning within it. She wanted to dance, to fill the cup to overflowing, she felt euphoric at the prospect. And as long as the door of the gilded cage was left open, and Gilbert would never close it, she would return to the cage again and again. But she must spread her wings. She was driving in Paris one night, she related to Bernice, when the raucous beat of African drums reached her. She felt a sudden need for excitement, a desperate urge to break out of the possessive cocoon which Gilbert had spun about her. She stopped the car outside a dingy nightclub called the 'Daughters of Isis" on the Rue Pigalle, known euphemistically as Pig Alley by the mackintoshed legions of American tourists. Smiling, she shouldered her way past the buskers and pimps on the sidewalk of the most notorious street in Paris. When the door closed behind her she ended a chapter in her life she would never be able to reopen. From that moment she prostrated herself on the altar of Bacchus. In a delirium of excesses she danced and drank herself into narcotic stupors. All of Gabrielle's lovers were strangers whom she forgot with the degree of assiduity she went looking for new ones. In her desperate search for love and pleasure she skirted with danger, like a fragile moth hovering about a flame of a candle. A few jealous lovers beat her, enraged at being summarily discarded. Did she naively believe, Claudel wondered, that love would be a concomitant of her pursuit of pleasure? In the end Gabrielle had subverted love to the nether realm of lies and deceit, to meaningless endearments from strangers. Her friend Bernice said Gabrielle was like a meteor blazing across the night sky. Claudel didn't agree with the analogy, there was no sorrow or tragedy in the wake of a meteor. Gabrielle died alone. Except for her grieving husband and Claudel no one attended her funeral. Dead she was an embarrassment to all, best quickly forgotten.

Claudel paid for his drink, left the nightclub and walked back to his car. Soon he was crossing the Bois de Boulogne to pick up the autoroute to his home in Ivry La Bataille. He thought of Solonge waiting for him at home. She would be fretting, wondering why he was late. He pressed on the accelerator and was soon lost in the traffic going West.

THE END

GUEST OF THE STATION

by

JOHN FLANAGAN

I CAN'T RECALL THE EXACT moment when I decided to travel to Baghdad Iraq. It was after some soul-searching and wondering what useful purpose I could serve in that beleaguered country. I felt I had led a privileged if mundane life, I wanted to do something worthwhile, a gesture to help alleviate the trials and tribulations of my fellow man.

The Iran-Iraq War in 1980-1988 had taken the lives of 150,000 Iraqi men women and children with 500,000 wounded. In the year 2003 a monumental scale of suffering subsisted in Iraq under the dictatorship of Saddam Hussein. Under his regime 4,000 children were dying every month from sanctions, hunger and disease.

In February 2003 I was watching the evening television news in Dublin Ireland. A bulletin interrupted to announce more saber-rattling of the US and coalition armed forces. Vivid images of the 1991 Gulf War were still fresh in my mind. Hospitals would again be overcrowded with the eternal victims of the insanity of war; the innocent, the elderly, women and children.

After the destruction in New York of the Twin Towers on 11th September 2001 all available intelligence, it was reported, pointed to Iraq as the culprit. No less a world statesman than US General Colin Powell would testify before a United Nations assembly that Saddam Hussein had weapons of mass destruction. This deception damaged General Powell's pristine reputation and gave carte blanche to President George W Bush and his administration that began beating the war drums in earnest. In a few weeks he had aroused his Republican henchmen and the Pentagon hawks in a frenzy of blood-lust that would not be appeased. Right-wing media fanned the flames, igniting the passions and fervour of sane rational men until the whole populace, it would seem, was hell-bent on going to war.

British Prime Minister Tony Blair proved the darling of the Washington conservative caucus. Singlehandedly Mr. Blair had mollified the unease of the British people about the war and sold them on the US idea of the invasion of Iraq. A battalion of spin doctors could not have surpassed what the Prime Minister accomplished for the USA in one fell swoop. He was invited to address the joint houses of Congress as a result of which he was awarded the Congressional Gold Medal. His speech garnered sympathy from uncommitted nations and helped expedite US hostilities in Iraq. He was given a standing ovation by an excited George W Bush and his inner circle of Dick Cheney, Donald Rumsfeld, Karl Rove, Paul Wolfowitz and Richard Perle. Deputy Secretary of Defense Wolfowitz and Defense Policy Chairman Perle were Washington's quintessential power brokers whose pervading influence insinuated itself into every facet of government and industry. Oil and media barons, war mongering Pentagon hawks, munitions salesmen and mercenaries-for-hire consultants were all gainfully employed by the two gentlemen. They were among the first to jump up and applaud the speech of the Prime Minister.

Prime Minister Tony Blair's address to Congress was in essence Uriah Heep-like obsequiousness and rightly scorned by the British press. The trouble was the British Press didn't really understand him. At the end of his speech to Congress he had been chortling with glee, his iridescent smile firmly locked in place until he read the morning newspapers. One British newspaper had the temerity to refer to him as George Dubya's poodle. But no matter what they thought of him Tony was determined that this would be his year, a year of achievement and reward. He had made earnest efforts to heal his unhappy relationship with Her Majesty Queen Elizabeth. He was uneasy in his relationship with Her Majesty, she had proved to be not nearly as malleable as his Cabinet colleagues. He felt she saw right through him and judged him harshly. Without her he could never hope to achieve his life's most fervent ambition; Tony wanted to be a Lord. Surely the Queen Mum would relent after his rapturous reception in Washington, would see his singular place on the world stage and would now make him a Lord.

All of the frenzied rhetoric and finger-pointing at the stunned Iraqis turned out to be a ploy to obfuscate the true motive of the invasion; the acquisition of Iraq's oil. Had it not already been revealed that the erstwhile USA Vice President Cheney with the sobriquet Dick threw maps and charts upon his desk and with a marker and grandiose flourishes cut swathes across Iraq's oil fields, pipelines and refineries before the war even started? He delineated vast oil tracts that after the invasion would be the spoils of war. It was Iraq's misfortune that some of the largest oil repositories on earth were within its borders.

I went to Iraq as a private citizen to help victims of the unfolding war. I had no special gifts or qualifications other than an Arabic phrasebook and a diploma recently acquired to teach English. I felt there had to be something useful I could do, however small.

Getting from Ireland to Iraq was a challenge in itself. The coalition forces invaded Iraq on 20th March 2003. On that day I was stranded in the Frankfurt am Main airport in Germany as the Amman Jordan flight had been cancelled. When a second flight was cancelled I decided to take a chance by flying to Cairo Egypt and thence to Jordon. As luck would have it I got one of the few remaining seats on a flight to Baghdad.

When I arrived in Amman Jordon, the spartan Iraqi consular office was under siege. An endless queue of journalists, television and camera crews jostled with expatriate Iraqis in a desperate bid for visas before the Iraq-Jordon border was closed. It was now two days into the invasion of Iraq. Engagement between coalition and Saddam's main forces built to a gradual climax until an opening salvo sent streams of terrified refugees speeding towards the Jordan border. My application for a visa was lumped together with the many foreign journalists who crowded the consul office. When I explained the purpose of my visit I was told to have a photo taken and return. After that I was given a Red Crescent Hospital I D card. For $200 I got a place in a beaten up old Volkswagen Beetle bound for Baghdad, a distance of about 1,000 kilometres. I shared the car with Salim the driver and three very distressed Iraqi businessmen.

In the early hours of Sunday 23rd March '03 we were driving East 100 kilometres inside the Iraqi border when a sudden explosion ahead shook the road and made the car shudder violently. The shocked Salim fought to control the careening car and finally brought it to a stop. He adamantly refused to travel any further until daylight. He had been driving all night by moonlight without lights on the car so as not to attract helicopters or fighter jets. I could understand how his nerves would be frayed. At the next farmhouse he wheeled the car off the road and cut the engine. There we sat, huddled up uncomfortably in the old Volkswagen and waited.

At dawn the golden tip of the rising sun suffused the Eastern horizon with tints of gold and purple. Meteor trails described white arcs across the silent cavern of the sky as stars flickered and succumbed before the approaching day.

At daybreak two buses pulled up beside the Volkswagen. The passengers, all men, wore long Arabic gallabiyyas and hijab headscarves alighted from the buses. Some of them carried antiquated long barreled rifles but most were brandishing semi-automatic Russian Kalashnikovs. Quietly and quickly as if with a sense of urgency they stacked the weapons and formed orderly straight lines. Facing South towards Mecca they commenced to recite the early morning Fajar prayers. In the dawn light I could just make out the noticeably different features of Pakistanis, Sudanese and Turks in the group. After prayers they collected the weapons and ambled casually over to our Volkswagen in small groups. They were a fierce motley looking group exuding intense gravitas. Being the only European I became a reluctant object of attention. Fortunately for me I was wearing the Red Crescent Hospital I. D. card on the lapel of my jacket. In a whisper Salim said they were Mujahadin, militant volunteers who came to join the forces of Saddam Hussein.

When we recommenced our journey we found the source of the explosion that shook the road the night before. A missile from an American helicopter had hit an overhead bridge, spreading chunks of twisted steel and concrete over the road. With just enough room to manoeuvre Salim drove the Volkswagen through the debris and we continued on our journey.

Later, driving at speed along the endless desert road we came upon burnt out vehicles; the occupants nowhere to be seen. It was eerily silent save for the crackle of dying flames licking about the hulks of the scorched vehicles. A burnt out tractor-trailer lay on its side, its cargo strewn about the road. In the desolate landscape of blinding sun and sand, the blackened wrecks of trucks, buses and cars dotted the Amman-Baghdad highway.

On the outskirts of Baghdad columns of thick bluish-black smoke spiralled up to the sky like giant tornado spouts; the skyline was peppered with the brackish cylinders of smoke. Teams of soldiers were digging deep trenches, filling them with black crude oil and setting them alight. Caught by the wind the smoke spread to form an ominous looking cloud that darkened the city. Every street we passed through reeked with the stench of oil. It was an eerie cataclysmic scene not unlike an eclipse of the sun. According to Salim the drifting blanket of smoke over Baghdad was an attempt to confuse the memory-guided computers of incoming scud missiles. The foreboding dark skies proved for me at lEast a portent of things to come.

I checked into the Al Fanar Hotel on Abu Nawas Street in Baghdad. It was just 30 metres away from the Palestine Hotel that would share center stage in the drama of the USA invasion of Iraq. It seemed all the journalists and television crews in Baghdad were crammed into the Palestine Hotel.

It was here I had the great pleasure of meeting famed war correspondent Robert Fisk and his wife, Irish Times correspondent Laura Marlowe.

When I had unpacked my bag, showered and had a meal I took some time to plan how I could make the best use my time. I decided against linking up with any of the numerous charitable groups that filled the Al Fanar Hotel. The International Red Cross had offices nearby as did the Red Crescent, the Iraqi equivalent of the Red Cross. Medicine Sans Frontiers had a presence here. I could have joined any one of them as a volunteer. I decided instead to join a group of anti-war missionaries visiting bombed sites and hospitals.

The US invasion of Iraq was not only an illegal war under international law, it provoked a virtual religious pogrom in Iraq between opposing Sunni and Sheiia factions of Islam. For almost 1400 years, since the death of Prophet Muhammid a schism divided Islam; tensions simmered over rights of ascendency. The ideological rift was contained by an uneasy mutual toleration over the centuries. The Baath party in Iraq overthrew the established government in 1968 and a year later Saddam Hussein became President. The Baath party was overwhelmingly Sunni and under Hussein's rule there began a brutal reign of murder and torture of Sheeias and Kurds.

Like most Irishmen of my generation I had never known what it meant to be in a war. The thought, the idea of war with its inhuman savagery could not impinge on my consciousness any more than it could with most men; the idea of war was just that, an idea, a vague concept, neurons floating around in my brain. A description of war at best evokes empathy; it cannot make it truly perceptible to the mind, to the blinding flash of an incendiary device sundering flesh and bone with body parts descending to earth at varying points of the compass. With my cosseted background I was very ill-prepared for what I was about to face.

I stood among the twisted ruins of a bombed out house in Sadr City, a poor Shiia residential suburb East of Baghdad. On the previous day the house was hit with a missile from an American fighter jet. The mud-brick and plaster family home was obliterated, the family dead with the exception of a 15 year old boy who had been taken to hospital. I was among a small group of American anti-war missionaries who came to assess what damage the bombing caused and to help the surviving teenage boy. Shocked neighbours gathered around the flattened debris that was a family residence the day before. I looked around at the faces near us; the hatred in their expressions was unmistakable. There was also confusion. Through the missionaries' interpreter, an Iraqi asked why, if the American jet fighters were bombing houses, American missionaries followed up to pacify the sick and wounded? The onlookers swelled to a crowd and the mood was turning ugly. Voices were raised and fingers were pointed to our group. The nervous interpreter insisted we leave. We piled into the small bus and not without some difficulty got back to the hotel.

After a week had passed in the Al Fanah hotel the guests got to know each other mostly through the gatherings at mealtimes. We were a disparate lot but agreeably sociable and courteous. I lost count of the nationalities sitting around the tables. It was hard to reconcile the prevalent calm and formal good manners of the hotel guests with the fact that the country was at war and bombs were dropping on Baghdad.

There was one guest who stood out by reason of his anonymity. He sat alone at a single table removed from the other guests. He had a noticeably grey aspect. He wore a grey suit, had grey hair and moustache. His grey grave face never changed its wry expression; he was gruff to the point of rudeness. I never saw him raise his head to respond to a greeting from any of the guests. From time to time, sitting behind his newspaper I noticed him scanning the faces of the diners. Before much longer I would have reason to regret ever having laid eyes on him.

As harrowing as it had been visiting the bombed house in Sadr City nothing prepared me for my visit to the children's ward in Baghdad's Al Kindi hospital. Rana Adnan, aged 15 years, had head wounds and lung contusions. She had been lacerated with pieces of shrapnel from a Cluster bomb; her right leg had been amputated from the knee down. Rana was the calming influence in her family though suffering the most. Her sister Nada's eyes were focused on her, lying motionless in the next bed 9 year old Nada was swathed in bandages. Through a Doctor I learned they did not know that another sister, 8 years old Fatehah had just died from her wounds. Rana's father had been killed. Her mother was sitting on a chair beside Rana's bed with her face buried in her hands and muttering incoherently. Despite the decimation of her young life Rana was struggling to talk to her mother to offer words of consolation. I was left with a feeling of utter helplessness, of futility at being unable to help any of them. I wanted to beg their forgiveness for my gender, for the barbarism in man that could perpetrate such obscene violence against their angelic innocence. The Cluster bomb that hit Rana's home was made to explode in mid-air, to pop out little bomblets loaded with napalm or serin nerve gas or packed with shrapnel that could penetrate ¼ inch steel plate. Many bomblets didn't explode until they were picked up by children. Rana and her family were part of the 'collateral damage' referred to by US President George W. Bush.

The screams coming from the children's ward were ceaseless and after three such visits I could take no more. I left some toys and other small gifts with the receptionist in the hope that some would recover well enough to enjoy them.

Bombs were pounding Baghdad from my first night in the hotel. A scud missile dropped in a nearby street, pulverizing the fragile ancient walls and buildings of this oldest of cities. The shock waves put the heart crossways in me as I sat in the middle of my room on the third floor of the Al Fanar Hotel with pictures and mirrors oscillating like pendulums on the walls. There was commotion in the hallway as the hotel staff shouted for guests to go to the basement where a makeshift shelter had been built. As I sat immobilized in my armchair I tried to assess my chances for survival in a crowded basement where tons of rubble would descend if the hotel got a direct hit. I decided to stay put. I stretched out on the bed with an English tabloid and read accounts of the war going on around me.

Over the next couple of weeks I volunteered to work with Red Crescent hospital workers in a food warehouse. Sitting in a circle we filled plastic bags with two kilos each of lentils, rice, powdered milk, sugar and couscous. An ambulance picked me up in the morning from the hotel and brought me back in the evening. The Saddam regime, seeking to boost the morale of the citizens broadcast daily of the plentiful food supplies available for all Iraqis. In fact shops and stores were running out of supplies. When the Iraqi Communications Center was bombed on 28th of March Saddam Hussein could no longer cajole the alarmed citizens and they took matters into their own hands. At first shops were broken into for food but as law and order deteriorated in Baghdad looting began on a massive scale. I passed literally hundreds of Iraqis pushing every conceivable mode of makeshift handcarts, prams and trolleys, all loaded down with plunder. Total anarchy prevailed as armed criminals, released from prisons to help repel the invaders instead went on a pillaging rampage. Sunni and Sheiia militias were forced to mount armed guards on their respective Mosques.

On Friday 4th of April I finished up at the food warehouse and returned to the hotel. Vital power installations had been bombed during the day and we were now at the mercy of the hotel's generator. As there were no telephones, no television and no hot water I decided to call it a day. I had a cold meal by candlelight and turned in early to get a good night's sleep. Or so I thought.

At 2:30 AM in the morning a series of heavy knocks on the door of my room woke me from a fitful sleep. At first I thought I had slept through another air raid. The knocking persisted and in a stupor I got out of bed and answered the door.

The man I opened the door to, I was to find out later, was a Captain in Saddam Hussein's Mukhabarat, Iraq's Secret Police. There were four men with him, dressed as he was in plain clothes with one holding a Kalashnikov rifle strapped to his shoulder. To a man they sported the hallmark hijabs and mustaches of Saddam's regime. Coming up the rear was the grey man I had seen in the dining room. Seeing him didn't surprise me, the Secret Police very likely had an agent in every hotel in Baghdad. The intruders pushed their way into my room and surrounded me, indicating for me to get dressed. After I got over the initial shock I felt this was no more than a case of mistaken identity, that they were looking for someone else. Still half asleep I hurled my choicest and loudest Irish expletives at the ragtag group. The leader did not take too kindly to my outburst although he probably didn't understand a word I had said. The one carrying the Kalashnikov hooked his thumb into the strap of the weapon, removed it from his shoulder and made a movement towards me. He stopped when the Captain raised his hand and told me to get dressed. I suddenly realized the danger I faced, that resistance would be futile. When I asked why I was being arrested, he said I had been seen signalling to an American aircraft flying over Baghdad earlier in the day. I told him I was at the food warehouse all day, that I had witnesses to prove it. He was unmoved and in broken English told me to continue dressing. I was so dumbfounded I lapsed into silence and felt more uneasy by the minute. These were Saddam's Gestapo, attached to the Ministry of Internal Affairs. In the 24 years of Saddam's reign the Mukhabaret had buried thousands of political dissidents in unmarked graves after sadistic rituals of torture and brutality. A doctor attached to Baghdad's Red Crescent hospital, where photographs of Saddam hung in every ward, later talked to me with anger in his voice about the Police Captain. I believe he could only do so because the Doctor was a highly respected Sunni in his community and a member of Saddam's Ba'ath Party.

From time to time I looked over at the Police Captain who was arresting me as a spy. His face had lapsed into a permanent sneer as if reflecting the moral depravity to which he had descended. His lustreless eyes expressed that feral cunning by which nature often compensates for lack of intelligence in ambitious men. I would later learn, imprisoned and in his custody, that the Captain was ostracized from the lives and affairs of ordinary men. He could not take his family to a restaurant because of the loathing and fear his presence provoked with his bodyguards sitting close by. Waiters hovered nervously while attending his table. No one outside his band of felons would condescend to meet or consort with the wives or children of members of the Secret Police. The lowest levels of social misfits, criminals and thieves spurned the Captain as a pariah more through contempt than fear. This served to increase his rage and savagery against the Shiia and Kurd prisoners in Abu Ghraib prison. Like the fallen angel Belial the Captain could only function effectively among the denizens of his underworld. Crude and uneducated he would have been promoted for his zeal in exterminating enemies of the State. His swarthy, emaciated face was filled with disdain as I got dressed. Watching him reminded me of the final denouement of the Portrait of Wilde's Dorian Grey. I didn't find it very reassuring to know that the regime employing these misanthropes was falling apart at the seams, that in a little while they would be living in terror of reprisals from their victims. They had to be ever vigilant; the ruling Sunni Ba'ath party in which the Captain served was a mere 15% of the population of Iraq, they were completely outnumbered by Shiia's and Kurds.

With the grey man leading the way I was frog-marched out of the hotel and put in a waiting car. I was driven North along Abu Newas Street. The car then turned left across the Jumhuriya Bridge over the Tigris river. After about an hour's drive I was taken from the car and put into a cell in a blacked out police station.

When my eyes grew accustomed to the gloom I looked around me with a sense of disbelief. The cell was 3 by 5 metres with a steel door and a barred window. The stench from previous occupants of the cell was nauseating in the confined space. In a corner was a metal bed on the floor without a mattress. I paced the cell until I heard in the distance the cry of a Mu'azzin calling for early morning prayers.

As daylight filtered into the cell what I saw filled me with fear and anxiety. A steel hook hung from the ceiling. My imagination ran riot when I saw two electrical wires with exposed ends coming down the wall. Later, sitting on the floor with my back to the wall I could hear the sound of sporadic 30 caliber machinegun fire not far from the station. Through the cell window I saw vapour trails of American jet fighters criss-crossing the sky. Bombs began falling followed by a barrage of anti-aircraft fire. Outside my cell window I saw two police sentries peering over a sandbag dugout. When night came I lay down on the metal springs of the bed and managed to get a few fitful hours of sleep.

When I awoke on Saturday morning 5th April I tried to convince myself I was having a nightmare, that I would awake in a few moments tucked away in my own bed at home. But it was all too real as bulbous cockroaches scuttled across the floor. At the same time a small green lizard ambled leisurely up the wall. I started to tear madly at my wrists which were a mass of red weals. Mosquitoes were buzzing everywhere. I jumped up and took off my jacket and by waving it around I managed to clear most of them away through the barred window.

In the afternoon I heard the sound of laughter nearby as a plainclothes Secret Police officer opened my cell door and beckoned me out. He tied my hands behind my back with a nylon strap. The laughter came from three regular police guards who were standing in front of me in full battle fatigues, helmets and rifles. I looked at them in amazement; their country was being bombed, American tanks were already in West and South of Baghdad and here they were, telling each other jokes and howling with merriment. The plainclothes officer caught their eye and they immediately lapsed into silence, adjusted their uniforms and stood at attention. The officer pushed me to the police car and unceremoniously dumped me in the back seat. Once in the car the guards' joy was unsurpassed as they weaved through busy Baghdad streets with sirens blazing and lights flashing. I was fairly sure I was the cause of their merriment. The ever-vigilant police had captured a spy. I was an uplifting spectacle for the besieged Iraqis; they were having a field day showing me off as they shouted and waved to passers-by. We finally drove in through a gate and pulled up in front of an ominous looking prison building. The massive walls were interspersed with high barred windows, some with hands gripping the bars. One of the guards, more talkative than the others, told me I was being transferred to this prison. At the time I had no concept whatever of the infamy attached to Saddam's prisons.

It transpired that the prison authorities would not accept me because the guards had forgotten to make out paperwork on me, quite possibly because none of them could write. When they returned me to my original cell the guards were in a more despondent mood.

On the third day in the cell I was handed a packet of biscuits by one of the guards. He said that when I finished eating them he was going to kill me. He walked away and I heard him guffawing and joking with his pals, obviously telling them what he had said. I ate the biscuits because I was hungry and when he came back he pointed a rifle at me through the cell window. I think I had already got into a mind-set that I would not leave the station alive. I don't know what I felt but it was wasn't fear or panic any more, it was more a sense of disbelief about my predicament when I stared up the barrel of the rifle. When he pulled the trigger on an empty magazine and laughed I felt it would be an ignoble end to lose my life at the hands of such an imbecile. In the afternoon I was put into a larger cell. This cell was also encrusted with filth but it did have a hole-in-the-ground toilet of sorts and running water. The barred window looked out onto a corridor and I had a broad view of the station courtyard. There were no beds in the cell, which meant I had to sleep on the concrete floor. It was then that the shooting started. I could both hear and feel the rumble of tanks and personnel carriers less than half-a-mile from the station. The Iraqis rifle fire was making a feeble response to the power and artillery of the US military forces. Through the barred door I saw some police guards rapidly vacating the station and the few who remained changed into civilian clothes. Divested of the intimidating aura of guns, helmets and uniforms the guards became little men in shirtsleeves fearing for their lives. In a frenzy of activity, weapons and office files were loaded into cars and driven away. One officer and the three guards who had escorted me to the prison remained. The officer handed each guard a wad of Dinars, gave some instructions and quickly left in the remaining police car. The three guards were looking at the bundles of money and didn't seem to know what to do next. When machine gun fire rang out nearby they ran into the station office. From there they crouched down and looked out into the corridor towards my cell, one head above the other. It was like looking at Moe, Larry and Shemp. I'm sure at first the guards were swelled with pride at the notion that they were left in charge of a dangerous international spy, the reality being that the officer who just left most likely saw them as the most dim-witted and expendable of all the police at the station. They came down to my cell unarmed and stood outside facing me through the bars. The one who had threatened to kill me took from his pocket a crumbled piece of cake wrapped in tissue paper. He handed it to me and told me with a straight face his mother had made it for me and that he wanted to be my friend. The scheming wretch knew he had to face the possibility of capture by the Americans and would have to explain my presence in the station. I was still wary of them. In the volatile situation anything could happen. At the end of the day the guards handed me in a mattress and blankets that were now in abundance in the empty station. I managed to get a few hours' sleep.

The next morning I awoke with a start. An American tank and a machine gun mounted Jeep were blasting away just one street from the station. Two of the police guards had fled and the one remaining, the one who had threatened to kill me and gave me the piece of cake was in a state of ill-concealed terror. He opened the door of my cell and I ventured out into the corridor leading to the exit gate. I went into an office, picked up a telephone receiver and handed it to the guard. I got him to call the Red Crescent headquarters. I was put through to an English speaking doctor to whom I gave my name and location and was told to stay put, that someone would come to collect me. The terrified guard told me his name was Ahmad and he followed me around the station like a lamb. I was now his protector. He sat down, dry lipped and nervous. I hadn't an ounce of sympathy for him. He had pointed a rifle at my head and threatened to kill me, even if there were no rounds in the magazine.

An ambulance from the Red Crescent hospital came to the station to pick me up and the doctor I had spoken to on the telephone got out to greet me. Ahmad asked to be taken along. The doctor nodded towards the ambulance and told him he would drop him near his home in Sadr City. It meant running the gauntlet between pockets of Iraqi soldiers and the Americans bearing down on them. On the way an American tank shell hit a bridge we were passing under and covered the car in rubble and white dust. There were scenes of jubilation and chaos in Sadr City, the district where Ahmad's mother lived. Predominantly Shiite muslims lived here. They had been terrorized by Saddam's regime and now were openly welcoming the US Forces. Nonstop fusillades of shots were fired into the air. They were also venting their hatred and lust for blood against Saddam's police and the remnants of his retreating army. All roads led North. For Sunni Muslims the road East to Sheeia dominated Iran was fraught with as much danger as the road North where militant Kurds seeking vengeance were massing on the Turkish border. Ahmad got out of the ambulance onto the sidewalk and mixed with the yelling throngs of people. He cut a lonely figure with his plastic bags filled with Dinars and food he had appropriated from the station kitchen. His disassembled rifle was hidden from view in a blanket. Anyone in the frenzied mob about him would cut his throat to get the weapon from him.

After a few days of rest and recuperation I packed my remaining belongings and prepared to leave. I dwelled a lot on all that had happened.

What seemed to stand out most were the screaming children swaddled in bandages in the Al Kindi hospital and the decimation caused by the Cluster bombs raining down on Baghdad.

It all seemed too surreal to be true but in fact it was all too terrifyingly real. I wondered where the US and other developed countries find ample amounts of sadistic fiends who have no qualms about making such bombs; bombs when dropped away from a war zone are especially designed to shred innocent non-combatants limb from limb. I tried to put myself into the mind-set of one of those gentlemen, a bomb-maker who found his life's vocation in the Pentagon in Washington DC. Before I go into the Cluster bomb and its special effects on random children playing in the street, I want to tell you about Mike.

Mike lives in an upscale suburb in Washington DC in the USA. There are manicured lawns and London style lampposts on every avenue. Nannies with engaging European accents push perambulators past gardens ablaze with swaying blooms. Mike lives in a two storey house with his wife Adeline and their two grown sons. He is a chemical engineer having graduated from the Massachusetts Institute of Technology in Boston Ma. The garden at the back of the house is Mike's pride and joy. There are goblins and elves figurines decorating his garden along with miniature water fountains and a rock-pool filled with exotic fish. Mike is a White Anglo Saxon Protestant and a pillar of the community. He is a Chapter leader in the Boy Scouts. He plays golf on weekends and attends PTA meetings with his wife. With a passable tenor voice he is a member of his Church choir. It's at cocktail parties that Mike shines. He is urbane, entertaining. When asked about his work Mike gets a laugh when he describes a boring non-descript job in the government that he can't quit because the money is so good. He winks at his wife who smiles and nods her head. She has believed the lie for 18 years.

Mike and his background is a pseudonym for the countless ghouls and profligates who earn their livelihood making Cluster bombs for a munitions corporation under contract to the Pentagon. His work has been mentioned in dispatches by Pentagon Generals for his innovative ideas that made the Cluster bomb a resounding success. The deafening silence of the American media about the invention of the lethal bomb made the task that much easier. The Cluster bomb proved highly lucrative for the munitions dealers;

over 200 banks vied with each other to finance the $40 Billion project. Already 10,000 bombs were dropped on Iraq. Photos were shown to Mike after an air strike to prove the effectiveness of the bombs. Mike felt humbled, grateful. He had recently modified the tiny parachutes of the bomblets that ejected in midair from the main Cluster bomb. The gaily colored ribbons were an invitation for enemy children to pick up and play with; the parachuted bomblets were designed to explode precisely at that moment. He modestly brushed aside the praise heaped on him by his Pentagon colleagues.

On Monday 30th of June 2003 the Israeli newspaper Ha'aretz reported that the Palestinian Prime Minister Mahmoud Assas met with US President George W Bush. Not especially earth shattering news until . . . , President Bush told Prime Minister Assas that God had spoken to him personally. He didn't elaborate too much. President Bush didn't say if God was sitting or standing or how He was dressed when they chatted away. The US President told Prime Minister Assas that God had told him to hit back at Al Qaida and he did. He then said God told him to invade Iraq and he did. The presence or otherwise of Weapons of Mass Destruction had nothing to do with it.

Thus commanded by God to invade Iraq, the US President George W Bush resolved to make the Iraq invasion his personal Crusade. Above the screams and slaughter of the innocent, the leader of the free world would have heard an opening fanfare of clarion calls rising to a spirited crescendo of choirs of angels urging him on to war.

Deputy Chief of Staff Karl Rove was seated at his desk in the White House. Beads of copious sweat trickled from his expansive forehead and down his chubby cheeks. The wily strategist whom the President acclaimed as the architect of his election to office had lost his famed aplomb. For the first time since his boss took office he felt worried, even scared a little about what recent events portended. He was trying not too successfully to limit the damage caused by the President's tete a tete with God. Favours were called in from right wing media tycoons to sit on the story but it proved too big to cover up entirely. Karl stood up. He went to the window and looked out at the White House grounds. He knew George too well to believe he was serious or telling the truth about God talking to him. He frowned and shook his head as if trying to convince himself. No. George was too much of a political animal to talk about God or the truth in a serious vein. No one knew better than George that truth was always a matter of expediency, it was a cherished principle of the Oval Office. And yet . . . , since he said God talked to him the President was becoming truculent, of late his eyes had the intimidating gleam of the redeemed sinner. It didn't bode well. Karl reached for the telephone.

Secretary of Defence Donald H Rumsfeld replaced the telephone back on the receiver. After his conversation with Karl Rove he was feeling grim and angry. He picked up a pencil to recommence working on the most favoured of the poems he had ever written.

> There are no unknown known knowns
> There are unknown known unknowns
> There are . . . .

He ran a pencil through the text in a pique of temper. His creative urge was gone. He slumped back in the armchair and stared into the dying embers of the log fire. Over on his desk was a pile of unopened letters that needed his attention. Lawsuits were impending over this

Aspartame business. He was expecting it; it had been a risky business putting the drug on the market in the first place. It was now public knowledge that Aspartame was proved to be a neurotoxin that had been connected to many deaths. It was too bad about the deaths but he didn't feel responsible. He was the Chief Executive Officer of G.D. Searle Inc, the company that produced Aspartame. The reason they hired him was because of his powerful political connections. Searle Inc needed him to persuade the food and drug administration to rubber stamp what proved to be a poisonous artificial sweetener. Once the FDA marketed Aspartame he made a fortune almost overnight but he had to tiptoe through a political minefield. Some democrats in congress with nothing better to do with their time were calling for his resignation. That didn't bother him; he thrived on confrontation. What did bother him was the telephone call minutes ago from his friend Karl Rove.

He stood up, picked up the poker and tried without success to rekindle the fire. He poured himself a nightcap, resettled his spectacles back on his nose and sat back down. Karl was right, a way had to be found out of this mess about God talking to the President. The Defence Secretary emitted a long breath through pursed lips and allowed a wan smile to ease the grim aspect of his features. Spin, that was the answer. With the right spin from a friendly media source there was no such thing as an inviolate fact that could not be turned on its ear. This business about God had made the President the laughing stock of the entire world. What the hell was George thinking about, making a remark like that in public? Didn't he know the newspapers would have a field day with it? The democrats and liberals were beating it to death. All serious world leaders now saw President George W Bush as a clown; a very dangerous clown. He had made suspect everyone connected to him. The exception being of course the deadly duo, Wolfowitz and Perle.

While executing the functions of their office dutifully and with deference to the trappings of the Presidency, Deputy Defence Secretary Paul Wolfowitz and his close friend Defence Advisory Board Chairman Richard Perle had not one iota of regard or respect for George W Bush personally. He was, to the two Merchant Princes who wielded great intellectual, political and industrial power, a country bumpkin, a Texas redneck out of his depth in the Oval office. But he served their agenda to dictate US Foreign Policy in the interest of Israel all the better for that. It was the neoconservative hawk Wolfowitz who first advocated the invasion of Iraq to which President Bush acquiesced a year later. The White House was in nervous disarray with cabinet members reluctant to confront the powerful Wolfowitz / Perle cabal. The Foreign Policy strategy of Wolfowitz and Perle was for the United States to invade every country that was a threat to Israel. Apart from helping Israel both men made more money than Croesus with their connection to Soltam, the Israeli weapons manufacturer.

When North Korea, Iran, China and Russia opposed further US hegemony in the Middle East, the region became a tinderbox ready to explode. Since 1948 when Israel was declared a sovereign state the US poured billions of dollars into its fledgling economy. With over 200 nuclear warheads in its arsenal, Israel was carefully nurtured by the US as a front line of defence against a volatile Middle East.

On 1st November 2005 President Bush convened a meeting in Bethesda Maryland to discuss the Pandemic Influenza Strategic Plan. It received huge media coverage with many house members attending. The purpose of the meeting was to perpetrate a hoax on a gullible public that should have brought charges of criminal conspiracy. President George W Bush, using fear and panic tactics said millions of Americans could be killed by an impending avian flu pandemic. A staggering $ 2 billion was appropriated from government to spend on a drug called Tamiflu that was proven in an independent laboratory to be ineffective against the avian flu virus. The drug was eventually stockpiled. Overnight the President's friend and Secretary of Defence Donald H Rumsfeld became a multimillionaire. Rumsfeld by sheer coincidence had been the CEO and a major stockholder in Gilead Sciences Inc, the maker of the drug Tamiflu.

Lest we forget Vice President Dick Chaney's service to his country and his fellow man. During his tenure he found time to award contracts to Halliburton Company valued at $ 20 billion and worth millions to himself personally owing to his large shareholding with the Company. VP Cheney was the driving force behind the degradation and torture of prisoners in violation of Article 1 of the Geneva Convention. The effect of the antics of the White House incumbents on average law abiding Americans was palpable. A sense of apathy, of lethargy swept over this great land in the wake of an illegal war against Iraq based on subterfuge and deceit and the obscene torturing of prisoners. Overnight it seemed America lost its moral and ethical imperatives that once made it envied and admired throughout the world. The Bush White House inner circle had led the country to the precipice of a new dark age.

When I arrived back at the Al Fanar Hotel I discovered everything of value had been stolen from my room: passport, visa card, money, camera and clothes. The clerk told me that the Secret Police returned the night of my arrest and removed everything. I was not surprised that such men would also be common thieves. The grey man was no longer around. I was told by the Red Crescent doctor that the Mukhabaret Captain and his band of brigands were fleeing for their lives.

I wound up my affairs in Baghdad. The local office of the International Committee of the Red Cross furnished me with new travel documents to take me to Jordan, to London and back to home sweet home.

THE END

THE WAKE OF THE TACOMA

by

JOHN FLANAGAN

IT HAS BEEN SAID THAT Irish people generally fall into two distinct categories with regard to travelling away from home. There are those who are homing pigeons by nature and would never be happy anywhere else and those born with an incurable wanderlust who can't be happy anywhere. I'm not sure into which camp I fall; I do know however that when the Irish economy hit an historical low the need for me to leave Ireland became a necessity. The truth is I was happy at home. My wife liked me most of the time and my two kids were coming along fine. Some months before I had found a mangy dog wandering the streets of Dublin. I brought her home, scrubbed her, named her Sally and she proceeded to displace me in the family affections. Since reaching a certain age the furthest I wanted to travel from home was to my nearest watering hole or to take Sally out for her evening constitutional.

I set my sights on the USA having lived there before. The economy was buoyant enough and I was confident I would land on my feet. The day arrived too quickly for my departure. I have always had an abhorrence of airports and train stations and the inevitable wrenching goodbyes they lead to.

When I arrived in Logan airport in Boston I was still in an emotional fugue. I was leaving everyone and would not see them again for a long while. I was re-enacting a centuries old ritual of the Irish diasporas dispersed to the far corners of the known world. Feeling somewhat downcast and sorry for myself I headed straight for the airport bar to see if I could alleviate my miserable disposition. Within an hour I felt as if Christopher Columbus' endorphins were surging through my veins. I spent the next two hours trying to get out of the airport and finally found my way to a Greyhound Bus depot where I boarded a bus for Portland. Maine.

The journey North to Portland Maine was uneventful. Darkness fell and the bus became a cosy capsule speeding through the pitch black night. Passengers slumped in seats, twisting and turning until most nodded off and fell asleep. I arrived in Portland at 2:30 in the morning and took a room in a rundown hotel, the only hotel I could find open at that hour. I was too tired to care what the room looked like as I switched on a bedside lamp. I threw my bags on the floor and myself on the bed and fell fast asleep.

I awoke early the next morning and as my eyes became focussed I saw an antiquated sparsely furnished room into which Raymond Chandler might incarcerate some of his underworld villains. The linoleum tiles in the bathroom curled up at the edges and wallpaper, sodden with fungus, adorned the walls and the clanking water pipes. Floorboards creaked under me when I got out of bed and went to the window to greet my first day in America. When I parted the curtains, perhaps a bit too vigorously, a cord broke and they collapsed in a pile of dust. When I finally pulled the shuttered windows open and looked out my head came to within inches of the building next door. I picked up my bags and decided anywhere had to be better than this. I paid the bill and later found a cleaner hotel in another part of town at a reasonable rent.

After three days of visiting the Job Centre I got a job selling tickets in the local bus company and remained in Portland, Maine for the next few weeks. The salary was not really good in the economically depressed New England states generally. One day when it was quiet in the depot office I was chatting with one of my fellow workers, Hermes, at the ticket window and the subject got around to the State of Alaska. Hermes said he was planning to go to Alaska. The very sound of the name aroused my curiosity, conjured up visions of the great wilderness depicted so graphically in the novels of Jack London. Curiosity gave way to yearning until finally I became obsessed with the idea of seeing for myself the last great wilderness left on earth. I had to see it all before I returned home; there would never be another chance like this. Hermes had said the job situation in Alaska offered great opportunities. That clinched it for me.

In a fever of excitement I bought a map of North America and Alaska, spread it out on the table and plotted my course. To get to Alaska meant a journey of thousands of miles by bus to Seattle Washington in the NorthWest. From there I would take a flight to Anchorage Alaska where, according to Hermes, jobs were more plentiful. And so one Saturday morning I left Portland and began the long journey East to Seattle Washington.

I crossed the Northern United States by Greyhound bus on Highway 90 from Albany New York. Days and miles sped quickly by. The scenery in places was stunning, breath taking in its scope and color. Deer and antelope crossed the highway frequently when we reached South Dakota and Montana. I saw herds of Buffalo in Wyoming which the driver said were privately owned by ranchers. When we climbed the acrophobia-inducing Rocky Mountains bottomless ravines seemed to fall away from the roadside. The landscape changed from mountain ranges to flat tablelands extending as far as the eye could see. Each evening the one constant presence looming before us was the enormous bronze globe of the sun as it sank into the Pacific Ocean. Atmospheric dust and light created illusions of distance and size, reducing and expanding the fiery red sphere. At times the sun was like a huge disk hovering just a few miles in front of the bus. Moments later it seemed to shimmer and reduce in size with heat waves emanating from it as if from a furnace. Early one morning the bus pulled off the road for breakfast just outside Butte Montana. I went off for a short walk to a nearby forest just to stretch my legs. As I looked up the sun's light was diffused in the aspen's foliage and lances of blue beams fell down from the forest's ceiling. I was rooted to the spot, immersed in the primal beauty of the forest that was almost spiritual. I felt my professed agnosticism was undermined more at such moments than any theological argument I have heard. I was shaken from my reveries by the honking of the bus. It was time to press on with the final leg of the journey.

When I arrived in Seattle I lost no time in getting to the airport where I booked a flight to Anchorage Alaska. My funds now were getting a little strained and I was anxious to get working.

The flight from Seattle to Anchorage took me over a wonderland of ice-capped mountain ranges. The winter snows were yet to fall and the valleys between the mountains were as green as you would find anywhere in Ireland. Age old caribou trails weaved their way like threads of gossamer through the passes. Pink fireweed and purple lupine wildflowers carpeted the tundra like an enormous patchwork quilt. We flew over Juneau, the Alaskan capital, named after a prospector who panned a fortune in gold in 1880. The city of Juneau grew from the ensuing gold rush to the area. Today there are a few lone stalwarts out in the hills panning for gold. But the sense of adventure that the old timers experienced is long gone. Many of the panhandlers ended their days disgruntled and disenchanted in the Alaskan Missionary Centres for the aged and indigent.

As luck would have it the bottom was falling out of the job market when I arrived in Anchorage. Hermes had got it wrong. I was furious with myself for putting so much faith in the words of a stranger but I had to admit the prospect of seeing Alaska influenced my decision. The economic recession was especially onerous as it coincided with the onset of winter. When I was interviewed by Mrs N Woodard at the Job Centre she explained that this recession looked like being the worst for many years. She blamed it on the world wide decline in the demand for oil. State spending was already being cut and the building industry was grinding to a halt. "For Sale" signs abounded on private houses, cars, boats and single engine airplanes. The crowded Job Centre, bulging at the seams with oilmen and loggers bore grim testimony to the interviewer's words. I found myself walking along the docks and wharfs having to face the possibility of returning to Seattle to look for work. I passed a moored 300 Ton fishing trawler with the sign "Hiring" along with a telephone number. When I called the number the ship's owner asked me to meet him at Fishermans Wharf. He didn't seem a business type, he was very casual and pleasant. The interview didn't last long. The owner said the ship was leaving the following day and he was a deckhand short.

No, I told him, I was never on a fishing vessel before. No, I didn't have a police record. No, I didn't do drugs, yes, I was healthy. That seemed to satisfy him enough and he gave me the job. It was with some trepidation the following morning that I walked up the gangplank and joined the Motor Vessel Tacoma.

There was a time in my life when I was young when my Mother said I should never wander too far from home. Her words came ringing back to me as the crew converged in the small galley of the ship. It was for a pep talk by the Captain before the voyage began. He came stumbling down the steps from the wheelhouse emitting a proliferation of obscenities at a deckhand whom he had caught drinking. The fact that the Captain himself was tottering on his feet and reeking of whiskey didn't seem to bother anyone. He was huge and rotund and hairy with his cap cocked over his right ear. He turned to face the motley crew' of which I was now a member, around the galley table. There were two gap-toothed Eskimos who only talked with each other, two fierce looking Tlingit Indians one of whom was on the run from the law. The two Eskimos, like the Tlingit Indians only consorted with each other. They were devoid of initiative of any kind and only moved when directed. Like the Indians they were drunk most of the time, the beverage of choice being rum and whiskey. There were two fresh faced students Mark and Scott from Cincinnati who had just graduated from college and wanted to see 'life' before returning to University. Van Halen was of German descent and came from Chicago. He was moody and kept to himself. He was given to outbursts of rage when he was upset. Being strong and burly he was given a wide berth by the rest of the crew. I don't know what drugs smell like but there was always a suspicious aroma around when Van Halen was nearby and smoking. The only crew member Van Halen was comfortable with was Santos, a jovial smiling extrovert from Mexico who was liked by all the crew. Andy from Tucson was the Boatswain, or Bo'sun. There were nine deckhands including myself. The only crew member I had a problem with who could send a shiver up my spine was the cook, a girl named Rosie. I judged her to be about 35 years old. She drank beer from a bottle and kept a flick knife in her back pocket. If she had at any time in her life been blessed with those charming qualities that define the fairer sex they were lost on me.

The Captain gave his pep talk while swaying back and forth, his speech slurred and peppered with hiccoughs. The little I gleaned from it was that there was to be no drinking or drug use during working hours. At the end of it he looked at me, introduced me and said I was to be berthed in the forepeak starboard. As I stood there wondering what he was talking about Rosie shouted at me that it was on the right hand side at the front of the ship and that I was to move part of my anatomy there immediately.

Early the following morning the mooring lines were unslipped from the bollards and we set sail for Dutch Harbour in the Aleutian Islands. Dutch Harbour is a 1500 mile long chain of islands dividing the Pacific Ocean from the Bering Sea. Here we stocked up on supplies and the Tacoma was given a final maintenance check of engines, crane, winches etc. We then set course for Nelson Lagoon where the real work began. The Tacoma was a fish processor primarily but she also harvested salmon. The Captain paid cash for cut-rate hauls of fish at each port of call. In Nelson Lagoon local fishermen were soon filling the ship's totes with King Salmon, many of the salmon weighed well over 100 pounds. They were aptly named for the salmon is king in Alaska, followed by lobster, halibut, shrimp and crab.

Through it all Rosie kept the meals coming and established order in the galley by yelling and threatening. One day when I asked her for paper and envelopes to write home, which I was told was common practice on board, Rosie seemed to snarl. She was saying no but her head reared up and her mouth twisted as she answered with an expletive. I hoped I had caught her at a bad moment and that this was not her normal disposition. From then on any time our paths crossed I was caught between a desire to hide somewhere or jump overboard. She gave no quarter in the galley. If you were late for meals you got burnt leftovers thrown at you. I was having lunch alone one day when Rosie sat down beside me. I felt cornered at once as she was between me and the galley door. She said she heard I was from Ireland and asked if I was from the North or South. When I said the South her lip curled into a reasonable facsimile of a smile and said her grandmother came from Kerry. I thought that made a lot of sense.

During the voyage, bald eagles, almost extinct in the lower 48 States swooped down for entrails as we processed the salmon. In the almost pollution free Aleutians the great bird thrives. A giant walrus circled around the ship while we took on fresh water in Herendeen Bay. The worse experience I had was when I went for provisions when we made a stopover in Kodiak. I was one of the few deckhands on board whom Rosie trusted with money. Perhaps it was because I was sober a lot of the time. Late one night I left the ship with a grocery list and walked to a store which was about a half mile away. About halfway there I saw a movement near a wire fence and what appeared to be a rubbish dump. In the dark it looked like a horse and as I wondered what a horse was doing in Alaska rummaging in a dump in sub-zero temperatures I drew level with it. The 'horse' was an enormous Kodiak grizzly bear. In the light from the docks I saw it looking my way. My feet never touched the ground as I ran the remaining distance to the store. I leaped through the door and sat down, panting and gasping from my effort. The store assistant came over with a smile on his face and said it was an old and harmless bear that came down from the hills to the refuse dump every night.

On the 2nd week out the weather turned foul. The transfer of hauls of fish from the boats to the deck of the ship was backbreaking work; in heaving turbulent seas the work became perilous. As eight to ten foot waves crashed over the bulwark and flooded the deck the stacked totes began to break loose with the violent pounding movements of the ship. The totes rammed into the sides of the deck. Spilled salmon gyrated in a frenzied dance of death on the deck as the two Tlingit Indians, sliding and falling with every step forward tried in vain to recoup the slippery fish. They were yelled at by Andy the Bo'sun to push the scattered totes against the header chute and fasten them down. The fish in the totes had to be beheaded and gutted, packed and refrigerated with all possible speed. It would be a daunting task even if all the deckhands were sober; as it was only the two college kids, Mark and Scott and I could claim that dubious distinction. On the heels of the Indians the two Eskimos also slipped and fell in an effort to retrieve the up-ended fish. A last boat was being unloaded and it risked capsizing as it scraped repeatedly against the bulkhead of the ship in the choppy sea. The Tlinket Indians, both drunk, could not stand straight and were thrown repeatedly to the deck as the waves swept over the sides of the ship. Everyone was on deck except Rosie who was in the galley, and the Captain was in the wheelhouse struggling in vain with the drift of the ship if the zigzagging backwash in the wake of the Tacoma was anything to judge by. Once darkness fell it would have been impossible to continue without the brilliant arc lights illuminating the deck. Under the pitch black night the Tacoma was a giant bubble of yellow light undulating on the raging sea. The violent gyrations of the ship caused an oxygen bottle to break loose and was crashing dangerously about the deck. We were concerned that it would blow until one of the Eskimos went out and lashed it down. Palettes of cardboard boxes went tumbling over the side. Van Halen came running up from the hull to say lethal ammonia was leaking from a burst freezer pipe. The Bo'sun went back down with him to try and solve the problem.

It was about the time when the pandemonium was at its height, when the totes were careering about the deck and the Tacoma was buffeted by swells and rough seas, with half the deckhands tripped out or otherwise impaired that I had this sense of dread, that something bad was going to happen.

The Bo'sun yelled at the college kids and me to help pick up the scattered fish. It was like trying to pick up wet blocks of ice and took us two hours to clear the deck. After that was accomplished I took my place with the rest of the crew to form what is known as the slime line. Santos was in charge of this operation as he had the most experience. The fish were unloaded onto a chute, beheaded by Santos and passed on to the adjoining tables to be gutted and cleaned. They were then thrown down a second chute to the lower deck and set on trays in a blast freezer. After a few hours the fish are bagged and packaged and stored in the hold until such time they are off-loaded onto a Japanese cargo ship at sea at a prearranged location. I'd never worked so hard in my life with the schedule calling for 16-18 hour shifts. What drove me on was the thought of the $10,000 paycheque waiting for me at the end of the voyage. The entire crew was promised a percentage of the haul and we had harvested a huge catch.

Santos was working at a breathless pace to keep the gutters and cleaners busy at the tables to his left. It was then it happened, suddenly and without warning Santos' life changed forever from that moment. With the fish chute filled to overflowing, ominously reducing his space to manoeuvre, Santos' right hand slipped forward as he lost his grip on a heavy salmon. Even with protective gloves his hand shot with such force into the header blades his thumb and middle fingers were severed from his right hand. A heartrending scream from Santos brought everything to a sudden stop. Every crew member dropped what they were doing and rushed to his aid, such was the measure of his popularity. His hand was quickly bandaged and his arm put in a sling. The Bo'sun gave him antibiotics and pain-killers. When Santos went into shock he was carried bodily to his bunk where Van Halen watched over him. The Captain telephoned Nelson Lagoon village and a lifeboat was dispatched to pick up Santos and transfer him back to the village. From there he was flown to Anchorage and made a connecting flight to Seattle. The last anyone heard was that he had flown home to Cancun in Mexico.

The strength-sapping pace began to have its effect especially into the final weeks of the voyage and the advent of the winter Solstice. Fights broke out among the crew in the last week of the season. There was one especially nasty fight between an Indian and Van Halen. A crew member threw a knife at the feet of Van Halen who picked it up. At that point the Captain pulled a gun from his pocket and roared them into submission.

When the fishing came to an end the entire crew were physically exhausted. But for the injuries to Santos they would have been jubilant, tired as they may have been. Each had a cheque worth $10,000 waiting for them.

I stayed with the ship when it made the long journey South to its home port in Seattle. From there I flew home and regaled everyone around the fireside about my journey to Alaska.

THE END

THE BISHOP

by

JOHN FLANAGAN

"Marc."

Marc's wife Solonge, called out to him from the rear window of the cottage. "It's Inspector Brunet, he's in the living room."

Marc Claudel turned around from where he was working in the garden, stood up and waved to his wife. He looked up at the sky. It was a beautiful warm summer's day with not a cloud to be seen. So much for his plans for the garden today. He shook his head as he scanned the rich pastureland surrounding his cottage home. It didn't help that Inspector Brunet lived in the nearby town of Evreux. He shrugged and decided to stop thinking in such a negative way, the Inspector had his own job to do.

He washed the earth from his hands and dried them with a handkerchief, hoping that just maybe the Inspector's visit might be a social call but that was unlikely. When he entered through the kitchen the frown on his wife's face confirmed the worst. Solonge liked the Inspector but she had already interpreted his grim demeanour as a bad omen.

She knew somewhere a crime had been committed, some serious infraction of the law that would place her husband in harm's way. She had known the nature of his work when they married but it was no less harrowing each time he was contacted by the Surete Nationale in Paris or had a visit from Inspector Brunet. Unfortunately the Inspector believed he served the interest of security better by not always telephoning when he came bearing bad news.

"A very tragic and difficult case Monsieur . . . ," began Inspector Brunet after they were seated in the living room, "two nights ago at about 11:00 P.M. in Evreux, Armand Coit, an elderly man in his seventies, shot and killed one Emile Boulet, a man about his own age. The whole thing is inexplicable. By all accounts they were friends, they knew each other all their lives. But first let me say Monsieur that if this was a straight forward homicide the local police could have handled it, but ah well, it is complicated. Chief Inspector Prejean asked me to brief you."

"Why does he want me on the case if it's a local killing?"

"Here is the problem. This matter . . . , how shall I put it, it requires a delicate hand, there's so much involved. Armand Coit and the man he killed and four other men, including His Eminence Bishop Auguste of Evreux joined local Resistance Units after Germany invaded France in the 2nd World War. When the war ended they were all personally decorated by General de Gaulle down there in the Town Hall. Bishop Auguste was just a young cleric at the time studying for the priesthood; his name was Pierre Etienne. I was there that day, of course I was just a kid at the time but I'll never forget the military band, the pomp and ceremonies, de Gaulle pinning the medals on the heroes of the Resistance. The scene was joyous, festive. After the ceremonies when de Gaulle came out with the decorated Resistance fighters and stood on the steps of the Town Hall thousands applauded them. Many people cried that day. Those men helped restore French pride after all the humiliations of the war. It was a great day for the town of Evreux and for France . . ."

The Inspector stopped talking abruptly as Solonge came in and placed a tray with coffee and biscuits between them. When she left he resumed.

"Eh Monsieur, there is a report being drawn up at the station on all of this, it just occurred to me perhaps you would rather read about it than listen to me . . . ?"

"On the contrary Inspector, I'm sure I'd learn much more from you than going through a lengthy police report. Please, continue . . ."

The Inspector, feeling pleased with himself went on with renewed vigour.

"After the war the Resistance Fighters married local girls, with the exception of course of Bishop Auguste. He went back to the Jesuit seminary in Paris to study. He lost touch with everyone and well that's about it. Everyone else just settled back into the community. Three went back to their family farms and well, just got on with their lives. Pascal Ribaud did well for himself, he seemed to have come into a bit of money and bought a small hotel on Rue de Pannette in Evreux."

"Did they keep in touch with each other over the years?"

"They were like brothers after what they went through in the war. They played petanque, they went fishing together. As the years passed they attended their kid's christenings, always there for each other. Except, as I said, Bishop Auguste. After his consecration he took up residence in Evreux. From that time he sort of distanced himself from his former compatriots in the Resistance. But one must make allowances for his rank and position. Evreux is a large diocese and being a Bishop must leave little time for socializing with old comrades in arms. But the veterans themselves, they are all in good health, considering their ages."

"What are your thoughts about what happened; does Coit seem like the kind of man who would murder someone?"

The Inspector shook his head.

"Armand Coit is the most likeable person you could meet. He's a shoemaker by trade, he has a small thriving business in Evreux that he runs with his two sons. He specializes in running shoes; he's also a time-keeper for the Evreux Athletic Club. Overall he's very well liked and respected in the local community. Coit is sort of semi-retired, he stays in the back of the shop and helps with the running of the store. Many of the top professionals go only to him for shoes. On top of that he's a decorated war hero. I can't imagine what turned him into a murderer."

"Does he have a criminal record?"

"Coit?, clean as a whistle. And that goes for all of them. They were just simple farm lads when the war started."

"Can you take me up to the time when they last met, before this killing."

The Inspector took a notebook from his pocket and turned over some pages.

"Ah, here we are. On Saturday evening last the four men with their wives and families visited Pascal Ribaud at the hospital in Evreux. He had angina and was recovering from a stroke. At about 6:15 P.M. he said he was not feeling well. He believed he was dying and asked for Bishop Auguste to hear his confession. From what I've found out everyone was surprised because Ribaud was not religious, he never went to Church. Still, he was born a Catholic and I suppose he didn't want to die outside the Church. Ribaud incidentally was a cousin of the murdered man Emile Boulet. When Bishop

Auguste arrived he cleared everyone from the room and heard Ribaud's confession. Ribaud died soon afterwards, at 7:14 P.M. to be precise, according to the hospital records. Later the same night Armand Coit shot Boulet."

The Inspector closed the notebook and put it back in his pocket.

"That's all I have Monsieur," He said, "We are holding Armand Coit at the station pending charges."

"I'd like to talk to him, what would be the best time?"

"Early tomorrow morning would be best Monsieur. By 9 '0' clock he will have finished breakfast and there will be no public visiting until the afternoon."

When Claudel entered the Evreux Police Station the following morning Inspector Brunet was waiting and took him to a holding cell on the ground floor. He opened the cell door and locked it when Claudel went in. Armand Coit was seated alone at a table and peering intently at a chess set. Claudel waited until Coit looked up suddenly and got up from the table. He approached him with his hand outstretched. While they shook hands Coit gestured towards a second chair at the table.

"Forgive my manners Monsieur, I get so carried away with this game I lose all sense of time. Please, have a seat."

Claudel sat down facing Coit and looked over the chessboard.

"Who's to play . . . ?" He asked.

"Black . . ." Said Coit.

Without saying a word Claudel moved a piece. As Coit quickly countered the move Claudel looked into the darting eyes of the older man. Deep crevasses ran from the corners of his eyes and spread to his temples. The weathered face bore the ravages of time and torture. The bridge of his prominent nose was misshapen where it had reset badly after being broken. His fingernail beds were discolored and rippled where the nails had been torn from his fingers while he was a prisoner during the war. But the mutilations and scars inflicted when he was an 18 years old youth had not dulled the lively and inquisitive eyes as he mulled over Claudel's last move on the chessboard. With a smile he made a move that won him the game. Claudel threw up his hands in mock despair.

"You must be an important man to have an Inspector open the door for you," Said Coit in a voice strained with age. He smiled as he put the pieces into a box and folded the chessboard.

"Monsieur Coit, my name is Marc Claudel of the Surete. I've been asked to look into this matter in a sort of . . . , advisory capacity, the reason being your Resistance activities in the 2nd World War. The government wants to make sure, among other things that you have a good legal defence. If you have no objection there are some questions I would like to ask you . . ."

"Very good Monsieur, I will help you all I can, up to a point. If you find me uncooperative with some issues you will make allowances I hope for an old man and not pressure me too much . . ."

"Anytime you want me to leave you have only to ask me. I'll make my enquiries elsewhere."

"Fair enough Monsieur. I can't ask for more than that. But perhaps I can save you some time by telling you I am guilty as charged. At home I had an old German Luger pistol along with some ammunition since the end of the war. I always kept it cleaned and greased but I never knew I was going to use it. I shot Emile Boulet dead at point blank range."

"Can you tell me why . . . ?"

"No Monsieur."

"Have you talked with a lawyer yet?"

"I don't want a lawyer . . . , I don't need a lawyer. Everything is simple and straight forward, I killed Boulet and no one else is involved . . ."

"Well I hope you understand if you maintain this silence you could spend the rest of your life in prison . . ."

"It's not a decision I made lightly at my age."

"I just don't understand. After all you've done for your country. You are a national hero. Do you want to be branded as a common criminal, is that the legacy you want to leave your family?"

"Monsieur Claudel I know you have good intentions and you want to help me but there is nothing more I wish to say . . ."

Claudel spent some more time with Coit and they played another game of chess. When he stood up to leave he was no wiser about why the old man had shot Emile Boulet. When the guard was opening the cell door Claudel turned to Coit.

"Is there anything you need?"

"I was hesitant to ask you but yes there is something. If I could get some runners magazines, I like to keep up with how our local lads are doing . . ."

"Of course, that should be no problem at all. Goodbye."

Jules Heniot was one of the Resistance veterans Claudel wanted to speak with next. Heniot was a heavyset articulate man who had a good retentive memory given his advanced years. He lived alone in an apartment complex in the town of Houdan, a suburb to the West of Paris. When Claudel knocked on the door he was greeted almost effusively by the elderly corpulent widower. Jules Heniot was pink-cheeked, he had moist translucent eyes, he was almost completely bald and appeared to be in robust good health. He had a breezy, jovial nature and welcomed Claudel warmly. There was something Claudel noticed about his eyes, a sadness lurking in them that was almost but not quite concealed by the bonhomie exuberance of his personality. He walked with the aid of an ivory tipped cane, one of a few concessions he made to his advanced years.

When the perfunctory civilities had been dispensed with he led Claudel to a small living room where they both sat down. Claudel explained the reason for his visit.

"And so I would be very grateful for any help you can give me." Said Claudel, "perhaps you could tell me what happened in Pascal Ribaud's room in the hospital?"

"What do you mean?"

"Well, who was in the room?"

"Everyone, it was really crowded. All my old comrades and their families were there. We arranged to visit Pascal together and cheer him up after his stroke. But he wasn't looking too good and we cut our visit short. Just as we were leaving he called me over to his bedside and whispered in my ear. He asked for Bishop Auguste to come and hear his confession. That surprised the hell out of me because he was a confirmed athiest. Since he was young he hated the Church and got more radical as he got older." Heniot sat back in his chair with a wry smile playing about his lips. "I remember a service in the Church in Dreux many years ago, that was before the war when Pascal was still attending Mass and anyway . . . , he started haranguing the priest who was serving the Mass. It was over some minor infraction by the priest, something to do with him overstepping his authority with the local soccer team of which Pascal was the captain. Pascal was frog-marched out of the Church by some of the guild leaders shouting at the top of his voice. He was always bitter about that afterwards. So when he asked for

Bishop Auguste to go to the hospital and hear his confession I figured old Pascal had finally lost the plot . . ."

Claudel was making entries into a notebook and it was some time before he realised Heniot had stopped talking. He looked up to see the old man was seized in a paroxysm of silent laughter as if living again the incident in the Church. He seemed on the verge of hysteria but no sound emitted from his closed lips as he shook quietly on the chair. His infectious mirth transmitted itself to Claudel who found himself smiling. Heniot reached into his pocket and took out a handkerchief as tears flooded his eyes. As he dabbed his eyes he heaved a great sigh and in a moment sat still and silent. Grief and distress then took hold of him, distorting the serene expression that was normal to his character and temperament. Tears again flooded his eyes, tears of bitterness and inner pain. Claudel waited as the old man purged his mind of memories and was breathing easily again. He dried his eyes for the last time, gave his nose a final blow and put away the handkerchief. He sat erect in the chair.

"Excuse me Monsieur, as the years go by I cry too easily . . ."

"I don't want to cause you any distress . . ."

Heniot waved his hand in the air.

"I'm alright now. Where was I . . . ,? Yes, you were asking me about Pascal. Someone left the hospital and went to get Bishop Auguste. He came over quickly, shooed everyone out of the room and heard Pascal's confession. I sat down outside in the corridor to make sure they weren't disturbed."

"Did you leave at any time . . . ?"

"Not for one second . . ."

"What happened then . . . ?"

"The Bishop was in there for about half an hour. Then he came out of the room looking very distressed and calling for a doctor. He said Pascal had lost consciousness while they were praying together. I ran to get a doctor. He went into Pascal's room and pronounced him dead."

That evening Claudel was stretched out on the sofa staring listlessly at the television set. Solonge was in Ivry La Bataille helping with the arrangements for an upcoming flower show. The three dogs were lying on the floor, watching him, full of expectation. He stretched and went to the window and looked up. There was an hour's light left in the sky. He turned to the dogs.

"Ok, let's go."

The dogs leaped up with delight. The highlight of the day was this running up to the copse of oak trees on the rise behind the cottage. The neighbouring farmers were used to the well disciplined dogs running through the fields. They gambolled through the copse as Claudel sat on a fence and pondered his next move in the murder of Emile Boulet. Further questioning of Armand Coit would elicit nothing from the intractable war veteran. If his torturers couldn't break him in wartime he would not be intimidated by a nosy government agent in time of peace. Coit was not an ordinary man and age had not weakened his character or resolve. But for all that the mystery of Boulet's death had to be resolved. If mitigating circumstances could not be proved in the defence of Armand Coit he would go to trial for murder. He put two fingers to his lips and brought the dogs back with a long shrill whistle. When he was back in the cottage he stretched out on the sofa again and stared at the ceiling. Solonge returned, filled him in on the news of the flower show and set about getting the evening meal ready. He remained motionless as the room darkened and night fell over the countryside. Inspector Brunet had told him that Armand Coit and the man he later killed, Emile Boulet, were seen talking amiably in the corridor of the hospital while they waited for the arrival of Bishop Auguste to hear Ribaud's confession. A few hours later Coit shot Boulet dead. Claudel sat upright suddenly. Could the confession of the dying Ribaud be in any way connected to the murder of Boulet ?

In the vestry of the 12th century Cathedral of Notre Dame in Evreux the Sacristan Pierre Galushon folded the last of the laundered surplices and placed them neatly in an airing cupboard. He opened the vestry door and peered out over the heads of the congregation and checked his wristwatch. The twelve 'o' clock Requiem Mass was just ending. The cathedral was crowded as Bishop Auguste turned around on the altar to bless the congregation and bring to an end the special Mass offered for the repose of the souls of Pascal Ribaud and Emile Boulet. Galushon looked at his watch again and dolefully shook his head. It would be well into the afternoon before he could lock up and go home. He opened the vestry door wide in anticipation of the Bishop and the six altar boys coming in from serving the Mass. Even after 28 years as a Sacristan in Notre Dame the presence of Bishop Auguste still filled him with uneasiness. Since the day of his consecration the Bishop had never condescended to speak with him, it was always to him: not even the most casual remark about the weather issued from the imperious Bishop and he doubted sometimes if the Bishop even knew his name. One Christmas eve the Bishop handed him a bottle of wine and muttered something about Christmas. Before he had time to thank him the Bishop had turned on his heels and was gone. He in turn had given the bottle of wine to an old age pensioner who sometimes fell asleep in the shadows close to the radiators.

The altar boys entered the vestry preceding Bishop Auguste. Galushon closed the door behind them. While

Bishop Auguste went to his changing room the altar boys blew out the flames of the candles they carried and placed the holders in a rack. Normally they would stay and chat with Galushon, full of giggles and mischief, talking non-stop about soccer and girls. But never while Bishop Auguste was around. The vestry, the Bishop had fastidiously reminded them was as sacrosanct as the altar and as deserving of their respectful silence, that they should not shed their piety as they did their surplices. The Bishop was at the sink in his changing room. With a stiff nailbrush he scrubbed his hands until they throbbed. This aggressive hand washing never failed to amaze Galushon. It was like a fetish with him and made no sense since the Bishop never got his hands dirty. The soft lily-white hands were as bloodless as the marble hands of the statues in the transept of the Cathedral. The running water stopped. The Bishop talked to Galushon through the partially closed door as he dried his hands.

"Go to my housekeeper. Tell her to prepare coffee. I'm having a visitor this afternoon."

His words, calculated and sparing were spoken as if the life and being of the Sacristan assumed relevance only at the moment of his being summoned to service by the Bishop. Galushon could never quite shake the feeling of being irrelevant in the presence of the Bishop.

"Yes Your Grace."

He put a coat on over his surplice and picked up his walking stick. At a leisurely pace he went to the Bishop's residence and delivered the message to the housekeeper Madame Bremond. By the time he got back to the Cathedral the Bishop had already left. He uttered an audible sigh of relief that bordered on euphoria as he put away the discarded vestments and then tidied up the vestry. Within an hour he had locked up the cathedral doors and was walking towards his home on Rue Josephine. He would be free until evening Benediction.

At 2:30 P.M. in the bedroom of his residence Bishop Auguste was kneeling before a votive lamp and a statue of the Blessed Virgin Mary. He murmured a final prayer, stood up, closed his breviary and kissed it. He was in a foul mood and had earlier snapped at his housekeeper not to prepare coffee for his expected guest. This Surete agent might prove to be an ignorant lump of a fellow, there would be no sense in prolonging his visit by entertaining him. He went to the window that overlooked Rue Charles Corbeau and drew the curtains over. He stopped when he caught sight of Galushon, instantly recognizing the hunched shoulders bent over the walking stick. His face grimaced with contempt as the Sacristan disappeared from view. He silently invoked God's forgiveness for the pusillanimity of the moods his thoughts gave rise to. He must say penance again, strive to be more forbearing towards Galushon and all he and his kind represented. It was no doubt the imminent visit of this detective that had his mind in a quandary. If they only knew! His own superiors, his congregation, the police, how could they be expected to understand that what he did over a half-century ago was for the glory of France and our Holy Mother the Church? The deaths of Ribaud and his cousin Boulet were tragic corollaries of the struggle to preserve the sanctity of the Church Incarnate. The secrets within him were like malignant growths that threatened to spill its festering pus into every fibre of his being. If his past was brought to light in this liberal democracy it would be men like Galushon, crude and unsophisticated dullards who would sit in judgement on him. Men with as much merit and individuality as amoeba in a sea of plankton, would be named a jury of his peers. It was such men who brought

France and the Church to its knees in that satanic Revolution of 1789. In forming the First Republic the Sans Culottes had irreversibly usurped the power of the Holy See of Rome and distanced man from God. Since the baptism of Clovis in 496 AD, in victory or defeat France had been the envy of the civilized world, indeed the very soul of France had been moulded by Kings of the Capetian and Bourbon dynasties. He saw the French Revolution as a progression of social evils that began with Martin Luther's Protestant Reformation in 1530. The besieged Church was further pounded in 1884 by the publication of Karl Marx's Communist Manifesto. That perfidious document had caused great social upheaval and dissention among the Catholic laity worldwide and had lasting ramifications for the Church to the present day.

Bishop Auguste let the curtain drapes fall back in place. He went to the piano and sat down. Spreading his hands out like fans before him he pressed on the cuticle of a fingernail that flushed vivid red for an instant. They were his mother's hands, sculpted to perfection if slightly spatula tipped from a lifetime of playing the piano, his only passion next to the Church. It was an agony no longer having her to confide in. She was the only one to whom he could lay open the innermost secrets of his heart and mind. She knew everything about him collaborating with the Germans during the war yet she never judged him or ever stopped loving him. He had never fully recovered from her loss. Soft dulcet notes resonated throughout the rooms as he lightly touched the piano keys without playing; his thoughts taken up by the plight of the Church and the challenges it faced. It would survive, he confidently predicted to himself, as it had survived incalculable challenges in its long history.

Unlike France he mused, as his fingers caressed the piano keys, Catholic Germany had never lost its soul. Germany!

That paragon of hope to the world. Why was the Church in France diffident about which side to ally itself when by the summer of 1940 a German victory was a foregone conclusion? Top German and French industrialists, eager to unite, had formed their own entente cordial. In 1936 French Industrialists helped finance the German Nazi Party, paving the way for a dictatorship under Hitler. All of Europe could have been freed of Communism and Freemasonry and the machinations of the Jews. Furthermore a German victory could have seen the restoration of the French monarchy. Alas . . .

He ran his pristine hands over the piano keys and gently touched the first notes of 'Jesu, joy of mans desiring'. Playing Bach took him a step closer to the divine, to God and hope and forgiveness. Bach was spiritually elevating, an antidote to the accursed banality by which his life was surrounded. At Mass he endured the foul odours of tobacco and cheap wine on the breaths of mendicants as he dispensed the Blessed Eucharist. For his sins of pride he imposed harsh disciplines upon himself just short of severe self-flagellation, as much as his aging body could endure.

Bishop Auguste was widely respected in his See but not unequivocally loved. When he condescended to make himself available in the confessional most parishioners sought another priest, the severity of the Bishop's penances was something to be avoided. On Holy Days he executed the sacred ritual of the Mass with a mercurial air as the assisting acolytes moved nervously about the steps of the altar, striving to avoid making eye contact with him.

He stopped playing and moved listlessly about the room, pausing before a mirror to adjust his silver-rimmed spectacles. His long thin face accentuated his prominent aquiline nose. Heavily hooded eyes glinted under thick eyebrows. His remaining hair, thin and white was swept back from a broad rounded forehead. His wide mouth was usually crimped in a long resolute line. At 76 years of age he was physically fit owing to a daily regimen of exercise and a strict diet. He had adamantly refused to retire and his superiors bowed to his wishes because of his excellent health and his status as a decorated hero of the Resistance.

He took a handkerchief from his pocket and wiped beads of perspiration from his nose and forehead. Who was this Marc Claudel from the Surete Nationale, what could he know? He shrugged his shoulders slightly as if to reassure himself. For the first time since the end of the war the dread of discovery no longer tormented every waking moment of his life. With the deaths of Ribaud and Boulet there was no one left to connect him to the sins of his past. The past. That great amorphous void that consumed all that ever was and all that ever would be in its gaping maws. He felt free, finally free after all these years. As for this detective, he must not appear to be discommoded; the police could be canny enough in their own blustering way. A knock on the door broke his train of thought.

"Yes?"

His housekeeper opened the door.

"Your visitor has arrived Your Grace. He's in the reception room."

Claudel was standing by the window of the reception room when the Bishop went in to meet him.

"Good afternoon Monsieur Claudel," Said the Bishop airily as he indicated a chair at the far end of a large oval-shaped table, "please be seated."

Claudel was completely taken aback when he moved forward to shake hands and was left with his hand in mid-air as the Bishop ignored the gesture and sat down. Claudel ignored what he considered a slight, and decided to make allowance for the ageing Bishop, not being certain at this point of the well-being or otherwise of the Bishop's mental acumen.

"Thank you for seeing me Your Grace," Said Claudel, "as I explained briefly on the telephone I am enquiring into the death of Emile Boulet. First I would like to ask you a few questions about Pascal Ribaud. As you were the last person to see him alive I . . ."

"Pascal Ribaud was suffering from angina," Said the Bishop abruptly, "he died in the hospital. Why is an agent of the Surete Nationale interested in him?"

"There are circumstances . . ."

"Aren't our local police competent enough to handle the matter?"

"The government has a special interest because, like Your Grace, he was a hero of the Resistance . . ."

A clock's pendulum ticked away the seconds and magnified the silence in the quiet room.

"I don't understand, what is it you wish to ask me?"

"Would you mind telling me what happened when you arrived to hear Ribaud's confession?"

"There's not much to tell. When I arrived at the hospital Ribaud didn't look well. His breathing was laboured, his voice was weak. I heard his confession immediately."

"Did anyone inform the doctor . . . ?"

"The doctor had already seen him. I assumed that's why he looked so weak, because he had been sedated. I prayed by his bedside until he stopped breathing."

"Was there anyone else in the room?"

"I think there might have been some people around . . ."

"Are you sure Your Grace? The reason I ask is that Jules Heniot said just you and Ribaud were in the room. He said he waited outside in the corridor, to make sure you were not disturbed. He seemed sure about that . . ."

The Bishop became irritated. He tapped the polished table with his fingertips.

"It's possible, it's possible. I can't recall every detail. Now perhaps you will answer me a question. I'm curious. What manner of man am I dealing with, what religion are you . . . ?"

"Your Grace," Said Claudel at length, "I came here on a serious matter . . ."

"Indulge me . . ."

"Well since you ask, I'm what you might call a lapsed Catholic . . . , I don't practice anymore . . ."

"Hm, a stray sheep. As for being lapsed, it will never be too late to return to the fold."

"About Pascal Ribaud Your Grace . . . ,"

"I don't know what you want me to say unless it's to divulge what a dying man said in confession," The slightest degree of testiness registered in the voice of Bishop Auguste, "the confessional is sacred, as a Catholic, even a lapsed one you should know that . . ."

"Your Grace may I respectfully remind you that I am a law officer. You can answer my questions now or under subpoena before a special judicial enquiry. It's up to you, I don't mind one way or the other . . ."

The Bishop felt the blood rushing to his face. This was so unexpected. He had thought his title and office would have been sufficient to induce some degree of subservience in the detective.

"When this interrogation is finished you'll regret taking this line of questioning with me, I'll see to it personally . . ."

"You were saying you heard Ribaud's confession, what happened then?"

"When I was praying by his bedside he seemed to fall into a deep sleep. When I was leaving I tried to wake him to say goodbye. That's when I noticed he had stopped breathing. I sent for a doctor immediately . . ."

"Did he say anything in his confession that I should know about?"

The Bishop shook his head and sat more upright in the chair.

"All Pascal Ribaud wanted was a general absolution for his sins. He was so weak he talked for no more than a few minutes. He died at peace with himself."

"Thank you Your Grace," Said Claudel standing up, "if there is anything else you might remember please contact me . . ."

Bishop Auguste nodded curtly without answering.

They walked to the front door. Claudel did not extend his hand as he said goodbye. He turned briskly on his heels and went out into the street. As he closed over the heavy panelled door Bishop Auguste's face grimaced and he briefly closed his eyes. Hurriedly he went upstairs and locked himself in to his bedroom. He went to the sink, picked up the fingernail brush and turned on the hot water. With feverish intensity he scrubbed his hands until he could no longer withstand the pain of the scalding water. The plight of the suffering souls in purgatory, for whom he prayed daily, helped him endure the agony.

He pulled his hands out from under the hot faucet and clung to the edge of the sink, breathless and weak. Plenary indulgences thus striven for in the sight of God were never wasted. As he dried his hands he stood by the window and looked over the ramparts of the ancient Cathedral. His Cathedral, his world, within which parameters all was conformity and order unlike the chaos beyond its walls. He remained still and lost account of time until the pain in his afflicted hands eased away. A calming tranquillity gradually displaced the turmoil of his soul. He raised his closed fists and dug his knuckles deeply into his eyes. Dear and Merciful Father guide me through my hour of need. That it should come to this. He looked up at the overcast sky. Rain was forecast. It would be a welcome relief for the parched flower beds in the public gardens in Rue Jean Juares. He knelt down and spent some moments in prayerful meditation. Feeling suddenly elated he went to the piano and began to play Chopin's 'Preludes'.

Claudel was in a quandary. Seldom had he been so perplexed about a case. In the study of his cottage he stood before a blackboard. With a piece of chalk he underscored and put a question mark behind Bishop Auguste's name. He felt there was much the uncooperative Bishop was withholding. He wrote on the blackboard.

6:15 P.M.   Hospital patient Pascal Ribaud asks for Bishop A to hear his confession.

6:35 P.M.   Bishop A arrives. Takes confession. Jules Heniot sits at Outside door.

7:10 P.M.   Bishop A calls for a doctor.

7:14 P.M.   Doctor arrives. Ribaud pronounced dead.

10:50 P.M.   Armand Coit shoots Boulet.

The telephone rang in the hallway. Sologne opened the door.

"It's for you Dear, Inspector Brunet."

He went out and picked up the telephone.

"Good morning Inspector."

"Good morning Monsieur. I am calling from the station. I just wanted to let you know we took care of Armand Coit, he's got all the running magazines he needs . . ."

160

"Excellent. There's some questions I'll need to ask him later."

In the afternoon Claudel drove to the police station. When he entered Coit's cell the elderly prisoner shook his hand energetically.

"Thank you for the magazines. Let's sit down shall we." He brought over a chair and sat beside Claudel.

"Monsieur Coit . . . ," Began Claudel.

"Oh please, let's not be too formal . . . , my name is Armand, everyone calls me Armand."

"Ok, Armand it is. First let me say I'm not going to ask you questions you've already refused to answer. What I do need is a sort of overall picture of your activities with the Resistance . . ."

Coit slowly pushed back his chair and stood up slowly, breathing heavily. The expression of innate amiability that was part of his character changed to one of rancour and distress as he paced about the cell. He finally sat down on the edge of the bunk bed. His breathing eased as he became pensive. Claudel placed a hand on his shoulder.

"I can't tell you how sorry I am to put you through this but I have to know. You've got to let me help you. Also I know is it was all a lifetime ago. If you can't remember, well then, there's nothing can be done about it."

"To be honest I'd have a hard time remembering what I did yesterday, or a week ago . . . , but, I remember every moment of my time with the Resistance. That's all crystal clear in my mind . . ."

"How did you become involved with the Resistance?"

"After Germany invaded France in 1940 I was one of 24 locals who joined up. We were part of three platoons, eight men to each. They made me a leader of the 1st platoon. Bishop Auguste, he was Pierre Etienne then, was made the leader of the 2ⁿᵈ platoon. The leader of the 3ʳᵈ platoon was Rene Degrande, he was among 18 of us who were captured or executed by the Gestapo."

"Eighteen out of 24, your losses were high . . ."

"That's right, by the end of the war there were just six of us left . . ."

"What was your mission, what accounted for such high losses?"

"I just don't know. Because of our youth we were kept out of the line of fire by the older men. Our job was to deliver Resistance newspapers. There was 'La Voix du Nord' put out by miners and textile workers. There was the 'Verities', 'Combat', 'L'Humanite and 'Le Coureur de L' Air'. The Coureur was printed by General de Gaulle's Free French staff in London and parachuted into France."

"You couldn't have been much more than a teenager at the time . . ."

"We were aged 16 to 20 years old. Old enough. We were soon older than our years . . ."

"Inspector Brunet told me you lost your parents, a young brother . . ."

"Yes . . ."

"You were arrested by the Germans, how did that happen?"

"We were in the town of Mantes, delivering newspapers. We had turned into a quiet side street and all of a sudden we were surrounded by German soldiers. It was obvious they were expecting us. The newspapers were hidden under panels along the floor. They knew exactly where to look for them in the old Renault we were driving. Two of us escaped. I was taken to Paris as a guest of the Gestapo for a week."

"Who were the two who escaped . . . ?"

"Pierre Etienne, he is now Bishop Auguste, and Pascal Ribaud."

"All of your men were picked up?"

"At one time or another, yes."

"What did they do to you . . . ?"

"Well, the Gestapo didn't bring me to Avenue Foch for Schnapps." He held up his hands. "they pulled my fingernails out. I think the only reason they let me live was because they decided I was too young to know anything. When I was with my platoon I didn't get home very often. My mother cried so much she could hardly talk. My father wanted to help deliver the newspapers but I wouldn't hear of it because of his ill health. One night I went home and the Gestapo were waiting for me. I had a pistol and I could have got one or two of them. But I didn't want to risk retaliation against my family so I escaped in the darkness. The next day I heard they had shot my parents and my brother . . ."

He stood up shakily, leaning on a chair. Claudel made a move to help him but he waved him aside. Claudel stood beside him.

"Your family will have died in vain if you don't bring everything into the open. You'll be seen as a demented elderly man who just lost his mind and shot someone . . ."

"It was Boulet . . ."

"What . . . ?"

"Emile Boulet. It was him. He was the informer, the traitor among us. From the time he joined the Resistance he had been working for the Germans."

"When did you find out . . . ?"

Coit lapsed into silence. He was about to speak but decided against it.

"Don't stop now," Said Claudel, "how did you find out and from whom . . . ?" Coit stared mutely at the floor. "Bishop Auguste told you, didn't he?"

163

When Coit looked at him Claudel knew he had guessed right. The old man shifted uneasily and sat back down on the chair. He nodded his head as he took a Gauloise cigarette from his pocket.

"Yes . . . , it was His Grace . . ."

Coit paused as he lit the cigarette and coughed weakly.

"My grandkids never let me smoke. They give me hell so I have to smoke in secret when they're around. They're always fussing over me. I wish they were here right now."

"What did Bishop Auguste say to you?"

"When Ribaud died in the hospital the Bishop telephoned me later that night. He asked me to meet him in his residence near the cathedral . . ."

"Go on . . ."

"I went there and saw him. He told me that Ribaud confessed that his cousin Boulet was the collaborator during the war. The word of a consecrated Catholic Bishop was good enough for me. I went back to my house to get my handgun and I shot Boulet."

"Tell me about Bishop Auguste; how did he become part of the Resistance?"

"As I told you he was a seminary student in a Jesuit college in Paris. His name was Pierre Etienne. As he was born locally in Nonencourt he became part of the three platoons formed in this area. His job like everyone else was delivering underground newspapers. His education and leadership qualities were soon noticed and he was made a platoon leader."

"Let me ask you something Armand. Why do you think Bishop Auguste told you about Ribaud's dying confession?"

"Why shouldn't he? We were comrades in arms, leaders in our platoons . . ."

"I was wondering about his motive for telling you . . ."

"I've just told you . . ."

"Bear with me for a moment Armand. Let us suppose that Bishop Auguste had kept his oath of silence regarding the confessional as indeed he was supposed to. In a few years the man you shot, Emile Boulet, would have died a peaceful death and that would have been the end of it. Now, as a result of what the Bishop told you, Boulet is dead and you are an accused murderer. Bishop Auguste risked serious censure from the Church by divulging a dying man's confession. He could have been forced to retire in disgrace if what he did was found out. Why would he want to risk all that?"

Coit's face darkened as he looked at Claudel.

"I'm not sure I like the way this conversation is going. What are you saying? He is a man of the Cloth, a catholic Bishop . . ."

Claudel was forceful in answering Coit. He raised his voice slightly.

"You said all the men in the 2nd platoon he commanded were arrested and killed, everyone except himself."

"But you could say the same thing about me. Why are you so antagonistic towards the Bishop. He's not an easy man to warm to, I'll grant you that. But put those crazy thoughts out of your mind. Maybe it will convince you if I tell you he was also arrested and tortured by the Gestapo."

"What . . . ?"

"That's right. They took him to the same place they took me; to Gestapo headquarters on Avenue Foch in Paris. Two weeks later a black Citroen Limousine, the kind the Gestapo liked to drive, drove to a street in Evreux and threw Bishop Auguste out on to the footpath. He was a terrible bloody mess but still alive. He had broken ribs, he was cut badly. They used hot pokers on him . . . , this man that you doubt so much."

This unexpected revelation caught Claudel by surprise. All he could do was stare at Coit dumbfounded.

"Tell me something Armand, who took care of him after that . . . ?"

"What do you mean . . . ?"

"Who dressed his wounds, took care of him, that kind of thing?"

"The Jesuits . . . he wouldn't let anyone else near him. He asked to taken back to the Jesuits in Paris. They nursed him back to health. He remained there until the end of the war."

There was a prolonged silence between the two men. Claudel got ready to leave. They shook hands.

"I'll be back before you go to court. Goodbye Armand."

"Goodbye my friend."

The police car came to a stop outside the residence of Bishop Auguste in the shadow of Evreux cathedral. Inspector Brunet turned off the engine. Claudel got out of the car and walked slowly, thoughtfully up the steps. He pressed on the doorbell and after a few moments the heavy door creaked open. Madame Bremond curtsied and led him to the same room he had been shown to on his first visit. He sat down and waited. He was still waiting 20 minutes later when Bishop Auguste came in and sat opposite him. There were no greeting this time from either man, not even a hint of effecting common courtesies. They had become two mortal adversaries circling each other before locking horns. The Bishop's manner was brusque and impatient as he took out a handkerchief and proceeded to polish his eyeglasses.

"I hope," Said Bishop Auguste, "that you have a good reason for coming here without an appointment. Haven't you heard of the telephone . . . ?"

"Your Grace, I have some more questions to ask you."

"It's not a convenient time for me. I'll have my secretary set up an appointment for you."

He replaced the eyeglasses on his nose, looked disdainfully at Claudel and made a movement to stand up.

"Sit down Your Grace . . ."

The resolute tone of Claudel's voice unnerved him. He found himself slowly sinking back in the chair. Moment by moment his resolve and composure ebbed away. His head slumped on his shoulders and a distant, vacant expression settled on his face. Claudel's voice became a grim monotone, distant and hollow as if from an echo chamber. He lifted his head to face Claudel but all he saw was the terrified face of Pascal Ribaud struggling helplessly as he suffocated him with a pillow in his hospital bed. The detective was talking but he couldn't hear him; he just saw the silently moving lips. In recurring dreams lately he saw over and over the sinister contempt on the face of the young Gestapo officer after he pointed out the house where Armand Coit and his family lived. He betrayed them all. All those brave fresh faced youths of the Resistance. When unbeknownst to anyone he had joined the Resistance when the war broke out how was he supposed to know he would compromise a secret Concordat entered into by Pope Pius X11 and the Third Reich? His old tutor in the seminary in Paris, Brother Jean Baptiste Duperiot, a Jesuit acclaimed in the arts of artifice and guile had enlightened him and pointed out the blunder he had made in joining the French Resistance movement. Brother Baptiste taught him to see how his Resistance activities could benefit the Church by helping Germany to win the war. The enemy for the Catholic Church was not Hitler and the Third Reich, it was the more menacing threat of world Communism. Hitler feared and hated the Bolsheviks, the Church was of the same mind; together they could defeat

JOHN FLANAGAN

the Godless arch-enemy. If evil triumphed man risked losing his soul in the abyss of Communist World Order. The young platoon leader Pierre Etienne would have to summon every last morsel of courage in order to transfer his loyalties from France to Germany in the service of God and His Church. Brother Baptiste explained how Monsignor Eugenio Pacelli, who would later become Pope Pius X11, instructed his priests to become members of Italys Fascist Party. He was told of the Concordat between the Holy See and the Third Reich. Pope Pius X11 pushed for and signed a Concordat between the Holy See and the vice chancellor of the Third Reich, Franze von Papen. In the Vatican prayers were offered for the health and well-being of Mussolini and Fascism. From that moment the Catholic hierarchy pledged allegiance to Hitler and the Nazi regime. The bête noire that drove the fervent Pope Pius X11 was the sundering apart of the Papal States by the Communists in 1848.

The voice of Claudel penetrated through the visions.

"Your Grace, I'm trying to help clear Armand Coit's name," Said Claudel, "by showing that he was provoked into killing Emile Boulet. That you, Your Grace, unwittingly as it may have been, indirectly caused Boulet's death by revealing what had been confided to you in the confessional . . . ,"

"What . . . , what . . . ?"

"You can understand how a defence attorney might argue that way in a court of law.?"

"You will never see me in a public court. I am a consecrated Bishop . . ."

"Your privileged rank in the Church does not exempt you from the law. You can answer my questions now or I'll have you arrested."

The Bishop felt the blood rising and flushing his pallid skin.

"Very well, get on with your questions."

"Why were you in such a hurry to tell Armand Coit that Boulet was a collaborator during the war?"

"It was a mistake on my part obviously. I had no idea he would get a gun and shoot Boulet."

"Armand Coit is very loyal to you, did you know that? He became upset when I questioned him about you."

"About me . . . ,?"

"About your role in the Resistance . . ."

"I could have given you that information myself."

"He said you were one of the best men they had."

"Those days are not something I care to dwell on . . ."

"I must admit I was getting nowhere until Armand Coit relented and told me it was you who named Boulet as the informer. And that threw me into another quandary. I asked myself over and over, what was your motive for telling him?"

"He had a right to know . . ."

"I have to tell you Your Grace since I first met you, you didn't fit my simple definition of what a hero is. Take Armand Coit for instance. He's my idea of a hero. There's unstated greatness in everything about him, just getting on with his life after what the Gestapo did to him. He's in a police cell facing a murder charge and one of his biggest concerns is that I should not discommode Your Grace in any way . . ."

"Are you going to tell me your reason for coming here?"

"I'm coming to that. Do you know Armand Coit became very defensive about you? And I know he would not believe me if I told him he played right into your hands when he shot Boulet. It's what you counted on and why you told him. Boulet was the last man alive who knew you were . . . , what, a Gestapo spy?"

"You're mad . . ."

"I felt I was getting close to the truth but it was still only guesswork on my part. Then Armand Coit stopped me dead in my tracks just a few hours ago when he told me you had been picked up by the Gestapo . . . , and tortured."

Bishop Auguste's face became a frozen mask. He stared in silent rage at Claudel.

"What exactly happened when the Gestapo arrested you? Armand Coit told me they broke your ribs, used a knife and pokers on you, left you a bloody mess and when they were finished with you they dumped you from the back of a car, right out there on the street."

"I've no intention of reliving that horror again. I want you to leave here now. I'll consult with my superiors and let your office have a statement . . . ."

His eyes widened in disbelief when in the next instant Claudel stood up and drew a pistol from his jacket holster. He pointed the weapon at the Bishop's forehead.

"Stand up." Said Claudel grimly.

The Bishop stood up and backed to the wall with his hands raised.

"What are you doing . . . , have you lost your mind?"

"Strip to the waist . . ."

"You're mad. This is the end of your career. You'll be ruined after this . . ."

"I never really liked the job that much anyhow. Now strip to the waist or I'll tear those clothes off you myself . . ."

The Bishop slowly unbuttoned his Cossack and collar. He undid his shirt and stripped to the waist. Claudel waved the pistol.

"Now turn around, slowly."

When he had done so Claudel replaced the pistol in his holster and sat down.

"Get dressed . . ."

Bishop Auguste dressed and sat down shakily on the chair. All remaining defiance had left him.

"There's not a scratch, not a mark anywhere on you," Said Claudel, "when the Gestapo threw you out of that car you were covered in blood that was not your own. You were taken to the Jesuit seminary in Paris so that no one could see your so-called wounds. It was an elaborate charade by the Gestapo and the Jesuits to cover your role as a collaborator, that's how valuable you were to them."

Bishop Auguste's eyes glazed over. His shoulders heaved as he began to sob in stifled gasps. He buried his face in his hands. After a few moments he stared distractedly at Claudel.

"My whole life has been devoted to the Church, and to France . . ."

"Do you want to tell me why you murdered Ribaud?"

"He hated me, he hated the Church all his life. He was an atheist, a man without principles or morals. In the hospital he didn't want me to hear his confession, he just laughed at me. He was suffering and in pain but he summoned up enough energy to laugh at me. He said he just wanted to live long enough to expose me in front of the remaining veterans of the Resistance. Then he said something that decided for me what I had to do. He said he told his cousin Emile Boulet about me being a collaborator. He started to shout for the others to come into the room. Fortunately for me Jules Heniot didn't hear him. The scandal would have done irreparable damage to the Church. I was left with no choice. I pressed the pillow on his face until he stopped breathing."

"How did Ribaud find out you were betraying them to the Germans?"

"I was driving the Renault truck the night we delivered the newspapers in Mantes. The Gestapo stopped the truck.

They arrested Armand Coit while Ribaud and I made a run for it. They caught up with me and surrounded me. Of course the Gestapo knew who I was and didn't harm me. In the darkness they couldn't find Ribaud but later he told me he was hiding behind some wooden pallets not 10 feet away. He heard me talking to the Gestapo Lieutenant and watched as they let me walk away. He just put two and two together."

"What I don't understand is, if Ribaud was as bad as you make out, why did he wait until now to expose you as a traitor . . . , he . . . ?"

"Because it was the way his mind worked, because he could turn it to his advantage. Oh he went about it very cleverly. He bided his time, he let the dust of the war years settle down before he made his move. Then one day he travelled to Paris, to the Jesuit seminary where I was studying and he didn't ask, he demanded to see me. He told me he knew I was a traitor, and if I didn't agree to some terms he would put before me he would expose me to the media, to anyone who would listen. It was blackmail pure and simple and there was not a thing I could do about it. I talked with Brother Baptiste who advised me that it would be best to agree to the terms he wanted if they were not too outlandish."

"What was it he wanted?"

"Money of course, what else with a man like that. How do you suppose he bought that hotel on Rue de Pannette? For the past 50 years, year after year I've deposited money into his bank account."

"You know I'm trying to see the world through your eyes but I can't find any redeeming qualities of character in you to excuse what you did. That younger brother of Armand Coit was 14 years old, a child, his name was Yves, when the men you served, the Gestapo, put a bullet through his head at point blank range. If you can't see the horror of what you did I pity you."

Bishop Auguste clasped his hands together. When he spoke his voice was barely audible.

"Cardinal Leclerc . . . , he's in Rouen . . . , he'll know what to do."

"I know exactly what to do Your Grace," Said Claudel moving towards him, "get your coat, you're coming with me."

"What . . . , where are you taking me . . . ?"

"I'm arresting you for the murder of Pascal Ribaud and for complicity in the death of Emile Boulet."

"But you can't do that. You are on Church property. We have our own ecclesiastical courts."

"Your courts are subject to the secular laws of France, as you must be aware. I have a police car outside. Now don't make me force you . . ."

The tiring Bishop placed his hands on the chair rests and pushed himself up. He went to the window and looked at the police car parked outside.

"It's true then . . . , it's come to this."

"Let's go Your Grace. There's nothing more to be said."

"What will happen to me . . . ?"

"That's not for me to say."

"It will be in the newspapers?"

"Yes, I would think so."

"Can't you please call Cardinal Leclerc . . . ?"

"You can call him from the station."

"As God is my witness I meant well. There was never any question of personal gain. Every sou I ever owned I gave to the poor of the parish . . ."

"Your Grace . . ."

"Yes, yes, just give me a few moments. I'll get my coat and breviary."

He left and went up to his bedroom as Claudel waited by the front door. Seconds ticked away marked by the pendulum of the grandfathers clock in the hallway. The sudden crack of a pistol shot shattered the silence. Claudel ran up the staircase and charged into the bedroom. Bishop Auguste lay slumped on the floor. He was already dead as Claudel searched for a pulse.

Claudel and Inspector Brunet were seated on a bench in the public gardens in Evreux. As was his custom whenever he visited the gardens the Inspector had a bag filled with breadcrumbs. He delighted in the ritual. Claudel smiled as the Inspector began feeding the pigeons.

"Are you trying to emulate Saint Francis?"

"Well Monsieur, I love this. I come here most days during my lunchbreak. I've often thought what a wonderful life it would be if my wife was half as happy to see me as these pigeons."

They laughed together like old friends, comfortable in each other's company and enjoying the warm evening. The Inspector turned to Claudel.

"Armand Coit's trial is coming up in three weeks; how do you think it will go for him?"

"Considering the circumstances I'm pretty sure the court will acquit him."

"I hope so."

"I hope so too."

THE END

THE FIANCEE

By

JOHN FLANAGAN

As an Intelligence Officer attached to the Ecole Militaire in Paris, Captain Marc Claudel did his job efficiently if without much inspiration. Two more years would see him free to retire to his cottage and garden in Ivry La Bataille in Normandy. Free to cultivate his roses and go hunting with his dogs. Free to listen to his choice of music in a more appropriate setting than a noisy military barracks. He had never married nor had he given much thought to the matter, having decided long ago he would never subject a wife to the isolation from society that army life entailed.

He was seated by an open window on the third floor of the Officers Club on the Champs Elysees. It was such a beautiful day down there in his beloved Paris. Close to the trees lining the boulevard, the morning's drenching rain would leave its indelible aroma of lavender and chestnut. In its great overture to summer, nature was obtruding itself everywhere in a rhapsody of color and light. It happened every spring yet it never failed to fill him with a sense of the incomprehensible beauty of life despite its trials and unending chaos. He closed the window abruptly. There were too many problems to be this daydreaming could wait for another day. He realized his present mood was ill-suited to his purpose. For the first time since he knew the Legrande family he wished he was not so intimately friendly with them. He sighed, regretting even thinking such foolishness. General Roget Legrande, his wife Odalie and their son Paul were lifelong friends. They would continue to be so long after this scandal had blown over. He went to a side cabinet to pour himself a drink but decided against it. It was too early in the day for such indulgence and he suddenly felt a twinge of shame that he needed a drink to face the task before him.

Before a mirror he patted down his hair and adjusted his necktie. At 38 years old his brown hair was rapidly turning grey. He was just under six feet tall with hazel eyes, a strong prominent nose and a wide full mouth. His appearance in army uniform was at variance with his character. Eighteen years as a professional soldier had failed to subdue an inherent refinement in his nature. He was essentially a pacifist, constrained by family tradition dating back three generations to a life of military service. His slow ascent through the ranks, even in a peacetime army was spoken of in whispers. He would never shine like his illustrious forbears who were all decorated or mentioned in dispatches up to the time of his father's service in Algeria.

The library in the Officers club was closed today, ostensibly for cleaning purposes. It was to be used instead for a meeting by top army officers and concerned government ministers to defuse the crisis caused by Major Paul Legrande and his Syrian fiancée Solonge. Claudel sat down at a table and took a file from his briefcase that had been given to him the night before by an Intelligence Officer of the Ecole Militaire. As he read through it he shook his head again in disbelief. The file contained personal details concerning Major Legrande and Solonge Peera from the moment of their first meeting in a hotel lobby in Damascus in Syria. It ended with a cheap Parisian tabloid newspaper, L'Echo, running a front-page story of Solonge Peera having love affairs with two foreign diplomats while engaged to Major Legrande. Wild champagne parties and foreign spies were alluded to in the L'Echo, causing a public outcry embarrassing to the army and the government. Claudel closed the file slowly, thoughtfully. Of course he knew about the rumors, every officer and enlisted man in the regiment knew about the rumors. He could think of nothing else lately because of his concern for the Legrande family. He had never met Solonge but he had known Paul since they were cadets together. He knew the good qualities of his character and the value he put on his family's good name, his pride in serving with the military.

The door of the library opened and four men entered the room. They were dressed in casual clothes and each looked preoccupied as if he would rather be somewhere else. He recognized General Nicolas Galen, second in command at the Ecole Militaire and his aide, Lieutenant Antoine Beausang. In deference to the General, Claudel made a move to stand up when he was waved back down. When they were seated he was introduced to Jules Manin of the Foreign Office and Stephan Castilloux, a Cabinet minister. After the introductions the General looked at Claudel.

"Captain, I hope this impromptu meeting does not inconvenience you too much but you will appreciate the gravity of this situation. By the way, why the uniform? This meeting is off the record."

"I had no idea Sir."

"It's not important. You've been briefed, right?"

"Yes sir. I got the file last night."

"Good, good. We're going to need your help on this. We feel your friendship with the Legrande family will facilitate matters. It's a delicate situation that needs the upmost diplomacy and tact. Among other things we're concerned about national security, and well, we'd be grateful for your cooperation."

"I'll do everything I can Sir."

"Thank you Captain. You'll be given free rein to deal with this. Have you met this woman Solonge Peera?"

"No Sir. I was invited to their engagement party but for some reason I couldn't make it."

"You'll need to meet her at some point," said the minister Stephan Castilloux, "this is some mess, do you agree?"

"Yes Sir, it is but . . ."

"But?" Said the General.

"How credible can that story be, coming from a newspaper like that, I mean considering Major Legrande's background . . . ?"

"Captain, let's not mince words," said the General, "L'Echo is a mud-raking rag, I wouldn't use it for cat litter. The problem is this story has caught the public imagination. The bigger newspapers won't go after the story if we give them our assurances there's no truth to these allegations. But we can't. And they can't ignore the public interest in this."

Jules Manin was shaking his head.

"This could not have happened at a worse time. I don't want to sound like an alarmist but we must put the lid on this business. The public is volatile enough with the high unemployment figures and the farmers blocking the Ports."

"We want to know if this is a storm in a teacup," said Stephan Castilloux, "or if that woman and Major Legrande are involved in espionage like the newspaper said."

"I can't speak for the woman," said Claudel, "but to suspect Major Legrande of spying is, well, it's preposterous."

"I want you to know Captain, I was against getting you involved for that very reason," said Jules Manin, "I think you're just too involved with the whole family to handle this with any kind of impartiality."

"Sir, as far as I am concerned it will give me a chance to clear Captain Legrand's good name."

"What we have so far is this," said Lieutenant Beausang, "Major Legrande's fiancée is a Syrian national. Since coming to Paris she has made contact with a German diplomat and later with a Syrian diplomat. She has no record. Whoever she is working for, our Intelligence people could dig up nothing in Damascus. Just parking tickets, fines for speeding, nothing more . . ."

"Maybe that's all there is," said Claudel.

"No no," said the Lieutenant with mounting enthusiasm, "this woman is a professional. I'm convinced L'Echo has uncovered an espionage ring. Getting engaged to Major Legrande was part of a well laid plan."

"What proof have you got," asked Claudel irritably, "have you something I can work with or are you just guessing?"

He looked at the young Lieutenant steadily. He was no more than a fawning clown, trying to impress the government ministers and ingratiate himself with the General.

"No . . , but . . ."

"So let's deal with what we know," said the General, "since there is a security risk we have to look at everything, every detail. It's really all conjecture so far, we have no proof of anything," he said this with a barely perceptible turn of his head to his Aide, "but we must find out if there's any substance to these allegations."

Claudel was about to answer General Galen when the Lieutenant piped in again.

"Did you know that every year for the past six years Major Legrande went to the Middle East, visiting different countries?"

"I'm aware of that. He visits the sites of old battlegrounds, all the way back to the crusades. He's an expert on the subject," said Claudel.

"He's never published anything."

"Excuse me?"

"Oh I'm just thinking out loud Sir. If he's such an expert like you say, why has he never written about it?"

"Lieutenant," said Claudel with some impatience, "I like dogs. I've always had dogs. Does that mean I should publish a paper on dogs?"

The General suppressed a smile. He wasn't very fond of the Lieutenant and was glad to see him put in his place.

"I'm inclined to believe Major Legrande is an innocent dupe in all of this. His record is good. But it begs the question, what kind of man is he to let his fiancée party alone with other men, is he a damn cuckold or what?"

"Sir, has this woman been questioned," asked Claudel, "or the two diplomats?"

"No," cut in Jules Manin, "only as a last resort do we want to question those diplomats. They have immunity status anyway and don't have to talk to us. It's important to keep in mind that this could develop into a major international scandal."

"How do you want me to handle this Sir?" Claudel asked General Galen.

"There's just too many loose ends to give you a defined brief. The Surete will give you all the help you need. What I want is you're feelings about all of it. If it proves to be no more than a juicy piece of gossip the newspaper uncovered, then it will all blow over in time. But we must know one way or the other."

"I'll get on to it right away Sir."

"Good. I thank you on behalf of us all."

The General rose to his feet and everyone stood up with him. They shook hands with Claudel and quickly left. Alone again in the library he put the file into his briefcase. Could it possibly be true he wondered, Solonge Peera's meeting with Paul in Damascus was part of some incredible plan? If that was the case Paul was an innocent dupe, he would never willingly bring such dishonor on his family.

Major Paul Legrande had graduated with honors from the Ecole Militaire to become one of the youngest army officers in France. When he was promoted to Captain and became a Company Commander he imposed the same rigid standards of discipline and conduct to his own life as he did to his subordinates and became greatly respected if not altogether admired by the rank and file for his qualities of leadership. All who knew him felt he was destined for greatness. Each summer since he graduated from Officer Cadet College he visited the Middle East to indulge his favorite hobby, visiting the scenes of famous battlegrounds of the Crusades. The previous summer he had gone to Damascus, the site of one of the great sieges of the Second Crusade. One evening, in the foyer of the hotel where he was staying the course of his life was changed completely. Solonge Peera had just left the reception desk and had stopped momentarily to put a letter into her purse. Her beauty immobilized him and he halted, unable to pass her. The books and maps he was carrying slipped from his grasp and tumbled in a heap at her feet. She bent down with him and helped him retrieve the fallen items. He was staring dumbly at her all the while, too enamored of her to utter a word. She left him in the foyer on his knees, smiling and amused by his dilemma. Only when she had gone did he recover his senses. He left the items at the reception desk and followed her out to the busy street. She had just taken a taxi and was pulling away from the curb. She looked back at him, smiled and was gone. Back in the hotel he asked the receptionist if she happened to notice the young lady who had just left. She said yes and if the gentleman wished he could see her in the hotel the following day and pointed to a sign near the exit door. The stunning woman he had just seen was the owner of the hotel flower shop.

The next day he went into the shop and introduced himself to her formally. He had to prove very persuasive to overcome her initial reluctance but she was impressed with his bearing and genial manner. In the end she accepted an invitation to dine with him that evening. In the next few days he forgot completely his reason for coming to Damascus. He met her family. Solonge had inherited her charm and dazzling beauty from her mother. Her sense of humor and vitality came from her father, a gregarious self-made man with a thick full beard and a loud laugh. In business he was tough and difficult to deal with. He had made his fortune in his early years building bridges for the government. Umar Peera counted himself lucky in life in nothing as much as his wife and daughter. The two women adored him. Her parents were upset but understanding when after three months Solonge told them she had decided to go and live in Paris.

When Major Legrande returned to Paris after meeting Solonge, he had an immediate irksome problem to deal with. His girlfriend Katiyana, whom he had met a year before at a party in the Officers Club, was waiting to greet him. She was the daughter of Russian immigrants and worked as an interpreter in the Intelligence sector of the Ecole Militaire. After meeting Major Legrande, Katiyana soon became obsessed with the idea of marrying him. He was a scion of one of the most respected families in France and would introduce her to the type of society and lifestyle after which she craved. Within hours of their meeting she realized he was a principled man with the kind of flaws she could mold to her advantage. Most promising of all he was malleable and to a woman of her guile and tenacity it would be just a matter of time for her to become Madame Legrande. Katiyana's father was a silversmith. He made his living engraving hunting scenes on the trigger housings of valuable shotguns. Her mother gave piano lessons to help make ends meet. As Madame Legrande, Katiyana would never again have to pinch sous and make do with a skimpy wardrobe. The very thought of penury terrified her and she had been determined from an early age to rise above the impoverished gentility of her parents. There was never any demonstration of love or affection in her family. Her parent's life in Russia had aged them prematurely and made them lethargic. In the raising of Katiyana they tried hard to inculcate in her the need for forbearance and patience but as she matured she became a firebrand with a violent temper.

When Major Legrande walked through the arrival gate of the Charles de Gaulle airport in Paris, Katiyana immediately sensed something was wrong. In the taxi from the airport he hardly spoke. When they arrived at his apartment on Rue Marbeuf he told her he no longer wished to continue the relationship. Throwing all caution to the wind he told her of meeting Solonge and how she would be coming to Paris to join him. It took some moments for it to occur to the smoldering Katiyana that she would have no future with Major Legrande. In a blind rage she struck him across the face and while he sat nursing a bloody nose she began systematically to smash everything breakable in the apartment. She was screaming when the concierge banged on the door and threatened to call the police if the disturbance continued. By the time Katiyana stormed out, the apartment was littered with broken vases and picture frames and valuable artifacts he had collected on his journeys to the Middle East. It was days before he got the apartment back to a semblance of order.

Solonge arrived and took up residence in the comfortable three-roomed apartment in Rue Marbeuf adjacent to the Champs Elysees. From that moment Major Legrande was oblivious to everything but the heady bliss of being in love. She became so central to his life that no happiness could be imagined without her being a part of it. They became engaged on the evening of the day when he brought her to his home to meet his parents and a few invited guests. His father, General Roget Legrande and his mother Odalie warmed to her immediately. Watching her from across the room mingling with his relations and friends, Major Legrande had never been so happy. When he returned to his military duties after an extended leave, the men in his Company noticed a change in him. The old aloofness was gone. There was a new engaging pleasantness in his manner, a jauntiness to his step. In the euphoria of his new found bliss he meted out promotions to enlisted men on the lEast pretext and had to be cautioned by his superiors. Every moment he could get away from the garrison he spent in Rue Marbeuf. Solonge had transformed the apartment with a Middle Eastern décor. Persian carpets and tapestries covered the floors and walls. Elaborately patterned fabrics adorned the armchairs and sofa. When he took to wearing a caftan in the apartment, she would call him her Sultan, her Caliphe. What rewards could heaven offer he wondered, compared to spending his life with this adorable creature? Love spun a web about him from which he did not wish to extricate himself, she bound him to her with every gesture, every smile. Five minutes after leaving her he would feel a sense of deprivation, a knot in his stomach, a loneliness as if his life was to no avail without her. The intensity of his adulation made him ever more emotionally dependent on Solonge for his happiness. She could plummet him to the depths of despair by a frown or raise him to ecstasy by the merest suggestion of a smile. She could weaken his strongest resolve with a single tear.

Solonge had brought a photograph album from Damascus and one morning when Major Legrande did not have to report for duty until later that day, they were going through the photographs. While they were thus engaged a white envelope slid from the album and fell to the floor. When he reached down to retrieve the envelope she quickly took it from him and grasped it guardedly in her hands. She quickly put the envelope in a drawer in which she kept her jewelry, locked it and put the key in her purse. She explained to him they were just old photographs which had become faded and torn.

Later as he changed into uniform and prepared to go to the garrison, Major Legrande wondered why the incident of the photographs loomed so large in his mind. He wanted to see the contents of the envelope but he had no right to insist. She should have shown him what was in the envelope he reasoned, as he felt there should be no secrets between them. He shrugged, no doubt she would show him the photographs if he asked. This afternoon he had to take part in a full dress rehearsal for a military parade, taking his company in a march past visiting dignitaries to the Ecole Militaire. Solonge had left earlier to go shopping. He left a note for her, locked the door of the apartment and walked the short distance to the Champs Elysees. He stood on the footpath and hailed a taxi. The taxi took him to Avenue George V. and crossed the Seine at Pont de l'Alma to Avenue Bosquet. They had passed Rue de Grenelle and were in view of Ecole Militaire when he realized he had left his briefcase back in the apartment. In it were special orders concerning the military parade which he needed. He directed the driver to immediately return to Rue Marbeuf. As the taxi slowed down on Rue Francoise 1er. to turn into Rue Marbeuf a black Mercedes Benz limousine with diplomatic plates and a miniature German flag flapping in the wind passed them by. Major Legrande gasped as the two cars passed closely together. In the back seat of the chauffeur driven car, her head thrown back and laughing, was Solonge. A man was talking to her and he was also laughing. It all happened in a few seconds. His thoughts were agitated and confused as he got out of the taxi and told the driver to wait. He ran up the stairs and let himself in to the apartment. In the bedroom Solonge's clothes were scattered everywhere. She did that sometimes when she was in a hurry. He picked up the briefcase and paused at the door. As he turned to leave his eyes fell on the dressing bureau in which Solonge kept her jewelry. The drawer was partly open. He walked over to the bureau. The white envelope, the one she had acted so strangely about was lying under her jewelry. He looked at it for a few moments before he reached in and took it out. Tormented lately by feelings of jealousy he was pondering over the envelope when he was startled by the ringing of the telephone. He put the envelope on top of the bureau and picked up the telephone. It was a friend, a fellow officer from the garrison. He listened for a few minutes without saying a word. When he put the telephone down he was staring about him as if disorientated. His friend had just told him to go out and buy a tabloid newspaper called L'Echo, he also said something about Solonge which he couldn't make out. He went out to the street, paid the waiting taxi driver and found a newsagent where he bought a copy of L'Echo. He stopped on the street and stared blankly at the headlines and photographs. Back in the apartment he sat down with his heart beating wildly and held the newspaper in front of him. On the front page Solonge, his Solonge, his fiancée was in two photographs with two different men. The headlines read 'Spy Scandal Rocks Government'.

Emile Mahe, the L'Echo reporter who broke the story was not an accredited journalist but an advertising salesman with a turn of phrase and a penchant for ingratiation which he could somehow cloak beneath the façade of a practiced sincerity and a warm handshake. With a skill born of long experience he had fabricated a resume in order to obtain an interview with the editor of the newspaper Bernard Chesnel. Monsieur Chesnel, an obese rambunctious individual who spent a great part of his day pirouetting in an enormous swivel chair between his desk and the coffee pot behind him, never bothered checking the resume. If Monsieur Mahe was prepared to sell advertising space on a commission-only basis, why then he could also put him to use cleaning the office, answering the telephone and making coffee. The regular hacks of L'Echo treated Mahe with ill-disguised contempt. But since they themselves for a variety of reasons were unable to find work with the larger Paris dailies they could not object when the editor of the tabloid began to send his toady out to cover a lost dog or a purse snatching. L'Echo made its profits on sleaze and titillation. The more lurid private lives of film stars and famous personalities were all grist for the mill of L'Echo.

Mahe was alone one night in the office when the telephone rang. The butt of an unlit Gauloise cigarette hung from his lower lip as he sat back in the chair with his feet up on the desk, his head nodding from lack of sleep. He groped for the telephone and put it to his ear, his eyes still shut. The caller informed him that a vanilla envelope had been dropped into the mailbox at the front door and immediately hung up. He went down and retrieved the envelope and read its contents.

The following night Mahe was seated at a table in a restaurant in Montmartre. Sitting next to him in a rumpled suit and unkempt hair the photographer from L'Echo was changing a lens on a camera. A few tables away Solonge Peera and a man were engrossed in conversation. With precision timing, photographs were surreptitiously taken of the couple. A few nights later they followed Solonge from Rue Marbeuf to the Hotel George V. where she dined with another man. Major Legrande was photographed leaving the Ecole Militaire. It was a simple matter to determine that the two men with Solonge were attached to foreign embassies in Paris.

When Mahe presented the photographs to Bernard Chesnel he grandly attributed its origin to his natural flair for a story, never mentioning the manila envelope that fell into his hands. More material was promised to Mahe on a condition of anonymity of its source. The editor was incredulous but he wasn't about to look a gift horse in the mouth. The story was sensational given the ingredients of two diplomats, a military officer and at the center of it all, a beautiful woman. The possibilities were endless. A hurried staff meeting in L'Echo was convened. This time the usual concoction of invention and innuendo was taken to extremes to shock and astonish. When the issue arrived at the newsstands the story caused an immediate sensation followed by public outrage.

Darkness had engulfed the apartment on Rue Marbeuf. Shadows darted about the walls as a neon sign across the street flickered on and off. Major Legrande sat in an armchair in the bedroom, his head spinning in a dull alcoholic fugue. On the carpet beside him was the copy of L'Echo, which had fallen from his fingertips. Beside it was an empty Vodka bottle. Sometime before he had been dimly aware of someone pounding on the door. He knew there would be hell to pay when he reported back to headquarters. The telephone had rung continuously through the day and into the night.

Finally the door opened and Solonge walked in, not knowing he was in the apartment. Because of his involvement with the military parade she was not expecting him back until the following day. After switching on the bedroom light she screamed with fright when she saw Major Legrande in the armchair. In a moment she was beside him, embracing him. She sobbed quietly with her head on his shoulder.

"I am so happy you are here, but why do you sit in the dark like this?" she said, "oh Paul, have you seen those dreadful things in the newspapers . . . ?" His face was grim, unyielding. When he didn't answer she moved away from him slowly and sat on a chair. Neither of them spoke for a few moments. A sadness clouded her face as she dried her eyes. "Paul, say you don't believe it, that you believe in me. I am innocent of those terrible things."

"What kind of a fool do you take me for?" She stared at him in disbelief as reached down and picked up the newspaper. "is that your photograph with those two men or not?"

He crumbled the newspaper in his fist and threw it away.

"Yes, but none of those things they say are true. It's a terrible mistake. They are not spies. It's so ridiculous, all of it."

"Who are those men . . . ?" He shouted.

"Please don't talk to me like that. You never raised your voice to me before . . ."

"Stop being evasive and answer my question. How many others are there?"

"Others? What are you saying to me?"

"I saw you in a Mercedes today. You have good taste in cars, I'll say that for you."

"It was a friend. His name is Heinrich. He had just arrived in Paris, and he telephoned me . . ."

"We are engaged to be married and you are running around with men I don't know."

"My dearest how can you say these things to me? I can explain if you will only listen . . ."

He stood up and paced about the bedroom. As Solonge tidied away her dresses he gave vent to his anger again.

"My superiors will crucify me. I know they will. This will reflect badly on my career, not to mention my family. You don't know what you've done getting involved with those people whoever they are. You've ruined my life."

She stopped packing and sat on the edge of the bed.

"Your life, your family, your career," she said with emphasis on each word, "not once have you asked me how I felt, what this has done to me. I thought you loved me more deeply than that. I really thought you trusted me."

"What's the point of anything after this . . ?"

He kicked away the newspaper at his feet.

"Yes Paul, you are right. Yes, what more can be said? You trust and love someone or you don't, it all comes down to that."

"Put yourself in my position, can't you see how it looks?"

"You condemn me out of hand and ignore me when I try to explain . . ."

The Major's dilemma was that he wanted her to be innocent but he lacked a trusting nature. In the end it was the doubt within him that presumed her guilt before she could prove her innocence. His doubt clarified everything for Solonge. It had not occurred to Major Legrande that the values and principles ingrained in his otherwise good character diminished in proportion to his loss of self esteem through jealousy and obsession. Often when they strolled together on the Champs Elysees, in a city of beautiful women, Solonge would cause men to gasp and stare as she passed sidewalk cafes. And if an ardent admirer raised a glass or whistled she would smile back. Such moments were excruciating for Major Legrande for he wanted to be the sole object of her attention and the only source of her happiness. He could no longer condone her independence if he found her exercising choices at variance with what he wanted. Since they had become engaged to be married he had adopted a proprietary attitude towards Solonge as if she belonged to him, much as his watch might.

"Were they lovers, those men in the newspaper?"

She stood up and walked away from him and gripped the back of a chair. She stopped crying and dried her eyes. When she spoke her voice was low and hoarse but the nervous tremor had left her.

"No Paul, I have no lovers. I have been called such terrible names today. Of all the knives yours goes the deepest. You were the first man in my life. I ran up here from the street believing I would be safe in your arms. No hugs, no kisses, just accusations like the newspaper."

"I want to believe you. I really do love you . . ."

"You love me? What kind of love is it that crumbles at the first sign of trouble?"

"You were not completely honest with me. I've had the feeling you were keeping things from me."

"Hush Paul, I've had enough for one day."

"That white envelope . . ."

"What?"

"The envelope you were so secretive about . . ."

"What envelope . . ?"

"Don't sound so naïve. You know very well what I'm talking about."

"Is this a game you are playing?"

"There's something in that envelope you don't want me to see," he went to the bureau and held up the envelope, "what else is there about you I don't know?" He approached her, "I want to see what's in it."

As Solonge looked on he tore open the envelope. Several photographs spilled out into his hand, each one cracked and yellowing with age, all of them showing older members of her family. In his agitated state he was furious because he had not found something to justify this intrusion of her privacy. He slumped back into the armchair. Solonge twisted the engagement ring from her finger and placed it beside him. She took two suitcases from the wardrobe and began filling them with her clothes. When he looked around and saw the ring he jumped up and grabbed her arm.

"No, no, not this . . , you can't leave me. What are you doing? I love you, don't leave me I beg you . . ," he closed the suitcase.

"Paul, if you don't let me finish packing I will just walk out of here. Now please, I cannot help listening to you but do not interfere with me again. Get out of my way."

"Solonge don't.., oh God I will die without you. It can't end this way," he sat on the bed and held her hand, "how can you walk away from me like this?"

"It is better this way," she removed her hand from his and continued packing, "you are a good man, a kind man. You would make the right woman a good husband. But I know now I could never marry you."

"Solonge please, we've been so happy. Do you want to throw all that away . . ."

"It would be better for your career, and your family. If you believe those accusations how could you defend me against them? Now let me finish, I have a lot to do."

"You won't reconsider?"

"No, I have made up my mind."

"What will you do, where will you stay?"

"I will send you an address and telephone number, you can send me the rest of my things."

Claudel pulled into a parking lot on Boulevard Garibaldi and walked the short distance to the apartment of General Roget and Odalie Legrande. This would be one of the few occasions when he would miss the game of chess with the General, there were too many pressing issues to allow for that pleasant distraction.

They lived in a spacious apartment on Rue Françoise Bonvin, chosen for its proximity to the Ecole Militaire where the retired General and Odalie had commissary privileges. Odalie opened the door and led him through to what she called the war room. The entire wall in front of the General's desk was covered in maps. Red lines marked off military engagements in the 170-year history of the French occupation of Algeria. Another wall was covered with photographs of comrades in arms, regimental colors and pennants. The General was hunched over a writing pad when Claudel entered. He was more like a son to them than a friend and one of the few people who did not suffer the invective of the General when he was in a bad mood. Odalie joined them as they shook hands and sat down.

"General, Madame," said Claudel, "I'm sorry I can't stay long."

"No need to apologize old fellow," said the General, "this has been a tough one for you."

"I'd no idea what I was getting into, I haven't been home for three days."

"Is there any way we can help?"

"Well, thank you, but no. I'm glad to say it's almost all over except for a final report for General Galen. I've spent the last three days at the Surete. There were teams of detectives working around the clock. Everyone connected with L'Echo was brought in and questioned."

"And what did they find out," asked Odalie, "about Solonge I mean?"

"She was cleared completely. The whole story was a fabrication."

"That poor girl, how awful it must have been for her."

"Yes. But it's all over now."

"How is she, have you seen her?"

"No, I still haven't met her. Once the Surete discovered the truth they didn't question her."

"I knew it all the time. She's so nice, such a lovely girl," said Odalie, "but what happened, why was she picked on of all people?"

"There's no easy way to tell you. It was Paul's old girlfriend Katiyana, she was the cause of it all."

"Katiyana?" Said Odalie, shocked, "it's not possible."

"A rum sort that one," said the General, "I felt she wasn't all there."

"She confessed to everything right away, caved in completely under all the questioning. There was no espionage, no spy ring. I think she just went a bit crazy at the thought of losing Paul; hell hath no fury, etcetera, etcetera."

"Oh dear," said Odalie.

"I spent some time with her," said Claudel, "she cried for the most part. Her main concern was the shame it would bring on her parents."

"But what I can't understand," said the General, "is how all of this ended up in a newspaper."

"Well L'Echo is not a newspaper in the real sense, no responsible journalist would work for it. Katiyana did her homework. She knew that with L'Echo the truth was just a side issue. She worked for army intelligence so she had access to everything to concoct a palpable story. The paper is printing a retraction of the story in the next issue.

"Huh," said the General, "it's the lEast the cretins can do. By the way, who are those two fellows in the photos?"

"One of them is her uncle, her mother's brother, he's a minor official in the Syrian embassy. The other man is Heinrich Ritter, a longtime friend of her father. That's all there is to it. The best piece of news of course is that Paul has been cleared of any wrong-doing."

"We are so relieved," said Odalie reaching out and touching the General's hand, "he telephoned just a little while ago. Oh, have you heard about him and Solonge?"

"Heard what?"

"They have broken off their engagement. I can only suppose this awful pressure has been too much for them."

"I'm sorry to hear that. But they may get back together when all this publicity has died down."

195

"No," said Odalie, "she has already left the apartment. She is returning to Syria. She called me on the telephone to say goodbye."

"What will become of Katiyana now?" Asked the General, "It was serious enough what she did, digging into the army files and all that. Will she be charged with anything?"

"Well, there were charges being drawn up against her but it was decided to put the whole matter to rest. It would only prolong public interest if it dragged on in the courts. She has lost her job at the Ecole Militaire but she's free at lEast to get on with her life. Incidentally she telephoned Paul from the Surete office when she was being questioned."

"What?" said the General and Odalie together.

"That's right. She was in the next room, I could hear her crying quite a bit."

"I expect she just unburdened herself," said Odalie.

"Marc," said the General, "you've worked wonders. A difficult job well done."

"I'm just happy it's over. All I want is to get back to my dogs and my garden."

"Will you be seeing Paul?" asked Odalie.

"Yes. I'll go by the apartment on my way home."

"Give him our love and tell him not to worry. We can all begin to relax again."

As he drove to the apartment in Rue Marbeuf, Claudel was ecstatic. He never thought one day he would play the role of cupid, a match-maker. Solonge was alone and no doubt miserable, Paul would be pining and unhappy and he was going to try to bring the two of them together again. It would be a fitting conclusion to his involvement in the whole affair. Like Bottom the Weaver, there was enough of the romantic in his soul to love a happy ending. He wished he had met

Solonge, it would have better suited the plan he had in mind. But first he would get them back together, then he would spring his surprise. He was still in army uniform and when he arrived in Rue Marbeuf three reporters rushed over to him as he got out of the car. He politely brushed them aside. Next week they would be gone when L'Echo printed the retraction and the Surete officially closed its file on the matter.

When he rang the doorbell to the apartment and was greeted by Paul Legrande he was not surprised to find him in a somber mood. He expected the break-up must have left him devastated. But when he heard a noise coming from the kitchen he guessed that they had already reconciled their differences and there would be no need for him to play cupid after all. And now at last he would get a chance to meet Solonge. When they were seated Paul offered him a drink which he refused as he had a long drive to his cottage in Ivry la Bataille. He thought his friend was acting peculiar in a way he could not pin down. He seemed to want to confide something but he kept looking towards the kitchen and changing his mind. Claudel decided he would cut his visit short, no doubt the couple wanted some privacy so soon after their ordeal.

"Well," said Claudel as lightly as he could, "what a relief for everyone that it's all over."

"Yes Marc, we owe you so much."

"Oh nonsense. It was just a matter of time before the truth came out."

"Perhaps, but it was the way you did it. You caused the lEast amount of pain for everyone."

"Paul, there's something bothering you. What is it?"

"Oh nothing . . ."

"Look, shake yourself out of this mood. It's time for celebrating. I'm having some guests at the cottage this weekend. Why don't you come along and bring Solonge with you? It's supposed to be a super day weather-wise. We'll have breakfast in the garden . . ."

"Oh, tomorrow morning, well eh . . , let me see eh . . ."

"I'm patching up the stonework on the orchard wall, I thought you might like to help me. We'll have a few glasses of wine and talk about old times, what do you say? And I'm planning a surprise of sorts that I can't tell you about now but, how should I put it? Well, if you and Solonge were there . . ."

"Marc you know ordinarily I'd jump at the chance but . . ."

You see General Galin wanted me to reassure Solonge that she will be helped in every way possible. I thought you could explain things better than me . . ."

A woman's voice coming from behind startled him in its nearness.

"Captain Claudel, how are you?"

Both men stood up and turned around. Claudel could hardly believe his eyes. It was Katiyana. It was with some difficulty he kept his composure and greeted her politely.

"I know I am the last person in the world you expected to see here," she said,

"I couldn't help overhearing you from the kitchen. I just wanted to say I'm glad Solonge is being helped. Paul and I were just talking about her."

"I hope you are feeling better now . . ."

"All the pain and anguish I've caused, how can you show me such civility? I know I would be in serious trouble with the law but for your help . . ."

She went back into the kitchen, closing the door behind her.

"You look surprised Marc," said Paul as they sat down.

"Surprised, surprised Paul ? Shocked would be more like it. I thought it was Solonge in the kitchen. Why didn't you tell me?"

"I was trying to work up to it when she came in. I know how it looks since she caused all the trouble in the first place. Her mother telephoned me in the early hours of the morning. She said Katiyana was distressed and talking about suicide. I went over there and she was in a bad way. I managed to calm her down. I found her so changed. We talked for hours and decided we'd try to work things out between us . . ."

"What about Solonge, you seemed so certain."

"And so I was at first . . ."

"Tell me, I have little experience in these matters as you know, but I'm just curious. When you read the newspaper did you really believe Solonge was having affairs with those men?"

"Yes I did."

"And before that, had she ever given you a reason not to trust her?"

"No, not at all."

"Then why . . ?"

"I don't know Marc, I really don't. I no longer believe she did those things but is that because she has left me and I am no longer jealous? I often wondered can a beautiful woman be faithful to just one man when so many lavish attention on her?"

"If I remember correctly Proust asked a similar question of a lady friend. She said it all came down to character."

"Whose character, the mans or the woman's?"

"She said it all depended on the man's character. But a beautiful woman who was also virtuous would want to be faithful to just one man, don't you think? What value has beauty without virtue? And from what you told me, Solonge had it all, so what happened?"

Paul shook his head dolefully.

"To her credit she had a loving warm nature but at the same time she was always so positive of what she wanted. I found it very unsettling at times. She was so . . . , imperious."

"Well my friend," said Claudel, standing up, "I have always taken Napoleon's advice about women. He said the only way to deal with a woman was with one's hat, grab it and run like hell,"

They smiled and shook hands.

"I've been asked to tender the government's regrets to her personally," said Claudel, "we don't want her flying out of the country with only unhappy memories of France."

"That would be a wonderful idea. I know she would appreciate it. Is there any way I can help?"

"Have you some way of contacting her?"

"Why yes. She gave me an address in Montparnasse, and a phone number."

"Would you mind telling her that we are very concerned about her welfare and want to offer every assistance.

"I'll have my mother pass on the message,"

Claudel said goodbye to Paul and Katiyana. He left the apartment, picked up his car and joined the Friday evening exodus from Paris to the Western suburbs. The traffic was heavy after he navigated the Arc de Triomphe and drove down Avenue Victor Hugo to Boulevard Suchet. At Porte de Saint Cloud a light rain began to patter on the windscreen and he turned on the wipers. After a few kilometers the rhythmic beating of the wipers had a soporific effect and he lowered the windows to clear the drowsiness overcoming him. He needed to clear his mind to think over the past two weeks. It had been an honor he supposed, to have been appointed a sort of troubleshooter for the government, to have the highest offices of state at his beck and call. The whole administrative machinery of government had been mobilized into action, because of a woman's jealousy. And now this incredible turnabout of Paul and Katiyana. The unfortunate Solonge, so far from home, was the real loser in all of this.

When he arrived at Pontchatran darkness was falling and he turned on the lights. At Houdan he turned right for Ivry La Bataille and was able to make up some time on the deserted road. What accounting was there he wondered, for the folly of human nature when it came to love? Sober intelligent men like Paul became suddenly bereft of all reason when caught up in the throes of passion. From what he could see and judge, love was neither constant nor enduring. He had only contempt for the habitual romantic. As far as he was concerned a romantic was a sycophant, one of life's also rans, often using the pursuit of love as an excuse for accomplishing nothing else with his life. As for women, he admired them totally and without reserve. He admired them as a gender. They were infinitely kinder, more humane than their male counterpart. And whereas they could be fiercely patriotic it was not endemic in their nature to put on uniforms and slaughter each other in trenches. Love alone was the raison d'être for a woman's existence and she sometimes created chaos it its name.

As he crossed the Eure river at Ivry La Bataille the rain eased and he began to feel elated when he saw the lights of his cottage in the distance. He had a house-keeper, the wife of a local farmer who looked after the cottage and took care of the dogs. He paid her a generous wage and she was happy to work for such an amiable and easy-going gentleman. She would attend to everything and leave the cottage when he arrived home in the evening. She had telephoned him earlier to say his guests had arrived and she was preparing dinner. As he drove up the gravel path he could hear the dogs barking excitedly at his arrival. He went in and joined his guests.

Early the following morning Claudel was working in the orchard while his guests slept. He went to the open window of the kitchen, reached inside and turned on the radio. The soft lingering notes of Schumann's Traumerai suffused the scents and odors of the garden. Myriad colored blooms swayed in a developing warm breeze. On mornings like this a cloistered silence pervaded the walled orchard where he was working. Only the occasional barking of the younger dog, a black Labrador, broke through the stillness. Claudel contemplated his lot. This was what he had planned for during his military career. The life of a country squire, solitary and genteel, consummately rounding off his ideal of a purposeful life. Surely Voltaire would smile benignly on his little acreage where he tended his garden. He had no need of a Cunegonde to complicate this best of all possible worlds.

Just before noon when he was putting the finishing touches to the wall one of the dogs growled quietly. Soon a car could be heard coming up the drive, the gravel crunching loudly beneath the wheels. A few seconds later a bell tinkled at the orchard door. He held his hands under a faucet, washed them clean and dried them with a handkerchief.

When he opened the orchard door nothing in his life prepared him for what he saw. He had erected an archway from the gravel path leading to the orchard door. The apex was a trelliswork of vines and flowers through which sunlight penetrated in lances of shadow and light. The archway door was a step higher than the orchard. As she looked down at him Solonge Peera was framed in a garland of roses. The warm midday sun, the scents, the cloudless azure sky conspired in the illusion before him. Her large oval shaped eyes held his gaze, waiting for him to speak. She had violet colored eyes, full rounded lips and the nose of Helen. She was dressed in a loose fitting burgundy colored skirt, white high-heeled shoes and a white silk blouse woven with patterns of white roses. Her blouse had a high brocaded collar from which hung a single string of white pearls with matching earrings. Her shining black hair was piled high in a chignon and secured with a mother-of-pearl clip. Thin bracelets of gold and green jade decorated her wrists. Beneath the gaze of her searching eyes he felt himself reduced to a mere image out on the periphery of her vision, as if his ego and the whole substance of his being had vanished. For the first time in his life he was speechless. He heard her voice as if from afar introducing herself. She followed him along the length of the garden to a table beside a willow tree. With his handkerchief he dusted off a chair and she sat down.

"May I offer you something to drink, I have iced tea, or coffee if you prefer?"

"Thank you, no."

"Very well . . . ," he started to sit down.

"Oh but please, you have something."

"Not unless you join me."

"In that case yes. Iced tea would be very nice."

"Good. I'll be back in a moment."

He went into the cottage and immediately attended to his guests. They had already breakfasted and were sitting in the living room. As he prepared the iced tea in the kitchen, he looked out at Solonge sitting forlornly beside the willow tree. He fumbled with a glass which fell broken in the sink. He took several deep breaths.

The damn woman was making him lose his composure. Some egregious force was insinuating itself on his emotions against which his deductive reasoning could not hold forth.

Such madness had tormented the brave Mark Anthony, made him flee the wrath of Octavious Caesar and the blazing sea of Macedonia, to relinquish his power and honor and become beauty's plaything, an iniquitous wretch robbed of his wits by love, left kneeling at the feet of Cleopatra. No woman would ever have such power over him. But why was he shaking at the knees? With the iced tea ready he stopped for one more look at Solonge through the kitchen window. When he went out he set the tray on the table.

"I hope it's to your liking?" he said when he had sat down.

"Yes Monsieur, it's very nice. Thank you."

They were silent for a few moments. She raised her head and looked about her.

"I smell jasmine."

"Why yes, that's it over there by the wall. It's a sensitive plant . . ."

"It needs lots of sunlight . . ."

As the early morning breeze died away the plaint dreamlike chords of the Schumann's Traumerie resonated in the still air of the orchard. He wondered if he played the strident brass and percussions of Wagner would he be less traumatized by her beauty. He took her for a walk through the garden.

"You spend a lot of time here," she said, looking about her.

"I like being out here . . ."

"That's the secret, your footprints are everywhere. May I . . ?"

She went to a nearby rosebush to look at a white rose. He stood behind her as she sniffed the fragrance. Not knowing he was so close she stepped back as she turned around and for an instant their faces were just inches apart. She dropped her eyes as he stepped back. They continued walking.

"The garden has given back every moment you spent here," she said.

"It's kind of you to say so. You seem to like roses."

"Especially roses. My home in Damascus was always full of flowers. I took my degree in botany. My favorite flower is the white rose . . ."

"Mine is the red" he said.

For the first time a suggestion of a smile played about her lips.

"We will not like each other . . ," she said and watched him for a moment, wondering if he would grasp her meaning.

"But only if you are from the House of York . . ."

She smiled broadly now, her lips sliding back over her teeth.

"Or if you are of the House of Lancaster."

The ice was broken. They went back to the orchard and sat at the table. She became suddenly graven faced as she spoke to him.

"Monsieur, I regret I cannot stay very long, I have so much on my mind. I feel I know you, having heard so much about you from General Legrande and Madame Odalie, and of course Paul."

"I'm sorry you must go so soon. But first let me tell you the L'Echo will be writing a public apology for the story. I don't know if you have taken legal advice but you could sue for substantial damages."

"No Monsieur, I just want to put all that business behind me."

"I see. But if it's any consolation the L'Echo won't last much longer, most of their advertisers have pulled out. I've been asked to convey to you that you can remain in France as long as you wish . . ."

"I cannot stay any longer."

"Please hear me out. You were very badly treated, I . . , eh, we want to make amends . . ."

She thought some time before answering him.

"To tell you the truth I have been happy here. Very much. Maybe it's something in the air in Paris. If things were different I would be very tempted to stay. But I'm concerned about my parents. They telephone me every day and I have not heard from them in over a week. I've called all my relations and no one knows where they are."

"Perhaps they took a vacation?"

"Never, not without telling me. They know I would fret if I did not hear from them."

"You sound as if you get along very well with them."

Her face lit up as she spoke.

"Oh they are wonderful, no girl could ask for better parents. My father worries about me when there is nothing to worry about. It was not easy telling them I was living with Paul, they were very strict with me all my life. He was the first man I had ever been with. You may laugh perhaps in this age of promiscuity . . ."

"It's all the more regrettable you've been treated so badly. There's something I've got to ask you. Is it true you're father shot at the reporter from the L'Echo?"

She smiled again, almost gleefully.

"He told me he was just having fun and shot into the air. The reporter was rude and he just ran him off," she put a hand to her mouth as she smiled again, "when he read about me being a spy my mother said he laughed so much he had tears in his eyes. He laughs like a horse, you could hear him in the next village," she stopped smiling and became quiet again, "you see my parents have complete trust in me, I expect no less of any man in my life."

For a few moments each were engrossed in their private thoughts. With his solitary, almost ascetic lifestyle, his dislike of socializing and party-going Claudel had almost no experience of women and less of love. In the time that had elapsed since he met Solonge his life he was thrown into emotional turmoil. He had shortness of breath and even at this moment his heart was racing wildly. He had been going about his business and now, as he turned and found her looking at him with her large expressive eyes, he couldn't bear the thought of her leaving. She stood up from the table.

"And now I must leave you. I have to get the first available flight home. I cannot sleep worrying about my parents."

Solonge was at a loss to understand Claudel's behavior in the next few moments. She was already moved by his compassion and sympathy and he had stirred feelings in her that surprised her and yet here he was, aware of her distress, smiling and waving a handkerchief in the air. Two figures appeared at the kitchen door. A woman's voice and a man's deeper voice called out her name in unison. Solonge spun around, her face filled with incredulity and disbelief.

"Maman . . , here? Papa . . , here?"

She gasped, too overcome to speak and with tears welling in her eyes she ran past a beaming Claudel into the outstretched arms of her parents. They clung to each other, Solonge and her mother crying uncontrollably. Umar Peera's great arms enfolded his wife and daughter as he turned to Claudel and smiled. Claudel returned the smile as Solonge came running back to him, her face radiant with joy.

"You . . , you did all this, you brought my parents to me . . , you?"

"Well I . . , oh, it was about time something nice happened to you."

He was taken totally by surprise when she reached up and kissed him on the cheek and ran back into her mother's arms. Umar Peera patted his daughter's head gently.

"Is she not a jewel?"

"Yes," said Claudel, smiling and raising his voice slightly, "a precious jewel."

Claudel led them back into the cottage where they would have some more time together. He pottered about the kitchen listening for the voice of Solonge coming from the living room. He felt elated, joyous. He would never let her go.

THE END

SHAY ELLIOTT. A SPORTING LIFE

by

JOHN FLANAGAN

ON A COLD BLUSTERY NIGHT in September 1951 the 18th Annual General Meeting of the Dublin Wheelers Cycling Club was held in an antiquated Georgian tenement house in Pearce Street. Dublin. Ireland. The sturdy oak door groaned when I pushed it open and I found myself in a dank musty hallway. Rays of weak yellow light filtered in through a grimy fanlight as I groped my way in the semi-darkness. Ghosts of a more leisurely era accompanied me up a creaky staircase of shining banisters rails, mildewed lace curtains and brass stair rods. When I entered the meeting room I was met with the clamouring voices of cyclists from the racing and touring sections of the club. I was asked to identify myself which I did and was duly impressed with the formality of it all. I found a seat and sat down. Behind a long table a grim faced committee was trying to impose order on the unruly throng. I had just turned 17 years old and was about to become a member of the famous cycling club.

JOHN FLANAGAN

If I could back-pedal for a moment to try to give an idea of Dublin in the late 1940's and early 1950's as a backdrop to the immense popularity of bicycle racing in Ireland

Post World War II Dublin was in the throes of social unrest caused by high unemployment, poverty, and unending labour strikes. Roaming gangs, in particular the Animal Gang out of Gardiner Street and the Hawks Nest Gang from Dominick Street terrorized the inner city. Parishes were seldom ventured out of. Every crammed tenement house bred Artful Dodgers and other candidates for nearby Mountjoy Jail, known colloquially as 'the Joy'. In this landscape a descent to the nether regions of crime and incarceration was a rite of passage; fragile blossoms withered on the bough in the arid environment of the inner city. Established families lived in dread of being separated from lifelong neighbours and resettled in the new outlying 'Corpnoration' estates of Cabra, Drimnagh and Finglas; areas according to writer Brendan Behan, where they ate their young. In desperation thousands took to the mailboats from the North Wall to begin new lives in Great Britain, Canada, the USA and Australia. Winston Churchill was heard to quip that Ireland could have the six counties of the North if the Irish returned Liverpool and Birmingham.

Infectious bacterial diseases were rampant in Dublin. In 1948 Ireland had the highest infant mortality rate in Europe. Over 10 % of the lower income groups, mostly children, died of or were infected with tuberculosis, chickenpox, diphtheria, whooping cough, scurvy, scabies, measles, mumps and ringworm. In 1950, five years after the end of World War Two and six hundred years after the 14th century Renaissance, Ireland was the last medieval jewel in the Vatican's crown. The Knights of St Columbanus were feverishly proscribing the most gifted writers and intellectuals of Western civilization from Huxley to Sartre. The power and prestige of Archbishop John Charles McQuaid rivaled that of the Jesuit monk Torquemada in the reign of Ferdinand and Isabella of Spain in 1483. And if Dublin lacked Auto-da-fe's and garroting, heads rolled nevertheless when John Charles invoked Article 44 of the Constitution, which he co-authored, and flexed his political muscle; witness his scuppering of the Mother and Child scheme of the innovative Minister of Health Dr. Noel Browne. But for all that and the penurious squalor of the inner city we were a happy lot. Knowledge, however modest, would have had to accept a measure of guilt for its acquisition if it compromised the serenity of our blissful ignorance.

It was an age of innocence, of sodalities, penny candles and midnight Masses, of miraculous medals and regular sightings of the Venerable Matt Talbot and the Blessed Virgin Mary. Pompous Bishops emblazoned in gold vestments served Mass, glowing in the candle-lit luminescence of the High Altar of the Pro Cathedral. Angelic altar boys in black soutanes and white surplices chanted Latin hymns in candlelight processions amid the crumbling tenements of Marlborough Street. At 16 years old we played spin-the-bottle, drank fizz and had a first shave with a Macs Smile. A Kingston shirt made all the difference when with a tremulous heart one savoured a first kiss.

Dublin's inner city in winter was like a setting for a Becket play. Beneath the claustrophobic dome of the night sky the buckling walls of decaying tenement houses were buttressed up by massive wood beams. Whole families often occupied one single room. The nefarious glimmer man made his nightly rounds dimming the sputtering gas globes of fin de siècle lampposts in streets lost in shadow and despair.

Dublin's gothic skyline always seemed less pervading in the darkness than in the harsh light of day.

This was the setting then that brought one to the sport. Bicycle racing offered a chance to travel, to breathe fresh air, to escape the grim environment of a Dickensian Dublin.

Every Sunday morning in the social season, (that is the non-racing time of year) I left the myopic confines of Parnell Street and cycled with the Dublin Wheelers into the countryside. The Clonee / Dunshaughlin / Navan / Trim circuit was most favoured for touring. Apart from the occasional farm tractor the roads were usually devoid of traffic. Mulhuddart and Clonee were sleepy villages awakened only on the day of an all-Ireland final or horseracing at Fairyhouse. After Black Bull the Navan Road weaved in cloistered silence under canopies of oak trees. Church bells tolled in the distance in a Turner landscape of flocks and herds and startled wildlife. The spinning tyres of the bicycle wheels alone disturbed the pastoral stillness.

Once my cycle racing career was launched in 1952 I rode with bravado and feared no one. Initial failures only served to intensify my insatiable greed for trophies and public veneration and unabashed I climbed hills with the indomitable spirit of Sisyphus. By the time I discovered I couldn't go for a message on the bike I was already too committed to turn back. Whilst my Dublin Wheelers clubmates cavorted in the Crystal and Metropole and Balalaika Ballrooms I wore out my John Bull tyres training on the Swords, Howth, Clontarf circuit in the dreary depths of winter. Big miles and ambition would circumvent my lack of natural talent, I was certain of it. I knew one day I would join my hero Fausto Coppi in the Bianchi team. We would share podiums in Paris and Rome while the monk Bartali seethed with rage.

In the rough and tumble sport of cycle racing many events ended in flared tempers and angry exchanges. In the longer, tougher races hardworking roadmen were plagued by opportunist sprinters and trackmen who often stole the fruits of victory in the last 20 yards of a race, having 'sat' on a breakaway group for 20 or 30 miles. All that was about to change as a different caliber of rider, more forceful and aggressive ushered in the new decade of the 50's.

John Lackey and Shay Elliott were among those riders who made life very difficult for the sprinters and hangers-on. Lackey aptly fit the popular axiom 'savage roadman' which he himself coined. The winner of over 200 races Lackey was perhaps more intimidated than any other rider by Elliott's presence in a race. It was more than the aversion a proud man feels in ceding to an adversary; Elliott's pure class mesmerized him. Lackey was a talented Salieri, living his life in another's shadow. John was not gifted anatomically, as Elliott was for the unnatural sport of cycling racing. His wide shoulders hindered him aerodynamically and he had a peculiar habit of twisting in the saddle to maximize his final rush to the line. But what he lacked in finesse he more than compensated for by being fiercely combative. An intensely private man he hid his feelings behind a veneer of jovial buffoonery, a hail-fellow-well-met Falstaff whose loud bellowing laugh echoed in pelotons and dressing rooms. After he retired from racing Lackey went on to organize and direct multi stage races. His own life was to end in very tragic circumstances.

No one who knew the Elliott family in the early 1950's could possibly envisage the series of tragic events that would befall each family member barely two decades hence. Shay's father Jim owned a garage and filling station on the South Circular Road in Kilmainham. Dublin. After some difficult years the business was at last turning around and doing well at about the time Shay's amateur career was taking off. Jim had been a champion racing motorcyclist in his day with many successes. He was a tall man, patrician in bearing with a strong face, an aquiline nose and silvery hair. One would never guess that this gentle mild mannered man had been engaged in the savagery of the Irish Civil war. Shay's mother Nell was a member of the Cumann na Mban. Some stories Jim shared with me including his friendship with Liam Mellows were vivid moments out of the history of the Irish struggle for Independence.

Nell, nee Ellen Farrell, was a gentlewoman from an old Westmeath family. She was an avid gardener and a great cook as I would happily discover. When the family moved to Crumlin, a suburb of Dublin she went everywhere on an old 'upstairs' bicycle complete with front basket. In later years she confided many stories to me of when the family was young and their horizons so bright with hope. When Nell met Jim Elliott she got caught up in his world of fishing and wildfowling as indeed I would in time. She once remarked to me that she seemed to spend all of her life plucking feathers. Always prim and sedate as a young woman it was Jim's love of wildfowling that brought out an adventurous streak in her. On many a night Jim took Nell with him while 'lamping' for rabbits on the plains of Kildare. She sat on the car roof with a spotlight and lit up the pitch-black fields where Jim was hunting. Rabbit soup and game were high on the culinary agenda when the boys were young. She was thrilled about Shays successes on the bike and went to watch most of the races he was involved in. I believe it was Jim and Nell's unwavering encouragement and belief in him and that formed the core of Shay's inner strength. The eldest brother Eddy, staunch and dependable would be a great support when Shay retired from cycling and returned home from France. Younger brother Paul would also prove to be a champion cyclist; in 1970 as a member of the Bray Wheelers he would win both the National Championships and the Tour of Ireland and in the meantime, a devoted wildfowler, he was emptying Wicklow of fish and game. In the early '50's the family lived in Old County Road in Crumlin. Later they moved to Shaymallee in Kilmacanogue. County Wicklow. (Nell named the house after Shay's win in the Tourmalet stage of the 1954 Route de France.)

On the 19th Dec.1959 Shay married Marguerite Geiger, a blond Strasbourgoise. Their son Pascal was born to the untold delight of Jim and Nell. Eddy married Bridie. In 1962 Shay came 2nd in the World Championships in Salo di Gardia in Italy, sacrificing the race in the interests of Jean Stablinski; a strategy he would sorely regret. In 1963 he took over leadership of the Tour de France, wearing the coveted Yellow Jersey for three days. And despite running disagreements with Jacques Anquetil over his function in the Saint Raphael-Geminiani team, fate seemed at last to be according him a more positive role. His career was at an all time high. His cup runneth over. The gods however were about to set in motion a sequence of events that would decimate the entire family, a reversal of fortune that was merciless and swift in its execution.

Shay was born in Rathfarnham Dublin on 4th June 1934. Later the family moved to 96 Old County Road, Crumlin. At age sixteen in 1950 Shay began a six year apprenticeship as a metal worker in a Dublin garage.

Just around Shay's 16th birthday it was discovered that he had a fine singing voice. Their neighbour was the celebrated violinist Geraldine O'Grady and they could hear her rehearsing in the house next door. If Shay was familiar with the piece she was playing he sang along with her, with gusto according to Nell. Just how fine Shays voice was I had occasion to hear. On a Sunday evening in the autumn of 1952 the touring section of the Dublin Wheelers stopped for a brief repast in O'Hagans Tearooms in Portmarnock. After tea the club members sat about the hall and, as was the custom, a song was called for. An embarrassed silence ensued, almost everyone hoping to avoid the spotlight. A clear resonant tenor voice suddenly filled the dining room. It was none other than the bold Shaymo, singing like the proverbial lark. He just thrilled the fair sex of the club and left the racing men, myself included shaking our heads. It was a final ignominy; he was not only cleaning up in the races, he could sing into the bargain. The richness and promise of his voice caused a dilemma in the Elliott household. Nell envisioned a singing career for him and wanted to have his voice trained while Jim sided with Shay who wanted to devote his time to racing. Nell was finally won over, the deciding factor being the acne Shay suffered from; the cycling seemed to be having a gradual healing effect. Within a year the acne cleared up completely.

When he was 17 years old Shay joined St. Brendans sports club in Donnybrook Dublin. His brief sojourn with St. Brendans was not a happy one. One night he was playing alone in the billiard room when an older club member, a little over the top, made a slighting remark about him being there and asked him to leave. Shay quietly replaced the billiard cue in the rack and walked out of the club. Soon afterwards he joined the Southern Road Club and began to train and race for the club. On 1st April 1951 he won a first novice award, recording 1hr 21mn 58sc for a 30 mile Time Trial. The SRC disbanded in February 1952 and in March of that year Shay joined the Dublin Wheelers. As a member of 'The Wheelers' his superlative talents took wing. On 21st April 1952 he recorded his first open win, a 30 mile open handicap on the Navan Road. On 10th June 1952, just after his 18th birthday he won the Grand Prix of Ireland from the legendary Jim McQuaid and a field of 100 riders. On 27th June 1952 he won the Mannin Veg trophy race in the Isle of Man, winning from Paddy Boyd of Liverpool and in the same year added the Raleigh Dublin-Galway-Dublin 2 day stage race to his growing palmares.

The 1952 June evening in the Phoenix Park when Shay won the Grand Prix cycle race from Jim McQuaid remains vivid in my memory as if it was yesterday. There were clouds overhead but they were high and the evening was bright and clear. I was on the roadside near the whitewashed finish line opposite the cricket ground. On the last lap of the race Shay had broken away from the peloton with two other riders and the peloton was quickly closing the gap. Shay zoomed across the finish line just seconds ahead of Jim McQuaid. The race was a spectacular event with literally thousands of on-lookers lining the course. Cycling up to the Phoenix Park to see the race I passed crowds of people mostly walking. They had taken CIE buses to Parkgate Street to see the race. A decade before television came to Ireland there was great nobility attached to champions when bike racing was open air theatre. Later television would reduce the drama of sporting events to a small screen in the living room.

The attention resulting from his exploits on the bike often proved hard for Shay to handle as an 18 year old; he was wont to act the prima donna on occasion. From the moment he discovered he had a facility for winning races he ceased to be a team player. I saw team mate and international rider of repute, Donal O'Connell angrily remonstrate with Shay for chasing him down. The Team Award never concerned him;

217

his eye was always on the main prize. He also developed an ill-advised habit of placing his little finger in the extended hands of fellow riders offering congratulatory handshakes. It was a denigrating gesture that cost him some admirers. At any rate his father Jim put short shrift to such idiosyncrasies in his son's precocious formative years. Many riders who competed with Shay in his early years were divided as to his personality and character. Some found him aloof, others vindictive; others again said he was gentle to the point of shyness. Depending on the setting he was all of those things. Good manners and a natural refinement were endemic in Shay's nature but they did not define him; he did not take politeness with him into a race. The moment the flag dropped in a bike race he rode with a grim single-mindedness often with scant regard for the niceties of fair play. In the 1954 Tour of Ireland stage race he approached the stage end into Cork having broken away from the peloton with British rider Bernard Pusey. They agreed to sprint for the finishing line side by side. While Pusey was reaching down to choose a gear for the sprint Shay was gone in that instant and beat the Englishman to the line. I finished fifth and afterwards asked Shay how the stage went for him. He told me he 'got the drop' on the Englishman. At the crowded dinner table that night Joe (Joe Joe) Mc Cormack said Shay would chase his grandmother around the parlour for a medal. While everyone laughed Shay smiled and modestly shook his head.

Shay was 5 feet 6 inches tall with a stocky build, strongly muscled legs and narrow shoulders. He had a full corpulent face and a sallow complexion that remained ashen even after years of racing in sun-drenched lands. His acutely arched eyebrows, long thick nose, piercing eyes and swept back hair gave him a Mephistophelian aura. Off the bike Shay had an ungainly way of walking that was often the target of good-natured ribbing; he leaned forward on his instep in a sort of rolling gait with his heels barely touching the ground. In contrast, in full flight on the bike he was a verisimilitude of aerodynamic grace. His powerful legs and short upper torso facilitated the best position possible to compete in the most unnatural of sports known to man. With this formidable advantage he also brought to the sport a ruthless will to win that was at variance with the bland smiling amiability of his character off the bike.

A racing cyclist, seen in the abstract, hovers over two large narrow wheels with angled steel tubing jammed between his legs. Balance is crucial to remain upright but is cavalierly disregarded once mastered. The rider then propels himself forward with his two feet strapped to two revolving cranks. It falls to the lot of a favoured few to achieve grace or symmetry balanced on such a contraption. The Italian rider, Il Campione Fausto Coppi perhaps best epitomized the fusion, the harmony possible between rider and bicycle. A man of gentle and modest disposition Coppi weaved his magic by playing the waiting game in a bicycle race. He waited for the steep mountains or for the moment when his adversaries succumbed to pressure and soared away to leave them floundering in his wake. Coppi became an immortal during his lifetime.

In 1953 at age 19 Shay was nominated to ride in the 3 lap Manx International in the Isle of Man. British rider Les Willmott won but it was generally accepted it should have been Shays race. I was riding in the two-lap Viking Trophy on the same course and I remember the commotion after Shay had crashed when he was about to catch Willmott. There is a notorious sharp bend at Governors Bridge at the bottom of the mountain. Shay hit the turn at speed; his tyre rolled off the wheel and down he came. He picked himself up and rushed to the line on a borrowed bike to finish fourth. His father Jim had glued the tubular tyre to the wheel rim but he had not used enough adhesive. He was in the doghouse for months when Nell found out what happened. The next momentous occasion was the 1954 Tour of Ireland. As a result of finishing 2nd overall and taking the King of the Mountains prize he won a month's stay at the Simplex Training Camp in Monte Carlo in the South of France. In 1954 he also competed in the 10 day Route de France stage race with team members Karl McCarthy, John Lackey, Derek Quinn, Terry Carmody, Tony Duggan and myself. Joe Loughman and Gerry Duffin were managers, Paddy McQuaid drove the team car. When Shay won the Col de Tourmalet mountain stage and finished 4th overall the French press sat up and took notice for the first time.

Shay reported to the Simplex Training Camp in Monte Carlo in February 1955 and came to the immediate attention of Jean Leuliott and Mickey Weigant, two of the most influential names in French cycling. In a 'friendly' training spin on a hilly circuit Shay had dropped a group of riders that included French star Louison Bobet, a two time winner of the Tour de France. The camp was riveted by the incident as it was known Bobet was looking for early season fitness. (He went on that year to win the Tour de France for a third time.) As a result of his stay at the camp and his impressive dossier Mickey Weigant offered Shay a month's trial, room and board, with the Paris based Athletic Club Boulogne Billancourt. The terms of the offer with ACBB were explicit; either he impress in that month or he was out. But the canny soigneur had seen enough to assure him the talented Irish newcomer would be around for longer than a month.

During his stay in Monte Carlo Shay had the great good fortune to become friendly with Jean Tchamassanian, a fellow club mate of the ACBB. Jean lived in Paris and had just begun his military service. When he returned home he invited Shay to go with him and meet his parents. The family was immediately enamoured of the quietly spoken expatriate and as he was looking for accommodation they offered him Jean's room. The house was in the old village of Passy in Paris. After his first classic win the neighbours on the street where he lived were usually to be found leaning of the windows to welcome him home after a race. Thus began one of the happiest periods of Shay's career.

I've heard it said that the chauvinist French hate everyone in Europe except the Irish. Perhaps the fact that our tiny isle produced four Nobel Prize winners for literature impressed the haute couture minded French. The Dublin expatriate James Joyce had set the Parisian literary salons on its heels with the publication of 'Ulysses' in 1922. Dubliner Samuel Beckett endeared himself to French hearts for his heroism in the French Resistance in the 2nd World War and in 1954 took Paris by storm when he launched his surreal stage play 'Waiting for Godot'. And history shows the newly formed First Republic came to the aid of Wolfe Tone and the Irish insurrection of 1791. At any rate the French seemed favourably disposed to another Irishman Seamus Elliott, storming the bastions of their national sport.

Shays 1955 debut in the French amateur races created a sensation. The Paris-Evreux road race, finishing on a stiff climb outside the town of Evreux in Normandy was the most prestigious event on the calendar. Shay won the race from a field of 200 riders, thus ensuring himself of a professional contract. In the Grand Prix de Boulogne he finished the race on his own ahead of the peloton. In all he won the incredible total of five amateur classics and was placed in many others. In November of the year on a banked wooden track in Brussels he set a new world record for the 1000 metres flying start. In December he failed in an attempt to break the hour record but enroute he created a new world record for the 10 kilometres. Not many professional riders had come close to the quality of his victories as an amateur. He rode with panache and flair and tactical brilliance, winning in every conceivable way, in mass sprints, in lone breakaways; he was fearless in descents and a formidable climber. The French sports fans and media were enthralled by him. They were flattered by his struggle to come to grips with the language and so admiring of him when at the end of 1955 he was conducting interviews in French. These were the halcyon days, some of the most rewarding days of his life, scaling the dizzying heights of fame and living the dream for us at home.

France embraced him as one of their own. And when he married Strasbourgeoise Marguerite Geiger on 19 December 1959 he became like a favourite son. After victories he was feted and plied with garlands of flowers, acclaimed and toasted at receptions in his honour. His exploits were written about in newspapers and magazines all over Europe. Under the astute guidance of public-relations conscious Mickey Weigant he became as well known as the great professionals whose ranks he was about to join. His feats brought him into the company of the legends of the sport. Shay's mother Nell said she got 'weak at the knees' when Shay introduced Fausto Coppi to her. Shay hunted game and wild boar with his 'copain', his pal Roger Hassenforder, the irascible jester in the court of King Jacques Anquetil. Hassenforder often broke away in a race, dismounted, grabbed a camera from a reporter and photographed the peloton as it passed by. Shay partied and played cards with Rik Van Looy, Andre Darrigade, Louison Bobet, Charley Gaul, Jean Stablinski,

Raphael Geminiani and the mercurial Jacques Anquetil; Maitre Jacques the team leader with whom Shay would have an unsettled relationship over the next decade. Nell was also delighted that Shays taste in clothes remained quintessentially Irish, favouring brown tweeds and brogues. Tongue in cheek Jim said he was decked out like the jockey Johnny Roe.

It should be added here that the names of drugs and stimulants of any kind had not entered the vocabularies of Irish racing cyclists. When the names of Coppi, Koblet, Van Steenbergen and other heroes became linked to drug taking there was a sense of incredulity, of disbelief on our part. Our despair diminished when the allegations went unchallenged by the legendary riders. I saw two friends become involved in a heated argument over Coppi's involvement or otherwise in taking drugs and they ceased to speak with each other from that day forward. In the end we were forced to face the inevitable truth even as we swore at the messenger with all the passion and vehemence of betrayed youth. In time we saw our heroes ignominiously toppled from the pedestals upon which our misplaced reverence had ensconced them. The ascetic Fausto Coppi, whose exploits surpassed the winged Icarus in his lofty flights over the cols indeed went too near the sun and proved to be all too human.

No one who knew him could ever accuse Shay Elliott of naivety; his astuteness and intelligence was evident on and off the bike. But the day he stepped into the charnel-house of professional cycling he was as an innocent abroad among the strychnine-laced doppelgangers masquerading as sportsmen. In his early days as a top-flight amateur in France he had heard of trade team sponsors, team physicians and managers putting unrelenting pressure on professional riders to produce wins whatever the cost. Sponsors took the view that cycle racing would cease to exist without their backing. Professional racing, they insisted, provided the majority of riders with an income well in excess of what they would earn on a farm or punching tickets on a bus. This harsh reality made the average riders of the peloton willing victims to the overtures of corrupt physicians who had forgotten where they put their Hippocratic oaths. That drugs were used to secure wins was still in the realm of public speculation. It was only when several riders died; Tom Simpson's death in the 1967 Tour de France was the most widely reported, that the lid blew off the bubbling cauldron of the widespread use of drugs in cycle racing. Any lingering illusions fans may have entertained about the well-being of the sport were quickly dispelled when in 1967 Jacques Anquetil took center stage and made a public announcement. Speaking with the imperious effrontery to which his fans were accustomed he informed the French public that they were naive to believe races could be won without drugs. He mistook either the tenor of the times or the adulation of his fans. His remarks were considered outrageous and as a result calls were made for a judicial inquiry into all levels of the sport. Doctors especially were pilloried for their shameless disregard for the health of the riders. The uproar resulted in the International Olympic Committee publishing a list of banned drugs in 1968.

Shay was invited to ride with the Helyett-Leroux-Potin team in February 1956. His new teammates were Andre Darrigade, Roger Darrigade, Miguel Poblet, Francois Mahe, Pierre Brun, Gilbert Scodeller, Raymond Hoorelbecke and captain Jacques Anquetil. Shays outstanding previous season as an amateur barely impressed the battle hardened professionals in the peloton. Brilliant amateurs had too often been touted by the media as the next Rik van Looy or Louison

Bobet only to fade to oblivion in the professional ranks. In his first few races Shay was 'allowed' to spread his wings. He wasn't overtly helped but as a new boy his team gave him the freedom to earn his spurs. In the Grand Prix de l'Echo d'Alger in North Africa in March 1956, in just his second race as a professional he finished in 1st place. A week later he won the Grand Prix de Catox in Marseille and followed this up with a win in the Grand Prix d'Isbergues. Several more wins came in quick succession. Considering his impressive debut Shay could have been forgiven for believing that with this powerful team behind him there was nothing he could not achieve in his professional career.

Jacques Anquetil was five months older than Shay when they teamed up, just 22 years of age. Incredibly he had already been a professional with La Perle Cycles for three years, winning the Grand Prix de Nations time trial each year. At this point in his career all of France hoped that Anquetil was the saviour whose coming was fervently awaited. In the decade following the 2nd World War France desperately needed a hero to inspire a resurgence of French pride after the harrowing years of German occupation. Louison Bobet seemed the obvious choice; he had won an unprecedented three Tours de France. But Bobet was 31 years old, he lacked charisma and accusations of stinginess had followed him throughout his career. He lacked what Anquetil radiated, an aura of invincibility. Anquetil was France incarnate; he was arrogant, petulant and proud. And if he was ruthless in terms of team discipline and loyalty he also had a reputation for honesty and fair play. As a cyclist Anquetil possessed flawless class. His prodigious talent was demonstrated in November 1956 when he broke the world hour record of the Campionissimo Fausto Coppi at the Vigorelli track in Milan, Italy. He had the elegance and poise of Koblet, the grace of Coppi, the raw courage and grit of the diminutive giant killer Jean Robic. Among other of Anquetil's attributes was his ability to motivate and inspire his teammates, even if solely in his own interest. The son of a fruit grower from Normandy, Anquetil ruled over the new team like a feudal lord over his fiefdom.

Before the racing season got under way in 1956 the Helyett sponsors, riders and soigneurs held meetings to discuss tactics and strategy, all fine-tuned to serve the needs and aspirations of team leader Anquetil. The first bitter pill Shay had to swallow was when he was told he could no longer orchestrate his own wins unless it was sanctioned by Anquetil. The concept he first had of his role as a professional now seemed naively idealistic. He learned of the practice of races being 'given' to riders, a sort of reward for loyalty and service. Usually it had to do with a rider competing in a kermesse in his own hometown. With the unstated consent of the peloton he was free to break away alone or win a sprint finish from a few breakaway companions. It made a huge hero of a local lad and everyone went home happy. The two Isle of Man Manx Trophy races in 1959 and 1964 were 'given' to Shay. That is to say his strong team controlled the peloton and facilitated the win for him.

When he made a flying visit to his parents' home in 1964 prior to the Manx race I cycled out to Kilmacanogue to see him. He told me in a matter of fact tone he would probably win the race. The Isle of Man was considered Shays backyard, his 'turf'.

Shay rebelled instinctively against the constraints Anquetil imposed on him but he was hesitant to let his feeling be known. He was deeply troubled as he wanted to be part of Helyett; the ACBB and Mickey Weigant especially had taken a personal interest in getting him placed with a good team. Shay found Anquetil's public persona to be aloof but he was cordial and friendly with teammates who were unswervingly loyal. In the end Shay felt he would have had to sacrifice too much of himself to make his relationship with Anquetil less tenuous. He was consigned the role of a domestique and he couldn't pretend to be happy about it. For over nine years of racing and training with Anquetil Shay was never privy to the warmth of personality that he knew to be a part of Anquetil's character. There were ample opportunities to reconcile their differences. They were at countless after-race parties where the wine flowed freely and Shay all but bared his soul to his team leader. They drove the highways of France with Geminiani, Van Looy, Darrigade, Riviere, Hassenforder and Stablinski, their Mercedes cars bumping off each other at speeds of 160 KPH. An uneasy peace prevailed but the pride of both made the rift unbreachable. Shay excluded himself, as later would the German rider Rudi Altig, from the Great One's inner circle.

His chief nemesis in the team was his former best friend Jean Stablinski, now Anquetil's second-in-command. An undercurrent of ill will between the two riders erupted in a dramatic confrontation in the 1965 Paris-Luxembourg race. Shay was leading the 4 day stage race when Stablinski, and Anquetil, latched on to a small group which detached itself from the peloton and was meandering up the road. None among the group posed a threat to Shay's leadership and he watched unconcerned as the escapees inched away. Shay reasoned that his teammate would sit on the group and contest the finish, possibly even win the stage without endangering his grip on the race. But the wily Stablinski was ambitious and wanted more than a stage win. In what would become known in cycling annals as an infamous act of betrayal Stablinski whipped the stragglers into a cohesive working group that powered away from the peloton. The fast-moving 'eschapees' took Stablinski into overall leadership on the road and to final victory of the race. Immediately afterwards the incensed Shay quit the team realizing Stablinski could not have 'stolen' the race from him without the approval of team leader Anquetil and manager Geminiani.

Quietly and without fuss Shay packed his bags and accepted a place with Raymond Poulidor's Mercier BP Hutchinson team. Raymond Poulidor, 'Poupou' was and remains a treasured possession of France. In 2003 President Chirac decorated Poulidor with the Medal of Honour. His tally of 189 professional wins makes him one of the all-time greats of the sport. He was also dubbed the 'Eternal Second' by the media owing to his riding in the shadow of the legendary Anquetil. The fans respected Anquetil, they adored the populist Poulidor. Softly spoken and taciturn with the swarthy features of a boxer he welcomed Shay as a new teammate. Shay responded by winning 7 races for his new team.

I lived in the tiny village of Saint Andre de L'Eure in Normandy in the years 1960-63. Spirited arguments about cycling often broke out in the time-worn Inn where ancient oak beams criss-crossed the smoke-stained ceiling. I especially loved the noisy Friday night atmosphere in the Bar during the running of the Tour de France. I sat huddled among the locals under an erratic TV set as the songs of Edith Piaf and Jacques Brel blared in from the bagatelle room. Choking on the rank incense of Gauloise cigarettes and the pungent odour of garlic I cut baguettes with a penknife, inserted slices of local cheese and washed it all down with glasses of rich red Beaujolais. It was pure bliss. But I digress. The general consensus about Shay among the clientele in the Bar was that he should have joined a more modest team as a 'protected' rider and concentrate on the classics. Like the Belgian Rik Van Looy and Andre Darrigade he had the build of a 'flahout', a roadman. His stocky build and massive legs were ideal for the one-day classics but he would never soar up the cols in the manner of lithesome Fausto Coppi or Charley Gaul.

On 22nd January 1966 Shay opened a small hotel / guesthouse in Loctudy on the coast of Brittany amid much fanfare helped by the presence of some of his famous peloton colleagues. He named it the 'Hotel Irlandais'. Nell and Jim voiced concern about the hotel. They felt that professional advice should have been sought to apprise its viability, its investment potential before he risked his life savings in a business of which he had no experience. And the timing made the venture more suspect in their eyes. Shay had joined Poulidor's Mercier team. How could he supervise the running of an hotel while he was still tied to a cycling regimen that took him to all corners of Europe for weeks on end ? Mismanagement, attempting to run the hotel in absentis and bureaucratic red tape put paid to all his cherished hopes. After a decade as a professional cyclist he watched his savings and dreams dwindle away to nothing.

Shay's star as an amateur had been a straight trajectory into the heavens; similarly as a professional he began with a run of spectacular wins. And though he ended his career with 57 races won he was never to win a classic. A run of incredible bad luck had befallen Shay dating back to his amateur days in France. I can't recall him ever crashing in races at home in Ireland. He almost crippled himself for life in the 1955 Route de France when he crashed into a roadside marker stone and shattered his right knee. Stripped freewheels, mechanical malfunctions and punctured tubulars deprived him of victory when it was most assuredly his. He accepted his misfortunes stoically and fought on. But in the battlefield of the peloton there were other debilitating factors to undermine his resolve. He had to contend with Machiavellian intrigue when he took matters into his own hands and won races in defiance of Anquetil, Geminiani and Stablinski who now had Anquetil's ear. He felt that the mundane races 'allocated' to him were a sop to quench his thirst for bigger game. The German Rudi Altig and hunting colleague Roger Hassenforder saw the brilliance and potential in Shay but they could not alter the intractable team strategy set by Anquetil.

After the Stablinski incident a withering disillusionment about professional racing set in, even as he was winning races for Poulador's Mercier Team. Cycling would lose its aura of romance, its charm, something that never seemed possible until that moment.

Years later on a cycle spin with him to Edgewardstown in Co. Longford he recalled this low point in his life and smiled suddenly. He said he wished he had been more careful about what he had dreamed of.

By 1966 Shay's marriage had taken a turn for the worst and at 32 years of age time was making big inroads into whatever options might be left open to him. In the latter part of his career the racing circuit became a frenzied carousel from which, due to the gathering storms in his private life, he was unable to extricate himself. With cycling commitments taking him all over Europe, visits to his Paris home were like pit stops in a car race. The marriage was severely strained at the time of his last full year in 1966. By the end of his career he had won stages in the Giro d'Italia in 1960, Veulta a Espana 1962/1963, Tour de France 1963, 2nd World Championships 1962 and had career total of 57 professional races. Shay wound up his affairs in France and returned to Ireland.

Shays father Jim had opened a garage and panel beating service in Princes Street Dublin, and he wanted Shay to come back and be part of the business.

Shay returned to Dublin, reeling from the breakup of his marriage, the loss of his hotel in Loctudy and the sudden demise of his cycling career. The Bray Wheelers Cycling Club under the chairmanship of Joe Loughman accorded Shay the hero's welcome he so richly deserved. Joe was the heartbeat of the Bray cycling community. I won't attempt to sum up his magnanimity and character in a few words. He merits an entire chapter unto himself in that he was an author; 'Trusty Steeds And Rain Like Stair Rods', an avid historian and a cycling coach without equal. Shay was made an honorary president of the club and was warmly received into their ranks. Within a short time he would be guest of honour and speaker at BWCC functions. After Shays death it was the BWCC that organized, funded and erected the splendid granite monument, unveiled by Nell, atop of Glenmalure mountain in County Wicklow. The BWCC inaugurated a classic annual bike race in his name. A closely-knit group of lifelong friends the Bray Wheelers Cycling Club made certain Shay would never be forgotten.

Nell and Jim, Eddy and Paul rallied around Shay, lessening his grief by sharing it. Jim had been in the motor trade for all of his adult life; he was widely respected and liked and was soon to put his knowledge and influence to work for his son. After a brief respite and rest for Shay they went to the family solicitors O'Hagan Ward in Dawson Street and proceeded to buy the property in Princes Street. The one-storey building was in a sorry state of disrepair but it didn't stay that way for long. Within a few weeks of creative block-laying, painting and cleaning it housed a thriving business with customers cars lined up outside in the street. Mick Fagin, Shays old cycling pal and a master carpenter built an apartment over the garage almost single-handedly. Another friend John Scahill put business his way and gave him expert advice. I replaced the broken glass around the place. Jim and Paul worked full-time in the garage with Shay. Eddy Elliott was a regular visitor and livened up the place with his bubbling good humour.

At the time when Shay returned home and the garage was up and running I was keeping myself in reasonable shape; cycling on the weekends and getting the odd spin in during the week. When we began cycling together Shay had hardly looked at a bike and wasn't in good form. He was sluggish and as we meandered along the Wicklow roads at a snail's pace I wondered how I could arouse him from his torpor. Little did I realize the Pandora's box I was about to open. All conversation ended one Sunday as I inched my bike past him and half-wheeled him from Rathnew to Ashford. It was a piece of impertinence that I knew I would have to pay for but when I saw a resentful glint in his eye I felt I had resurrected a competitive spark inside him. The pace picked up noticeably and I spent the remainder of the spin sitting on his wheel. It took a while but gradually he regained a semblance of his old self and my half-wheeling days were over. Not long after we went on longer forays, cycling as far afield as Arklow and Longford with me sitting in most of the time.

Princes Street Garage was a magic place to be. Each one of the Elliotts was unique and idiosyncratic, all gifted with a fine intelligence. The enigmatic Paul inherited his father's love of the outdoors and was an excellent marksman. At every opportunity he indulged his passion for wildfowling, fishing and golf and sporadically, bike racing. Paul had won the Tour of Ireland stage race, the National Massed Start championship and other important races, yet cycle racing was a sport he never totally committed himself to. His talent was immense and many knowledgeable riders believed Paul could have surpassed Shay if he had given himself over completely to the sport. But the fact was that if Paul had the choice between sitting in a duck-blind waiting for a flight of geese or riding the bike, the bike would lose out every time. I first met Paul when he was 14 years old. He was already developing the strong personality traits that would characterize his later life; his conversation even at that early age was measured and thoughtful. That is not to say he was without humour, I was often a victim of his practical jokes. In contrast to Shay and Paul, Eddy was the extrovert of the family, you knew the sparks were going to fly when he came through the garage door. His conversation was peppered with jokes, often falling flat in the company of unresponsive Paul. In appearance Eddy and Paul were very much like their father Jim while Shay resembled Nell. In the garage Jim and Paul and Eddy spoke with the authority of experienced engineers and I often sat there feeling like the village idiot because much of what they discussed was over my head. Eddy's interest was car engines. Years ahead of his time he talked about running a car on methane gas extracted from the offal of pigs. As for Paul, one day I found him intently studying the strewn parts of an old radio. When I asked him what he was doing he loosed on me technical jargon about diodes, capacitators and resistors. Another time I found him machine-tooling precision parts for a broken outboard engine and he got it running perfect. He made his own harpoon gun for underwater fishing. I was intrigued because their formal education was as basic as my own, that is Grammer School, and Nell told me they had never formally studied subjects in which they showed this marked degree of expertise. They seemed possessed of knowledge they had not acquired through learning and I wondered if they had what in epistemology is known as 'a priori' knowledge, knowledge that is independent of experience. Coleridge made the point that forms of thinking revealed by experience, (a priori as opposed to empirical) must have pre-existed in order to make experience possible. Eddy and Paul seemed to exemplify that notion. Shaymo on the other hand knew how to turn the key in the ignition, that being the limit of his mechanical expertise and close enough to mine.

When the wildfowling season opened in November 1968 Shay and I cycled the 67 miles to the Hotel Edgeworthstown in Co. Longford. A friend was there to meet us with suitcases, guns and dogs. After a late meal a card game was set up that went on to the late hours. It was the first time I played cards for money and as luck would have it I cleaned up. The game was Blackjack, or 21, and to give the others a chance I took hits on 17 or 18 and still managed to win. I thought it very funny watching Paul shaking his head as I pulled in my winnings time after time. He had a dry acerbic wit and rarely smiled whereas I found it hard to keep a straight face in his company. He was intense and close-lipped and adhered to a scrupulous moral code. In all the years of our acquaintance I rarely heard him indulge in gossip or malign another person. Nell once asked me how it was that Paul was so popular since he was so reclusive and hardly spoke a word. I was at a loss to explain how Paul captured the hearts and minds of so many of his contemporaries as so very few pierced his stoic reserve. His Bray Wheelers teammates were zealously protective of Paul when he wore the leadership jersey going into the last stage of the 1970 Tour of Ireland. On the final stage Irish champion Peter Doyle, a clubmate and one of his best friends, strung the entire peloton out in a straight line all the way from Monaghan to Dublin to ensure Paul won the race. Often when out on cycle spins with Paul barely a couple of sentences would pass between us for hours at a time, yet I cherished his company. When in a rare mood of levity he joked and smiled it was as if the sun came out and you waited patiently to hear everything he had to say. We remained close friends up to the moment of his own tragic and sudden death.

At 4:30 AM the following morning after the late night card game I was standing with Shay in a duck-blind on a small Island on the Shannon, swathed in waterproofs under drenching rain, waiting for the first flight of geese. We had found our way to the deserted island with the aid of a hand held compass and rowed silently through the choppy waters. In the pre-dawn darkness the treacherous Shannon echoed to an unceasing cacophony of local and migrant wildlife. We partook of a little poteen, a present I got from Nell, fortifying ourselves one might say against the harshness of the morning. As a result we were in the very best of moods and quite oblivious to the stormy weather. Among the fondest memories I have of Shay were the mornings we spent in a duck-blind with the foam-flecked black Shannon waters swirling about our feet. Talking and laughing in the rain, our animated chatter caused birds to veer off and fly away. In that tempest strewn milieu of raging Shannon waves and torrential downpours time seemed to slow and to petrify the image forever in memory.

In other more serene settings cycling through Wicklow Shay would recall epic moments of his career. He shrugged off the ill luck that deprived him of a classic among the 57 professional races he had won. He had accomplished great things. Much of it had been inspiring, elevating; the bliss of meeting Marguerite for the first time and the birth of his son Pascal, the audience in the Vatican with Pope Pius X11, the family of Madame Tahmassanian who befriended and practically adopted him in Paris, the joy and pride of Nell and Jim in all he accomplished.

When Shay stepped back on Irish soil after a decade of racing as Ireland's first professional cyclist the reception he received left much to be desired. The Irish media and CRE, the Irish cycling authority, all but ignored him. Gone was the remembrance of times past when he captivated all of Europe with his exploits. The news reports of his achievements had never been more than perfunctory in Irish newspapers. When he established a new world record for the 1000 metres Flying Start in Belgium in 1955, a tiny photo and a few nondescript column inches in the 'Evening Herald' newspaper underplayed that remarkable achievement. Shay's role as a public relations emissary for Ireland was in itself significant and worthy of note. At a time when France was mired in a lingering xenophobia after the war years Shay carried a breath of Irish culture to remote hamlets and villages on the professional racing circuit. Ireland couldn't ask for a more cordial ambassador-at-large. He had qualities of temperament the French applauded. He was softly spoken and unpretentious while his friendliness was tempered with a slight reserve; a gentleman by all accounts and a weekly communicant in catholic France.

Ten years of exhaustive physical and psychological pressures took their inevitable toll. As his adult character was forged on the anvil of professional cycling, Shay was like a soldier returned from the trenches when he came home. Wasn't it Orwell who described sport as war without the shooting? He was much quieter and profound, more introspective; it would take him a full year to reconcile to the sweeping changes in his life. Marguerite was making the occasional journey from Paris to Dublin at this time. There was great hope that the rift between them might be healed but it was not to be.

In 1970 the British firm Falcon Cycles invited Shay to participate in the marathon London-Holyhead road race. It was a big event on the calendar and all the British professionals and top amateurs were scheduled to ride. Shay accepted the invitation. While Jim and Paul held the fort in Princess Street he threw himself wholeheartedly into an intensive training program that included long stints pacing behind a motorbike. I thought the whole idea of his participation in that race was ill conceived given the short time he had to prepare. The six to nine months he needed to get fit after a long layoff were reduced to three to meet the tight schedule. On race day he wasn't even close to the fitness he needed to contend with the 275 mile one day marathon from London to Holyhead. He finished well down the field in 21st place and took a terrible hammering. That was the last attempt he made at any kind of competitive cycling.

Jim Elliott took ill and was confined to St. Stevens hospital where he died on 21st April 1971. Shay died just 2 weeks later on 4th May 1971.

The interior of the Dublin City Morgue on Ushers Island reflected the grim purpose it was designed to serve. It was dank and foreboding, reeking of chemical vapours. The table upon which Shay was laid out filled the small room. He was dressed in a brown and red chequered shirt and grey trousers. He looked for all the world as if he had fallen asleep and might awaken at any moment. Nell and Paul, Shay's wife Marguerite, Bridie, Eddy and I stood over his body each of us trying to come to terms with his sudden death. Marguerite cried quietly as she caressed his forehead. Nell's face was an implacable pale mask. Having buried Jim 2 weeks before, she had lapsed into a quiet inconsolable despair. In a few days she would recover her strength and will to live from a sense of duty to Paul and Shay's son Pascal, at the time living in Mulhouse in France. Marguerite had agreed for Pascal to come to Ireland and live with Nell and Paul when he reached the age of sixteen years.

In an extraordinary epilogue to Shay's death his dog Kim, a Springer Spaniel and an inseparable companion, crossed the road at Kilmacanogue just days after Shay died and was killed by passing traffic.

Father Jack Lynch of Kilmacanogue parish, an energetic and likeable young priest worked wonders to help Nell through the funerals and burials of Jim and Shay. Saint Mochonogs, the small Church at the bottom of the Long Hill was filled to capacity for the funeral mass. The mourners, the majority of them local cyclists spilled out to the winding driveway leading up to the Church.

Within a few short years I flew with Paul to Mulhouse in France to attend the funeral of Shay's son Pascal. He had been working as an assistant waiter in a local restaurant to earn some money as he prepared to leave for Ireland. He commuted back and forth to the restaurant on his motorcycle. The one day when he did not wear his helmet he skidded in the rain and crashed into the back of a van. He died instantly. He was 16 years old, a lovely mischievous lad my own son's age who dreamed only of Ireland, Nell and Paul and the two hunting dogs. The active and adventurous life he hoped to share with Paul was far removed from the stark circumstances of his life in an apartment building in Mulhouse. I remembered an occasion when I was visiting Nell and Paul in the new house Weirview in Dodder Road,

Rathfarnham. We were sitting in the living room while Pascal, on holidays from France was out in the back garden playing with the dogs. Nell smiled at me as Paul shouted out to Pascal that he wanted to talk to him. Pascal came in and sat down. Paul, in his usual somber and grave manner told him that he had met the girl of his dreams and he'd be getting married in a week, selling the dogs and there would be no room for Pascal in the house. Paul then picked up a newspaper and said he was looking for someone to buy the dogs, Luddy the Springer Spaniel and Flash, the English Pointer. Otherwise, said Paul, they'd have to go to the Dogs Home as his girlfriend didn't like dogs. The unfortunate child stared disbelievingly at Paul as his lips began to quiver. He hugged the dogs in a state of shock. With a loud wail he began crying and threw himself in Nell's arms. When Nell explained that Paul was joking Pascal rushed at him and in a moment they were wrestling on the floor.

To the utter despair and disbelief of all who knew him Paul drowned in a boating accident on the Shannon at Lanesborough. Co. Longford on 9th January 1988. Nell died in June 1989 to be followed by the sudden tragic death of Eddy Elliott on 29th August 2000.

Much has been written of the circumstances of Shay's death. There has been speculating by journalists who never met Shay nor known the circumstances of his death. Why should anyone insinuate his death was other than an accident, or appear to be privy to details unknown to his own family? The coroner for the City of Dublin Dr P.G. Bofin in his post-mortem held on 14th May 1971 made no such inference. Not a single journalist who rushed to judgment bothered to enquire about the faulty Luigi-Franchi shotgun that was the instrument of Shays death. He used the shotgun every time he went wildfowling. He was sentimentally attached to the

Luigi Franci shotgun having won it as a prize in the 1963 Tour of Spain cycle race.

The barrel of the 12-gauge shotgun had what is known as an improved cylinder choke. It was designed to disperse a wide spread of light shot ideally suited for clay pigeon shooting or the elusive snipe. In this case number 7 or number 8 cartridges are used, fairly light as loads go. Shay used the Luigi Franci almost exclusively for geese and mallard, game that require a heavier shot load. For this he used Magnum and number 3 cartridges. The higher powder charge affected the timing of the shotgun's bolt action and by the end of the 1967 hunting season the cartridge ejector was malfunctioning. I had occasion to use the Luigi-Franchi as did John Scahill and we both found it unsafe to use. Paul wouldn't touch it because of its lightness and faulty mechanism. On the one occasion I used it a cartridge jammed in the trigger housing. We advised Shay in no uncertain terms to either drop it in the Shannon or take it to a gunsmith. He was safety conscious to a fault but in this matter he couldn't see the inherent danger of the piece.

With the trigger mechanism thus affected, the most singularly lethal aspect of the shotgun was that when the safety catch was disengaged the firing pin would click forward if the gunstock was subjected to a sudden impact. That is to say the shotgun could discharge without the trigger being pulled.

During the week Shay lived in the apartment above the garage in Princes Street in Dublin, going home on weekends to Kilmacanogue. The garage had already been burglarized twice since it opened. It was Shay's habit to keep the loaded shotgun and a rifle by a window overlooking the back of the garage with the intention of scaring off intruders. His body was found under the back window of the wardrobe closet.

Eddy and I scrubbed the wardrobe clean after Shay's body was removed to the Morgue. We put his clothing into tea chests and disposed of them. The coroners report showed that death was caused by trauma to the liver and heart. The wound was consistent with Shay falling over the shotgun as it discharged. The faulty mechanism of the Luigi-Franchi shotgun was the cause of the death of Shay Elliott, not a self-inflicted wound.

Nell's last words to me were to the effect that Shay would never leave her like that. I hope there the matter will rest.

Nell passed away a year after the death of Paul on 3 July 1989. I was living and working in Boston when I got a last letter from her. She wrote mostly about Paul, how she missed cooking for him, looking after him, her isolation and sense of loss. I cannot help but think of Nell when I hear a refrain from one of Moore's melodies—the last rose of summer, all her lovely companions faded and gone. I think Nell willed herself to her final resting place. The words of Earnest Dowson come to mind;

> They are not long the days of wine and roses:
> Out of a misty dream our path emerges for a while
> Then closes within a dream.

THE END

UP AT THE PALACE

by

JOHN FLANAGAN

JIM DUNNE ALIGHTED FROM THE 45A bus at the terminus in Dunlaoghaire Co. Dublin. He adjusted the strap of the tool bag across his shoulder and tapped the top pocket of his jacket to make sure he had not forgotten his glass cutter. Jim was 56 years old, a glazier by trade. As he was already late he walked briskly towards the Sisters of Mercy convent on the Croften Road in Dun Laoghaire. Last minute holes had to be cut in window panes for the emplacement of ventilators in the convent's new wing. A simple enough job for him, he could finish early and book a couple of hours overtime. He pushed open the door of the building contractors office and prepared to say hello to Chris Cowan the foreman of the site. Chris was a good friend and had been for most of his life. They had much in common; they were the same age, followed Manchester United soccer club, played on a darts team and both were politically liberal. Jim entered the office with smile lighting up his face. He stopped abruptly when he saw Chris engaged in a hushed conversation with a young Priest, his face grim and tense. The Priest he was talking to was visibly nervous, his hand quivered as he made entries into a notebook. He looked around and closed the notebook when Jim entered the office. Chris stood up from the desk.

"Jim, give me a couple of minutes will you? I'll talk to you later . . ."

Jim left the office and walked along the seafront road. He wondered what caused Chris to be so upset and hoped it was nothing too serious. While he paced the seafront road he looked back and saw the Priest leaving the convent grounds. He retraced his steps and went back to the site office. Inside Chris motioned him to a chair while he went over and locked the office door. He sat back down at his desk, his face a mixture of anxiety and fear.

"Well Chris, are you alright, has someone died or what. What was that Priest doing here?"

"The Priest, do you know what he was doing . . . ?"

"Jasus Jim, I don't have a clue . . . , and why is there nobody working on the site, where's the crew?"

"I'll get to that . . . , the Priest that was here took my confession, he swore me to secrecy over something that happened in the convent early this morning . . . I still can't believe it . . ."

"What . . . ?"

"Jim you're my oldest friend. I can't keep this locked in . . . , I can't, I just can't . . ."

"Tell me, what happened Chris?"

Chris Cowan looked down at his clasped hands and slowly shook his head. He waited for a few moments and then stared at Jim.

"You've got to promise me Jim, this is just between you and me . . ."

"Chris, what the hell happened . . . ?"

Chris stood up and went to the architect's plans pinned to a board. He pointed with a pen to the convent wall.

"This is the new wing we've attached to the Nuns convent. It was almost complete. This morning we poured the last of the concrete over what we thought was a solid foundation in the kitchen. Well the floor was anything but solid. There was a hidden cellar below that was not shown on the original plans of the convent. Anyway, the floor collapsed from the weight of the cement. I got a ladder and a flashlight and climbed down into the cellar. That's when I found them . . ."

"Eh . . . ?"

"Fetuses . . . , dead babies fetuses in rotted black plaster bags. Eight of them, I'll never forget it as long as I live. I nearly got sick, I couldn't help it. After that I climbed back up the ladder and pulled it up after me. I told the carpenters to put up a barrier around the kitchen so no one else would see what was down there. I then sent for the Mother Superior."

He paused to catch his breath. He sat down as his hands began to involuntarily shake. Jim took out a packet of Woodbine cigarettes, handed one to Chris and took one himself. He struck a match and lit the cigarettes.

"The Mother Superior . . . , well, she's a brusque no-nonsense kind of Nun," he continued, "the first thing she did was send all of the men home except me. I wanted to call the police. She said I would do nothing of the kind, that I was to wait here in the office and someone would come to talk to me."

"Good God Almighty, dead babbies in bags?"

"Just as I said, there were eight of them, the tiny little bones all decomposed . . ."

"Real human babbies, how can that be . . . ? Naw, bags of rotten meat is what you saw, you said yourself it was under a kitchen . . ."

"They were wee babies Jim, I saw them with my own eyes . . ."

"Jeez, is that why the Priest was here?"

Chris nodded.

"When the Priest arrived I was surprised they sent someone so young, he's just about 25 years old, still wet behind the ears. I took him to the kitchen where the Mother Superior was waiting for us. After I fixed the ladder to go back down to the cellar I rigged up a strong lamp to see whatever else might be down there. The Mother Superior gave us dust masks to cover our mouth and nose. Then we put on plastic gloves. I went down first with the lamp and they followed me. By the time the Mother Superior and the Priest reached the end of the ladder I tied the lamp cage to a hook on the wall and turned on the light. The look on the face of the Mother Superior was resolute and unflinching as the bags burst open at the slightest touch and spilled the fetuses around her feet. The stench was putrid coming from the bags. Her steely eyes swept around the rest of the tiny cellar as she adjusted her face mask. I felt my stomach heaving and on the verge of getting sick but I managed to keep my mouth shut. The young Priest was not nearly so composed or calm as the Mother Superior when he saw the decomposed bodies. I thought he was going to faint. Strangled gasps of air came from him and his shoulders shook and finally he retched and vomited. I went to him to try to help but he was in a terrible state and he just waved me back. The Mother Superior ignored him as she took the lamp from the hook and continued searching every nook and cranny of the confined space. Finally she straightened up.

"'There's nothing more we need to know'" She said to me, "'another building contractor will be coming here to finish the work. Your employers will be informed. If Father Murray is up to it, he will counsel you before you leave the convent's property.' "With that she went up the ladder leaving the Priest heaving and vomiting in the cellar. After he cleaned himself up the Priest came here. He cautioned me not to say a word to a living soul. I was just thinking he had no right, no authority over me to caution me about anything. But I went along with him after what he went through getting sick in the cellar and all, and he really didn't seem a bad sort. Well Jim, I'm going home and I'll be glad to see the last of this place. First I'm going to Downey's Pub in Georges Street to have a pint and a hot whiskey. Why don't you join me?"

"Begod I will, no better man." Said Jim, readjusting his toolbag as he moved towards the door with his friend. "Who would have thought, innocent little babbies come to an end like that, who would have believed it?"

In the cold waiting room of the Catholic Archbishop's Palace in Drumcondra Dublin, Father Murray took a handkerchief from his pocket and on a wintry morning with temperatures down to near zero, he wiped the perspiration from his brow.

Father Tadgh Murray, aged 25 years was the second youngest of a family of six children. Since the beginning of their 30 year marriage his parents, Frank and Beatrice were famously weekly communicants and strict practitioners of the faith, in the local parish church of Saint Francis Xaviours in Gardiner Street, Dublin. Tadgh's father was a timorous self-effacing civil servant in Dublin Castle with just two promotions over the past 25 years. Frank Murray was at a difficult, unsettling stage of his life. He felt he was losing his way in coping with the exigencies of life to the extent he sometimes felt invisible to all around him. Of late the substance of his being appeared to wear away as if by attrition. It wasn't an overt or suddenly noticeable change

in his nature or character; it was a slow barely detectable
erosion of his self-awareness and identity, in the debilitating
daily monotony that was his life. He didn't know who he
was anymore. He felt he had lost touch with himself in the
rearing of six children, in his dour put-upon existence in the
Civil Service, in the ceaseless haranguing from his harpish
wife and the interminable prostrations at the altar rail to
receive Holy Communion; merely to save face. The ritual
of shaving every day assumed a relevance beyond its simple
execution. The few quiet moments before the mirror seemed
to reinforce the fact of his existence, it buoyed his flagging
spirits for a while, it made him feel less hollow. His son
Tadgh was the only one in the family who ever had time
for him, and he had lost him when he became a Priest; the
close caring bond between them vanished when his son gave
his life to God. Since his ordination, Tadgh had become
other-worldly, aloof almost. He knew Tadgh wanted to be a
classical pianist, he had taken to the piano since he was seven
years old. At 16 he was giving recitals at the Father Mathew
Hall where he was given rapturous ovations. He had been
pushed into the Priesthood by the obsessive colluding of
Frank's wife Beatrice. Having a quiet, almost shy disposition
in his early years he was too weak to confront his mother's
strong will. At his ordination her tears of joy filled Tadgh
with shame that he could have ever wanted to act contrary to
her wishes. All of Frank's other children were doing alright
for themselves but he found himself unable to care about
them. His eldest son Sean was coming up for promotion in
the Garda Siochana. Sean Murray's induction into the police
force was taken for granted. In school he had been a bully
since early childhood and being big and burly in his prime
his chosen career surprised no one. It was a blessing from
God, his wife Beatrice said, not many families were blessed

as they were. In the cloistered red-bricked terraced houses in the shadow of Saint Xaviours Beatrice immodestly flaunted her family's enviable status in the community. Having a Priest and a Garda Siochana in the same family was the dream of every devout Catholic mother in Ireland.

In the waiting room Father Murray was fidgeting uneasily with his handkerchief when a young novitiate came into the waiting room and politely informed him that the Archbishop would see him. Following the novitiate he heard a piano playing faintly which sounded clearer as he was shown into a spacious room.

"Father Murray, Your Grace." Said the novitiate. He retreated and closed the door behind him.

The window curtains were partially drawn in the large conservatory blocking out much of the daylight on a bright and chilly midwinter's day. It took some seconds for Father Murray's eyes to adjust to the muted lighting. A chandelier and several table lamps illuminated the darker recesses of the room that was richly decorated with brocaded leather armchairs, settees and walnut tables. Sitting at a piano His Grace the Archbishop Charles McQuaid, was playing a medley of Irish tunes. He was dressed in a long black alb, a red surplice and wore a pectoral cross. His grave taciturn expression relented for a moment when he looked up, smiled briefly and motioned Father Murray to an armchair. Father Murray immediately went to the Archbishop, kneeled down and kissed his ring and sat down. When he was seated he stared incredulously at what appeared to be a deformed young man dressed in a black soutane and a tasseled cap, attempting to dance to the Archbishop's playing. The features of his ruddy childlike face twisted with mood changes as he struggled to coordinate his erratic movements to the music.

"Father Murray" said the Archbishop, stopping playing, "come here would you?" Father Murray joined him at the piano. "this is Joseph . . ."

Father Murray extended a hand to Joseph who contemptuously brushed it aside. He ran to an armchair in a dark corner of the room and curled up on it. He face was twisted in a sneer as he looked back at the Priest.

"Father Murray, you'll have to excuse Joseph", said the Archbishop, "he's been through a lot of trauma in his young life. We are trying with God's help to rehabilitate him. Even with me he throws these tantrums. He's constantly casting aspersion on my Priests and staff . . ."

"Haaa . . ." Said Joseph in a raised rasping voice from the corner, "being privy to God exacts a pretty price my Lord . . ."

"Enough . . . , enough Joseph, I'm tired . . . , you try my patience . . ."

"My ire is not as yet half driven my Lord, wait, just you wait . . ." he lapsed back into a resentful silence

The Archbishop turned to Father Murray.

"You see what I have to put up with Father. At any rate be patient with him. Please stay with him for a little while, I have to go now and say my office. When I come back I want to talk to you about your visit to the convent in Dun Laoghaire among other things. I have a mission for you regarding the media pressure our Church is facing at the moment; you could be of great service to me."

"It would be an honour to help in any way Your Grace . . ."

"We'll talk later . . . , in the meantime please play for Joseph. Something more soothing than the ditties I play, a piece by Mozart perhaps, yes, that should calm his feverish mood."

There was a knock on the door.

"Yes, come in." Said the Archbishop.

The young novitiate entered.

"Your Grace, Archbishop Aldo Zanini has arrived from the airport. I've shown him to the guest room. He said he'd like to rest for a few hours and join you for supper if that's alright"

"That will be fine. Thank you."

The novitiate bowed his head and withdrew.

The misshapen dancing youth was Joseph Carboy. Joseph was 15 years old, one of 395 children placed under arrest by the Garda Siochana and incarcerated in the Artane work camp for no other reason but that he bore the unforgivable Irish social stigma of being a homeless orphan. Joseph's family had abandoned him: his mother had absconded to Liverpool with a boyfriend, his father was eking out his final days in a half-way house afflicted with pneumonia and substance abuse.

When Joseph was 16 years old he took up residence in the Archbishop's palace in the Dublin suburb of Drumcondra. Many eyebrows were raised within the Archbishop's immediate circle. His critics, who were legion, both religious and secular, struggled to divine the ulterior motive that must reside in the puzzling action of the scholarly Archbishop. The mentoring of Joseph, was in fact a consequence of a traumatic spiritual crisis in the life of Archbishop McQuaid. Lately he felt elements in the foreign media had begun to expose the running of children's internment camps, operated by the catholic church and the Irish State. This latest maelstrom of public hostility towards the church caused him the most anxiety since his election to office. Traditionally he could count on the Irish media, especially the Irish Press newspaper with its De Valera connections, to keep all sordid details out of the purview of the general public. Since the children's prison camps were first established by the church, few newspaper reporters had pierced the church's veil of secrecy protecting the issues of clerical child abuse and forced labor in the camps; and now in the term of his Archbishopric, it seemed as if overnight the clandestine operations were in the public domain. He had prayed fervently for answers, answers that would solve problems and preserve the integrity of Holy Mother the Church. He still recoiled from slights hurled at him a decade before. He felt an enduring shame in not being nominated for a Cardinal's hat in 1953, a wound that still festered; he was convinced beyond all doubt it was because of Pope Pius X11's innate dislike of him. Of late the Archbishop felt his inept handling of the work camps and in particular Artane, had incurred God's wrath. He wanted to atone, to make amends for the cruelties and molestations inflicted by his Priests, the Christian Brothers and Nuns on children in the camps. It would be through Joseph, he decided, that he would make amends to God for his mistakes and errors of judgment in office. God would understand that showing concern for Joseph marked the beginning of a personal spiritual odyssey for the Archbishop, a fervent cry to invoke God's mercy by nurturing and caring for the malformed child Joseph had become, because of the sadistic cruelty of one Brother Stanislaus,

As Archbishop McQuaid left the room the soft, haunting, elegiac tones of Mozart's piano concerto No. 21 for keyboard was played in andante by Father Murray. The strains of the music followed him to his private oratory where he kneeled and prayed. After an hour he pushed himself up wearily from the prie-dieu, sighed and paused to look at his reflection in a mirror. As he peered closer the pink fleshy pouches sagging beneath his tired eyes seemed to expose the very essence of what he had become; he was spent, worn out, a shell of his former self. An inner awareness, a light that had carried him through his formative years had died. He was bereft of the ambulatory veneers behind which he once sheltered, from whence he could metamorphose into varying facets of his self that the moment required; he had lost his verbal dexterity to navigate through the labyrinthine subterfuge and guile of his adversaries. His shoulders slumped. Before God he wanted to atone, to make amends for the cruelties inflicted on helpless children in the camps.

He put out the light in the oratory and crossed the corridor to his private study where he picked up a manila folder. He then retraced his steps to re-join Father Murray and the irascible Joseph.

When the Archbishop left Joseph and Father Murray alone in the conservatory the young Priest continued playing Mozart. Joseph's eyes were clamped shut with his hands pressed against his ears as he curled up on the armchair. As the music surged his eyes opened slowly and blinked, his hands fell from his face. A light came into his eyes and face while easing away his unrelenting grimacing sneer. He was breathing deeply as he succumbed to the final diminuendo of the piece. Father Murray heard him and anxiously turned around. He stopped playing immediately. Joseph excitedly waved a hand towards him.

"No, no," said Joseph as he sat on the edge of the armchair, "don't stop. Play, Priest, play."

Father Murray looked at Joseph for some moments. He turned around and brought the music to a finish.

Joseph had become quietly introspective. He left the armchair and joined Father Murray at the piano. He stared at the Priest for a few moments. Gradually the belligerent posture endemic to his nature reasserted itself.

"How long have you been a Priest?"

"About two years now . . ."

"I would never have thought a Priest could play Mozart like that . . ."

"You think little of the clergy Joseph . . . ? I'm sorry if life has not been too pleasant for you . . ."

"Don't patronize me Priest. You are here about the convent are you not . . . ?

"I'm here to see His Grace . . ."

"My Lord discusses everything with me. T'would suit your purpose to curry favor with me."

"I'm sorry Joseph, I don't wish to talk to you about the convent. Or to curry favor with you for that matter . . ."

"T'is a pity Priest, you would learn a lot. For instance, that paragon of feminine virtue the Mother Superior from the convent was here to apprise my Lord of bags of newborn cadavers found in the convent in Dun Laoghaire . . ."

"What . . . , His Grace has discussed that with you . . . ?"

"And more besides. He's sending you to the Artane work camp, that's why he wants to see you . . ."

"What . . . ? I know nothing of this."

"Why do you suppose it matters what you know or don't know. You'll go on doing what you are told, won't you Priest?"

"What right have you to address me in such a manner?"

"What right? Oh I have every right. I talk to my Lord as I please, why should I not amuse myself with one of his minions . . . ?"

"You may say what you want to His Grace, I've no intention of sitting here and being spoken to like this . . ." He stood up.

"Ho ho, what have we here, a Priest with spunk? I never would have believed it."

Father Murray came closer to Joseph and looked down at him as he prepared to leave.

"Please tell His Grace I'll be in the waiting room when he wishes to see me . . ."

"Oh sit down Priest" Joseph snapped in a loud voice. "Sit down or I'll have you sent to the missions . . . ,"

"I have a good mind to report your insolence to His Grace"

"I'll tell him myself if you don't. Let me explain something to you Priest, I am the sole object of My Lord's obsessive desire to have greater communion with God. I am his conduit, his means to consummate the harmony he seeks with God. So he indulges me beyond measure. I mock him when he prays, I insult him and his friends, not that he has many. I shout at and scare his students. All the while he shows deference and kindness to me even as I snarl at him and hate him."

The shocked Father Murray moved slowly back to his chair and sat down. He seems slightly dazed.

"You hate him," Said Father Murray. "you hate His Grace the Archbishop?"

"With every fiber of my withered being . . ."

"But why, I don't understand . . . ?"

"Because he's a Priest . . . ," shouted Joseph.

Silence pervaded the room as they stared at each other, each absorbed with their own thoughts. After a few moments Joseph stood up and walked about the room snickering and laughing dementedly.

"Riddle me this Priest. In the most remote krall in darkest Africa witch doctors rattle small bones, fling them to the ground and deduce solemn portent from their configurations. We Christians are more civilized. We extol worshippers to drink the blood and eat the flesh of Christ by proxy, thus making cannibals of us all. T'is enough to make a horse laugh don't you think?"

Father Murray couldn't prevent himself from smiling.

"I don't think it's meant to be taken quite so literally . . ."

Joseph raised a hand and pointed a thumb to his back.

"Not a pretty picture, am I Priest?"

Father Murray shook his head in a state of bewilderment.

"I . . . ," stammered Father Murray.

"I wasn't always like this." Continued Joseph. "I was a normal child, before my father became a dipsomaniac, before my mother . . . , well, she went away with someone. The Gardai Siochana came and arrested me. Took me to Artane work camp where the clergy locked me up and threw away the key."

"You were in Artane?" asked Father Murray.

"For two years until I was almost 16 years old. That's where I got this . . ." He pointed again to his back. "I was in good physical health when I arrived at the work camp. The group I was sent to was under the control of a psychopath, a Christian Brother, now there's an oxymoron if you're ever looking for one, anyway his name was Brother Stanislaus. The group I was with made and repaired hob-nail boots and shoes. My job was to nail studs into the leather soles until I learned to cut the leather. We numbered six in my group. Brother Stanislaus hovered around the work bench slapping his three-foot bamboo cane against his leg. Bloodstains smeared the uniform shirts of many of the children where the cane had cut into their backs. Everyone had been hit regularly with the cane and my own time was not long in coming. I was doing a bad job of aligning the studs on the boot soles. I was bent over a last one day when Brother Stanislaus struck me with the cane. That was the beginning of my nightmares."

"But didn't anyone report what Brother Stanislaus was doing?"

"Yes, some did and I was one among them. When I went to the Sisters of Mercy offices Sister Teresa put a bandage on my back and then she boxed my ears when I told her what Brother Stanislaus had done. She told me not to tell anyone else. The next day I was at the work bench, just myself and two other children. Brother Stanislaus burst into the room in a rage because I had reported him. The two other children huddled together frightened out of their wits. He told them to get out and bolted the door from the inside. Brother Stanislaus chased me around the work bench. I was terrified but I was a robust child, quick on my feet and stayed out of the range of his swishing cane. The iron shoe lasts on the work bench protruded up from the bench so I was able to grip them as I ran around the bench eluding Brother Stanislaus. He was gasping for air, seething, spittle formed on his lips. He paused and looked down at me cringing at the other side of the bench. He threw away the bamboo cane, bent down, gripped the heavy work bench and heaved it over on to me. When I fell a last caught me on my back and broke three vertebrae in my spine. I passed out and when I recovered consciousness I was in a hospital. Because of my weakened immune system I contracted scarlet fever and tuberculosis; Kyphosis gradually deformed the curvature of my spine to the extent that when I was returned to the camp Brother Stanislaus smiled at me and called me a hunchback. Soon afterwards My Lord the Archbishop was visiting the camp and brought me here to the palace. His physician attended to me and took me to the Mater hospital. It was a slow process as I was in intensive care and needed surgery. Gradually I was restored to general good health except I was left with this hump on my back and I was brought here to the palace. After that My Lord put me on an intensive program of private tuition. I had four different tutors. It seemed my broken body hid an alert mind that had never been challenged. I was able to assimilate lessons in history, mathematics, music and literature."

"I'm not being patronizing when I say I'm truly sorry for the agony you must have suffered. But, if you'll pardon my asking, why do I not see much appreciation in your attitude to His Grace?"

"I am merely his penance for his sins of omission while he protects the sadistic Priests and Christian Brothers in the work camps."

"Now wait just a minute Joseph, you go too far . . ."

"Too far is it, are you saying you really don't know what the Catholic clergy do in the work camps, the mental and physical cruelties they inflict on children?" Joseph yelled loudly, derisively at Father Murray. "It's only in deference to your naivety and innocence that curbs the full extent of my wrath. Too far . . . , haa . . . Here's something for you to contemplate. His Eminence, His Grace, His Lordship knows about the abuses and torture, the beatings in Artane. He condones it all by the fact of his silence. My Lord lost the plot long ago."

"I don't believe that for one moment . . ." Said Father Murray.

"Do you think I am interested in what you believe Priest," Said Joseph, "you are one of them. But you will see for yourself when my Lord assigns you to Artane. You will meet Brother Stanislaus and other Brothers and Priests on their nocturnal sorties to the children's dormitories and hear the beatings and screams in the night. When you get to Artane Priest look deep into the children's eyes and you will smell the fear; the sense of hopelessness and abandonment, if you have eyes to see and ears to hear. Then you will return here most likely and add your voice to My Lords in a chorus of denial about your findings in Artane. Alas we must not tarry, I hear footsteps; my Lord comes . . . , farewell Priest."

Joseph turned and exited through a rear door seconds before Archbishop McQuaid entered the room.

"Hmm . . ." Said the Archbishop, closing the door behind him. "Joseph has left us I see . . ."

"Yes Your Grace, he just left . . ." Father Murray still felt shaken after speaking with Joseph.

"It's just as well, I would like to speak with you. Please sit down."

The Archbishop and Father Murray sat down facing each other.

"First off, well . . . , I'm sure I don't have to caution you in the matter of the convent, upmost discretion must be observed at all times. It's crucial to keep what you have seen and heard highly confidential. Can I count on you for that?"

"Absolutely Your Grace. I do have a concern . . ."

"Which is . . . ?

"The foreman of the building site at the convent, he is the one who made the find of the, eh . . . , remains. He was very distressed of course. He is a quiet family man, a steady type. Well Your Grace, I'm concerned he might indulge in loose talk or go to the police . . . , or the newspapers . . . , before we can clarify what it all means."

"You need have no concerns on that front Father Murray, the Garda Siochana have always been a staunch and dependable ally of the church. And as for the Irish newspapers, leave them to me; it's the foreign press that concerns me the most. You need not concern yourself any further about that matter in the convent. Reverend Mother Imelda knows what has to be done. She will take care of it." The Archbishop opened up the manila folder he brought with him. He leafed through typewritten pages for some minutes.

"Father Murray . . . , I have received very good reports of you since your ordination. It seems you have impressed your teachers. An honours degree in English literature," he said, flipping over the pages. "honours in classical music, an interest in archeology, thesis on Thomist realism, . . ." the Archbishop slowly closed the manila folder. "The church is fortunate to have such a luminary in its ranks . . ."

"It's kind of you to say so Your Grace."

The Archbishop replaced the pages in the folder and set it aside. He sat back in the armchair and clasped his hands together with his two index fingers joined under his chin.

"Father Murray, you must be aware of the severe pressure the media and many prominent writers are putting on our Holy Mother the Church. As we speak our enemies are mounting offences against the Kingdom of Christ. We have to show strength and resolve now more than at any time in our long and illustrious history. The fight will be long and arduous but we will prevail for God is on our side, Gloria in excelsius Deo. I asked you once before Father Murray, if you will join us in this endeavor to defend the church."

"Yes your Grace."

"What I would like you to do is go to our industrial school in Artane. Spend a few days there, size up the situation and report back to me. I will have my secretary draw up a letter for you. You will be acting in my stead; no one will question your authority. Tell no one of the purpose of your visit. Contact only me if you have any problems whatsoever. Do you have any questions for me now?

"No Your Excellency."

"Good, well if there is nothing else . . ."

Father Murray rose from his armchair. He went quickly to the Archbishop, kneeled down before him and kissed his ring. He left the room and made his way to the parking lot where he got into his car. He drove out of the palace grounds and linked up with the busy traffic on Drumcondra Road.

Later that evening Aldo Zanini the Archbishop of Detroit strolled leisurely into the empty private quarters and dining room in the West Wing of the palace and waited for the arrival of his friend Archbishop McQuaid. He had changed into clerical attire in deference to Archbishop McQuaid whom he knew to be a stickler for formality; he would have preferred to wear his more casual slacks and a white open-necked shirt. He could hear the busy movements of the staff in the nearby kitchen. The polished walnut dining table was very tastefully laid out with Celtic linen tablecloths and napkins, antique silverware, Belleek china and Waterford cut wineglasses. A log fire burned brightly. Moving to a drinks ladened sideboard the Detroit Archbishop peered intently at labels on wine bottles. Holding a bottle up to the light he nodded his head slightly in silent assent of what he saw. He smiled suddenly and muttered to himself,

"Charlie likes to live it up."

As he waited in the dining room for his host his eyes came to rest on a door. There was something odd about the door; on his last visit it had been an ordinary wood paneled door. Curiosity got the better of him. He went to the door to find it was made of solid steel. Intrigued yet cognizant of his status as a guest he looked about him quickly and tried the handle. The door was locked tight. He was immediately beset by qualms of conscience and wondered how it would look if he saw caught in such a compromising act. He moved quickly away from the door.

He felt very much at home in Dublin, he liked to visit Ireland having made many visits in the past few years. He wished his present visit could be more congenial but . . . , he shrugged his shoulders, he would be facing that ordeal soon enough. The Detroit Archbishop was the only person with whom the austere Archbishop McQuaid had formed any degree of friendship. They were student clerics together since the early days of their vocational training. Of Italian descent, the Detroit Archbishop had returned to the Vatican after his ordination. He wielded great influence in the Vatican court being a distant relative of Eugenio Pacelli, the present Pope Pius X11. It was in this privileged social circle that he learned that the Pope harbored a great dislike for the Dublin Archbishop. Upon being nominated as Detroit Archbishop Aldo Zanini kept in touch with Archbishop McQuaid and visited him whenever time and opportunity allowed. The odd circumstances that led to this visit caused him some discomfort but it was not something over which he had control. Unbeknownst to Archbishop McQuaid he had come to Dublin at the behest of Pope Pius X11 who had selected him as his emissary to deliver an urgent personal message to the Dublin Archbishop.

Aldo Zanini was an amiable, boisterous giant of a man. He was 6ft. 3in. tall, weighed 230 pounds, and was of substantial girth. His voice was a natural and melodious basso profundo. Not a single controversial incident has ever sullied his exemplary record. At age 56 years the Archbishop has managed to step-toe through the minefield of litigations and lawsuits against his Detroit archdiocese. Victims of molestation by his clergy were awarded millions of dollars and drained his coffers almost dry. The Archbishop had little to concern himself with personally apart from the financial burden placed on his church. Throughout the media frenzy Aldo Zanini acquitted himself of his duties in the manner he had conducted himself all of his adult life; equitably and honourably. He had counseled his errant clergy; he had listened to their litany of vile and sickening confessions of abuse of small children. The offending Priests, Brothers and Nuns in time stopped confessing to him when it became known that the Archbishop began reporting their hideous crimes to the civil authorities in Detroit. His parishioners continued to love and respect the extrovert bishop who punctuated his sermons with levity and humor. Among close friends he was not remiss in peppering his conversations with execrations that were cheerfully attributed to his eccentricity of manner.

A faint knock on the door made him turn around quickly. Archbishop McQuaid came in and they approached each other with extended arms like the old close friends they had become. Aldo Zanini as always was the most effusive in their greeting, hugging and patting the more physically timid McQuaid. McQuaid however, Zanini sensed, was not as jubilant as he had been to see him on previous visits. They sat down on two armchairs.

"Well Charlie," Said Aldo Zanini, "I'm sorry to say my visit this time will be very short, I'm taking a flight to Rome tomorrow morning. I was hoping to have enough time to see a bit more of beautiful Wicklow. Well, maybe next time around . . ."

"That's a pity," said McQuaid, "but as you say, next time. How long has it been since your last visit?"

"Oh, 1½ years or there about."

"There have been some sea changes in Ireland since your last visit . . ."

"I've already noticed. I arrived from Detroit just this morning. Starting with the airport and all the way into town I didn't see a single solitary priest or Christian Brother along the way, not one. I remember how it used to be, the clergy at one time proliferated the island of saints and scholars. They seem to have just vanished. The streets of Dublin seem oddly deserted without them."

JOHN FLANAGAN

"Perhaps," said McQuaid, "it's the price the church must pay now for the recent indiscretions of a few of our errant priests . . ."

"Well I'm sure it's a lot more serious than that. But tell me Charlie, how are you holding up, how you have been . . ."

"Well, oh you know how it is; these times are not easy for the best of us. You've had a long flight, did you manage to get some rest . . . ?"

"I did . . . , thank you Charlie."

"Is it too soon to eat . . . ?"

"No, not at all, I feel a bit famished"

"Good, I'll let them know . . ."

Archbishop McQuaid went to the wall and tugged on a bell-rope. After a few moments a liveried waiter came in from the kitchen.

"We'll eat now Thomas," said McQuaid.

The waiter bowed and went to the sideboard. He put two wineglasses and a bottle of vintage wine onto a salver, filled the wineglasses and handed them to the Archbishops. They sat at each end of the polished walnut table and were waited on by Thomas. The two Archbishops ate the entrée in silence, a silence which after some minutes assumed an obtrusiveness that detracted from the usual convivial banter of the two prelates. By the time the main course of the meal and dessert was ended a sense of inescapable gloom had curled into every cornice and crevice of the room and hung like a contagion over the lonely diners.

"Why do I have a sense of foreboding about your visit Aldo?" Said McQuaid.

The Detroit Archbishop looked evenly at his friend with a disturbed frown.

"You guessed right Charlie, I'm not the bearer of good news."

"Part of me was hoping His Holiness was reconsidering his offer of the Cardinals hat."

"No, nothing like that . . . ,"

"If you've finished your meal why don't we take our drinks and sit down over there." The two Archbishops stood up, moved to the armchairs and sat down. "So Aldo, let's not stand on ceremony, we have never done that. You've always been open and honest with me, tell me what's going on . . ."

"Charlie, you've made some bad decisions regarding those Irish work camps for kids, it's . . . , well it's downright bizarre. It wouldn't happen in any other country in Europe, it certainly couldn't happen in the USA, kids arrested because they are orphans or whatnot, interned and used for slave labour. The Vatican is not pleased. And this molesting of children by the clergy has redounded on His Holiness Pope Pius."

"I'm handling the crisis to the best of my ability." Said McQuaid. "My foremost concern is to preserve the prestige of our Holy Mother the Church in getting through this . . ."

"These are historic times we are living in," said Zanini. "here I am euphemistically titled a prince and defender of the church and I can tell you without fear of contradiction our 2000 year old edifice to the glory of God is in jeopardy of turning into a house of cards. The church in Ireland, the most precious jewel in the Vatican's crown is tumbling down around our ears because of Irish pedophile Priests and Christian Brothers here and in the US. You know I'm here as a locum tenens on behalf of His Holiness the Pope, but I'm also here as a friend. I feel I can help you if you'll level with me . . ."

"Aldo I'm at a loss to understand the crimes my clergy are alleged to have . . ."

"Alleged . . . ? We're getting off on the wrong foot here Charlie. There's nothing alleged about what's going on in your work camps in Ireland . . . , it's in newspapers all across the civilized world. There are copies of lawsuits piling up daily on a desk in the Vatican to prove it. Do you want me to draw you a picture where you've gone wrong, what you've allowed to happen; why the Holy Father is so incensed with this mess that you allow to go on unchecked?"

McQuaid seemed stunned by the Detroit Archbishop's heated words. His put his wineglass down slowly and stared into the crackling fire. He spread his hands and then joined them together in a sense of desperation.

"I tried to alleviate the suffering of the children . . ."

"Like hell you did . . . , you know what's going on better than anyone. Not a single incident was reported to the police . . ."

The Detroit Archbishop suddenly got up from the armchair and paced about the room. He went over to the fireplace and stood with his back to the blazing fire. His face became crimson as he fought to control the agitation rising within him.

"Charlie, there's a few things we have to sort out before I get back to the Vatican starting with that Artane work camp. As I said before I want . . . , no, I demand you be forthright with me otherwise you're on your own. The Vatican is very well informed about what is going on in Ireland. You see at the behest of His Holiness, an Irish Priest, a former staff member of yours has been keeping the Vatican informed of your every move."

"Are you telling me you've planted an informer here . . . ," asked McQuaid, "one of my own priests?"

"Because we had to, because we couldn't get a straight answer out of you. Ok, tell me your thoughts, your reasoning behind sending a priest and a Christian Brother who abused young kids just two weeks ago, to remote parishes in the west of Ireland? You sent no warning to the parish priests about the obscene crimes they committed so they are free again to begin preying again on unsuspecting children."

Zanini stopped talking and slowly shook his head. He grimaced as he walked towards McQuaid who seemed to shrink in his seat as the Detroit Archbishop towered over him. McQuaid made an effort to straighten up in the seat and effect a defiance.

"Have you any idea," said McQuaid, "what the enemies of the church would do with that, if we turned our clergy over to the civil authorities? I made decisions that were in the best interest of the church even if I made mistakes, can't you understand that . . . ?"

"The fiends who molested those children should not be a given a free pass or handled with kid gloves, which is what you've been doing."

"Everything possible is being done," Said McQuaid, "I've thrown the whole weight of my office behind this urgent matter; I will resolve it I promise you . . ."

"I have to tell you Charlie, His Holiness the Pope is looking at a short list of successors to your office."

"You cannot let that happen Aldo, I've given my life to God and the church . . . , please, there's so much yet to do. Just tell me where I should start."

Aldo Zanini spread his arms wide in exasperation.

"I'll give you my recommendation; the rest is up to you . . . The Catholic Church is disgraced in the eyes of the world because of the Irish work camps, concentration camps some wags in the Vatican call them. In those camps you put young kids who never broke any law. First of all I want you to draw up new rules and regulations, a code of conduct for your clergy. From this moment on if it's proven beyond doubt that any of your Priests or Christian Brothers again molests a child they will be de-frocked and sent packing. And that's not the end of it, they will be reported to the civil authorities, prosecuted and tried and hopefully locked away in cages where they belong. Even that would not be sufficient punishment for any man who abuses children. Am I getting through to you Charlie?"

"But that's . . . , can't we council our clergy, show them the error of their ways. With help, professional help . . ."

"They are ogres . . ."

"It's easy for you to point a finger. You said you'd help me find a solution, all I'm getting from you is endless criticism."

"I'm not criticizing you Charlie, I'm accusing you on behalf of His Holiness of gross negligence. I know for a fact you used your influence with the Irish Department of Justice and the Garda Siochana to help your clergy avoid prosecution."

"You've no idea what it's like here . . . , I honestly tried to contain that type of aggression in the camp and I've been giving it my undivided attention of late."

"Listening to you Charlie I don't know whether to laugh or cry. Try to see yourself through the eyes of His Holiness the Pope. Every civilized country is focused on Dublin since the world media began reporting of assaults of children by your Irish clergy. Now the media are looking into the functioning and legality of the work camps. I want to talk about the work camps. You've been selling the produce of the labour of children aged 10 to 16 years old in workhouses where they made boots and shoes, they made bread and pastries in bakeries, they farmed the land and you never paid them one penny. The kids in your camps are in virtual rags, the food is substandard, there is no recourse to medical help after being abused, beaten and whipped by your Priests and Christian Brothers. I don't think it's overstating it to say you personally are running a slave labour camp in Ireland. You were a co-signer with Eamon De Valera of the Irish Constitution. You are the most feared and influential cleric in the whole of Ireland Charlie, politicians vie with each other to do you favors, so don't tell me you are only marginally involved in the running of these work camps"

Archbishop McQuaid looked abstractedly at the neatly manicured nails of his long pointed fingers. He realized, being interrogated by Pope Pius X11's locum tenens left little room to manipulate their friendship to his benefit. He was visibly cowed by the verbal assault of the Detroit Archbishop.

"Aldo . . . ," He said, shifting in his chair, "I admit I made mistakes, I delegated responsibility to the wrong people. They let me down . . ."

"I'm not going to let you sidetrack me on these important issues . . . , that slave labor camp is a stain on the fair face of the church. You've got to clear that up, that's not negotiable. I want to move on to something else; the sacrament of confession, or the misuse of it . . ."

"The confessional . . . , am I hearing you right. What are you talking about?"

"That practice of pederast Priests and Brothers who confess to each other has got to stop. It's farcical beyond belief; an obscene sacrilege against the holy ritual of the Confessional where God's love and mercy is invoked to expunge the soul from sin. Think of it. A few Hail Marys or Our Fathers for penance and an abusive Priest obtains a state of grace. Confessor and penitent exchange seats in the Confessional in a sort of macabre musical chairs and proceed to exonerate the foul crimes of each other. They are free to molest in perpetuity with a clear conscience."

"Can I say something, or do you prefer I just sit here and listen . . . ?"

"Go ahead Charlie, if you've anything positive to say I'd appreciate it . . ."

"Let's be reasonable about this." Said McQuaid. "I know there is room for improvement but the fact is the camps are viable business concerns and generate equitable returns. Profits go back into the coffers of the church, I would have thought that should be taken into consideration."

By the grim expression lighting on Aldo Zanini's face the Dublin Archbishop immediately regretted his choice of words and thought to qualify them. He decided that silence would serve him better.

"I'm glad you brought that up," Said Aldo Zanini, "I'm curious about how much profit the work camps earned . . . , say last year. I mean in total for the, what is it, about 40 children's work camps throughout Ireland? The reason I ask you is there's no record of any transfer from the Dublin diocese to the Vatican exchequer. You have always given me the impression you are strapped for cash, on the verge of bankruptcy . . ."

"Aldo my office staff is overburdened having to cope with lawsuits and . . ."

"That's because of your clergy assaulting children, right . . . ?"

"I have had to close some churches, others are in a state of disrepair and need refurbishing. I've been at my wits end trying to cope with demands on my meager resources." Archbishop McQuaid attempted to show a confident pose while sitting. With a hand visibly shaking he took a sip of wine and smiled diffidently at the Detroit Archbishop. "But with the income from the work camps to help us we try not to cry poverty within earshot of the Vatican, I don't want the Holy Father to be burdened with my concerns . . ."

"Let me see if I've got this straight Charlie. You're prepared to keep the work camps open, the attacks on kids and lawsuits notwithstanding as long as you end up with a profit?"

"Well I wouldn't put it that way . . ."

"I'm quite sure you would not."

"All I want is what is in the long term interest of Our Holy Mother the Church. And as for my clergy? His Holiness the Pope can rest assured I'll get the best psychiatrists available to counsel them, to take care of them."

"Would any of those psychiatrists be available to counsel the victims of your pederast Priests . . . ?" When the Dublin Archbishop elected not to respond, Aldo Zanini solemnly shook his head. "Charlie, this is the end of the road for you and me, I'm losing respect and regard for you even as we speak. I'll try to be a gentleman and figure it's all just been too much for you. I've known you most of my life Charlie and I just don't know what happened to you. There was compassion, kindness in your nature back then, when we were young Priests. Back then you would not have sanctioned what's happening in the work camps, or cover up for your sadistic clergy. You are an Archbishop, a disciple of God and you know what? There doesn't appear to be an ounce of human kindness left in you anymore. You had it in spades when we were students in the seminary. Do you remember those days Charlie? You had fire in your belly. You wanted to go to the missions, to the Third World and help the impoverished and the hungry. Look at you now, you let your clergy inflict psychological wounds in a child that never heals . . . , never ever heals, how does a child cope with that . . . , you really don't give a damn, do you Charlie ?"

The wan smile vanished from the face of Archbishop McQuaid. He looked at Aldo Zanini with some concern. He stood up suddenly, incensed, upset.

"Now see here, I will not tolerate swearwords in the house of God . . ."

Aldo Zanini looked steadily at McQuaid. A smile gradually spread across his wide face. He started to laugh out loud as McQuaid sat back down staring incredulously at the Detroit Archbishop.

"You know, we've been talking about some serious issues tonight Charlie. You've been pretty calm and composed about it all. And the only thing that gets your dander up, that gets a rise out of you is my foul language. Why don't you turn that sense of outrage on the work camps and stop crucifying those kids. That's what sickens me the most. You don't see them as precious human beings any more than your clergy does, for you they're just a number in one of your administrative folders. You're a cold fish Charlie, everything about your character and personality mitigates against the loving message of Christ. We are after all what defines us Charlie. You are a Catholic Archbishop but that is not what really defines you, in the greater understanding of our lives. In the well-spring of your life you are a camp Commandant of children's concentration camps; that is the sum total of who and what you are. Now why not put a sign over the gate in Artane that reads Arbeit Macht Frei, get yourself a topcoat and boots and a braided hat with a swastika?"

"I don't see the point of this conversation going any further. I made a mistake asking for your help." Said the Dublin Archbishop.

"Aw forgive me for blowing off a little steam, I never did learn to keep a lid on this temper of mine."

"All I want personally is to please the Holy Father and serve the church . . ."

"I will express your sentiments to His Holiness . . ." The Detroit Archbishop looked at his watch. "I'll prepare to retire; I have an early flight to Rome in the morning. There are just a couple of final points I'd like to clear up with you. You say you want to please the Holy Father which I'm very glad to hear. But don't you think, just between the two of us something pleasing, a gift say, should be offered to him?"

Archbishop McQuaid's eyes flitted uneasily for a moment as he bent down to retrieve his wine glass. He sipped the wine and tried unsuccessfully to smile at Aldo Zanini.

"I'm not sure I understand you, in what way . . . ?"

"Oh, say a gift as a token of your good will. You did say the work camps were showing a profit, didn't you Charlie?"

McQuaid's fingers tightened around the wine glass causing it to shake slightly. He replaced the glass on the table and fought to regain his equilibrium. He inhaled forcefully as he faced Zanini.

"Wh . . . , what, had you in mind, I . . . ,"

"We'll get to that. Before I leave I want to help you achieve peace of mind both with His Holiness the Pope and Our Sacred Father in Heaven, you would wish that, wouldn't you Charlie . . ."

A sense of uneasiness mixed with dread and foreboding took hold of the Dublin Archbishop

"Oh, of course, of course . . . , please tell me how I can achieve that blessed state . . ."

"I used harsh words with you earlier; I do apologize for that. I'm just genuinely concerned about your whole approach to the immense problems you face. I believe there is a solution to the work camps crisis, for that is what you have Charlie, a crisis, and it affects the Vatican. I am asking you to garner all your inner reserves of courage and bring this crisis to a positive conclusion."

Archbishop McQuaid now felt a sense of impending doom. He knew the Detroit Archbishop well enough to know he would be forced into an ultimatum of sorts that would cost him dearly.

"Charlie," Aldo Zanini continued, "I'm sorry to have to tell you but unless you clean up your act here within two weeks His Holiness will ask you to resign."

"It can't come to that, it can't, I just need a little more time . . ."

"Do you want to be loved and respected again? Well then pay your debts to God and to the children in your camps. Recover the innate goodness you had in you when you were young. You just went astray there for a while. You've been balancing on a razor's edge between darkness and light, succumbing to the wiles of Mammon, loving money."

Aldo Zanini moved towards the steel plated door he had been looking at earlier. He turned to face McQuaid.

"Charlie, tell me it's none of my business but I have to ask, what in the world is locked behind that steel door?"

When McQuaid involuntarily flinched, the perceptive Zanini smiled and looked at the door again.

"Charlie, indulge an old friend. My imagination is running wild . . ." He spoke in a jovial, humorous vein in language subtly phrased to obfuscate his true intent; he was determined to see what lay on the other side of the steel door.

Slowly, reluctantly McQuaid reached into the pocket of his cassock and took out a set of keys. His hand shook as he turned the key in the lock and pushed open the heavy door. He went in and Zanini followed him. The room was in darkness. McQuaid reached to his left and turned on a panel of light switches.

As has been ascertained for the reader, Archbishop Aldo Zanini was a man of stalwart character. He was large and impressive, also tough and resourceful. There had not been many times in his eventful life that caused him to be overawed, startled or overly surprised about anything.

As the room flooded with light Aldo Zanini was so stunned by what he saw it took him some time to recover. At first glance the mahogany paneled room appeared to be a small museum. Treasures and artifacts of every conceivable size and shape adorned walls and display tables. A log fire in a huge hearth spurted into life and was soon casting dancing shadows on the walls and ceiling. Going in front of McQuaid, Zanini walked boldly to the center of the room. In cabinets and display cases he saw glittering emeralds and diamonds. He stood before a wall on which hung two original oil portraits by Degas and Constable. Close to them the fans of two humidifiers whirred gently and occasionally released jets of moisture onto the portraits. He stared in awe around him, musing over several objets d'art exhibited in glass-fronted showcases. Solid gold Celtic pendants and crosses were displayed. He took out and examined closely a gold, jewel encrusted carved dagger. Beside it hung a lethal looking Arabian scimitar made of polished silver. He went to the mantelpiece and took down a French 18th century marble clock set in gold thread. He examined it at length and replaced it back gently on the mantelpiece. Beside it were antique Chinese jade figurines intricately woven with gold and silver filigree. Blue and white Ming dynasty porcelain vases adorned cabinets alongside ancient Egyptian papyrus scrolls. Priceless first editions of 17th century manuscripts were displayed with collections of rare gold coins. With an effort the Detroit archbishop dragged himself away from the treasure trove and faced Archbishop McQuaid. His face darkened. McQuaid again felt an unease that something inimical to his personal well-being and his purse was about to unfold.

"I never saw such beautiful treasures in my life. Why there must be a fortune tied up in here. I have to ask you, how did you pay for all of it Charlie?"

"Oh," said McQuaid. A haggard hunted look spread over his face. "I didn't get them overnight, as you can imagine, I've been gathering them over the years . . ."

"You know," said Zanini, "I didn't ask for this job but I've been stuck with it, you know that. I feel like a Grand Inquisitor asking you questions like this but I have to know the truth. I'm not a connoisseur of art by any stretch of the imagination but I'll hazard a guess as to their worth; with the two oil paintings I'd say . . . , about 20 million Irish Pounds. Is that any way close?"

"It was nearer to 26 million . . ." Said McQuaid.

McQuaid was beginning to wilt under what was becoming a no-holds-barred form of interrogation by the Pope's representative; it was this he feared most of all. He didn't expect the Archbishop of Detroit or the Holy Father in the Vatican to appreciate his dilemma. He had fallen under the spell of the treasure, the sublime mystique and allure of which he became helpless to resist. The resources of revenue over which he had control as Archbishop of Dublin had allowed him to accumulate wealth over time. When he found he had riches at his disposal he made his first purchase of a collection of diamonds and rubies, with a sense of heady adventurous joy. He locked himself into his study in the Palace and caressed the precious stones; he was transfixed by the lustrous hues, the hypnotic light and play of the jewels. His head swooned. Steadfast in his mind as he purchased more objets d'art with the passing of time was the certainty that the treasure was an endowment for the church and the Glory of God. Of late he became troubled when he thought of what might become of the treasure, even resentful that Pope Pius X11, who disliked him so much, would demand its transfer to the Vatican which he was entitled to do. Its vulnerability caused the Dublin Archbishop much grief as he was developing a proprietary attachment for the treasure he came to think of as his own.

"We could throw you to the wolves Charlie," said the Detroit Archbishop, "for what you've done. What do you think the media would make of this . . . , this Aladdin's Cave, if it became public knowledge? You an Archbishop embezzling 26 million Pounds of church funds to buy your own private museum? The very clandestine nature of it would cause endless embarrassment for the church and His Holiness. But I'm very glad to say it can all be kept under wraps. Cheer up Charlie . . . ," Zanini patted McQuaid lightly and condescendingly on the shoulder, "a sum of 26 million Pounds is paltry, a mere drop in the bucket to the Vatican exchequer. Let your mind be at ease on that point and later I'll explain it all away to the Holy Father."

McQuaid found the buoyant good humor of Aldo Zanini unsettling considering the grim repercussions his folly might have provoked. But he soon realized he had misjudged the American Prelate's disposition when he looked at the darkened flush on his face. They stood together before the display cabinets looking at the jewelry shimmering under the brilliant lights and leaping flames of the log fire.

"I've been thinking hard about what has to be done here Charlie. In one month from now I want you to announce your retirement. It will give you time to sort out what you want to do with your life from now on."

The Dublin Archbishop nodded his head. He counted himself lucky.

"In the beginning I wanted to beautify the church," Said McQuaid, subdued and contrite. "Then I became mesmerized by the jewels, the jade, gold filigree . . ."

Aldo Zanini reached into a display case and picked out a ruby and a large uncut diamond. He turned them over in his hand.

"You like these little baubles Charlie, what do they mean to you. How would you describe them?

"Oh, I couldn't. I'd be lost for words . . ."

"Try . . ."

"Well, they really are indescribable. Each one is different, unique in itself. The way they respond to the environment, to light and care is remarkable. It's a spell they cast that makes your head spin. They seem to have a propensity to make you happy, to radiate joy just by their mere existence."

"Now isn't that remarkable?" said Zanini after some moments, "that's exactly how I'd describe . . . , a child."

"What . . . ?" Said McQuaid abstractedly.

"A child Charlie, you were just describing the characteristics of a child, not intentionally of course."

"Oh, yes, yes of course. I . . . ,"

"And how many children do you have locked up in your slave labor camps Charlie, and for what? How was it you put it, for the equitable returns the camps generated." He spread his arms in front of him. "Every penny you took was filthy lucre. Blood money." He walked slowly around the room. "All of these treasures came from the helpless tears of infants. What will you do to atone for that? The children suffered the agonies of the damned in your camps, and you could have ended it all with a flourish of your pen. What does that make you Charlie, as a man; as a representative of God?"

Aldo Zanini acted calmly but his mood changed as his face became stark and vengeful. He pulled open the doors of a glass cabinet and took out the heavy scimitar. Raising the blade over his head he smashed Ming vases and chopped at priceless papyrus scrolls and manuscripts. He sent the scimitar crashing into the rare clocks adorning the walls, their pendulums clanging noisily to the floor.

McQuaid had collapsed into the armchair, staring disbelievingly at Aldo Zanini as he rampaged through the room. He raised his arm feebly and in a strained hollow voice shouted at Aldo Zanini.

"Stop . . . , stop, please . . . , don't, no more . . ."

If Aldo Zanini heard McQuaid exhorting him to stop he paid him scant attention. With his left hand he picked up parquetry boxes of jewels and gold coins and violently flung them into the depths of the blazing fire. With the exception of the Degas and Constable paintings he went on an orgy of destruction until not a single treasure was left intact. Fragments of splintered wood and shards of glass littered the floor. Dust hung on the air like a fine mist. Miniscule wisps of ancient papyrus and manuscript paper undulated beneath the whirring humidifier. The cook, the waiter and a maid rushed into the room to find the cause of the sudden explosions of noise, only to be shouted back into the kitchen by the bellowing Archbishop. He finally sat on the end of a display table until he recovered his breathing and composure. Standing up slowly he then sat in the armchair next to the terrified McQuaid and sat down. He threw the scimitar away from him. It hit the hardwood floor noisily and went spinning across the room. Both men leaned back into their seats and were silent for some minutes.

"The two painting, of Degas and Constable," said the Detroit Archbishop breathing heavily. "I want you to have them crated and sent to my room. I intend to bring them to the Vatican as a gift to His Holiness. Now tell me what did

I accomplish here tonight Charlie, any idea, no?" McQuaid had struggled to get to his feet and stood facing him as if petrified. "Well I'll tell you. This was your penance and your atonement for the damage you inflicted on the children in your work camps. If you can't see that they are the true treasures of God, I pity you."

McQuaid leaned forward and buried his face in his hands. He stayed that way, not moving until fitful sobs wracked his spindly frame. He removed a handkerchief from his pocket and dried his moistened eyes.

"Yes, yes, I think I understand now. May God in heaven forgive me, Christ forgive me. What was I thinking?" After some minutes he said quietly, almost under his breath, "Aldo will you hear my confession?"

The Detroit Archbishop stood up and brushed some of the dust from his cassock. He smiled gently as he reached out a hand to McQuaid.

"Of course I will. You'll be fine Charlie. You just didn't know what you were doing."

Father Tadgh Murray walked the along the gravel path that led to the complex of buildings that housed the Artane industrial work camp and detention center. The meager educational facilities of the camp were restricted to 18th century classrooms and desks in cold shoddy rooms. The reason for the existence and continuance of the vast network were the profitable workshops at its center; with learned skills and labour provided by the child workers. Their jailers, with Irish government collusion were of the Congregation of Christian Brothers and Priests assigned to Artane by Archbishop McQuaid.

Father Murray pulled up his overcoat collar to fend off the chilling wind. The morning was brisk, biting cold. It was the fifth day of the assignment Archbishop McQuaid

had given him to covertly assess the day to day running of
Artane work camps. There had been some developments in
that the Archbishop had recalled all the Priests in the camp.
The Christian Brothers, now in charge of running the work
camps closed ranks against Father Murray and impeded his
inquiries at every turn. He was seen as an interloper for the
Archbishop which in effect he was much as he disliked the
inference. His inquiries were not without some success. With
the authority delegated to him he pushed through doors of
classrooms and offices causing consternation and resentment
among the Christian Brothers staff. One evening as he walked
in a corridor adjoining the children's dormitories he heard a
child crying. He went to the door from which the sound issued
and turned the handle. The door was locked. Father Murray
backed up, raised his foot and lunged at the worm-eaten
door. The lock broke and he went into the room. A Christian
Brother was beating a child who was laying face down on a
sofa. The Brother froze still with a three foot bamboo cane in
his raised hand when Father Murray entered the room and
moved swiftly towards him. He backed towards a wall where
he tripped and fell to the floor. He let out a terrified yell as the
cane was snatched from him and Father Murray stood over
him ready to strike. The Brother whimpered and curled into
a ball on the floor. With a grimace of disgust Father Murray
threw down the cane and went over to the child on the sofa.
He was bleeding on the back of his legs. Covering the child
in a blanket Father Murray lifted him up and went to the
Brother still cowering on the floor.

"You . . . ," He kicked the Brother who backed away into
a corner, "How do I get to the infirmary. Speak up or I'll kick
the hell out of you . . ."

Father Murray rushed to the infirmary with the bleeding
child. Finding the infirmary empty he placed the child on

a table. He cleaned and bandaged the wounds and pacified him until the child's eyes closed from exhaustion and he finally fell asleep. Father Murray picked up a telephone and looked at his watch. It was almost 1:00 AM in the morning. He finally got through to Brother Adrian who was the Chief Administrator of the work camp. Having just been rudely awakened by the telephone from a deep sleep, Brother Adrian was in no mood to hear about a beaten child. He threw down the receiver and pulled the blankets over him to go back to sleep. When the telephone rang again and kept ringing he picked it up in a fit of rage. His initial outburst was tempered by the more ferocious verbal onslaught of Father Murray. He pulled himself up on the pillow and listened with mounting uneasiness as Father Murray promised to unleash the wrath of Archbishop McQuaid on Brother Adrian personally. Father Murray threatened to call the Garda Siochana Superintendent in nearby Coolock about the assault on the child which in turn would instigate what the Congregation of Christian Brothers feared most; a civil investigation of one of their own with the inevitable media blitz to follow.

In the room in which he beat the child and in turn was kicked by Father Murray, the Brother painfully got to his feet. Gasping for breath he limped to the sofa on which he fell heavily. He sat back and felt his bruised ribs where Father Murray had kicked them. He swore aloud and clenched his teeth and fists tight. For as long as he could remember he had a proclivity for inflicting pain on others but would run like the wind to avoid it.

Mary Mullins was a dour inoffensive woman. It was the dull clothing she wore that sometimes merited this erroneous impression. Before the onset of the present crisis in her life she was considered kind and personable. She never wore jewelry any more nor make-up of any kind. Her overcoat, her hat, her dresses and shoes were all of a singular drab theme. There was much more to Mary Mullins however than her gray exterior would suggest. Early in her married life she felt contented and fulfilled. Her husband Alec was loving and supportive in all her endeavors and had a good job as a life insurance actuary. Her seven year old son Kevin was a normal bright child. He had settled down well in his new kindergarten school and had made some friends. And then it seemed, without warning the happy cozy life of Mary and Alec Mullins was turned upside down. Kevin had hurt two small pupils in his class and kicked viciously at a teacher who tried to intervene. The incident left Mary and Alec in a state of shock, unable to understand or cope with the sudden belligerent behavior of their child. It marked the beginning of erratic mood changes in Kevin's behavior that would continue into adulthood and virtually ruin the social lives of his parents. They were shunned by friends and relations owing to the aggressive antics of Kevin. His malevolent compulsive behavior shook the stability of the home and the marriage of Mary and Alec. They took him to a child psychiatrist who prescribed tranquilizers which Kevin spit out and caused such a furor the parent's efforts subsided into helpless resignation. Alec Mullins found it impossible to cope with the situation. He became withdrawn and after his workday confined himself to the third bedroom of their small house in Clonliffe Road in Drumcondra. He filled the small bedroom with books and retreated to the sanctuary of the room to avoid the cantankerous mood swings of his son.

From the age of seven years Kevin Mullins became an intense and lonely introvert known for the ferocity of his temper tantrums. He was regularly picked on by the school bullies from whom he would run to the safety of the nearest

Brother. It was also noted about him that he showed violence only against younger children in his school. He attended Saint Canices Christian Brothers School on Dublin's North Circular Road where he contrived to ingratiate himself with his teachers. He accomplished this by expressing a love of the religious life and to all who would listen to him, his devout wish to become a Christian Brother. Almost immediately he accomplished his intention of escaping all corporal punishment by the cane wielding brethren of Saint Canices School. During his time at Saint Canices events conspired to form the core of his developing character that would influence him for the rest of his life. When it became known that he was a 'teacher's pet' he was given a wide berth by the school bullies who were terrified of incurring the wrath of the Christian Brothers. With the tacit concurrence of the Brothers he attacked bullies bigger and stronger than himself who never retaliated, ever fearful of being expelled from the school. By the time he was 15 years old Kevin Mullins would have been charged on several occasions with common assault by the parents of young children but for the timely intervention of the teaching staff in the school. It was about this time the Congregation of Christian Brothers sent recruiting postulators to Saint Canices. When he was interviewed Kevin Mullins stated categorically that he had a vocation; that he wanted to be part of the religious life. What tipped the scales in the fateful decision he made was the stifling thought of having to go on living with his elderly parents, Mary and Alec.

When Kevin told his parents of his decision to join the Congregation of Christian Brothers Alec Mullins exulted to the extent he was left almost speechless. Mary Mullins felt initially ashamed and then weak when Kevin said matter-of-factly that he would be joining the Christian Brothers and training to become a primary school teacher. He asked her to wash and iron his clothes and pack a suitcase for him. Mary and Alec attended to his clothing and packed the suitcase and, though they would not admit it even to themselves, with a sense of exuberant relief. When the time for his departure arrived Alec carried the suitcase out to a courtesy van sent by the Christian Brothers. Kevin impassively shook hands with his Father, nodded his head and said goodbye. He gave his Mother a placatory hug, turned on his heels and was gone.

When the van sped away into the distance Mary and Alec gave each other long endearing hugs. As they went back into the house Mary took a handkerchief from her pocket and dabbed her eyes. Alec let out a long sigh of relief.

Kevin Mullins was indoctrinated into the Congregation of Christian Brothers and transferred to a boarding school. He took religious vows of which he would be required to renew every year and as a novitiate he would wear the black habit of the Order. At age 17 years he was sent to a training college to become a primary school teacher. The regimented lifestyle of the Congregation of Christian Brothers appealed to his sense of orderliness and discipline. He applied himself diligently to his studies up to the day when he took his perpetual vows, at which time he changed his name from Kevin Mullins to Brother Stanislaus.

As Brother Stanislaus he was appointed as a teacher to a newly built school in Whitehall, a suburb north of Dublin. From the beginning he instilled a sense of uneasiness amongst the 7-14 year olds under his tutelage. Physically he had an unprepossessing somber appearance dressed in the black uniform of the order. As a teacher he was severe, unsmiling and demanded absolute silence and obedience of his pupils. In the classroom he strutted in the aisles with his three foot bamboo cane tucked under his arm. He caused young children to scream by hitting them across the back with the cane if he found them talking or being inattentive. The sensation of the bamboo slicing across a child's back, the scream of agony from the victim aroused sadistic impulses that he was helpless to understand or control. After several such incidents he was reprimanded by the school principal owing to threatened lawsuits by enraged parents. Because of his forceful method of teaching he was transferred to Artane industrial work camp. While being given a guided walk through the camp he noted the casual laissez-faire attitudes of the resident teachers. One Brother sarcastically remarked that teaching in Artane was the last recourse for troublesome Priests and Brothers who proved to be lacking in refinement and were challenged in the social graces. The Brother said the pupils in Artane, who were the labour force for the work camp, were societies cast offs; unteachable children, thuggish and hopelessly embittered against the teaching staff. It was said that there had even been cases where Brothers were physically attacked by the children under their care. Brother Stanislaus thrilled at the prospect of teaching in such a challenging environment. It was the happiest he had been since he became a Christian Brother. Unlike his previous teaching post he made friends with like-minded Brothers and Priests who weren't reluctant to use the cane or the strap against the ungrateful internees of Artane.

Having received assurances from Brother Adrian that the child in the infirmary would be attended to, Father Murray made his way back to the room where he had found the beaten child. The broken door pushed open easily and he went in. Brother Stanislaus was sitting on the sofa in front of a fire. He had a furtive, scared look when Father Murray walked into the room and closed over the broken door.

"If you lay a hand on me I'll call the police . . ."

Father Murray picked up a telephone and pulling the line behind him roughly threw the telephone onto the Brother's lap.

"Go ahead, get the police over here. I'll call them for you if you like. You'll walk out of here in handcuffs, I can guarantee you that. Do you know who I am?"

The Brother gathered up the telephone, leaned over and put it on a nearby table.

"Sure," He said, "I know who you are, everyone in Artane knows who you are. The Archbishop's spy."

"And you, who are you?" Asked Father Murray.

"My name is Brother Stanislaus . . ."

He stopped talking as Father Murray's eyes narrowed slightly at the mention of his name.

"I've heard about you too . . . ," said Father Murray.

"Oh, and what have you heard . . . ?" asked Brother Stanislaus.

"I've heard you're a rampant psychopath who likes to beat up defenseless children . . ."

"Do you believe everything you hear . . . ?"

"I do from my source. His name is Joseph Carboy, he lives in the Archbishop's palace . . ."

Brother Stanislaus sneered at the mention of the name.

"Huh . . . ," He said with a measure of contempt. "The hunchback, always answering back, that was his problem. I couldn't discipline the other workers because of him."

"He told me what you did, you crippled him . . ."

"I, I don't know what you you're talking about . . . He was an unruly child . . ."

"You up-ended a heavy work bench on a petrified child trying to hide from you. You broke his back."

"I'm a Christian Brother, a teacher, I'm not accountable to you. You can't touch me. From what I've heard Archbishop

287

McQuaid is losing influence in the church. The Christian Brothers are the real power brokers in Ireland, even the Vatican hesitates to confront the Congregation of Christian Brothers. But . . . , fine. You want me out of Artane? Ok, but I'll be transferred to another school, in another parish . . ."

"You're days of beating kids and teaching are over. You have a choice, follow my instructions or take the consequences. I want you to go now to Brother Adrian's office, he'll be expecting you. Tomorrow he will arrange transportation for you to be taken to the Congregation office in Marino. It will take a few days to formally discharge you of your vows. In the meantime they will provide you with accommodation, but . . . , you can sleep on the streets as far as I'm concerned. You won't be lonely, a few more Christian Brothers will be joining you . . ."

"If I refuse to go . . . ?"

"I'll have the police here in 10 minutes and show them the beaten child in the infirmary. They will arrest you and put you in a cage where you belong. Now get out of here before I throw you out."

In the waiting room in the palace of the Archbishop of Dublin, Father Tadgh Murray jotted down some final words in his notebook. He put the notebook into a briefcase, replaced the pen in his pocket and looked at the waiting room door with some impatience. He checked his watch again and shook his head; it was already 30 minutes past his appointment time. It was two weeks to the day since the Archbishop sent him to Artane to bring him up to date on the running of the work camp. He was about to make more notes when finally the novitiate knocked and entered to announce that His Grace the Archbishop would see him. As he followed the novitiate towards the West Wing and the Archbishop's quarters he saw a tall powerfully built figure coming towards him who seemed to fill the corridor. He was dressed in a dark grey suit, a white shirt and a dark blue necktie. By the deeply set eyes, aquiline nose and tone of his skin suggestive of a warmer climate than Ireland, Father Murray judged him to be Italian. As they passed each other the Archbishop of Detroit Aldo Zanini turned to him, smiled and nodded courteously.

Father Murray was surprised to see Archbishop McQuaid. His appearance had deteriorated and his face seemed puffed and ruddy. He walked slowly about his quarters as if disoriented.

"Who . . . ?" He said vaguely.

"It's Father Murray to see you Your Grace." Said the novitiate for the second time. He then withdrew and closed the door. Father Murray's attention was caught by a movement in a darker recess of the room. It was then he noticed Joseph. He was sitting sideways in a large chair with his right arm swinging back and forth over the side. In his hand was his tasseled cap. He sat quietly and stared at Father Murray.

"Oh yes . . . , yes." McQuaid waved towards an armchair. Father Murray sat down and McQuaid took a seat opposite him. "Forgive me if I seem distracted, I have a lot on my mind."

"If Your Grace wishes I can come back at a more convenient . . ."

"No. no . . . ," Said McQuaid, "I'm anxious to have your report. Tell me in your own words how you found the situation in Artane?"

"I regret to say I haven't anything very positive to say. In deference to Your Grace I may not be able to couch what I saw in Artane in appropriate diplomatic language."

"Be as blunt as you need to be . . . , just tell me what you saw . . ."

"I didn't have a chance to interview any of the Priests in Artane. They were withdrawn the day after I arrived. It left Artane completely under the control of the Congregation of Christian Brothers . . ."

"It was I who withdrew the Priests . . . We need not go into that. Please continue."

"Yes, Your Grace. From the beginning there was very limited cooperation from the Christian Brothers, it was as if they resented my presence in the camp. However I didn't let it deter me Your Grace as I had your authority . . ."

"Go on . . ." Said McQuaid.

"With my own eyes I saw terrible cruelties inflicted on mere children by ordained clergy. At midnight near the children's dormitories Christian Brothers scurried like rats in the corridors of Artane when I chased them down. Artane is a snake pit, a vile reign of terror for the frightened children of the camp. I cannot overstate it Your Grace. I regret to say the newspaper and television reports, the books written about Artane, well . . . , it's not just anti-Catholic bias as Your Grace had intimated, it's all true. This is obscene blasphemy against the church by its own missionaries of Christ, it beggars belief. There is at least one positive aspect of my visit to report. I sent four offending Christian Brothers to the Congregation offices in Marino. In your name, Your Grace, I set in motion the procedures to have them thrown out of the church, stripped of their vows . . ."

"Oh . . . ," Said His Grace, "Oh . . . I . . . , I wish you would have contacted me first on that . . ."

"Does your Grace wish me to explain the sordid nature of the crimes of those four Christian Brothers . . . ?"

"That won't be necessary . . ."

"Your Grace these Christian Brothers are not only wretches who vilify the church they are consummate thieves. They robbed the children. They robbed them of the divinity of Christ, of the power of God in the mind of a child. They robbed them of laughter and joy, they robbed them of hope."

The Archbishop looked at his watch as if impatient.

"And how did you manage to get the cooperation of the four Brothers to go voluntarily to the Congregation offices in Marino . . ."

"I threatened them Your Grace, in view of the serious nature of the crimes. There were other Brothers hanging about the dormitories who ran before I could identify them. With these four Brothers I was guided to their rooms by the sound of children crying. I barged in and confronted them. I gave each one an ultimatum. They choose to revoke their vows in preference to having a public trial and going to prison."

"That is all irrelevant . . ." Said McQuaid.

"Your Grace . . . ?"

"I detest that the word politics should raise its ugly head in matters of religion but the fact is I have come to certain decisions that you may find objectionable. These decisions need not concern you. Now, for the matter at hand. I asked for a written report, did you bring it with you?"

"Yes, Your Grace."

Father Murray reached down for his briefcase. He took out a plastic folder and handed it to the Archbishop who thumbed through it quickly.

"This is most important . . . , are there any other copies besides this?"

"I have a copy in my quarters Your Grace. Should you wish to make changes or . . ."

"I want to impress upon you that you must get that copy to me as soon as possible. Is that clear . . . ?"

291

"Abundantly clear Your Grace ... If I may be permitted to ask since I'm involved in this matter, what decision have you made that I might find objectionable ... ?"

"As I have said, it doesn't concern you ..." Said McQuaid.

"Your Grace, may I at least know ... ?"

"No, you may not . . ." Said McQuaid forcefully, "I am surprised at your insistance Father Murray, I will not be harried in this manner . . . That will be all, you are excused ..."

Joseph emerged from the darkened corner of the room and vaulted onto a nearby sofa next to them. He was playing with the tassels of his cap. As Father Murray stood up and prepared to leave Joseph jumped up and sat on top of the sofa.

"Oh tarry awhile Priest, and know the fruits of your labour My Lord wants hidden ..."

McQuaid turned on Joseph testily.

"I'm in no mood to indulge you now Joseph."

"Tell him My Lord, or I shall ..." Said Joseph.

"Leave the room this instant Joseph, or you'll go without supper tonight ..."

"I said tell him, My Lord ..."

McQuaid sat back in his armchair in a state of resignation and annoyance. He looked at Joseph and shook his head wearily.

"Sit down Father ..." He said.

Father Murray sat back down with a frown and a look of puzzlement on his face.

"There are things you just do not understand," said McQuaid softly and slowly. "Many decisions I face each day are filled with political ramifications and I have neither the inclination nor the energy to enlighten you at this moment ... , and this poor child ... ," indicating Joseph, "does not make the duties of my office any easier ..."

"Tell him My Lord . . ." Said Joseph.

McQuaid waved a hand at Joseph as if appeasing him and addressed Father Murray.

"You see, at present the church is facing confrontational issues with the Congregation of Christian Brothers who are seeking to establish an infrastructure independent of my authority. In the past decade they have become very powerful. From time to time I have to be seen to be, how should I put it . . . ? Conciliatory in our dealings with the Brothers . . . The upshot is . . . , well, the four offending Christian Brothers that you wanted to have disavowed, well . . ."

"What My Lord is trying to say is those four exemplars of Christian piety and virtue are presently free, enjoying the bracing air of Connemara in the most picturesque parishes you could imagine."

Father Murray rose slowly to his feet.

"What . . . , those criminals, after what they did. It's not possible, It can't be . . . , Your Grace . . . ?"

McQuaid got up slowly from the armchair.

"It's done. It's done and finished with and not a thing I can do about it."

"Your Grace, one of them was Brother Stanislaus. He was the one who broke Joseph's back . . ."

"I don't wish to hear any more about it . . ." Said McQuaid abruptly.

"Your Grace, don't you want to see justice done, for Joseph's sake?" asked Father Murray.

"Father Murray, I will try to make allowances for what you have been through but I must ask you to remember to whom you are speaking."

"Why don't you call the police Your Grace, turn the Christian Brothers over to the civil authorities for the crimes they committed."

McQuaid became visibly upset, flustered, grimacing. He made an attempt to intimidate Father Murray by inching closer to him.

"This is nothing short of impertinence; I did not expect this from you. Obviously I have misjudged you . . ."

Joseph leaped from one end of the sofa to the other. He placed the cap at a cocked angle on his head. He stared at Father Murray for a few moments and turned a crooked smile on the Archbishop.

"Methinks . . . ," said Joseph pointing his finger at Father Murray, "his anger is a bubbling volcano My Lord and being a gentleman hides it 'neath a façade of forbearance. Compared to it yours is but a trifle, a piddling thing . . . ,"

Archbishop McQuaid ignored Joseph with disdainful glances.

"If I want your opinion I will ask for it," He said to Father Murray. "I must again ask you to remember your place . . ."

"Desist My Lord and listen," Said Joseph, "t'is possible you may learn to your advantage . . . , this Priest can draw men closer to God with a few notes of music than your whole panoply of pomp and ceremony"

"Your Grace has said he came to an important decision, well so have I . . ." Said Father Murray.

"I have no interest whatever in anything else you have to say . . . , bring that file on Artane to my office the first thing tomorrow morning . . ." Said the Archbishop.

Father Murray stood his ground and held the Archbishop's gaze.

"Your Grace," he said, "In light of you aiding and abetting four criminals to escape from justice and facilitate their molesting other children I intend to make extra copies of the file and send them to national radio and television and the major newspapers around the country. First I will send a report to the police. Then I intend to write to the Minister of Justice urging him to open a Tribunal of Inquiry into the running of work camps in Ireland. It's my considered belief that the Catholic Church and the Irish Government should be taken to the Hague and charged with crimes against humanity. Finally I will volunteer my services as a material witness."

"In defiance of my express wish as your Archbishop?"

"Especially in defiance of your express wish Your Grace." Joseph sat on top of the sofa and waved the cap over his head.

"Aeii, aeii, aeii . . . , hark My Lord," shrieked Joseph while acrobatically jumping on armchairs and sofas. He threw the cap energetically into the air and caught it. "The enemy is at the gates, man the barricades, pull up the drawbridge, fill the urns with boiling lead. The end is nigh."

"Be quiet Joseph . . ." Said McQuaid.

A hint of nervousness crept into the manner and voice of the Archbishop. He gazed at the resolute face and stance of Father Murray. He had dealt with hundreds of problematic priests in his time and made them all subservient to his authority. This one was not as malleable as he had presumed.

"I want you to remain at your quarters until I send for you . . ." He said.

"No Your Grace I'm leaving my quarters. I won't be returning to the palace anymore. I'm relinquishing my vows as a Priest, I'll try to serve God in other ways . . ."

McQuaid seemed suddenly enormously saddened. His anger left him more frail than his appearance suggested. He seemed to physically deflate when he sat down with an effort. He motioned for Father Murray to sit beside him.

"You are leaving the church because of me . . . ?" He asked in a strained voice.

"I regret to say yes Your Grace . . . ," said Father Murray as he sat down. "Principally it was your office, that is you, that preserved Artane, and the outrageous brutality that went with it."

"Let the penny fall where it may," said Joseph, looking with concern at McQuaid, "but let us desist for the moment Priest. He looks fair in . . . ," Joseph walked around the armchair of McQuaid and placed a hand on his shoulder. "a recent visitor, a beneficent Inquisitor or sorts raked My Lord o'er the coals, trashed his treasure, confessed him and then seemingly set My Lord on a moral and righteous path but that didn't appear to last. Even that, mark you, failed to dislodge his dubious loyalty to the Christian Brotherhood. And now? it is fear and uncertainty sets his compass and fills his sails. My Lord has worn many masks, who can say with certainty where his true fealty lies, who could plumb his depth? In his time he could cut and thrust with the best of them, a tricky Priest he was in his prime. With age he became ill suited to his office; aye, no match for the guile and machinations of the Christian Brothers. But few are. Even the Jesuits pale by comparison. He worries about posterity and his legacy. The Brothers will write his history, that is his worst fear."

"Has His Grace taken ill?"

"He seems to have retreated to within himself. I think he is just exhausted. He will recover."

Archbishop McQuaid sat upright in the armchair with his arms extended on the arm rests. His eyes were slightly glazed over as he stared vacantly into the dying fire. He is lost in reverie and seems unconnected to his surroundings. Joseph went to the hearth and threw logs on the fire. It reignited and began to blaze again. He went back to the Archbishop and again walked around him patting his arm. Father Murray went to Joseph's side.

"I will leave now Joseph . . ."

"Goodbye Priest, you have almost restored my faith in human nature."

Father Murray smiled.

"Take care of yourself."

"Aye, aye," said Joseph, "I surely will and I'll take care of My Lord. I'm going to persuade him to take an outing by the seaside, that will bring back the colour to his cheeks. What will you do with your life priest?"

"I'll pick up where I left off . . . , I'll play the piano again, devote my life to music . . ."

Joseph moved to the piano.

"Can you play for me but one more time . . . ?" Said Joseph, indicating the piano.

"Joseph, nothing would give me more pleasure," said Father Murray as he went to the piano and sat down. He lifted the keyboard cover, turned to Joseph and smiled. "anything special?"

"Mozart's 21st if you please . . . , this piece invokes the presence of God. All the unease and brutality of the world take flight for a few divine moments . . . ,"

Father Murray gently pressed his fingers on the keys and began to play.

THE END

GOLD

by

JOHN FLANAGAN

SMALLHOLDING FARMER MICHAEL AVERY WAS very disgruntled. He had a problem to solve. Being a widower living alone in a remote area on a rock-strewn hilly pocket of land in County Wicklow, Ireland, there was no one to whom he could turn to for advice. Michael's wife Nora had died eight years before. His two adult sons, well-educated but without prospects, had decided to immigrate. Sean went to Sydney, Australia and Brian settled down in Seattle, Washington, USA. The problem began when, just days ago, Michael found a tiny morsel of gold in a stream on his small farm.

Michael was 50 years old. He had owned a small business in Wicklow town, a shoe shop that had thrived until a shopping center opened nearby, and all but decimated his trade. He was forced to sell the shop and opted for early retirement, a decision that proved fortuitous as it coincided with the rapid decline of the Irish economy. With careful husbandry he cultivated the land, stocking it with sheep and goats and poultry. He started a vegetable plot and planted an orchard. It was basic and rudimentary but it proved to be enough to provide for his sustenance, which was all he required.

Michael's character was such that he could not be described as being especially well-liked or popular among colleagues or acquaintances, but he was held in good esteem by a few close friends. If truth be told, he was seen as abstemious and frugal, even when his pockets were known to be full. He might be described as a deliberate man, careful in his choice of words, not given to jocular, robust camaraderie. When he became a member of the Wicklow Golf Club he enjoyed the game but he was hesitant to integrate socially with club members and was welcomed with some reservation. His nearest neighbors Pat Mulcahy and his wife Ailene, who lived a half-mile away, often dropped in for a chat. Michael always greeted them cordially, being of a mind that good neighbors were better than good friends; they were always close by when needed.

When the boys were young and Nora enjoyed excellent health the house was a source of great joy for him. The back field of the house rose up in an incline to a grove of fir and pine trees, wide granite rockfaces and boulders, thickets of purple heather, fern and heavy undergrowth. A stream trickled down the length of the field alongside a six foot high hawthorn hedge. In warm sunny weather the agrarian scene was idyllic; in midwinter rains, the stream, no more than 1½ yards wide at it widest point, became a fast torrent, gushing down to roadside drains.

His happiest years were when Nora was well enough to spend some time helping him set up his business. When his sons, Sean and Brian, were teenagers they also helped him in the shop. They were a close happy family of which Nora was the core, her natural good nature and humor buoyed him through the stressful years. The business provided a good living for the family and by careful management he was able to pay off the mortgage on the house. Every Christmas without fail two of his suppliers sent him gifts of a bottle of wine and a bottle of brandy. As the cache of drink increased Michael made a wine rack where the bottles aged and gathered dust in the cellar over the years. Only occasionally was a bottle opened when the odd guest arrived; but that was when Nora was alive, and the boys had not yet departed to foreign parts.

Michael had been a middle-distance runner when he was younger and had continued running for exercise well into his fifties. He combined running with weight lifting and calisthenics, which prolonged the grace and power of his middle-aged physique. He had indulged in the sport of wrestling when he was younger, and successfully competed as an amateur in several tournaments. His favorite pastime was hunting small game with his two dogs.

For a long while after the death of his wife and the departure of his sons, Michael lived in a state of morbid disbelief. Thankfully the funeral of Nora was a quiet orderly affair, devoid of the boisterous wake and carousing of most funerals. His sons Sean and Brian had returned from overseas to attend the funeral, stayed for a couple of days and were abruptly gone.

For the first six months of living alone, he found the loneliness almost unbearable in the remote region of Wicklow. Following the loss of Nora, further bad news followed quickly. Some years earlier he had bought shares in a telephone company that showed promise initially but rapidly fell. The shares of the telephone company he invested in diminished by 85% of their original value. His generous settlements on Sean and Brian to help them settle abroad cut further into his dwindling savings. Thus began a time of continuous worry and concern trying to balance the financial demands on himself and his small estate against his only source of income, his small pension the meager returns on his smallholding farm.

November of the year arrived. The weather became almost continuously windy with showers and overcast skies. Michael's depressed mood lightened somewhat with the arrival of the shooting season. His dogs, an older English Pointer and a Springer Spaniel seemed to instinctively know the season was upon them, and spent most of the day staring at Michael from the sofa and issuing impatient whimpers. Finally when he took down the Purdy shotgun to clean it, the dogs ran excitedly around the living room.

Michael set out one morning after game, cradling the shotgun across his forearm. The dogs worked the stream and hedge, as he moved towards the trees and granite boulders above him. When the dogs flushed out a pheasant from the underbrush, they looked around at him in wonder when he failed to bring down the easy target. Beset by worries and problems, Michael's mind was not focused as the dogs went ahead and he continued up the hill. The rains of recent days had abated. Mild winds ushered banks of cumulous clouds across a cold blue sky, allowing glimpses of a weak mid-winter sun. The shallow stream sparkled in the morning light.

Michael was in the act of kneeling down and tightening a bootlace, when he stood up and found himself alone. The dogs had disappeared. Much surprised he pushed on up further until he was faced with the massive outcrop of rock that marked the boundary of his property. There was still no sign of the dogs. He sat down on a rock, put two fingers to his lips and blew long shrill whistles. Normally the dogs were so dependable; they never took off like that before, never roaming further than shot range. He could practically talk to them and for their part it was as if they could anticipate his every command. At last a movement in a thicket at the base of a rockface stirred, and a huge pheasant flew up and out of sight. There was still no sign of the dogs. Suddenly the dense thicket at his feet parted, and it looked as if the dogs walked out of the towering granite wall. They sat at his feet and stared at him as if wondering why he let another pheasant escape. Michael laughed out loud and kidded around with the dogs. As he turned to go back towards the house he looked again at the rockface from which the pheasant and the dogs emerged. Laying the shotgun aside he kneeled down and pulled the heavy thicket and wild gorse aside. He saw a hidden opening in the base of the wall and beyond it a dark tunnel that disappeared from view. Filled with curiosity he went down to the house and brought back a flashlight. The dogs were excited by the new turn of events and preceded him as he crawled on his hands and knees into the dark tunnel. After two minutes he found himself in a wide damp cave, about 9 feet high.

He stood up in a state of amazement and shone the flashlight around to get a perspective of the vaulted cave. It was gaunt and foreboding, claustrophobic. The earth beneath his feet was soft. Water was trickling down a wall-face and flowing over a strip of sand and gravel. Following the gradient of the hill, it careered into a hollow where the convex walls met, and the water disappeared. He became excited and wondered about the age and origin of the cave. He promised himself to return and rig up some lighting and really explore his new find. He was about to leave when he shone the light for a final sweep about the cave. The beam caught the bed of the shallow stream and he stopped dead in his tracks. He went back and stared down. A tiny pebble-sized yellow object lay glistening in the gravel beneath the crystal clear flowing water. Michael shooed the dogs away when they began to muddy the water. He bent down and picked up what looked like a particle of gold and scrutinized it under the flashlight. Judging by its texture and color he could but hope that it was of some value. He walked slowly and carefully around the floor of the cave. His heart pounded when he found another morsel of the glistening metal. And another. Several minute pieces were grouped together, others scattered and half buried in water and gravel. In a few minutes the batteries of the flashlight began to flicker and dim, and he was forced to abandon his efforts. With the dogs following, he scraped his way out through the tunnel and back down to the house. By that time he was in a state of feverish excitement and he had to force himself to slow down and think. He sat down in front of the turf fire until he regained some composure. Reaching into his jacket pocket he took out the 15 pieces of nuggets he had collected, and spread them out on the table before him. The excitement mounted within him again, as he dried and examined each piece. He was mesmerized by their gleaming yellow color and endless possibilities; and, being practical, the problems the find might engender. He had no idea of their value, guessing was useless. His thoughts went back to three months before when a party of geologists from the government run Exploration and Mining Division, took mineral samples from rivers and streams in the county. He took exception to them trampling over his property and their cavalier attitude towards him on his own land. Some heated words were exchanged. They threatened to call the police and left him in no doubt about the government ownership of all minerals found on his property. When they were leaving, night was falling as they loaded excavating equipment onto a truck. They drove away in the dark and left behind an assortment of tools and ten sticks of dynamite with a fuse, all wrapped in a plastic bag. He had been so incensed with their obnoxious attitude that he never called them, believing they would return. When they did not call back to recover the items, he put the dynamite in a small box and kept it in the cellar of his house. The grim warning of the geologists came ringing back to him; no minerals belonged to him, even on his own land. The injustice of such an arcane law infuriated him, it smacked of the oppressive penal laws of British occupation to which his forbears had been subjected. It was his land, bought and paid for, why shouldn't it be his gold?

As he rolled a piece of the precious metal between a thumb and forefinger he was beset by doubts, wondering if what he held in his hand was fool's gold, a gold look-alike which had misled experts in the field. He was forced to concede that apart from wishful thinking, he knew nothing about the shiny trinkets he plucked from the stream. He put away the shotgun and cartridges and settled the dogs down. For the remainder of the day and far into the night he was at his workbench in the barn, attaching spotlights to a generator.

The following morning Michael arose at dawn. He dressed, had breakfast and fed the dogs. They were excited, instinctively knowing something odd was going on. He donned his wellingtons and anorak. Out in the barn he loaded the generator and spotlights, tools, and cans of extra diesel onto a wheel barrow, and began the arduous trek up the hillside. The dogs were in a frenzy of excitement. When he arrived at the granite wall, he pulled back the thicket that hid the mouth of the tunnel. Standing on a small hillock he checked the surroundings to ensure he was not being observed. He smiled to himself for taking such precautions; he might as well be standing on the moon, his little plot of land was so barren and isolated. He dismantled the steering handle of the generator to give him more leverage to maneuver it through the confined space in the tunnel. Once inside the cave he started the generator and rigged up the spotlights to focus on the narrow stream. Taking a deep breath he bent down and set to work, gathering up shining morsels of gold until well into the evening.

The following day in his house, Michael made entries into a notebook and erased much of what he had written. He was considering the options open to him to convert the gold, if it was indeed gold, into cold hard cash. He could not take the pieces into Dudgeons, the jewelers in Wicklow Town. They were an old reputable company, where he had bought Nora's engagement and wedding rings. And though he was on a cordial footing with the owner/manager, it was more than likely they would be required to report his cache of gold to the appropriate authorities. In doing so he could very likely find himself in trouble with the law. In the end he decided his best course would be to authenticate the value of the smallest pieces he had found. He wrapped two pieces in tissue paper and put them in the inside pocket of his jacket. There had to be huckster shops in Dublin that sold cheap jewelry. He would simply ask one of them to assess the value of his gold.

Early next morning Michael opened the door of the house and looked up at the low close clouds. He got into the old Mercedes car and drove the 60 kilometers to Dublin. He was given the Mercedes from his father-in-law, when the old man's health deteriorated and he could no longer drive. The running of the stately Mercedes was one of the few indulgences he allowed himself in his otherwise Spartan life-style. A soft rain began beating down on the windscreen. His mind was in a quandary not having decided on any course of action, but going to the first out of the way jewelry shop he could locate. When he reached Dublin he parked the car in Bolton Street and walked towards the older backstreets of the town. In Capel Street, a myriad of small dilapidated old tenements and shops presented themselves to him. The contrast between the drab and ramshackle shops and houses was startling, compared to the glass frontages of nearby shopping centers. As he walked he stuffed his hands into his pockets. The day was bitingly cold as dark ominous clouds hovered over the city and a light mist hung on the air. He cursed himself for forgetting his trench coat, as old and worn as it was. He walked for an hour and began to have doubts about the sagacity of the venture when he reached the River Liffey, and turned left into Ormand Quay. It was there he saw the swinging circular sign ahead of him that read 'Curio Shoppe'.

It was more with the intention of getting temporary respite from the rain that made him step in under the curved granite arches of the old shop. He was tucking up the collar of his jacket when he turned around and looked into the window. The antiquated shop was a relic of a bygone era. The plate glass window was broken and boarded up with pieces of wood held together with wire. On the left side of the window a motley of sea-faring antiques were displayed; a ship's sextant, an old anchor, a rusted hawser. To the right a World War 1 British Expeditionary Force uniform with a Sam Browne belt, a holster and shoulder strap was shown beside a Masai warrior's shield and spear. African art in the form of an elongated head carved in mahogany was displayed next to it. A pith helmet and khaki jacket, a copy of a painting of an 18th century Man o' War, all spoke of the Great War and colonial expansion by the European powers.

The rain was pattering down steadily as Michael pushed open the door and went into the shop. A small bell jingled above his head as he closed the door behind him. Bookcases lined the wall opposite, before him was a glass-topped jewelry display counter. A small round table and chairs occupied a corner. Beside it a wood-burning hearth blazed away, giving the shop a cozy ambience. The owner/shopkeeper came in through a door behind the counter. He looked to be about 55 years old. He had an engaging pleasant countenance, with sharp alert eyes and a strong aquiline nose. His thick, grandee beard and hair was completely gray. He wore a polo-necked Aran sweater and a sleeveless leather jacket. A faint smile hovered about the corners of his mouth as he faced Michael across the counter.

"How I can help you." He said.

He spoke with a heavy European accent that Michael took to be German but wasn't sure.

"I was just admiring the items in the window; I've never seen anything like them." Said Michael.

"Thank you . . ," said the shop owner, "but you will pardon me for observing, the rain has made you look quite cold and wet. There is a warm fire there by the table. It's near my coffee break, I was just making it when you came in. If you are not pressed for time, why not sit down and I'll bring you out some coffee."

Michael sat at the table and in a few minutes the owner brought a tray with coffee and biscuits to the table. As they drank the coffee Michael smiled. He extended his hand across the table.

"My name is Michael Avery. I'm from Avoca in Wicklow."

"And I am Walter Hahn from Hamburg in Germany. Pleased to meet you."

They shook hands.

"You are far from home, Walter."

"Yes. My wife Imogen, and I fell in love with Ireland, and we have lived here for three years now. She left two months ago to go to Nice in the south of France. We have a house there. Imogen is a French citizen.'

"Well, that should be a pleasant change, away from the Irish weather."

"We hate to leave Ireland. But we don't have a choice."

"Oh . . ."

"We cannot go on, day after day, living in fear as we do." He pointed to the front of the shop. "Did you notice the hoarding around the window? That's the latest calamity, a couple of days ago. I'm glad my wife had already departed for Nice when it happened. After the pubs close at night, the drunks come by here in packs. They shout out racial remarks, throw rocks and run away."

As they drank the coffee both men gazed out past the windows.

"It's growing, this random violence," said Michael, "I've lived in Wicklow my whole life. It's not the same town, it's not the same country anymore. You would have really liked it in the old days. It was a safer, nicer place to be. People were gentle, civilized; you could sleep with your doors open. Strangers said hello to each other. Now," Michael shook his head resignedly, "drugs are peddled in every major city in Ireland. People get shot down in the streets in gang wars. It's as if something sinister has spread itself over the land."

Walter nodded.

"My windows have been broken four times since I moved in here. No foot police come around here anymore, it's too dangerous. I see a patrol car passing once a month and that's it. We can't go on living under siege like this. The Ireland my wife and I fell in love with, I'm afraid it's changing too much for us . . ."

"What will you do?"

"I'm selling out. I'll join my wife in Nice. And now my friend, you must tell me why you came into my shop, apart from sheltering from the rain . . . When I first saw you, you looked very stressed. I hope the coffee has made you feel better . . ."

"Of course it has, I feel much better now. Please, first tell me about yourself, you've obviously travelled a lot . . ."

"I was born in Hamburg. I was a sixth generation mariner in my family; the lure of the sea was predestined for me from the moment I was born. At 18 years old I joined an ocean going cargo ship. In a nutshell, I finished my education on board and worked my way up to become the ship's First Engineer. I met Imogen when my ship docked in the port city of Freetown, Sierra Leone in Africa. We were delivering a consignment of medical supplies. Imogen was a doctor, a gynecologist attached to Medicines san Frontiers. She tended to women and children in camps in the impoverished country. When I visited the camps and saw so much destitution and overburdened staff I resigned my post as engineer of the ship. I worked alongside Imogen in the camps. We fell in love and got married. Not long after Imogen and I were expelled from Sierra Leone. It was a country known for its valuable reserves of diamonds, gold and titanium ore. Imogen and I stood on the toes of some powerful politicians. You see, we wrote letters to the European press, about the dichotomies between the obscene abundance of the rich and the destitute poor. So, they booted us out. We decided to live quiet, peaceful lives in the land of Saints and Scholars, and came to Ireland. Yes, I've travelled; I've been around the world a few times with the merchant navy. I have a yacht in the Poolbeg marina down there," he nodded eastwards, towards the sea, "on Pigeon House Road. Whenever I feel landlocked I take it out, and run it up the coast for a few hours."

"Well, I've read Conrad," said Michael, smiling, "but I must say I've never set foot in a boat, unless you count a rowboat."

As they were talking a group of four noisy youths had gathered outside the shop door and stayed there looking in the window. When Walter went out to confront them they ran away while shouting racial slurs back at him.

When he was left alone at the table Michael was beset by doubts. He now felt ashamed he ever considered resorting to subterfuge, and lying to identify the morsels of gold in his pocket. Walter seemed, at least if appearance would have it, to be a likable person with good character. When he came back from the door, Michael finished his coffee and put the cup down.

"Walter, I have a confession to make. I came in here under false pretenses. I had a story ready to spin about finding pieces of gold somewhere in the hills of Donegal, just to have it evaluated. I didn't expect to be shown civility and hospitality . . ."

"Oh for nothing, for nothing. Look, let me help you if I can. Now what's this talk about gold?"

"I have a small parcel of land in a village called Avoca in Wicklow. To cut a long story short I found some pieces of what looks like gold. They could be just shiny bits of granite or metal, I just don't know. As the law stands if they are worth something, I can't keep them."

"Do you have them with you?"

"I have two pieces . . ."

"May I see one?"

Michael reached into his jacket, took out the folded tissue paper and handed a piece to Walter. He placed it carefully on the table before him. He stood up, went into a backroom and after a few minutes returned carrying a microscope. He sat down and placed the tiny piece on a slide under the microscope. Michael watched quietly as Walter operated the controls of the instrument. His face was impassive for some moments. After what seemed an eternity to Michael, Walter looked up and a broad smile spread across his face.

"It's the real thing. It's gold . . ."

"What . . . ? Michael was too shocked to speak coherently.

"It's gold alright, no doubt about it. Just a minute . . ." Walter went behind the counter, opened a drawer and took out an electronic weighing scale. He brought it back to the table and set it down. Deftly he placed the minutiae of gold on the scale, made a quick calculation on a notepad and pushed it across the table to Michael.

"Your piece of gold weighs half an ounce. At today's prices on the market that's what it's worth . . ."

Michael stared disbelievingly at the figure on the pad.

"I don't believe it, that was one of the smallest pieces I found, 450.00 Euroes, are you sure, it seems too tiny to be worth that much?"

"Oh I'm sure . . ." Said Walter. He pointed to the jewelry on display in the counter cabinet. "I dabble in jewelry, I know the price of it. But I must warn you Michael, you will have a struggle to get rid of it at half its value."

Walter refilled the coffee cups. They were thoughtful for some moments. He then told Walter details of the find.

"You know," said Walter, "you will have to be very careful. You know where you stand with the government? They have the legal rights to any gold or minerals found on your land. If somehow they found out you've got gold you could be prosecuted if you went near it. You could be hauled off to jail for illegal gold mining." Michael sat back and shook his head in exasperation.

"And that's not all . . . ," continued Walter, "if you go public with this, every ne'er-do-well with a bucket and spade will invade your property looking for gold."

"I suppose so, human nature being what it is. I try to make allowances, but what rankles me most is this claim the government has on any minerals found on my property. When I first bought the land I dug up every stone and rock so I could make the land arable. It's my land. Now the government can essentially steal it from me with a stroke of a pen."

"If I were you I wouldn't go near a bank; even a pawnshop. Leaving your ID anywhere could lead to all sorts of murky problems for you later. You could have the Department of Finance breathing down your neck."

"Yes, you're right of course," said Michael, "more's the pity. Well, I'll have to get rid of it somehow, even if it's only for a pittance of its value. The problem is I run a small farm. The cost of animal feed and just the bare necessities are spiraling out of control. I just want enough to run my small farm."

Walter smiled.

"From what you tell me you'll be able to do a lot more that that" Walter handed him back the gold. "Look, let me make you an offer. I'll give you 400 Euros for that piece of gold. And I'll hold on to it for you. If you can find a buyer who will pay you more I'll give it back to you. In the meantime you can stock up on your farm and keep it running."

"I couldn't ask for a better deal than that," said Michael as he pushed the piece of gold across the table to Walter.

"Come back and see me when you're ready. I get my gold from a supplier in Marseille for my own trinkets," he pointed towards the glass display cabinet, "he gives me what I want at a fair price."

"I don't know what to say. It's . . . , so generous of you."

"I hope," said Walter, "you will forgive me, but just one last word of caution, about your find. Gold, of all the precious elements on earth, seems to awaken the most primitive and darkest instincts in man. In its pursuit men have been known to lose their minds, and their very souls. I saw two sane, rational men, partners and close friends, turn viciously against each other over a gold claim in South Africa. One shot the other . . . , he's languishing his life away in prison."

"Oh, I'll be careful," said Michael, "I lead a quiet life. My family is gone, I don't get to see many people . . ."

"Good, I'm glad to hear it."

When Michael left Walter's shop, the evening was closing in over Dublin. The rain had stopped but low close clouds darkened the skies with a promise of heavier rain. His mind was in a quandary. The excitement he felt about the gold was rudely balanced by the seemingly insurmountable problems the find presented. He got into the car and drove around Dublin for hours hoping to clear his mind. He finally pulled up alongside the River Liffey on Burgh Quay. He turned off the engine of the car. Leaning forward he rested his forehead on the back of his hands over the steering wheel and uttered a deep sigh. If only his sons were here he could talk with them. If Nora was still alive she would know what to do. She was so practical. Normally he had a good head on his shoulders in dealing with problems, especially in business. But common sense seemed to have abandoned him under the weight of this latest pressure. After a few minutes he leaned back slowly in the car seat and looked about at the ceaseless maelstrom of traffic in O'Connell Street. He got out of the car, locked it and walked distractedly along the footpath parallel to the river Liffey.

Amid the winter solstice, the River Liffey, rising from beneath the dome of Kippure in the Dublin Mountains descended swiftly and angrily, through creeks and gullies sculpted from the pliant bogs by the plunging force of the water, on its way to the mouth of the sea. In stormy gales the washed residue of the peat bogs made this most ancient of rivers morbidly brown in color. The foam-flecked, swollen river undulated slowly, like a heaving behemoth trapped between the Liffey walls.

A withering North wind blew down as the first trickles of drizzling rain fell over Dublin city. Michael pulled his jacket collar up. He was in Gardiner Street when the light rain became a deluge and he hastily found his way back to the car. As he was about to turn the key in the ignition when his eyes fell on a Pub with a gaudy neon lit billboard advertising food, and he realized he hadn't eaten all day. He locked the car, walked across the street and pushed open the Pub door.

A deafening din of piped music rooted him to the spot as he stood inside the door and looked around the Pub. He was about to withdraw to find a quieter place to eat when he saw a smorgasbord displaying a tempting variety of dishes. He took a tray, filled it with food, sat down and ate hurriedly. He was now anxious to get home to feed the dogs and relish the peace and quiet of his house in Avoca. The pub food did nothing to alleviate his bad mood and in a short while he lapsed into a state of despair. Without thinking he made his way to the noisy crowded bar. He found an unused barstool and sat for a few moments with his arms resting on the bar. He gazed at the bewildering array of exotic bottles staring at him across the counter and finally ordered a hot whiskey.

He felt he needed something, anything to alleviate his foul mood. As the burning liquid seared through him he felt his breath was cut short; he coughed and put the glass back down on the counter. A coarsely dressed woman to his left turned her head towards him and sniggered. She was in her early 40's and seemed to have over imbibed judging by the animated tete-a-tete she was having with herself; she was mumbling distractedly in between sips from a glass of wine. To Michael's right, four men stood in a group talking vociferously to each other. Their heated vitriol was drawing attention from other bar clients; an older man amongst them restored a semblance of civility by raising a finger to his pursed lips. The younger men showed him a marked deference by instantly subduing their vocal zeal. They had the flat guttural accents of Dublin's North inner city. The conversation was not so much peppered with vituperative swear words as to be almost totally submerged in them.

Michael let some moments pass before he upended the remainder of his drink. He ordered another whiskey, put the glass down and sat staring in front of him lost in thought. He shook his head dolefully. It was sheer idiocy walking in the rain like that; it had resolved nothing. He was now more confused than ever about how to convert the gold he had found to cash. He suddenly felt nauseous and physically weak. He had a crushing headache, and the cold wet clothes clinging to him made his body tremble. It could not be said that Michael ever suffered a problem with drink. When Nora passed away, when his sons left home, as devastated as he was he dealt with it, and picked up the threads of his life. He never felt the need to drown his sorrows in alcohol. It has been established that he was abstemious, careful by nature. But tonight was different. He needed a drink and wouldn't object to some social interaction, no matter from what quarter it came. At the bar he wiped his hair dry with a handkerchief. He raised the second glass of whiskey to his lips and quickly emptied it. He ordered another. Gradually, almost imperceptibly he felt a lessening of the tension and pressure that assailed his frayed nerves throughout the day. His headache and discomfort lifted until, Michael believed, he was suddenly as lucid and clearheaded as he had ever been. He picked up the glass, mused over the amber opiate and took a swallow. It hardly seemed credible a few drinks could effect such a transformation in his thinking. He gave a senseless clownish laugh, emptied the glass and asked the bartender for another. What was this euphoric metamorphosis transcending his being, altering his psyche? Was it real or delusional rapture, juxtaposing its radiance on a mind that but a moment before was beset by grief and anxiety? He suddenly felt transported above the common weal of existence to a level of joie de vivre and aesthetic exuberance he had never experienced before. He was elated and filled with a sense of altruism towards his fellow man. He grinned broadly as he paid the bartender for his sixth whiskey and ordered a seventh. He found himself talking to the unkempt woman to his left and smiling and nodding to the group of four men to his right. Without knowing how or why, Michael became involved in their company. The older man shook his hand and said his name was Leo Mulvey. Introductions were mumbled as the men, who immediately fell silent when he joined them, diffidently shook the hand of the effusive Michael after Leo introduced them and bought a round of drinks. The woman at the bar was introduced as Emma, the sister of Leo. Two of the younger men, Gil and Pat, were Leo's sons. The third was his nephew Jikey, Emma's son. Jikey, at 18 years of age was the youngest member of the family and the most challenged in the social graces. He was short and barrel-shaped with a thick neck and a face that bore the scars of savage gang confrontations. Jikey evinced the charm and gravitas of a traduced bulldog. Besides being a creature of instinct and given to violent temper eruptions he was unused to shaking hands as it made him uncomfortable. He felt more predisposed to curl his hands into fists in his preferred mise en scene of battering adversaries into submission. When introduced to Michael, Jikey proffered his hand reluctantly and wondered why he had to shake hands with a culchie from Wicklow. For Jikey, everyone outside the Dublin Pale was a culchie; a breed at once mysterious and best not dallied with. He sullenly clamped his mouth shut and stepped back into the shadows behind Gil. He knew his Uncle Leo was 'working' the stranger. Whatever was going on with Leo nothing was ever as it appeared. Leo was proud of Jikey because recently he had contributed generously to the family coffers. Only three weeks ago Jikey had been released from Mountjoy prison after he burglarized an old couple's home and robbed them of their savings. Before he was arrested he made a cash donation to Leo. He also bought Leo a pearl-handled switchblade knife as a consequence of which he leapfrogged over Pat in the hierarchal structure of the family.

Michael's head was swimming and he never felt so good. He was jubilant and uncharacteristically verbose, humorous even, judging by the boisterous response of the company to his feeble jokes. He normally abhorred jokes, no matter the shade or hue. In the past he lacked the confidence to relate jokes without incurring some mocking derision for his efforts. His present dire attempt to be jocular was an effort to ingratiate himself with his new found friends; that and the expensive round of drinks he had been treating them to. He became so enamored of their company he failed to notice the intense avarice in the faces of his companions, as he peeled off Euro notes from the sum Walter had given him for the nugget of gold. The ensuing banter became mindless diatribe calculated by Leo Mulvey to establish a sense of rapport with Michael, or as much of it as his feral cunning could effect. By the time Michael polished off eight whiskeys he began to slur his words and lose his sense of equilibrium as the bar began to spin around him. He lost all account of time as the night drew on. Near closing time Leo looked at his watch and whispered into the ear of Jikey. Jikey went to the back of the bar to the Snug, a semi-private room for clients who preferred to drink in solitude. He quickly cleared three drinkers out of the room by jerking his thumb menacingly towards the door. He then nodded to Leo. With a friendly smile Leo suggested to Michael that they all retire to the Snug where they could hear themselves talk. Michael and his new friends retired to the Snug with drinks in hand. Leo and Pat cordially helped settle Michael in a chair when he appeared to be somewhat disoriented. Emma was noticeably tipsy and was escorted by Pat and her son Jikey. She had stopped drinking and now sat quietly, swayed a little and tried to look sober. By this time Leo had elicited some details of Michael's life from which he was forming a general picture in his mind of the fool that fate had thrown into his lap. He was smiling congenially at Michael when a bartender knocked on the door of the Snug, looked in and shouted.

"Last call gents, closing time in 10 minutes . . ."

The bartender left and closed the door behind him. Leo had by this time subdued his family members to silence by looks and winks. He turned to Michael.

"Well Michael," he said, "It's almost time to say goodbye. But let me say it has been a pleasure for me and my family to meet a gentleman like yourself . . , hasn't it lads . . ?" He turned and faced his family who acquiesced with a chorus of 'ayes' and other vocal blandishments. Michael waved his hand and babbled out incoherent words while his eyes were half-closed and his chin rested on his chest.

"Thank, thanks, it was great . . , great. No, no wait, one last round, on me, double whiskeys for everyone, where's the bartender, can someone . . ?" Leo nodded to Gil who went to the bar to order the round.

"That's most generous of you Michael," said Leo, "But I must say, emm . . . , I'm a bit concerned to tell you the truth . . . You said you were from where . . ?"

"Wicklow, Leo," mumbled Michael, "a little place called Avoca in Wicklow. About 65 or so kilometers due south from here . . ."

"Well now that's what bothers me Michael. You've spent a fair penny on me and my sister and the boys here. Well, I'm asking meself if you have enough money to see you home to wherever it is you come from. Won't your family be wondering where you are . . . ?"

"No, no one will be wondering where I am . . , not a single soul . . ."

And Michael proceeded to regale the company with the minutest details of his private life. "And so you see my friends, all that's waiting for me at home is two dogs that I have to feed."

Michael pulled back his jacket sleeve and looked dumbly at his watch. As he did so the bartender entered and put the order of drinks on the table. Reaching into his pocket Michael pulled out the much reduced wad of money. He handed it to the bartender who shook his head impatiently, counted off some money and handed the remainder to Michael who stuffed it carelessly into his pocket. The bartender lingered for a moment over Michael and smiled knowingly at Leo who was staring grimly at him. With a slight turn of his head towards the door Leo sent the bartender scurrying out of the room. Leo leaned towards Michael and took out a few Euro notes from his pocket.

"Michael, you take that. You've been very good to us but I'm worried about you needing some petrol for your car, you have a long drive home."

Michael was in the act of finishing off his double whiskey. He put the glass down and looked obliquely at Leo and the money in his hand. Michael's left eye drooped a little as he shook his head.

"No thanks, you're a real friend, but soon I'm going to have all the money I'll ever need . . ." he laughed maniacally, loudly. "and I won't forget my friends . . ."

"I think maybe you've had one or two drinks too many . . ," cut in Leo's nephew Jikey. He looked at Leo and froze. He backed away, realizing he had spoken out of turn. He slid back in his chair and lowered his eyes.

"Why that's great Michael," interjected Leo, smiling broadly, "me and my family are very happy for you . . ."

"It's the Gods honest truth Leo. Aah, maybe you don't believe me . . ?"

"Oh no Michael, of course I believe you . . ."

"Well, maybe you'll believe this?" Michael fumbled through his pockets for what seemed an inordinate length of time. Finally he patted an inside pocket and drew out a piece of folded paper. With shaking hands he pushed bottles and glasses aside and spread out the paper napkin. There for all to see was the nugget of gold shining in its center. An ominous silence fell over the room.

At this juncture Michael was quite detached from his surroundings, caught up as he was in the throes of an alcoholic fugue that left him unable to communicate except by the most basic of sensory mechanisms. He had lost control over his eye muscles one of which, his left eye, was oscillating like a pendulum in his eye socket. When he closed his eyes briefly from a surfeit of drink and exhaustion, his friend Leo was there to rouse him back to the present, his head inches from his own, smiling and concerned and asking endless questions.

A man of simple mien, deprived by drink of the use of his faculties, Michael was unaware of the perverse savagery Leo Mulvey and the men surrounding him were capable of.

Leo Mulvey was a small-time hoodlum who through swagger and braggadocio created a false illusion of confidence and courage. In truth he was cowardly, acrimonious and cruel. He owned and lived in a rundown scrapyard on East Wall Road in Dublin from which he sold parts from crashed or stolen cars and dealt in black-market contraband. Leo's scrapyard was close to the berths of deep water ships in the Dublin Port. One evening as he was disassembling a stolen car he was paid a visit by four foreign crew members from a ship docked in nearby Alexander Basin. He had difficulty in understanding them as they all had pronounced east European accents. What he did understand was the generous sum promised to him for his part in a business proposition. In short shrift Leo's latest enterprise was the smuggling and transport of illegal African emigrants, from ships in the Port into Dublin city. In all likelihood Leo could have gone on being a successful smuggler but for an incident that would prove detrimental to his health and well-being. One night he drove four illegal emigrants from a ship in Alexander Basin to an address in nearby Fairview in Dublin. When he arrived at the destination a stuffed envelope was pushed into his hands by one of his passengers. He had been forewarned by the sinister crew members who hired him never to accept money; never. There were people who took care of that. He knew instinctively it was money within the large manila envelope. Given Leo's character, greed and avarice overcame him; the smell of money was irresistible. He opened the fat envelope. He counted it and found he had 40,000 euros. He immediately sped back to his lodgings in the scrapyard. He threw his personal belongings into suitcases. He locked the gates, checked to see if he was being followed and drove to his widowed sister Emma's nearby council house where she lived with her son Jikey. In the parlance of the felons with whom he consorted Leo was holed up and on the run. A car was seen parked everyday outside the scrapyard with two, sometimes three men inside. After a month they no longer came but he could never be sure they were not still around. Leo wanted to go back to the scrapyard but Emma advised against it. Instead she proposed that the whole family move to Canada. She had a brother in Toronto who had started a house painting business and was doing well. He would sponsor them. With the money Leo was sitting on they could start a new life in Canada. Preparations were made, tickets were booked. It seemed a bright future awaited the enterprising family. However the plan was derailed by the continued greed and avarice of Leo Mulvey. On a fateful stormy night in a Dublin Pub he met the smallholding Wicklow farmer Michael Avery.

Since he was 15 years old Leo had been incarcerated in reform schools and finally Mountjoy prison. Nature replicated Leo Mulvey's genes with such acuity and precision that his progeny might be clones, given their predilection for crime and violence. His sons, Gil and Pat and his nephew Jikey followed in the family tradition. His sister Emma was equally bound up in his nefarious pursuits.

Emma was the first to react to the sight of the gold nugget in the center of the table and the first to break the silence. She picked it up, looked at it closely and put it back down.

"Holy God," she said, staring open mouthed, "is that what I think it is .. ?"

"It's gold alright," said Leo, "emm, I'm just asking as a friend, just out of curiosity where emm ... ," It was not often Leo Mulvey was lost for words. He had however to couch his language in words suited his purpose. "where did you get the likes of that .. ?"

"On my little plot of land in Avoca in Wicklow, it's no bigger than a postage stamp, but it's got a cave and a stream and lots of these in the water"

The Mulvey brood fell suddenly silent as Leo's squinting eyes searched their faces and nodded knowingly. He smiled and placed his hand on Michaels shoulder.

"Michael, put that away safely," he then wrapped the gold nugget in the tissue paper and placed it in Michael's hand. Quietly and persuasively he whispered to Michael, "Will you do me a big, big favor .. ?"

"Name it, name it .. , anything .. ?"

"Ah thanks Michael. I have a car outside. Now here's what I'd like to do. You've put away a fair few whiskeys Michael. As your friend I know you won't mind me saying that ..."

"Naw, not at all ..." mumbled Michael.

"Why don't you let me drive you home? My son Gil here will follow us in his car, it's an Opel van and when we drop you off he'll drive me home ..."

"You'd do that for me Leo? But it's such a long drive ..."

"Ahh, sure what are friends for Michael. We'd all be worried sick about you driving in your condition .. , now why don't you let me have your keys and I'll get you safely home .. ?"

Without another word Michael handed the car keys to Leo and got shakily, dumbly to his feet. Hands reached out to keep him standing as he stumbled and swayed and was frog-marched out of the Pub. Emma was similarly escorted by Pat and Jikey.

Strong winds and rain greeted the party as they exited the Pub and crossed Burgh Quay to Michaels car. Gil and Pat lifted and pushed the semi-comatose Michael into the passenger seat of the Mercedes and closed the door. Leo got into the driving seat and started the engine. Gil and Pat joined Emma and Jikey in the Opel van. Gil got onto the driving seat. Leo shook Michael into wakefulness. He had already fallen asleep with his head rested against the side window. It took some time to rouse him. Leo who was no longer smiling condescendingly, showed signs of impatience.

"Michael, Michael, wake up. How do I get to . . , what's the name of that place where you live?"

"Oh, Avoca. Go out to the N11, turn right at Kilmacanogue. Go up the Long Hill. Stay on the main road through Roundwood, Laragh and Rathdrum. You better wake me in Rathdrum, it gets tricky after that . . ."

"Ok, that's what I'll do, now get some shut-eye."

Michael, with his head rolling and swaying needed no encouraging. His eyes closed immediately and he fell into a fitful sleep. Leo pulled away from the kerb and adjusted his rearview mirror. Gil was right behind him.

Within an hour of leaving the city center Leo was ascending the steep gradient of the Long Hill in Kilmacanogue, County Wicklow. A grey mist reduced visibility and slowed progress by the time they reached the elevated plateau of Calary bog. Heavy wind and rain buffeted the two cars as they negotiated undulating roads and narrow bends going through Roundwood and Laragh. When they reached the narrow deserted streets of Rathdrum, Michael suddenly woke up, put his hand to his mouth while shouting at Leo to stop the car. As the car skidded to a halt Michael jumped out, staggered to the rear of the car and vomited. Gil pulled up behind him in the Opel van. Exposed out in the ferocious elements Michael stared about him in a state of disbelief as he became saturated by the gale force rain. It was as if he was living a nightmare from which he could not arouse himself. If the blinding high elevation wind, rain and freezing air caused him great physical distress it also brought an invaluable new awareness in its wake; he was no longer hopelessly drunk. While his mind grappled to understand the predicament in which he found himself, it was his memory that failed him. Fleeting images came of a sea of faces, ribald jokes and the forced laughter of strangers with glasses raised on high. He looked about him again. He knew exactly where he was, he had driven these roads countless times over the years. What he didn't understand was what he was doing out in the stormy night, getting sick by the side of the road, and a stranger was driving his car. And why was he bathed in the headlights of an Opel van parked just a few feet behind him? He ran his hands over his hair and face and wiped away the rain. He got back into the passenger seat of the Mercedes.

Leo looked sideways at Michael with a new sense of urgency. His concern at the moment was that the two cars could be spotted by a police patrol car.

"Well Michael, do you feel better? That was a lot of drink you put away . . . How much further we have to go . . ?"

Michael was sitting bolt upright in his seat. He didn't answer.

"Them 40 winks worked wonders for you," said Leo smiling uneasily, "you don't look any the worse for wear . . ."

"Who are you, and why are you driving my car, and who's that following behind . . ?"

"That's my family behind Michael, don't you remember? We were all drinking together in the Pub and we got worried about how you would get home. As soon as we drop you off my son Gil back there will drive me home. You were good enough to buy us some rounds of drink and things sort of got out of hand. We just wanted to make sure you got home, ok. Are we getting near where you live or what . . ?"

When Michael patted his inside pocket searching for the nugget of gold, the gesture was not lost on Leo.

"Everything ok Michael?"

"Go right at the next turn, follow it for about a quarter of a mile. You'll see a barn and a white house near some trees to your left. That's where I live. You don't have to go through the gate, I'll take it from here . . ."

"Ok, er, tell me Michael, do you have a telephone . . . ?"

"Yes, I have a telephone . . ."

The cars drove through the open gates and pulled up in front of Michael's house. Immediately the two dogs in the house started barking loudly. Leo got out of the car with Michael.

"Good watch dogs you have there Michael . . ."

"Yeah, and they're hungry. I haven't fed them all day." He reached out his hand for the car keys which Leo gave him. "Well, thanks for getting me home. I won't keep you any longer, you must be anxious to get going . . ."

"Sure, we'll be on our way right now. About the telephone. I'd like to telephone my mother Michael. She's elderly. She lives with us and she's a born worrier. She won't sleep till we're all home. I'd really appreciate it Michael . . ."

"Very well, wait here a minute," said Michael tersely and reached into his pocket for his house keys. He unlocked the door and pushed it open. He turned to Leo. "Wait here and I'll lock up the dogs, they're not used to strangers around the place . . ."

327

He went into the house and turned on the lights. The dogs stopped barking when they saw him and followed him out of the house and into the barn. He said some soothing words to them, and settled them down and leashed them to the kennels. After closing the barn door he drew the bolt across. Leo was already in the living room when he returned to the house. A resentful anger enveloped Michael as he pointed to the telephone in the living room. He felt something sinister with the presence of Leo in the house, a feeling he couldn't understand. When he looked away for an instant Leo snatched up a log from the fireplace, raised it high and brought it crashing down on Michael head. Michael groaned as his knees buckled. When Leo hit him a second time he collapsed unconscious to the floor. Leo tossed the log down and went outside. He shouted at Gil and Pat.

"Get the cars out of sight, put them in that barn. Emma, go inside and draw all the curtains. Jikey, look around for some tape and rope. Get moving . . ."

Early the following morning Michael opened his eyes with some effort. He felt something wet and clammy sticking to the side of his face. Blood from a two-inch gash in his head had streamed down the side of his face and dried. He was tightly strapped to a chair with duct tape spread across his mouth. The pounding headache from a hang-over was the least of his concerns as he became fully awake. Rays of early morning sunlight flooded the house. He was in the living room. The clock on the mantelpiece read 6.30.AM. He could see Emma in the kitchen, standing over the stove; he smelled cooking. Leo was stretched out on a settee with his eyes closed. Gil and Pat were dozing uncomfortably in armchairs. Jikey was sitting at a table watching him. He was fidgeting nervously as he turned and looked at Leo.

"Hey Uncle Leo, he's awake," When Leo didn't respond Jikey went over and shook him on the shoulder. "He's awake Uncle Leo," he repeated.

Leo opened his eyes, rubbed them with his knuckles and then stretched. He sat upright on the sofa and nodded towards Gil and Pat. Jikey crossed the room and woke them up. Leo pulled on the rope binding Michael to the chair and gave a loud contemptuous laugh. Gil and Pat and Jikey laughed. Emma, who was cooking food in the kitchen laughed; the house reverberated with laughter directed at the bound and gagged Michael. Leo reached into Michaels pocket and took out the small nugget of gold. He held it under Michaels nose.

"You know, it's dumb cretins like you that turn honest men to crime. It would be a sin not to take advantage of you, you begged for it. I've never met a more naïve fool in all my born days. What kind of a man do you call yourself? You're disgusting, you can't even hold your drink . . ."

Emma called out from the kitchen.

"Food is ready. All that idiot has is eggs in here, not as much as a sausage or a slice of bacon. He must live like a hermit . . ."

"Eggs sounds good to me," said Leo rubbing his hands together,

"ok, get some plates and cutlery on the table, let's get some food in our stomachs."

Leo, Gil, Pat and Jikey sat at the table. In a few moments Emma emerged from the kitchen with pots of tea and plates filled with fried eggs. She sat down and joined them and looked at Michael with a malicious grin.

"What do you say, should we throw the dog a bone?"

"To hell with him," said Leo.

For the next hour the five intruders into Michaels world sat at his table and ate his food. They looked at him with sidelong glances, filled with mockery and derision. Observing them from behind a mouth bound with duct tape Michael finally saw with clarity the perverse bounty he had reaped from his mindless self-indulgence the night before. Still, it defied belief that it should end this way. Before his eyes his own home, Nora's home where they had raised their two sons, was being defiled by derelicts who now plundered it, as if by divine right.

Leo finished his meal hurriedly and the others followed suit. He threw the utensils noisily on the table, wiped his hands on the tablecloth and stood up.

"Right, I want each one of you to pick a room. Bring out everything of value and stack it by the door, we'll load it into the van when we pull out of here. Emma, see if his wife left any jewelry or valuables behind. Check to see if there's a cellar or an attic. Me, I'm going to have a chat with our big spender here about where exactly he found that gold nugget . . ."

While Leo's family proceeded to ransack the house he brought a chair over to Michael and sat down facing him. Reaching forward he pulled back the duct tape from Michael's face. Michael held his head back and gasped in the sudden abundance of air. Leo watched him as his breathing calmed. At that moment Gil came in from a bedroom carrying a shotgun with a shoulder strap and a box of cartridges. He had a bulky plastic bag under his arm.

"Look what I found," he said excitedly, handing the shotgun to Leo.

"A Purdy, a side-by-side Purdey," said Leo admiring the piece, "it's a beauty. Where did a country hick like you get a gun like this . . ?"

"It was my wife's father who owned it . . , it's been in the family for years."

"Well, it's going to be in my family from now on," said Leo as he broke open the gun and looked down the shining barrels, "Beautiful. I like these old guns, they don't make them like this anymore," he examined it some more, inserted two cartridges into the barrels and snapped the gun shut. He placed it on the table and turned his attention to the plastic bag.

"You won't believe what's in there Pa . . ." said Gil.

Leo reached into the plastic bag and took out a round bundle. He held in his hand ten sticks of dynamite bound with nylon cord. Strapped to the side of the dynamite was a blasting fuse. Leo whistled through pursed lips as he looked at it.

"What the hell is this . . . ?" He said to Michael.

"That belonged to some government geologists who took chemical samples from all the land around here. They worked on my land. I found that after they left . . ."

Very carefully Leo replaced the dynamite into the bag and handed it to Gil.

"Be careful how you handle that. Get it out of the house. Put it out in the barn. That's dangerous stuff."

When Gil left, Leo reached out to the shotgun and ran his fingers over the intricate engraving on the trigger housing.

"Of course guns have their place but it would never be my weapon of choice," he reached into the inside pocket of his jacket and took out the pearl-handled switchblade knife. He pressed a button and a 6 inch thin steel blade flew open. He moved the point of the knife up Michael's cheek and across his eyes. "This is my weapon of choice."

When the knifepoint lingered close to his eyes Michael moved his face closer to Leo.

"Yes I could believe that. At night in the dark shadows, sneaking up behind some defenseless drunk and sticking it in his back. I could believe that alright . . ."

Leo jumped up enraged and lashed out with his foot. He caught Michael in the chest, knocking him back backwards. His head hit the floor hard leaving him reeling and dazed. He struggled in vain against the rope binding him to the chair. When Gil walked in Leo shouted at him.

"Pick him up," he snarled at his son.

Gil bent down and gripped the back of his chair. The problem was Gil was a pale pimply-face 23 year old stripling who wilted under Michael's weight and could not straighten his back despite his compulsive need to impress and placate his father. Leo went to his side and together they lifted Michael and the chair upright. Gil was left breathless from the effort and sat down at the table and glared at Michael. Leo again confronted Michael. He waved the knife in Michael's face.

"I'm going to ask you some questions. For your own sake, don't lie to me or I'll start cutting you."

"I've no doubt that you will . . ."

"Good, then we understand each other . . , now, how many visitors you likely to get calling here today . . . ?"

"No one visits here, ever . . ."

"What about telephone people, gas, electric . . ."

"I said no one. I pay my bills once a month when I pick up groceries in Wicklow. I live off the beaten track up here. My nearest neighbor is a half-mile away. He lives down on the main road to Arklow. I see him about two or three times a year at best."

Pat came running in excitedly from a bedroom carrying a Chinese tea caddy. He rattled it as he approached Leo.

"Look what I found on top of a wardrobe," he said as he opened the lid and threw the contents of the tea caddy onto the table."

Numerous pieces of gold bounced and rolled across onto the table.

"Good work . . ," Said Leo. He gathered up the pieces and put them into the tea caddy. "We've got a lot of ground to cover and not much time. Keep looking . . ."

Pat left the room.

"Where exactly did you find this gold . . . ?"

"Before I go into that . . , and I will, I'll tell you where to find the gold. I want you to do something for me. The dogs have not eaten since early yesterday. There's tinned food in the kitchen. Just open a few tins for them. The pointer is old, he has arthritis. I don't work him too much anymore, I'm worried about him . . ."

"Ok," said Leo standing up, "I'll take care of the dogs for you. Stay with him," he said to Gil, "use this if he gives any trouble."

With a quick motion he closed the blade of the knife and threw it onto the table. Gil's eyes glittered as he mused over the knife.

"Don't worry Pa, I'll handle him alright . . ."

"Don't get too carried away Son, he's got a lot to tell us . . ."

"Alright Pa . . ."

Leo strapped the shotgun over his shoulder and went into the kitchen. He put tins of dog food into a plastic bag and pulled some drawers open. He shouted back at Michael."

"I can't find a tin opener back here . . ."

"It's on the window ledge . . ."

Leo put the tin opener into the bag and went out of the kitchen towards the barn. At the sound of the strange step the dogs started barking.

Michael stared dumb-founded as Gil Mulvey sat at the large round oak table and with Leo's switch-blade knife carved his initials into the table that had been in his family for four generations. An uncle had made the round table and his aunt, a French Polisher by trade, had brought the surface of the oak wood table to a mirror-like finish. While watching the hunched shoulders of Gil as he cut away at the wood Michael felt a homicidal rage welling up inside him. He felt the blood surging through him, his face turned a shade darker, his cheeks flushed. The passion and intensity of his feelings were alien to him and swept aside any concerns he might have for his own safety or survival. He was breathing heavily as he strained against the rope binding him to the chair. The movement was seen by Gil who jumped up from the table and faced him. He opened the knife and put the point of it up Michael's nose and pulled on it. Not hard enough to draw blood but enough to subdue Michael's struggle against the rope.

"I'll cut your nose off if you don't stop moving . . ."

Michael exhaled and sat still on the chair. He had to curb his instinct to react against the outrages committed against his person and property. He was playing into their hands, putting his very life in danger by indulging in bluff and bluster when he couldn't even budge from the chair to which he was bound. Showing his anger was to their advantage. They had shown him what they were capable of; if he hoped to live through the ordeal he would first have to devise a plan. His breathing eased considerably as he relaxed back in the chair.

"Look, I just felt my arms were getting numb. I needed to stretch a bit. Can you loosen the rope a little . . ?"

"You try anything like that again and I'll tighten the rope more . . ."

The muted report of two explosions sundered the peace of quiet countryside. Michael thought at first it was a car back-firing but it was unlikely given the remoteness of that region of Wicklow. He didn't allow himself to dwell on the notion that was forming in his mind. Leo entered through the kitchen door while inserting two new cartridges into the shotgun. He came towards him and saw Gil standing by with the open knife in his hand.

"What's going on .. ?" he asked Gil.

"He said he was getting numb on the chair, wants the rope loosened ..."

"I'll keep an eye on him ..."

"What he needs is a good lesson Pa, so he won't try nothing."

"You go ahead. Keep looking around the place for anything worth taking ..."

"Ok Pa," said Gil and left the room.

Leo sat down in front of Michael.

"What were those shots out there?" Michael asked him, "did you do as I asked you, did you feed the dogs?"

"Hell, I never said I was going to feed the dogs."

"You said ..."

"I said I was going to take care of them which I did," he laughed, a vicious sneering laugh, "hell you ought to thank me, the damn dogs will never be hungry again ..."

Michael closed his eyes. He was unable to comprehend the mind of the man in front of him; his sadistic brutality in killing two helpless dogs. The die was cast for him personally. How could they let him leave the house alive? The only way for them to escape the clutches of the law would be to kill him and bury him. In the meantime Leo needed his help to take whatever gold remained on his land. A wild desperate plan began to take shape in his mind. As he mulled it over Leo shook his shoulder.

"Hey I'm talking to you ..."

"Uh, what .. ?"

John Flanagan

"I want you to show me where you found those gold nuggets. I'm going to turn you loose so you can walk around. I swear I'll gut you if you try anything . . . ,"

Leo flicked open the knife and cut the rope and tape binding Michael. He shouted to Gil and Pat who came in and joined him.

"If by some chance that neighbor comes by, the story is that we are prospective buyers and you are showing us over the property, got it?"

"Sure . . ," said Michael. He pointed to a powerful flashlight on the mantelpiece. "We're going to need that . . ." Gil took down the flashlight.

"Let's go . . ," said Leo.

After leaving the house by the backdoor they turned left towards the stream before heading up the hill to the back acre of the property. They were almost completely hidden from view by the barn and the trees encircling the house. From the stream Michael led them up the hill and stopped at the rock outcrops. At this point a century's old beaten track came to a halt at the base of massive boulders of rock and granite. He made straight to the cave where he had closed over the entrance with hawthorn hedging and brush. He threw aside the camouflaged cover, kneeled down and crawled through the dark tunnel as he had done before. Leo turned on the flashlight and followed after him with Gil and Pat in tow. Inside the vaulted cave they stood up. Leo shone the flashlight on the roof and walls to get a perspective of the interior. It was damp and eerily foreboding. The slow trickle of water echoed quietly over sand and gravel in the confined space.

"Is there another way out of here?" Asked Leo.

"That tunnel is all there is. The walls go straight up. It looks like it was hewn out of solid rock."

"Is this where you found the gold . . . ?"

"Right there in the water."

"How in hell did you find gold in here, it's so dark . . . ?"

"This cave faces East. The early morning sun shines directly into the tunnel and lights it up. Apart from that, as you can see I rigged up spotlights for the generator"

"Let's get out of here Pa," said Pat, "this place gives me the creeps . . ," he looked about him nervously, "look how dark it's got already.

For the rest of the morning and into the late afternoon Leo insisted on seeing the remainder of the property. He stopped and knelt by the stream running alongside the hawthorn hedge. He scanned every foot of the stream and motioned for Gil and Pat and Jikey to follow suit. Michael stood back watching them. Since early morning he had affected an attitude of acquiescence, of being seen to be helpful and accommodating. He was under no illusion about the danger he faced. For the sake of their own survival they would not let him go. He could identify each one of them. The plan he was conjuring up in his mind was fraught with risk and danger. He had seen the Opel van and the license plate; he could send them all to prison for a long time. Looking at them he felt his life was already forfeit. The idea entered his mind of making a run for it now as Leo and his cohorts searched the stream for gold. But Leo had the shotgun strapped across his back and his line of fire would be unimpeded in the open ground between him and the house. No, he reasoned, he would have to wait and bide his time for the right moment. When Michael eventually led them back to the house Leo took the flashlight from him.

"Gil, Pat," said Leo, "Tie him back in that chair. We've got a busy day ahead of us tomorrow. We'll pull out of here tomorrow night just as soon as it gets dark."

Gil and Pat pushed Michael back on the chair. They pulled tight on the rope until it dug through his arms and legs. Finally they pressed tape across his mouth. Leo and his family then turned in for the night.

Alone in the living room Michael's mind was racing. While he was being strapped to the chair he had bulked out the muscles of his arms and legs to gain even the slightest degree of flexibility in the rope binding him to the chair. When silence pervaded the house, he allowed himself to relax in the chair and felt the rope loosen a little about his body. With his arms tied behind his back he began to twist and rotate his hands and wrists to the extent that the rope would allow. He gyrated in the chair to move the slackened part of the rope towards his hands. After what seemed an eternity his wrists, raw and bloody, stopped throbbing as he slid the loosened rope down over his hands. For 15 minutes he sat perfectly still with the rope bunched up in his hands. He pulled the rope quickly from him and laid it on the floor. Finally he stood up and suddenly froze as the chair creaked. He heard the rush of feet and in a few seconds Emma opened a bedroom, saw him and shrieked loudly. Michael flung the remaining rope from him and made a dash for the door as another bedroom door opened. He was through the front door and was in the driveway when the houselights were turned on, lighting up the front gate that he was running towards. The shotgun exploded. As he reached the gate he felt shot pellets piercing his left arm and shoulder. He stumbled over and lay panting on the ground. He felt boots and shoes savagely kicking into his head and face. His ribs and back were pummeled as he rolled into a ball and tried to protect himself. Hands grabbed him and pulled him back into the house. The kicking started again. Finally a boot thudded into his head and he lapsed into unconsciousness.

When he came to, he found himself lying prone on the living-room floor, once again trussed up with rope and tape. Every bone in his body ached. His right eye was puffed up and closed over. His left arm and shoulder were without feeling. He ran his tongue around the inside of his mouth. Two of his side teeth were moving loosely to the touch of his tongue. Blood had congealed on his face and forehead. Leo and his family were sitting at the table, all drinking. Bottles of whiskey and wine were scattered about the table. Michael half-closed his good eye and remained motionless.

They looked his way occasionally and went on talking.

"Is he awake yet?" Leo asked.

"No," said Jikey," he'll be out of it for a while. We worked him over real good. He'll be easy to handle from here on . . ."

"Just the same," said Emma, "someone will have to stay with him around the clock from now on. There'll be the devil to pay if he got away from us . . ."

"Yeah, that's right . . ," said Gil.

"Boys," said Emma, "go ahead and get some sleep. Me and Leo have some talking to do . . ."

Gil, Pat and Jikey went into a bedroom and closed the door.

"I have a good idea what you want to talk about." Said Leo.

"Well, I hope so. If we want to cover our tracks there's no other way to handle this . . ."

Through his half-closed good eye Michael could see Emma looking down at him.

"Leo, I've stuck with you through thick and thin but I'm telling you now I don't like this, I don't like it at all. You're all I've got, you and the boys and I don't want to lose anyone . . ."

"You're not going to lose anybody . . ."

"Hush and let me finish. Every ounce of gold you take from this place will be worthless . . , unless you do away

339

with him," she nodded towards the motionless figure of Michael on the floor. "You've got to do him in and bury him somewhere up on the hill. We have to burn his car. Clear away tire prints and any evidence we've been here. Hell, I'll kill him myself if you don't want to do it . . ."

"I'll do it, I'll do it. Just leave it to me," Leo looked at his watch, "it's a couple of more hours till daylight. Why don't you catch some sleep? I'll keep an eye on him . . ."

"No," said Emma, "you and the boys have a lot of work in that cave. I'll watch him . . ."

Leo went into the bedroom. Emma filled up her empty wineglass, took a long drink and turned again to look at Michael. From the shadows he watched her every move until he fell into a fitful drowsiness, exhausted from pain, hunger and lack of sleep.

After a few hours he awakened to the sound of the backdoor opening and closing. Early morning light filled the kitchen and living room. Hands gripped him roughly and pulled him into a sitting position on the floor. He kept his eyes firmly closed and let his head loll about on his chest. Leo slapped his face roughly.

"No," he said, talking to Emma, "he's out for the count . . ," when Leo stood up he took out his switchblade knife and gave it to her, "here, take this. Make sure he doesn't move. Listen to me everyone. Maybe we'll get really lucky up in that cave. Have a quick look around and find something we can carry gold in . . ."

Gil, Pat, and Jikey went into the bedrooms. They pulled open closets and drawers and threw them noisily on the floors. Pat found a large black briefcase, upended the contents and brought it out to Leo. He inspected it, snapped it shut and handed it to Pat.

"Don't worry about that fool," said Emma looking at Michael, "he's not going anywhere," she handed Gil a plastic bag, "here's a thermos full of coffee and some sandwiches, they should last through the day . . ."

Leo, Gil, Pat and Jikey departed through the back door.

Three hours passed and Emma didn't budge from the table. Having to mount guard over Michael was causing her some frustration as she wanted to have a hand in the search for the gold. Her face twisted in a grimace as she banged a fist in anger on the table. There was nothing in her appearance or in the makeup of her character that was remotely attractive about Emma. She could never, in the most liberal interpretation of the word, be described as comely. She had sharp angular features and a sharp vituperative tongue that lashed out at anyone unfortunate enough to incur her wrath. Michael watched her every move. He scanned as much of the room as his limited vision would allow, without moving. He had seen Leo give her the switchblade knife and where she had laid it on the table. She was sitting now with her head rested on her arms but she was too restless and stood up from the table. She blinked her eyes drowsily and went over to Michael. She kicked at his feet. When she got no reaction she looked about and saw his bag of golf clubs standing in a corner. She pulled the driver club out of the bag and stood over Michael. She raised it up high. Even before the impact Michael knew he would be serving his own death sentence if he uttered a sound. He gritted his teeth and held his breath as the heavy club slammed into his leg. Not a sound emitted from him as he fell in and out of consciousness.

"I know you're awake damn you . . ," she said, "if I throw some boiling water over you, that will move you . . ." She kicked him in the arm that had been shot. It was all Michael could do to stop himself shouting out in agony. Emma went back to the table and sat down muttering and yawning. She threw the club away. After a few minutes she reached out for the wine bottle and poured herself a drink. The clock ticked away two more hours. Her head began nodding and her eyes were closing over when the back door burst open and Gil ran in.

He was excited and breathless. Under his right arm he was carrying the briefcase. He put it down on the table, unsnapped the locks and slid it towards Emma. She opened the briefcase and her mouth fell open.

"Is it, is it . . ?" was all she could stammer.

"Gold. Every last ounce of it." Said Gil.

The heavy briefcase was filled to capacity with nuggets of gold. Gil closed over the cover, snapped the locks shut and placed the briefcase on the floor. He jumped up from the table and headed back out of the house. At the door he stopped and looked back at Emma.

"Pa said to keep that in a safe place and be ready to leave here after dark. Can you believe it, they're still digging up gold in that cave. We're going to be rich, we'll all be millionaires . . ." He was about to go out through the door when he looked at Michael. He went over to him. "Is he still out cold, did you try to wake him?

As long as he's well tied . . , damn him, he could ruin everything for us . . ." He drew back his foot and kicked Michael in the ribs. He turned quickly and went out of the house. He made his way back to the cave and joined in the continued search for more gold.

Michael tried to shift his twisted body to ease the pain of the kick Gil had just given him. He feared a cracked rib as a searing ache spread across his side.

When Gil departed, Emma took another glass of wine. Slowly she began swaying and muttering incoherently. Michael guessed she was already well inebriated before she had this last glass of wine. He had no idea how he could try to escape, watched over as he was by a drunken harpie who was also planning his murder. He watched the clock as two more hours passed by and Emma dispensed with three more glasses of wine. She eventually shoved away her wineglass. Her head sunk down on her arms. Michael listened intently to the rhythm of her fitful breathing. When she eventually fell asleep he strained against the bonds and injuries that restricted his every move. Now there was a new sense of urgency in his desperate attempt to set himself free. There was no longer any doubt but that he was fighting for his life. The rope and heavy tape clung to him like a carapace without a millimeter of flexibility. Only his feet, and his wrists tied behind his back had any degree of movement. He lay on his stomach and by putting pressure on his shoulders he dragged his knees under his abdomen. By degrees he straightened up his back until he was in a kneeling position. Keeping his balance was crucial to his agonizing attempt to stand up. While watching Emma he took a deep breath, leaned back and heaved himself up on his feet. The first thing he felt was a dizziness that made his head reel. He shut his uninjured eye to stop the sensation of vertigo, of the room moving about him. His whole body trembled as he fought to maintain his balance. At last the sickening spinning stopped and he dared to breath freely again. He inched closer to Emma. Guttural noises emanated from her from time to time. Her hair was tangled and her mouth was agape. Michael had reached a point where he had to throw caution to the wind. He was two meters from the table where the pearl-handled switchblade knife lay close to Emma's hand. He shuffled closer to the table and stopped. He was faced with another crisis; the knife was in the center of the table. The way he was bound up he would have to somehow sit on the edge of the table for his hands to reach the knife;

JOHN FLANAGAN

that would run the risk of awakening Emma. He solved the dilemma by getting to the table, bending over it and picking up the knife with his teeth. He inched slowly to the living room wall, turned his back to it and slid down quietly to the floor. He dropped the knife from his teeth to his lap and maneuvered it to his hand. Suddenly it was there, he was holding it safely in his grasp. He flicked the knife open. The razor-like blade sliced cleanly through the rope and tape. He forgot the pain of his aching body and limbs, his broken rib, his shattered eye. He ripped the final remnants of the rope and tape from him. Free at last he deliberated for some moments. He then looked at the drunken form of Emma with hatred and outrage rising within him. He got shakily to his feet, closed over the knife and put it in his pocket. He went to the kitchen sink and removed his shirt. He sponged away the blood from the cuts and bruises covering his body. His left eye stung where the swelling had turned purple. He looked in a mirror and opened his mouth. With a thumb and forefinger he reached in and pulled out the two loosened teeth. He rinsed his mouth out, dried off put his shirt back on. A fleeting movement behind him made him turn suddenly just as Emma ran screaming at him with a golf club raised in her hands. Hampered by his injuries he barely managed to side-step her onward rush, kicked out and sent her sprawling to the floor. The shock of the fall seemed to have a sobering effect on Emma as she got quickly to her feet and picked up the fallen club. When she raised the club again Michael did nothing but sneer. She became immobilized and slowly lowered the club. She cringed when Michael came towards her, pulled the club from her hands and threw it on the floor. With her back to the kitchen wall a feeling of uncontrollable terror took hold of her as she faced Michael.

344

"Sit in that chair and don't move from it." Said Michael

Emma stared at him as if she was suddenly struck dumb. She felt she and her family had awakened some primal savagery in the soul of an affable, inoffensive gentle man. She put her hands to her temples as if the realization of what they had done only now dawned on her. He had been nothing but friendly and outgoing when he came into the Pub on Burgh Quay and cheerfully joined them. Perhaps he was naïvely generous and free with his money but he meant them no harm. And too naïve to suspect Leo and Gil, Pat and Jikey and herself had waited like drooling jackals in long grass for the right moment to strike. They had struck. They came to his home and plundered it. They savagely beat him, shot him and robbed him even of his soul, of who he was; for he could never again be the man he was before they came into his life. He stood over her as she sat resignedly, timidly in the chair and clasped her hands. She looked down at her hands.

"The keys of the two cars," he said harshly, "get them."

Zombie-like Emma stood up and faced him. She went to the room where Leo had been sleeping and retrieved the keys from the dressing table. She handed them to Michael.

"Follow me . . ." He said to her.

Michael left the house with Emma behind him. He pulled open the barn door and went inside. After he opened the boot of the Mercedes car he turned to Emma.

"Get in . . ." He said.

"What are you going to do with me . . ?"

Michael picked up a long-handled shovel beside the workbench and came menacingly towards her.

"Get in, or I'll kill you first and then put you in . . , it's all the same to me . . ."

Emma at this point was terrified with fear and climbed into the boot of the car. When Michael slammed the lid down she screamed for a few moments and then became quiet. Inside the dark space she pressed her hands against the steel lid of the boot and collapsed back; resigned at last to the whatever fate that awaited her. Some of the stark terror she experienced earlier left her as she closed her eyes and waited in her claustrophobic tomb.

Michael picked a corner of the barn and began digging a hole. He dug a meter deep. He went over to the dead dogs' cadavers, placed them in the hole and covered them over. He searched the barn to locate where Gil had put the dynamite. When he found it he went back to the house and carefully put the dynamite and fuse into a backpack. Reaching on top of the kitchen dresser he took down a pair of binoculars. He looked at his watch. It was 12.45 PM. He drew back the curtains of a back bedroom and with the binoculars scanned the rockface and granite boulders on the top of the hill. He couldn't detect any movement. He looked at the sky. In a few more hours midwinter darkness would begin to fall. He could not afford to wait that long. Donning the back-pack he stopped by the kitchen and put a box of matches in his pocket. He went out through the back door and headed up towards the hill.

As he neared the top of the hill he could hear the muffled sound of the generator. He was bent over in pain and was limping by the time he reached the cave. He took off the backpack holding the dynamite and laid it carefully at his feet. He had no idea how sensitive or dangerous the dynamite would be in handling it. He took out the ten sticks and bound them together with tape. Very carefully he inserted a blasting cap and fuse into one of the sticks. He went to the mouth of the tunnel and kneeled down.

Inside the cave Leo was standing facing a wall. With a claw hammer he was chipping at a gold vein he had found

346

in the wall. Minute chips and morsels of the precious metal flew off the wall and landed at his feet. Gil and Jikey were on their hands and knees picking up the pieces while Pat was searching for the last remnants to be found in the narrow stream. These were stored on the dry earth beside the generator. At this point the accumulation of the gold pile after hours of excavating had become an impressive mound. Leo stopped chipping, threw down the hammer and leaned exhausted the wall.

"Oh hell," he said and had to shout above the noise of the generator, "That's it, take a break. Let's open those sandwiches . . ."

Michael knelt before the tunnel entrance to the cave with his left knee on the ground and his left arm leaning on the granite wall. His right arm was swinging loosely, practicing the arc he would need to pitch the dynamite to the furthest point along the tunnel. Placing the dynamite on the grass he took the box of matches from his pocket. He looked up at the sky again. The wind had died down. He was in a thoughtful, reflective state of mind. He had cooled down; his raging lust for revenge had abated but was not entirely quenched. He was in no hurry to send four men to their deaths however much he considered their demise to be just and deserving. There was one glaring fact that removed all doubt about the decision he had made. If they were arrested and sentenced, it was inconceivable that Leo and his gang, at the expiration of a prison term, would not return to threaten his life and property again. He felt no sense of moral ambiguity in sacrificing the lives of Leo and his cohorts, to protect his own. Leo and his brood preyed on societies vulnerable and weak, he a coward at heart who found safety in numbers. And Leo knew the exact location where he lived in Avoca. Michael had guided him to it on that fateful night when he had been too drunk to know any better. In order now to effect some semblance of a life for himself he would have to capitulate totally to Leo's demands, and then run away. The most basic life forms put up a defense itself against attack. He believed it would be futile to call the police. How could he expect justice from the law? The law; that amorphous domain administered by societies rich and privileged few. In effect the law rewarded murderers and felons for the crimes they perpetrate on innocent victims; incarcerated thugs are provided with free accommodation and sustenance, educational opportunities and entertainment, with scant regard to the victims of their outrages.

Yes, Michael finally decided, as he turned over the box of matches in his hand, and withdrew a match; Leo and his brood would be back if they were subjected to the law of the land, and very likely bring more felons with him next time.

The sun was descending in the west, covering the towering rock-faces in shades of greyish blue. Michael lit the fuse and picked up the bulky roll of dynamite. He bent down one final time to gauge the angle and length of the tunnel leading to the cave. He drew back his right arm and hurled the dynamite as far as he could see in the gathering dusk. He pushed himself up and away from the tunnel opening and sped down the hill as fast as his shattered body would allow. He stumbled and fell on the steepest part of the hill and rolled down. Slowly and agonizingly he picked himself up to distance himself from the rock-face. He had fallen down when the dynamite exploded. He turned and looked up the hill. The entire hilltop erupted. Pulverized rock and granite tumbled down the hillside. Pine and fir trees were uprooted, caught and tossed like matchsticks in the avalanche. The inner walls of the cave had imploded. The resulting depression was buried under tons of shattered rocks, earth and falling debris.

Michael got to his feet and travelled the short distance to the house. Darkness had settled over the region as he closed the house curtains and rested back in the armchair. The silence seemed pervasive in the house as he looked about the living room. It was no longer the same room, the same house. He looked at the scattered cutlery, at the used piles of dishes and plates. He flinched when he saw the decimated round oak table, the crocheted table cover Nora had hand-made was lying in a heap on the floor. Everything that Leo and his progeny had touched they had profaned. It was as if some obscene plague had contaminated the sanctity of his home. He stretched to get some relief from his aching muscles. Darkness had settled over the region as he finished drawing the curtains across the windows, and turned on the lights. He missed the dogs. They would be alive today if it was not for his idiocy, but self-recriminations were useless at this point. He would have to make a visit to the hospital; a rib was broken he was sure of it. In the bathroom he swabbed the cuts and bruises with an antiseptic. Beyond cleaning the wounds, the pellets from the shotgun lodged in his arm and shoulder would have to wait. He soaked in the bath for an hour, dried off and got dressed. The clock chimed 8:00 PM. The nightmare wasn't over yet; something would have to be done about Emma. He put on an anorak, crossed over to the barn and switched on the lights. He opened the boot door of the Mercedes to find Emma cowering and staring at him, too petrified to move. She looked like a trapped animal with her disheveled hair, her wild eyes and distorted features. The thunderous roar of the explosion had rocked the car, throwing her into further terror. When she began to say something he cut her off.

"Get out . . ," he growled, "go up to the house. Clean yourself up, we're going on a journey."

Michael waited in the living room while Emma prepared to leave. She came from the bathroom combing her hair.

"When did you stop being a woman?" He asked her as he held open the door. "Let's go . . ."

He pushed her less forcefully into the backseat of the Mercedes and told her to lay down and out of sight.

He drove down to the link road in Arklow and joined the busy Saturday night traffic on the N11 main road going to Dublin. Rain started to fall heavily and he turned on the windshield wipers. The kilometers flew by quickly in the old classic car. Wicklow, Bray, Stillorgan flew quickly by. After fifty minutes he arrived at his destination; the rear car park of the Berkeley Court Hotel in Dublin. He found a vacant spot in a quiet shaded area, cut the engine and pulled on the hand brake. The rain was saturating with gusts of wind buffeting the car park. Michael got quickly out of the car, reached in the back door and helped Emma to get out. She stared up at him with glazed eyes. She climbed out awkwardly, leaning heavily on him for assistance. Dressed in a frock and light sweater she shivered in the downpour and made a futile attempt to brush her hair away from her face.

"I don't feel so frightened of you any more. I don't think you are going to hurt me . . ."

"Do you see those cars lined up over there . . . ?" He pointed past the black railings outside the car park. "Taxis. Take one. Get home, get in out of this rain. Do you have enough money for a taxi?"

Emma opened her purse and searched it.

"I don't know . . ."

"Here, take this . . ." Michael dug into his trouser pockets and took out a small roll of euro notes.

She stared blankly at the money.

"I'm so sorry, I'm so very sorry . . ."

"You better take this," He unzipped his anorak and helped Emma into it. She stood in silence as he closed the anorak and pulled the hood up over her head.

"Stop for a meal somewhere. You better get going now."

She walked tentatively towards the taxi rank, her legs still felt weak and cramped. She looked back once before she stepped into the taxi. He was watching her as the rain poured down on him. When she was gone he turned and got back into the car. He drove out of the car park and picked up the N11 highway going south. While his head reeled at moments when he recalled the tumultuous events of the past 24 hours, he had nevertheless, recovered clarity of thought. He was not overwhelmed nor did he harbor the slightest sense of remorse in taking the lives of four men who were intent on taking his own. They were buried forever under tons of rock and granite; the worms were welcome to them. And he was not worried about Emma sending police to his house. From the little he could remember of the events of the previous night Emma drank so much wine she had to be helped out of the Pub by Pat and Jikey. No, the likelihood was that she had fallen asleep in the car all the way to Avoca. When he finally arrived back at the house it was close on 11:00 PM. He put the house lights off and went to bed.

He awoke the following morning as fresh and alert as his injuries would allow. He called his doctor and made an appointment for the following day. He then rounded up everything in the house that was touched or used by Leo and his gang and cleaned and disinfected all of it. While the washing machine and dishwasher were operating he scrubbed the kitchen tiles and mopped the parquet floors. He finally sat down feeling exhausted, but satisfyingly so. Over the next few days he visited his doctor who sent him to the hospital in Arklow to have the shot pellets removed from his arm and shoulder. In answer to the surgeon's enquiry as to how they got there he said he was out hunting with a friend and was shot accidently, the broken rib and other bruises he got when he fell on some rocks. The doctor listened with some skepticism to his implausible excuses, thought for a moment and shrugged. As a GP he had heard some taller stories in his time.

The following day Michael hooked up the trailer to the small tractor he kept in the barn. He rounded up the livestock and ferried them to his neighbor's farm. Michael had decided to sell his house and offered the livestock free to Pat Mulcahy and his wife Ainne. He asked Pat to look after the Mercedes, saying that that he would return at another time to collect it. It took him two full days to clear the back field of fallen rubble from the hillside. His body was showing clear signs of recovery and by the end of the week he was no longer limping. He spent a lot of time on the telephone. He gave the keys of the house to the auctioneer with a telephone number where he could be contacted.

Early in the morning on his last day in the house Michael opened the barn door and loaded some personal belongings into Leo's Opel van. Amongst them was the heavy black briefcase, bulging with gold. He drove out through the gates past the large 'for sale' sign and was soon on the road to Dublin. Traffic was sparse and he made good time. At Merrion he turned right off the main road, drove to Sandymount and eventually pulled into the busy car park near to the Poolbeg Marina on Pigeon House Road. Walter was waiting for him.

"Are you sure about the car Walter, parking it here?"

"Well I picked this spot because I don't see any surveillance cameras," said Walter, looking around the car park. "no, in about one week they will start to put stickers on the car. In two weeks they will haul it out of here and that will be the end of it . . ."

Together they unloaded Michael's belongings and walked and towards the marina where the yacht was berthed. As Michael handed him the black briefcase fill with gold he looked at it thoughtfully.

"My friend," said Walter as if reading his thoughts, "we'll just stow that in the galley and forget about it. I've had my boat here for the past three years," he smiled reassuringly; "they know me as an old sea dog. We will be fine."

Michael looked up and there it was before him; Walter's yacht in all its regal glory. The 'Mangalore' was an old yacht, made of teak and mahogany from stem to stern. While Walter primed the engine and prepared to get under way Michael leaned over from the dockside and climbed nimbly aboard. To acquaint himself with the layout of the vessel he walked back and forth on the multi-varnished deck. He was awestruck by the sight of the scrubbed canvass sails, the shining brass, the orderliness of the tackle; the polished mahogany helm wheel and the two gleaming masts rising majestically above the deck. With impeccable craftsmanship and attention to detail, the old yacht had been lovingly restored by master mariner Walter, when he bought it. When he paused for a moment on deck, Michael's heart quickened when he felt the gentle undulations of the ebbing tide causing the deck to roll beneath his feet.

In the engine room Walter pressed the starter button and the 40 horsepower diesel engine roared into life. He put the engine in neutral and left it idling. He then attached an ensign flag to the stern of the yacht. After switching on the radio he made two calls; one to the harbormaster and one to his wife in Nice. When he emerged on deck he smiled when he saw an expression just short of rapture on the face of Michael.

"Finding your sea legs?"

Michaels face broke out into a broad grin.

"I'm trying Walter. It's going to take some time. This yacht . . , it's like being in a dream . . ."

"We have a favorable wind. Wait till you see her when I cut the engines and put her through her paces, out on the open water."

Walter turned and spread his arm towards the deck. He spoke as if the yacht was a living, breathing entity as he enunciated its virtues.

"It's a beauty," he said, "she's narrow with a low point of gravity. She's straight and true. Unless you sailed and owned a boat you'd never understand. A boat like this haunts you. I don't own the boat, the boat owns me."

He placed a hand on Michael's shoulder.

"We're ready to cast off. Can you go dockside and toss the ropes on board."

Michael stepped onto the dock, uncoupled the ropes and jumped back on.

"Now, coil them up neatly and tie them to the bulwark."

Walter went to the helm and put the engine in gear. The yacht inched away from the dock. He steered it out of the Poolbeg marina until they reached the sea. Walter cut the engine. He was in a jubilant mood as the sails were hoisted and billowed out before them. The 'Mangalore' sliced evenly through the moderately calm Irish Sea at 15 knots. He motioned for Michael to join him at the helm.

"There's a berth waiting for us at the marina in Nice. My wife and I are members there. We have a house in the hills above the marina. It's an old house but it's in good shape. It has a huge fireplace, in winter it's very warm and comfortable. I just talked to her on the phone. She told me to tell you she has an Irish whiskey waiting."

"I look forward to that."

"When we get to Nice, I have a project in mind that I'm really looking forward to. Take a guess what it is"

Michael shrugged his shoulders and smiled.

"I've no idea, Walter."

"I'm going to make a sailor out of you. And now that you are a very rich man, you can buy your own yacht."

"I think I would enjoy that very much."

The Mangalore sailed on a south easterly course towards a horizon of unlimited visibility

In the early dawn up on the hill behind Michael's house in Avoca, a lone deer was foraging in the dew moistened grass. It raised its head suddenly. Its acute senses had picked up a faint tapping that was not germane to the pastoral stillness of the morning. A weak, muffled sound followed, coming from beneath a pile of rubble at the bottom of a rockface.

The deer turned and ran. With a few leaps and bounds it disappeared into the safety of the woods.

THE END

ARSON

by

JOHN FLANAGAN

CLIVE KELLER WAS THE ONLY son of Edward Keller, a
successful property developer. A patriarchal figure, Keller
senior was renowned for his philanthropy and charity to
Dublin's poor and destitute. Clive Keller was born into very
privileged circumstances. As an only child he was cossetted
by doting parents from the moment he was born, in the
family mansion in Foxrock, an affluent surburb of south
Dublin. By the time he became a teenager his character and
personality reflected an indulgent, minimally disciplined
life. He was likable and confident and had every reason to
be; his powerful father hovered in the background ready
to remove any or all impediments to his son's well-being.
A sense of trepidation, of love and fear underpinned his
relationship with his strong-willed, charismatic father: Clive
Keller had a desperate need to please his father, to be found
worthy of being his son. He entered university with one great
concern; out of fear of incurring disfavor, he had decided not
to tell his father of the inner revulsion he felt at the thought
of business as a career choice.

At Trinity University Clive Keller exulted in a new sense of freedom. He excelled in the humanities; his discipline being impressionist painting. The idiom revealed a wealth of natural talent resulting in innovative themes ablaze with originality, color and light. It was the happiest time of his adult life. He was invited to lecture on his style and work, and by his final semester, his paintings were displayed in a public gallery in Dublin. It was a wrench at graduation, to leave it all behind. His business study results proved to be disappointing; his efforts being, unfairly perhaps, compared to his father's meteoric rise in business. The uninviting prospect that faced him for the rest of his working life was to live and exist within the restricted parameters, for him, of his father's business empire.

Before and after graduation Clive Keller spent a lot of time with his father on the local golf course. The convivial landscape lent scant relief to the serious nature of the topic his father was pursuing and detracted from his enjoyment of the game. Later in a secluded corner of the club lounge Edward Keller continued to ply his son with questions about how he would like to commence his business career, with any one of the companies he owned. Keller Senior did not express, nor by his manner ever show, except to his wife Rose, his mounting unease about his son's apathetic interest in his business endeavors. The trouble with Rose was she became aggressively defensive whenever he criticized their sons shortcomings. Keller was worried about the success of his business as the economic woes of the country deepened; he worried about his legacy. He loved his son but Keller senior did not seem to understand that the more unpalatable aspects of business could be inimical to the more sensitive mind. Keller was getting beyond exasperation with his timorous son. There were other personal factors for him to consider. Of late he had begun to feel light headed, his heart fluttered wildly. His doctor told him he had developed atrial fibrillation of the heart. He had followed medical advice to cope with the problem initially and then ignored it.

In the golf club lounge when his son prevaricated once again, Keller frowned and lapsed into a prolonged silence. He felt almost betrayed by his son's indifference to the business opportunity he was handing him on a plate; he didn't even have to earn it. He ended the conversation by insisting his son start on a modest level, possibly as an assistant within the Group until he got a good grasp of business management.

Two months after graduation Clive Keller, was sitting at a desk in an office on the 5th floor of Group headquarters building in Donnybrook, Dublin. He was staring vaguely at sheets of data and statistics he had just been handed by an accountant, and found them incomprehensible. His heart pounded, his forehead glistened with perspiration. Disgruntled he pushed the paperwork aside and clasped his hands. It seemed his mind could not function cogently, or come to grasp with the most mundane problems presented to him. It was as if his years of business studies at the university were a meaningless waste of time. His great fear of failure obtruded into every aspect of his daily life. He was trying to excel in a world not of his own making; for which he had no talent, even detested. He was proving to be glaringly inept to those around him. Associates who were asked by his father to clandestinely monitor his progress became hostile in time. He was sick to his soul; the person he had become was a stranger to him. He wanted to conquer the world of business with his father, for his father. He had the will and the intention and he had tried; more than he had ever tried to succeed at anything else in his life. He also knew he had no one to blame but himself. His father laid the world at his feet; it was there for the taking. He had squandered his father's love and regard for him by his laissez faire attitude to his business studies at university where he did just enough to get passing grades, nothing more. He knew he didn't lack intelligence. It was his lack of true commitment and interest that undermined his strongest resolve, with abject results. He retained almost nothing of what he learned in college; the newly acquired business knowledge seemed to have been commended to the deepest recesses of his mind from which he could neither retrieve nor recollect. No fire raged within him as it did when he faced a new canvas, when an inward vision guided the brush movements with such purpose he often stood back and gasped at the visual effect of what he had created.

Prior to his distinguished business career Edward Keller arrived in Dublin from the far-flung scenic village of Ballyroe in the dingle peninsula of County Kerry. With nothing more than a small suitcase that contained all his worldly goods and a tidy sum willed to him, he settled in a cold-water flat in Aungier Street in Dublin's south side. The year was 1987. In short shrift he acquired a small bottling plant in Rutland Place, a back-lane of the inner city. With the plant up and running he introduced himself to his local bank and was fortunate to find a manager appreciate of his talent and ambition. The bank financed his purchase of derelict tenement houses falling to ruin on Mountjoy Square. He got them for a minimal price, refurbished them and leased them out. After he purchased a clothing factory with 20 employees in Capel Street, he formed the Keller Group Incorporated. To the staid, closely-knit, club and lodge oriented businessmen who formed the core of Dublin social life, he was seen as an interloper, an unproved Johnny-come-lately. At a time when the Irish economy began dragging its heels Edward Keller was steadfastly accumulating property for the Keller Group. He had also somewhat of a contentious attitude in that he never even tried to interact socially with men he had to do business with. In time he earned the reputation of being tough and unyielding, secretive and closemouthed.

When Keller bought Wentworth Tech, the previous owners had prevailed with the publicly quoted company but closure became inevitable and the company was put up for sale. Keller was monitoring Wentworth Tech closely. When the price bottomed out he moved, a press wag later commented, like a predator sensing the kill. Buoyed up by the successes of his prior acquisitions, Keller was euphoric when he added Wentworth Tech to his coterie of growing companies. But buying Wentworth Tech almost proved the undoing of the burgeoning merchant prince. The clerks he had appointed to make a comprehensive inventory of the stock in the vast warehouse, and on which he based his bid for Wentworth Tech, had made grave errors in the report sent to Keller. Container-loads of defective computers, television and radio sets packed 25% of storage space of the vast warehouse. It transpired that Keller's staff had merely read the content labels of the locked containers and cartons, copying the details into the inventory report. When the error was discovered, it was too late for Keller to retract his bid, the deeds of ownership were already signed and stamped and lodged with the courts. The costly blunder placed the Keller Group in dire financial straits at a time when the banks had lost all sense of congeniality.

After almost 20 years of accumulating property and wealth, Edward Keller changed tack to adapt to new challenges in more turbulent seas, as the lingering malaise of the dying Celtic Tiger spread like a contagion through the land. Harrowing tales of bank foreclosures, bankruptcies, and panic selling abounded. Massive housing projects were abandoned almost overnight, deserted by feckless builders to become ghostly blights on the landscape. Across the country steel cranes hung over deserted buildings like giant praying mantises. And finally, as unemployment in Ireland reached 11%, the age-old scourge of immigration once more siphoned away the young and the able to foreign shores.

Keller retreated to his new home in Foxrock to consider his losses and options. He did something he rarely did during the week; he opened a bottle of whiskey, sunk into a sofa and poured himself a stiff drink. He half-emptied the glass and filled it again. He put the glass down as the fiery liquid burned his throat and gradually altered the normally concise symmetry of his mind. He made mental notes of how he should redress the situation from getting worse-if that was possible. As he eventually dozed off his final thoughts were how dire his situation was; he faced ruin. He must take drastic measures to limit the damage.

The following morning, feeling refreshed and with a new resolve, Keller dismissed the six clerks responsible for the debacle that cost him so dearly. He approached the banks again to take a second mortgage on his existing loan, but they were adamant, he had no collateral left to justify another loan. He thought he detected a note of contempt in the banks refusal, as if they had erred in helping him acquire Wentworth Tech. If truth be told they were appalled by his lack of judgment. The last loan extended to him had been to cover the warehouse insurance. He had insured with Northstar Insurance; no other underwriter would risk covering the potential fire hazard contents of the immense warehouse. Northstar Insurance, under the owner-chairman John Cobb, charged the Keller Group an exorbitant fee for insurance cover. In the event of accidental fire the policy would pay the insured the sum of 200,000 Euros.

Keller spent the next few weeks fending-off his creditors who had begun mustering at the gates. Bankruptcy and ruin stared him in the face as he sought to cope with new daily challenges. He held off hiring new men until the last moment, to replace the Wentworth Tech salesmen he had fired. A few days later he received a call from the personnel department. It was from a sales manager, Ger Kelly, who said he had interviewed some applicants for the sales department. The manager said it came down to making a choice between two final candidates. The one Kelly chose was named Sean Buchanan, who was 24 years old. Buchanan said to him in the interview that he hoped he wouldn't have to work too much overtime, he wanted to improve his education by going to night school. Kelly said Buchanan seemed to know the right things to say, he was a bit smart-alecky, overconfident perhaps, but good potential. He had been in sales, selling car parts, until he was let go when the company folded. He found him presentable and well-dressed, he had a fair knowledge of computers.

"Do you wish to see him, Mr. Keller?"

"No, I've enough to worry about. You take care of it."

"Very good, Mr. Keller."

Thus Sean Buchanan began a period of employment with the Keller Group of companies. He served in sales. His initial endeavors proved impressive. He had a natural persuasiveness with clients that was admired and envied by his peers. It was believed a promising future awaited him when the fluctuating economy stabilized and would grow again. Adversely the debonair salesman displayed a volatile temper on occasion; but he was always quick to apologize, and was mostly forgiven by the victims of his outbursts by reason of his generally affable persona. But Buchanan's tenure as a rising star with Wentworth Tech was neither long nor happy. Apart from his occasional tantrum, he could not control certain compulsions that formed destructive patterns in his young life and laid to waste his otherwise lofty ambitions. Sean Buchanan had a tendency to pilfer; a habit begun as a street urchin in Dublin and had never left him. The satisfaction he felt in getting something for nothing overcame, in time, his ever dwindling pangs of conscience. As he had grown into an adult Buchanan developed a very cynical attitude towards societal mores, and determined to escape the egregious environment into which he had been born. As a young adult he had managed to avoid incarceration and thus had no police record to hamper his employment prospects.

At the end of his first year with the Keller Group, Buchanan showed signs of a growing petulance and unease. He was upset about many things but most of all his income. His salary consisted of a fixed stipend, a moderate sum which in itself barely covered his outlay on rent, car repayments and his fine wardrobe in which he took special pride. The carrot for him was the generous commission Wentworth Tech paid it's salesmen on goods sold. This source of income was diminishing rapidly with the failing economy, filling each new day with new concerns.

It was part of Buchanan's job to keep account of computers and cell-phones. The electronic instruments filling the shelves of the Wentworth Tech warehouse beckoned to Buchanan, enticed him with the allure of the sirens tempting Ulysses to his doom. After a year with Wentworth Tech and by now a trusted employee, late one night he drove into the warehouse. The offices were all closed. He had keys as his job required he had access to the warehouse. He closed the steel door and looked about him furtively. The light from street lamps allowed him to find his way in the semi-darkness. Being lithe and athletic, he swiftly loaded ten personal computers into his car. He knew the company had no security guards as yet. They were in no hurry as the building was deemed as impregnable as a fortress with steel doors and barred windows. Barely daring to breathe he pressed a button and the exit gate slid open. After driving out he closed the gate and locked it. Without using his headlights he let the car careen noiselessly down a slight incline to the main gate. He followed the same procedure and locked the gate behind him. He turned on his headlights. He was soon lost in the traffic heading towards the city.

The discovery of the stolen computers was immediately hushed up within Wentworth Tech. At the behest of Mr. Keller the area was cordoned off much like a crime scene. The police, again at Mr. Keller's insistence, were not called in. The forklift driver who discovered the theft and the warehouse manager to whom he reported it, were each cautioned not to talk about the matter with anyone. They were left in little doubt of the consequences if they discussed it. Three weeks later, Mr. Eddy Flynn, the sales director, approached Buchanan while he was on his 10:00 AM tea break. Buchanan was leaning back in his chair with his feet up on the table. He was telling a joke that had his sales colleagues guffawing loudly. When he turned and saw Flynn bearing down on him he flinched for a moment, recovered his momentum and put his feet on the floor. He smiled broadly.

"Hi Mr. Flynn," he said, "what's up?"

"Boss wants to see you."

"Oh, what's it about?"

"Dunno", said Flynn, turning to leave, "maybe he's making you the CEO of the Group."

"He should be that lucky." Flynn shook his head. Buchanan was a smart-ass and too cocky, but there was just something about him he liked.

Buchanan walked the short distance to the Group headquarters building and went up the carpeted staircase to Keller's office. The secretary stood up and smiled. She preceded him, opened the office door and closed it behind him when he went in. Keller sat behind a large ornate desk in an office that exuded expensive good taste, not the least of which was an original oil painting adorning the office wall. He had bought the Cezanne when his star was in its zenith, when he had the Midas touch. In the last few weeks he had been looking more quizzically at the painting. He had bought it to impress his clients. Personally he couldn't understand what anyone saw in a bunch of fruit.

He motioned Buchanan to a seat with a wave of his hand. Buchanan sank down in the soft deep leather armchair and looked about at the affluent and tasteful décor of the office. He noticed an easel and blackboard with a covering over it. Then he looked at Keller whose graven features did not reflect the face of someone about to indulge in idle chatter. He did not think any more about having stolen the computers, as if it never happened. He disowned the notion because the theft had been executed so perfectly, what cause had he for concern? Keller stood up from his desk and sat close to Buchanan in the second armchair. Buchanan felt the hairs bristle on his neck being so close to his powerful boss. He tried to assume a confident air but found it impossible to do so. Keller was saying something but he couldn't hear him because of a nervous feeling enveloping him. Keller eased himself back into the armchair, looked at him and was about to speak when a soft tap on the office door gave Buchanan a start. The secretary entered carrying an envelope. Without a word she handed it to Keller and left. He opened it slowly, took out the letter. He spent a few minutes studying it before putting it in the inside pocket of his jacket.

"You've done this type of thing before," he said quietly, "haven't you?"

Buchanan's worst fears were realized. He collapsed inwardly. His defiance seemed to be seeping away. He couldn't think straight.

"What do you mean," he gasped, "what . . ?"

"It's all over for you, Buchanan," said Keller, "in the three weeks since the robbery I've had you checked out. I use a very savvy detective for that kind of thing. He doesn't come cheap, but he's very thorough. That music shop you worked in, in Grafton Street. You were accused when two radios went missing, the police were called but you were never charged. How did you get out of that one?"

A sudden unexpected defiance flared up in Buchanan. His face reddened as his hands curled into fists.

"I swear to God," he said in a raised voice, "the police went to my house in Drimnagh and found nothing. The shop owner said he wouldn't press charges if I paid for the radios, and that's just what I did, I paid for the radios to avoid going to court. But I didn't steal them. And he fired me anyway, the jerk."

Keller was looking at him now with a cynical, vacuous smile as Buchanan grew ever more apprehensive. The specter of police and courts, the claustrophobic confines of a prison cell rose up before him; a dark weight was descending on him, even as he thought about it. His breathing became stifled and his heart raced. He undid his tie, opened the collar and pulled it loose. For all of his adult life he had been tormented with a horror of dark and confined, enclosed spaces. Looking at him, Keller saw with a certain satisfaction, the blood draining from Buchanan's face. His intention was to break Buchanan, destroy his resistance, and make him compliant to his will, it was all crucial for the scheme he had in mind. No one would feel more incredulous than Buchanan, more disbelieving or dismissive of the notion that Keller saw, in him, the means of effecting a Phoenix-like resuscitation and revival of the fortunes of the Keller Group of Companies. First he had to petrify him to the extent that the thief sitting before him would squirm and be glad to placate his every wish. Fate had thrown Buchanan into his hands, and he wasn't about to look a gift-horse in the mouth. His detective had dug deep into the background of Buchanan. It seemed in his teenage years he had got lost in an underground tunnel and couldn't get out. It affected him so much he was later diagnosed with an anxiety disorder. He could function well in his social setting providing he avoided tight enclosed spaces. It was this fact alone upon which Keller sought to redress his business misfortunes.

"And the computers you stole from the warehouse," said Keller, "are you going to tell me you didn't take them?"

The intervening moments had given Buchanan a chance to regain his equilibrium. There was no proof, he guessed, that he had stolen anything. He was certain no one had seen him or heard him on the pitch-black night when he broke into the warehouse.

"I don't know what you're talking about."

"Oh, it's going to be like that, is it?"

"If you believe I stole from you Mr. Keller, you would have called the police and had me arrested already. At the very least you would have fired me. But you have no proof, and I'll go on denying it."

"I was hoping it wouldn't come to this, but you are forcing my hand." Said Keller. He stood up and went to a cabinet from which he took a cassette. He inserted it into a television VCR player. He turned off some office lights and closed the window blinds. With the room in semi-darkness he sat down and picked up a remote control.

"What is this?" asked Buchanan, his voice a little shaken.

"This? This is how to catch a thief."

With that he pressed the remote control. The dark television screen flickered and an image gradually appeared. For a few moments it was indistinct and vague. Suddenly a clear image of Buchanan could be seen carrying boxes from the shelves to a waiting car. He was seen moving quickly and looking at his watch. The image changed to a close-up of Buchanan's car and number plate leaving the premises, with the sign Keller Group clearly seen in the background. Keller shut off the television, turned the office lights back on and opened the window blinds. As daylight flooded the office Buchanan was staring dumbly at the floor. He was emotionally and physically drained. His shoulders were slouched forward with his head bent down on his chest.

"So you've known about this all along?" He asked Keller.

"For the past three weeks, to be exact," said Keller, "Probably what fooled you was seeing no security guards around. They're planned for, they just haven't got here yet." Buchanan registered no reaction in his drained, pallid face.

"But I'll tell you what we do have," continued Keller, "infra-red cameras with lens so small they're practically undetectable, the marvels of modern technology."

Buchanan lifted his head feebly.

"Have you called the police about, this . . . ?" he asked, indicating the television player.

"Not yet."

"Look, Mr. Keller, I still have the cash I got from selling the computers. I'll give it to you. I'll work for nothing for you so it's all paid off. I just want to stay out of prison, avoid being locked up . . ."

Keller laughed without mirth as he went to his desk and sat down.

"You know, I got it from a friend of mine, he's a Police Inspector whose job it is to put petty criminals like you away, you're a menace to society. From what he told me you won't have a life to get back to, after you've rotted away in prison for a few years. For starters do you really think any employer would hire a rotten apple like you, with time served and no references? Do you know what he told me, the Chief Inspector? Would you like to know what awaits you in prison, when I hand that cassette over to the police? They'll put you in a cage that's just a little bit bigger than my desk here. From the moment you set foot in your cell, hundreds of eyes will follow your every move, every day and every year until your time's up, a beaten and broken wreck, a burden to society. But before all that, first you have to become acquainted with your new cell-mates. Who gets the top or bottom bunk? That can be your first confrontation; it could end amicably or with a shank, that's the term I believe, shoved between your ribs."

Buchanan eyes were dull and lifeless as if he had retreated within himself.

"I don't want to talk about prison, please." He wrapped his hands and arms over his head, shutting away all sound. "Please, I,"

"Prison is the original house of horrors," said Keller. "the physical intimidation is bad enough, the real nightmare is when you finally go mad, lose your mind. The terror of the prison system is in the rate of suicides, 25% is the current figure. The fear factor dominates prison life; it's a jungle where roving jackals trap and destroy the weak and unwary."

With an effort Buchanan raised himself up from his slumped position and turned towards Keller.

"Mr. Keller, you don't have to try to scare me about small confined places, or any of that other stuff that goes on in prison. I suffer from claustrophobia, it's an anxiety disorder, since I was a teenager. Unless it gives you some kind of twisted pleasure to talk about prison, you can stop it right now."

"Oh, you misunderstand me-," said Keller.

Keller spent a few moments as if assessing the impact of his words.

"I don't think so," said Buchanan. There's something you want to say to me. Just spit it out. I don't want to talk to you any more than I have to."

Keller raised his head suddenly. This defiance from Buchanan came as a surprise, he hadn't expected the young thief to be so forthright. He picked up a pen and tapped lightly with it on the desk.

"Alright, alright. Look, I don't want to make it worse for you than it has to be. I'm here to offer you a deal to get out of this mess you've got yourself into. Just hear me out and you can make up your own mind. The fact is you committed an indictable offence, in the eyes of the law that makes you a criminal."

He paused to look at an open folder on his desk.

"I see you are just twenty-four years old. If I was to press charges against you, apart from prison time, if this became public it will put an end to whatever hope you have of finding a decent job, place in society. Let me reiterate, no one would ever hire you again. You'd be a felon, a pariah, for the rest of your life."

He stopped talking and looked intently at the sulking, brooding Buchanan. Beads of perspiration glistened on his brow. Keeler felt nothing but contempt for the silly, reckless thief who appeared to live instinctively, mindless of how a moment's thought or deed might adjudicate tomorrow. He put the pen aside and leaned forward with his elbows on the desk. He formed a pyramid with his fingers below his chin.

"At this time, you and I are the only ones who know about this crime and this tape. I can make it all go away as if never happened. That's what you'd like, isn't it."

Buchanan surfaced from the trauma into which he had lapsed. His head rose up. His eyes narrowed with distrust as he gripped the arm-rests of the chair. He licked his dry lips.

"Yes, yes, I'd do anything for another chance . . ."

"Alright then, I'll tell you what you can do for me, and you can tell me if we have a deal. Mind you, this is not a task for the faint-hearted. I wish I had more time for preliminaries, but I don't. So here it is. In exchange for dropping criminal charges against you, I want you to set fire to Wentworth Tech warehouse."

Buchanan didn't know what was coming from the powerful owner of the Keller Group of Companies. He felt too insensate to reply with some off-beat remark that could see him in jail before the day was through.

"What?" It was all he could answer with a growing sense of desperation.

"Don't make me repeat myself," said Keller with growing impatience, "if you insist on acting like a fool, I'll throw you to the wolves. Take a look at this blackboard."

Keller pulled down the covering from the blackboard and threw it aside. Several sketches and a long rectangle filled the blackboard. Keller picked up a pointer and indicated the rectangle.

"That," he said emphatically to Buchanan, "is the warehouse. Over here is the Utility Room. In it is the main fuse box with electrical circuits, cables etcetera. The Utility Room doubles as a janitor's closet. In it, besides his mops and buckets, are hazardous liquids and solvents. That's where you will set the timer to start the fire."

The whole episode, for Buchanan, was evolving into a vague insubstantial fantasy bordering on the bizarre. But he knew if he didn't comply with the dictates of this business mogul telling him to set the warehouse on fire, his expectations for any future would vanish. The mere thought of being locked up in a prison cell was again causing his heart to throb wildly and cut his breath short. He clasped his hands before him and tried to listen attentively. Keller sat on the edge of the desk holding the pointer and looked down at him.

"I want to know a few things about you. Tell me about yourself. Are you a drinker?"

"I take the odd drink."

"How about friends, do you have many friends, a girl friend? Why don't you answer me . . . ?"

Buchanan lapsed into a prolonged silence. When he didn't answer immediately, Keller lashed out viciously with the wooden pointer. He caught the unsuspecting Buchanan across the fleshy part of his upper arm. Even before the blow fell, the swift reflexes of Buchanan contrived to deny Keller the pleasure of seeing him cringe. He gasped inwardly but didn't flinch as the pointer cut painfully his arm. He stared grimly at his assailants face. Keller seemed partially stunned by Buchanan's phlegmatic reaction to what must have been a searing, hurtful blow. "If I ask you a question I expect to be answered. Do you think this is a game we are playing?"

"If it's all the same with you, can we get on with the details, how am I supposed to start this fire."

Keller sat back down and placed the pointer on his desk. He felt the striking blow he had dealt Buchanan had been worth it.

"A battery-operated timer will be connected to the wiring in the fuse box. It's a simple enough device that I'll set up myself. Today is Friday. In exactly two weeks from today you'll find your way in here and set the timer." He took a notebook and a thick white envelope from a drawer and placed them on the desk. He opened the notebook and peered at it. "Would I be correct in guessing you don't have a valid passport?"

"I have a valid passport . . ."

"Oh," said Keller, feigning surprise with raised eyebrows.

"That's right. I follow Manchester United. Sometimes I go over to see them play at Old Trafford." Said Buchanan.

"What I have here is a schedule for you to follow. First thing on Monday morning go to the office and hand in your notice to quit, to sales manager Ger Kelly, to take effect immediately. Don't get into any long drawn-out banter with him; just tell him you've had a better offer from another company. Cut the conversation short. Talk to no one about what you are doing or where you're going. From here on I want you to commit everything to memory, don't write anything down. At precisely 9:00 PM this Friday two-weeks, a timer will be set to activate at 11:45 PM on Sunday night. That's what time the fire goes off. The timer is a simple device, it will be all set up for you, all you have to do is turn a switch." He paused as he perused the notebook. "The rest of what's in here is about to rip your life apart. For both our sakes, I hope you'll be up to it."

"You mean when I set fire to that warehouse, it's not the end of it?"

"Just listen to what I'm saying. There's this, or prison. It's your decision." He looked down at the notebook. "On the Friday before you set the timer, get a suitcase packed and be ready to travel. Keep in mind you'll be away for a very long time. Keep the suitcase in the boot of your car. After you turn the switch on the timer in the warehouse, drive straight into town and park your car in O'Connell Street. Take your suitcase and get a taxi to Dublin airport. At the airport go to the reception desk. Tickets will be there for you. You will take a flight to London. A room has been booked for you at the Hilton Hotel in Heathrow, London. Questions so far?"

"What about the security cameras in the warehouse, how do I avoid them?"

"Don't concern yourself about the cameras; they won't be functioning while you're there."

"What about employees who might be working late?"

"That's taken care of. I've seen to it that all offices and the warehouse will be closed from 6:00 PM Friday until the following Monday morning. Satisfied?"

"Not quite. This airplane flight and the hotel in London; what do I use for money, because I haven't got any?"

Keller pushed the white envelope forward.

"That's probably more money than you've ever seen in your life. You're going to need every penny of it, until the dust settles on this caper."

"I've got just one more question, when do I come back?"

Keller thought for some time before answering.

"You don't come back . . ."

"I don't understand you, what's that supposed to mean, I don't come back?"

"I'm not going to argue or debate with you. This is the way it's going to be: if you don't like it there's the door." With that Keller sat back in the chair, waved a hand towards the door and folded his arms.

It would be fair to say at this point that the mind of Sean Buchanan was racing to keep apace of the myriad calamities in which his young life was suddenly mired. He often wondered, in moments of reflection, if he was not facing up to certain truths that his life should take such ominous turns from what polite society called the path of righteousness. He had taken stock of himself many times, and as often as not, he couldn't comprehend what he saw in his self-analysis. He knew he was an occasional, compulsive thief, he faced that truth. He wasn't happy about it, but there it was. It must be an inherited, fundamental fault in his make-up, his genes; so he only felt partially responsible for that flaw in his character. That was in the realm of psychology and too deep for his limited understanding of the science. He was also a liar, but not habitually so, just the same as everyone else; he found that was a consolation of sorts. Sometimes it was as if he had no direct control over his own life; choices were made for him that he didn't seem to initiate or condescend to. But the consequences were there and they exacted a terrible toll on his peace of mind. He didn't believe for a moment that he had a bad character. It was good and bad like everyone else; it all depended on prevailing circumstances. Most men were moral, or ethical, he decided, through lack of propitious opportunity. The more scrupled bore a mantle of sanctimony as a virtue, and became the greatest dullards on earth. His colleagues in the sales office were such men. Sedentary amoeba in a sea of plankton evinced more spark and passion than the average Wentworth Tech salesman.

But all of that had no bearing on anything as Keller faced him across the desk with his arms folded. He had just given him an ultimatum: he could set the warehouse ablaze, or go to prison for theft. Keller leaned forward on the desk and set his hands apart as if appealing to reason.

"What I mean by you not coming back is this. If you do this right, just follow my instructions, there will be no reason to suspect you had anything to do with it. When the fire takes off, you'll be in a hotel in London. Lay low for a few days in London. After that go to the American Consulate and apply for a work visa so you can travel to New York . . ."

"New York?" Said Buchanan incredulously.

"That's right. I have a partnership in the Carlisle Furniture Company in Manhatten, in New York City. I'll give you a letter with the details later. You'll get a job offer from the company. Take that letter with you when you apply for a work permit. When you get there you'll be given a minor position in the main office of the company. The people there are business colleagues of mine. They will help you find lodgings in a safe area. After that, when you start earning some money, you're on your own. You know, if you could put a rein on the more unsavory choices you make, this stealing from me for instance, you could really get your life together in New York. You were doing fine here, I got good reports about you. A good salesman is what I was told, and the figures were there to prove it. Can you tell me something, why did you steal those computers, were you that pushed for money?"

"Money had nothing to do with it . . ."

"Then why, are you a kleptomaniac, or something like that?"

"I, I can't answer that-."

"Well, whatever the reason you should . . ."

"Can we dispense with the lecturing, and get on with this. How long do I have to stay in New York?"

"Ten years."

"Ten years-?"

"That's how long it will take for the Statute of Limitations of this crime to run out, when the police close the file on the case." Keller looked at his watch quickly and continued. "I have to go now. Everything will be set up for you. Just follow my instructions and you'll be free and clear-."

"And what if for some reason it all falls apart, suppose the timer fails, what happens then?"

"You better hope, for your sake and mine that the warehouse goes up in smoke. Otherwise you'll rot in a prison cell and I'll go bankrupt-."

"Yes, but let's just suppose for a moment. What if someone got hurt, or possibly worse-?"

"How can I guarantee anything like that? I'm risking everything I've got on this going right"

"You're risking what? Its other people's lives you put at risk, not yours, to solve your personal money troubles. You know that the warehouse is packed full of explosive materials. There are council housing estates all around this area; a strong wind could scatter burning ashes for miles. People could be incinerated in their own homes."

"I'm telling you this fire has been planned with care and precision. The flames will be doused before the building is engulfed . . ."

"You hope, you can't be sure which way a raging fire will turn."

Buchanan stood up and towered over Keller sitting behind the desk. He picked up the money filled envelope and put it in his jacket pocket.

"You know, I worked for you for two years. I never knew who you were or what you were like. You were this larger-than-life image passing by in a chauffeur-driven limousine. Your name was everywhere, in every newspaper and television station. Edward Keller, benefactor to the destitute, champion of the poor. You contemptible hypocrite."

Keller, whose eyes were on his notebook, looked up suddenly. He looked shocked as he slowly stood up. His face flushed crimson as he faced Buchanan across the desk.

"What did you say?" He asked menacingly.

Buchanan raised his head back and laughed, a loud bitter, raucous laugh devoid of humor.

"What was that you said to me?" Keller repeated. He raised his voice only to be shouted down by the louder strains of Buchanan.

"You hear me. Go on, why not, set the world on fire. Who cares who gets hurt or crippled for life just so you'll walk away with your insurance money? That's what it's all about isn't it?"

"I'm warning you. One phone call from me and I'll have you arrested."

"You," said Buchanan, his voice a little lower now but with a vicious edge to it, "that front you show to the public, the do-gooder, the social magnate, that's not the real you. No, no, under your smiling public persona you have the ethics of a sewer rat."

For the first time in their caustic verbal exchanges, Keller's carapace of self-assurance had slipped. The angry glare left his face as his clenched fists fell limply to his side and unfurled. His voice mellowed as he assumed a less confrontational pose. He stared sullenly, silenced by the vociferous rage in the mocking, strident voice of Buchanan.

"You were asking about my friends," said Buchanan, "they are tried and trusted. I couldn't classify them as drinkers because, like me, they don't drink much. You asked me about a girlfriend. Nora was my girl next door since we were kids. We started dating since we were teenagers.

I know we would have married at some time or other, but
you see, something happened. A car accident, a drunken
driver, a stormy night and his car smashed into mine. Nora
was killed. And I, well, here I am at this point in my life
talking to a would-be-murderer who wants me to burn down
his warehouse for money. And I have to do it because I'm
claustrophobic and I'll become a basket-case if I'm locked in
a cell. I don't think Nora would be very proud of me."

He reached down and picked up the pointer from the
desk.

"And now that we are partners in crime, I want you to
know what it feels like to be whipped with one of these . . ."
Before Keller could react he raised the pointer above his head
and brought it down with every ounce of strength he could
muster, across Keller's arm. The out-of-shape business tycoon
shrieked in pain as his knees buckled and he fell backwards.
He tumbled over the chair and fell to the floor, gasping and
holding his bruised arm. Buchanan walked over to him.

"I'll do your bidding Mr. Keller," Said Buchanan, "and I
hope to God I never have to set eyes on you again."

With that he threw the pointer down on the prostrate
figure of Keller and walked out of the office.

Two weeks later, in the early hours of a Saturday morning,
North Dubliners awoke to the sirens of several fire brigade
tenders racing to the scene of a fire. In the sprawling suburb
of Santry the fire was already raging through the two-story
warehouse. As the fire-fighters deployed it was established
that the wind was blowing away from the adjacent housing
estate. Because of the heat and intensity of the fire the nearest
line of houses were ordered to be vacated, causing more
excitement than panic among the house dwellers. The well-
drilled firemen and police kept the encroaching crowds at
bay as the massive fire was steadily brought under control.

The burning warehouse was cordoned off as the fire died down. As the day wore on the yelling excited children and the inquisitive crowds thinned out as the tenders, the work completed, returned to base.

A spacious portable cabin was emplaced near the fire scene, as a headquarters office, to co-ordinate the various branches of investigation that was already underway. Police, fire and insurance interests had three desks in the cabin where all information relating to the fire was shared. A taxi driver reported the fire, and he was certain he saw a man running close by. But it was in the early hours of the morning and too dark to provide a useful description. Because it had attracted nationwide interest it was decided to concede a brief statement to the querulous newspaper and television outlets. Police Captain Noel Byrne, just recently promoted, was anxious to get through the fire investigation without mishaps. After four days of rummaging in the debris and ashes of the warehouse, he had found nothing to suggest arson. Captain Byrne was a studious, intense man, some would say dull; and thus ill-served by the general press corps demanding answers and reasons for the catastrophic fire. Pressure mounted daily on the beleaguered Captain as rumors of arson caught hold among the general public. He refused to be drawn out or indulge in idle speculation just to mollify the insatiable demands of the media.

On the following Monday morning Police Captain Byrne was finishing his address to assembled reporters in the crowded conference room of Jurys Hotel in Ballsbridge.

"And that's all we've got at this time, ladies and gentlemen." He summed up brusquely, "We are going through the warehouse with a fine-tooth comb. We'll get to the bottom of this I assure you. As soon as something breaks you'll be the first to know. Thank you."

Friday of the following week was the day designated to wind up the investigation of the cause of the warehouse fire. Fire Chief Ted Forbes and Police Captain Noel Byrne walked through the demolished shell of the warehouse. The special investigator for Northstar Insurance, Alex Quinn, had already combed through the site. He deferred making his report until Forbes and Byrne had completed their own. The cordoned off site left the inspectors free to sift through the devastation. Fire Chief Forbes and the Police Captain Byrne did not have a great liking for each other. Forbes felt the police officer was infringing on his area of expertise and that his presence was perfunctory. Besides, on this particular day Forbes had a personal reason for wanting to be alone at the fire site. He suggested they work separately. Byrne did not agree, suggesting they pool their knowledge and skills. Forbes baulked at this. He was about to become insistent when Byrne raised his voice and reminded him forcefully he out-ranked the fire Chief; that if he had a problem with that he could telephone the Superintendent of Police and verify it. Forbes relented and reluctantly followed Byrne in combing through the wreckage of the janitor's utility room. The area was of particular interest. It had contained flammable solvents and a fuse box; a possible source of ignition and sparks that could have generated a fire. All that remained was warped, tangled pipes and cables that had liquefied and fused in the intense heat. The two men were on their knees probing through the gutted mess, within feet of each other. The fire Chief turned to Byrne and pointed towards the pipes.

"There could be some batteries around here. They're very likely dead but I want to make sure. Can you do me a favor? There's an instrument in my locker called a powerscope, would you mind getting it for me? The locker's open. I pulled a muscle out jogging last night, it hurts like hell."

The police captain looked at him askance. He could only marvel at the audacity of the gruff, uncooperative fire Chief. He disliked him intensely and instinctively wanted to tell him to go to hell and get his own instrument. But the fact was the Chief had knowledge of fire safety and hazards far superior to his own. He stood up, turned abruptly on heels and headed to the locker room. When he was out of sight Forbes quickly took a wire cutter from his pocket. Reaching down he forced apart the congealed mass of burnt plastic, vinyl, and blackened wiring. Using the wire cutter he snipped away at a bulbous shaped cable. Working frantically he finally pulled up a foot long, shapeless cable. He cut away the PVS covering to reveal a timing device. Quickly he folded the timer and jammed it into his dungarees pocket. He threw handfuls of refuse over the area where he cut out the timer. He was finishing as Byrne came back and handed him the powerscope. He continued searching the area with Forbes by his side. Towards evening the fire investigation came to a close.

Police Captain Byrne sat at his desk in the cabin and packed away his computer. He filled his briefcase with reports relating to the fire. Being fastidious by nature he left the desk as he found it, everything cleared away. He patted the inside pocket of his jacket and retrieved some notes. As he read them a worried frown settled on his forehead. He shook his head slowly. He was in a quandary, not being certain about what to do with the notes. They related to the moments when he and Fire Chief Forbes entered the charred, smoking remnants of the janitor's closet. When Forbes had asked him to retrieve his powerscope, like an idiot he went back for it. He should never have left him alone like that for a moment. He had been gruff and uncommunicative, wanting to be alone. When he had got to the locker room he looked back and could spot Forbes in the distance. From his own locker he took down a pair of field binoculars, went to the window and focused on the Chief. He plainly saw him pick up a small round object attached to a blackened cable and put it into the pocket of his dungarees. Since the Chief did not bring the object to his attention, Captain Byrne saw no reason to question it, even though he was driven to near distraction regarding its identity. He picked up a telephone and called his superiors at Gardaí Headquarters in the Phoenix Park, Dublin. His investigation was complete; he would make his report and return to headquarters. He told his superior they were looking at the janitor's small space heater as the cause of the fire. No, there was nothing to suggest arson of any kind. He flattened out the notes he was reading and dropped them into the office shredder.

Fire Chief Ted Forbes, reacting to media and public unease, called an impromptu press conference in Dublin's historic Mansion House. The Lord Mayor of Dublin, with a residence in the Mansion House, did not officiate at the meeting but hovered in the background, greeting the more renowned of the attendees. The lines of people gradually filed in, with members of the press occupying the front rows. The general public, coming from every town and county, though well represented numerically, looked diminutive in the enormous, expansive Round Room of the Mansion House.

When Chief Forbes stepped up to take his position at the podium he faced a hostile media. He had been gruff and dismissive with the media generally in his eight year tenure as Fire Chief. He made no secret of the fact that he viewed the Press Corps, with few exceptions, as adumbrative imbibers, filled with narcistic self-absorption who would gratefully sell their souls for a by-line in a news-sheet. The Chief was known to be irascible and ill tempered; most of the reporters had suffered his invective at one time or another. His detractors in the media were happy to portray him to the public in a negative light. The problem for his accusers was that he was a decorated, fearless and able leader. On this day, in the aftermath of the warehouse inferno he gave the press more reason to be incensed when he announced the meeting would be brief and he would answer only a limited amount of questions. Chief Forbes had the authority to conduct the meeting in any manner he pleased. He had the right political backing to act without constraint in all matters concerning the Fire Department. The political party he subscribed to was in power; the Taoiseach and the Lord Mayor were personal friends. As he looked over a sea of faces his eyes went briefly to the front rows where the media sat. The outright expression of acrimony coming from some journalists was ostensible and gave cause for a smile to briefly brighten his face. He knew the public saw him in a more conciliatory way. He was a popular figure to the public at large. At the scene of a previous fire in the city center he had personally entered a burning house and rescued occupants trapped on an upper floor. His known eccentricity and tantrums were all forgiven as he was publicly presented with a medal of valor by the Taoiseach. The press could not touch him. He was inviolate: in his home, in his office. Unless one of the reporters dug too deeply. A fleeting shadow crossed his brow and his smile diminished; this was not the time or the place to entertain doubts. In his personal life he had made one stupid mistake which, if discovered, could bring ruin to him and to his family. He put the thought from his mind, coughed, and stepped to the microphone.

"Ladies and Gentlemen, honored guests," he began, "I am here to give an up-date regarding the fire outbreak in North Dublin. As most of you know by now, the fire was reported late on Sunday night, at 11:50 P:M, that was on the 18th Inst. A taxi driver returning to the city from the airport saw flames coming from a warehouse window, the property of Wentworth Tech in Santry. The results of the investigating team of Gardai, and my own team are now completed. With the widespread public concern over the massive size of the fire, no effort was spared to find the underlying cause of this terrible disaster. The damage to the property was devastating, the warehouse was completely gutted. If I may digress for a moment I just want to say I have been a fire-fighter most of my life and I've never seen such an inferno. The two floors of the warehouse were filled with timber, paint, solvents and ceiling-high wooden pallets. An entire floor was filled with bitumen-based building products. Tins of paint exploded in the white heat and catapulted over the flames. Steel containers in the warehouse were warped and buckled, crushed by the intense heat. A terrible calamity was averted by favorable weather; the high winds blew the flames away from the nearby housing estate. And though we had ambulances and medical personnel on hand, I am happy to say there were no injuries to report. Two elderly pensioners were overcome by all the excitement. They were taken to a hospital for checkups and returned safely home."

He paused as he referred to his notes and looked over the faces of his listeners as he drew to a conclusion. He coughed again.

"After the fire had been put down," Chief Forbes continued, "and we could move through the warehouse, the combined investigation of Gardaí and Fire Department and Northstar Insurance officers focused on the Utility Room area on the ground floor. We found the burned-out remains of a small space heater. Our experts were able to determine that an overloaded circuit caused a faulty electrical wiring to spark and ignite. The Utility Room was used to store paper towels, napkins and other combustible materials. In such an environment, the fire spread very quickly once it took hold."

Among the journalists, some heads shook in disbelief.

"I will try now to answer some of your questions. Please keep them brief. I still have a lot of reports to write out."

Several hands in the audience went up. He pointed to one of them.

"Yes Sir, how can I help you?"

"Your base is Tara Street, is that correct?"

"That's correct Sir, yes."

"I was just wondering as I live close to that warehouse, what if the fire got out of hand and reached the housing estate . . . ?"

"The fire stations in Malahide and Skerries were closely monitoring the fire. I had only to pick up a phone for immediate help. Next question please . . ."

A reporter in the front row stood up. He had been avowedly critical of the Fire Chief in the past.

"My name is Gerry Tierney of the 'Herald'. Can you explain why it took so long to get the fire under control?"

Chief Forbes instinctively wanted to upbraid the reporter he knew was indulging in grand-standing for public edification. He also knew him to be loud and boisterous in his cups, and of questionable character. Tierney had been often heard making ignorant, disparaging remarks about firefighters; men lounging around the station, watching television, playing cards; all a drain on the public purse. The Chief had invited him to make an unannounced visit, at any time, to his station in Tara Street. The reporter would see for himself the army-like discipline, the rigorous work-ethic demanded of employees in the Fire Service. But even that did not reflect the true merit of the men who risked being cremated in the furnace of a blazing building. Human nature being what it is, the Chief thought, the reporter's opinions too often reflected the public's *laissez-faire* attitude to the firefighter; after lives were saved, after their precious property was salvaged, the public's memory and gratitude was short-lived at best, once the danger was passed. He addressed the 'Herald' reporter.

"I believe I have already covered that question. The fire was of massive proportions. The substructure collapsed because of the weight bearing down on the second floor. As a precaution we pulled the men back when the roof began to cave in. That caused some delay in getting the fire under control." He looked at his watch. "I will now hand you over to a spokesman for the Garda Siochana. Thank you ladies and gentlemen."

Chief Forbes gathered up his notes and quickly left the podium. After a question and answer session with the police spokesman, the audience gradually left the Round Room.

One person lingered behind as the Mansion House hall emptied. Twenty five year old Leonard Cobb bristled with rage at the brevity of the proceedings. The fire Chief had answered only two questions from the audience. Cobb attended the meeting, wanting to learn more about the fire. It did not make sense, he decided, the warehouse was just recently built to accommodate the new shopping centers in Santry. How could it have faulty electrical wiring when just two months previous, the building had passed a government safety inspection? He knew that the warehouse was recently purchased by one Edward Keller who had insured the property for 200,000 Irish Pounds, a virtual fortune for Northstar to bear. The underwriter was Northstar Insurance under the chairmanship of his father, John Cobb. Cobb had just appointed his son Leonard, a brilliant wunderkind to the board of Northstar Insurance. The warehouse fire in Santry proved to be a financial disaster for the insurance company. Despite the most detailed analysis of the cause of the fire by the company's own investigators, no evidence was found to suggest arson was the cause. A settlement of 200,000 Irish Pounds was made to the Keller Group Incorporated. The effect of the award on Northstar Insurance co-owner and Chairman John Cobb was devastating. Against the background of the unsettled Irish economy, Northstar Insurance was forced into bankruptcy. The company, one of the oldest and most respected in Ireland, was founded by his forbear Augustus Cobb in the year 1879. John Cobb's health deteriorated until he finally lapsed into a coma; he succumbed to an ailing heart and died, a bitter broken man. His son, Leonard Cobb used all his energy and considerable business skills to try and rescue Northstar, to no avail. In time the death of John Cobb was attributed to stress, exacerbating a heart condition because of the warehouse fire, and the hefty award that went with it. Leonard Cobb believed differently. With every fiber of his being he believed the warehouse fire had been gutted by an arsonist. The odd behavior of Fire Chief Ted Forbes reinforced his suspicions. He became obsessed with uncovering the cause of the fire that ultimately led to the untimely death of his father.

Sean Buchanan was literally shaking as he passed through customs at Dublin Airport, enroute to London Heathrow. While his suitcase was being checked he shifted uneasily on his feet. He licked his parched lips while he dabbed with a handkerchief at his glistening forehead. The customs agent was looking at him steadily. Buchanan quickly averted his eyes, making himself an even more an object of suspicion. Finally, after surviving the ordeal of customs inspection he sank weakly into an armchair and patiently waited for his London flight. He stopped shaking and gathered his thoughts. So far so good! He hoped he would be safely ensconced in London by the time the Wentworth Tech warehouse erupted in flames. In the meantime he knew he would be a nervous wreck until he arrived intact in New York City. When he arrived in London, after he settled into the Hilton airport Hotel he confined his movements to within its parameters. In the hotel he bought a copy of the 'Irish Times' newspaper. He read of the spectacular warehouse fire in Santry, Dublin, with a voluble sigh of relief. He read that the fire was caused by a faulty space heater. The fire was put under control and there were no injuries. He was less apprehensive than he was in Dublin but still fretful about getting through the US customs at JFK Airport in New York City. On the morning of his departure he was sitting in the departure area, waiting to board the 747 airplane for his flight to New York. After a good night's sleep he was surprised to find an element of light relief in his mood and thought; an involuntary lifting of the angst and stress that had borne down on him since the night he set the timing device that started the warehouse fire. For the first time he felt he would not have to face the nightmare of being locked up in a concrete cell. Just thinking about it caused his heart to palpitate wildly. He stood up suddenly. It often happened when he dwelled too long about confinement in dark enclosed spaces. He went to the windows overlooking out to the airport's runways and looked up at the brilliant wintry silver orb of the midday sun. Staring into the radiant light sometimes alleviated the claustrophobic terror that often took control of his mind. The sun seemed to saturate, to drown, to immerse him in its dazzling winter light, keeping the endless black void surrounding the universe at bay. But this he knew would be but a brief hiatus from the demons threatening his sanity. What was the feeble light of the sun compared to the black oppressive night pressing down on earth from the illimitable reaches of space. There was no escape. Buchanan fell limply on a chair and closed his eyes. He reached up, unloosened his neck-tie and undid the collar button of his shirt. Gradually his erratic breathing, and his rational thinking returned to normal. An elderly, kindly faced woman sitting next to him was looking at him with some concern.

"What's the matter son," she asked, "are you feeling alright, can I get you a drink of water?"

The sound of her voice had an extra calming effect. He sat upright in his chair.

"Thank you, Ma'am. I'm ok now; I just got a little light-headed. Thanks"

He walked around for a few more minutes until boarding time. Entering an airplane was another hurdle he had to overcome, he knew he would be uneasy until he landed in New York. The London to New York flight proved not to be as arduous as he had expected. The continuous distractions of fellow travelers made the journey less onerous across the Atlantic Ocean. It was with a sense of relief he felt the giant 747 bounce on the runway in JFK airport when it landed in New York. His passage through US customs was uneventful. He had a valid passport, he had the offer of a job under the letterhead of the Carlisle Furniture Company in midtown Manhattan in New York City; plus he had a bank statement showing his account to be in credit. Lastly he offered glowing references from previous employment, the Edward Keller Group. From his office in Dublin, Keller had weaved a carefully spun web of concoction and half-truths to expedite Buchanan passage through US Customs; not from misplaced altruism but to absent himself, the further the better, from guilt by association with the warehouse arsonist. The placated customs official smiled and waved him through. After he collected his suitcase he boarded a shuttle bus that took him to a taxi-rank in midtown Manhattan. A Taxi took him to the Hampton Inn Hotel on West 39th street. Still a little drowsy from the long flight he signed in at the hotel. A porter preceded him to the elevator and took him to a room on the 10th floor. He tipped the porter, closed and locked the door and threw himself on the bed. He fell asleep immediately.

Early the following morning, totally refreshed, he showered, shaved and dressed. This morning he would be meeting the Projects Manager in the dining room. He drew back the curtains, raised a window and leaned out to look at Manhattan. A feeling of energy and exuberance throbbed through him as he looked down; full of wonder, on the busy, bustling metropolis that was New York City. He felt elated as he looked up at the skyscrapers, and heard the sounds reverberating up from the restless clamor of the city. Eagerly he hurried down the stairs to have breakfast and greet the day.

Hans Bauer, The Projects Manager of Carlisle Furniture Group based in Manhattan, called in, as arranged, to meet Sean Buchanan in the Hampton Inn Hotel. His boss, the Chairman of the Group, Elmer Curtis, had called him and told him to take care of the newcomer to the company. Curtis explained that Edward Keller, in Ireland, was a financial partner in Carlisle and needed help in getting Buchanan a job within the Group, however menial. He gave Bauer the chore of giving him a job and finding him accommodation; in other words, wet-nurse the newcomer until he could fend for himself. Bauer didn't like the idea of taking on Buchanan to work in the joinery shop. At 24 years of age

Buchanan was a tad old to begin an apprenticeship in the art of producing fine cabinet-making and carving period-pieces of furniture. He was under pressure in the factory, behind in schedules because he would never compromise the standards of excellence he demanded. He liked his job, a position he has held for the past 18 years. He had risen up through the ranks and was co-opted to the board of Carlisle. He was respected and liked on the factory floor. When Bauer had worked at the joinery bench, the best wood craftsmen in New York paid homage to his artistry and skill. In the corridors of power within the Group, Bauer had his detractors. The now retired founder of the Group, Mathew Lambert, greatly admired and liked Bauer for his expertise in fabricating the finest china cabinets, armoires and period-pieces the company ever produced. The remaining members of the Board were generally respectful of Bauer's work and standards of excellence, but some baulked at what they saw as time-wasting in Bauer's obsession with detail. And he had encumbered the Group, many felt, with unnecessary expense when he visited salons in the palace of Versailles near Paris. Plus he had caused a minor kerfuffle by examining King Louis 15th chairs with a magnifying glass in his hand.

As he faced Buchanan across the breakfast table he could almost feel the excess vitality exuding from the young Irishman. He was glancing with avid interest at everything that moved. His expression was animated and curious as if he could not absorb enough in one cursory glance. He finished his breakfast. His movements were quick and purposeful.

"So," said Bauer, "how was your first breakfast in the New World?"

"Very enjoyable, Sir."

"Do you find the hotel to your liking?"

"Where I come from I'm not used to this kind of luxury."

"Ok. Well, we have to find you accommodation. You'll be here for about a couple of weeks. We keep the room here for out of town guests. As soon as you are ready I'll take you to the Carlisle building and introduce you to some people. It's just a couple of blocks over, we can walk from here."

"Great. Could I have just a couple of minutes to brush my teeth."

"Sure. There's no hurry. I'll wait for you out in the foyer."

As they walked down 9th to 38th street towards the Carlisle Group building, the phlegmatic Bauer broke out into a rare smile as he observed the antics of Buchanan with his neck craned backwards, looking up in awe at the surrounding concrete canyons of Midtown Manhattan. He looked like an archeologist gazing at newly discovered wonders. Bauer liked what he saw in the raw energy, the irrepressible vitality of the young Irishman. He would like to harness such energy for the benefit of the Group. Still walking together on the sidewalks he made a snap decision. Although he had just met Buchanan, his exuberance and engaging personality would he lost on the factory floor in Carlisle. No, he would try to find a place for him in sales, somehow.

On reaching the Carlisle offices he took Buchanan on a tour of the building, including a prolonged visit to the bustling factory floor. Bauer introduced him to carpenters, joiners, carvers, French polishers and painters. All of them shook hands with Buchanan and had a brief chat about the work at hand.

"Hey," said a carver with a huge grin, nodding towards Bauer, "watch out for him, he's a slave driver." Bauer shook his head with a brief smile and led Buchanan to the elevator. They went to the top floor of the building where he introduced the newcomer to board members some of whom barely condescended to lift their heads up from the desk. When

Bauer reached the office of the sales director, Tim Scofield, he introduced Buchanan and then asked him to sit and wait for him in an outer office. When he finally emerged Bauer looked smugly satisfied with himself and nodded to Buchanan to follow him. After some more introductions they went to Bauer's office that looked out onto the joinery shop on the factory floor. He asked Buchanan to sit down and went to his desk.

"There are a few more people I'd like you to meet. But first, tell me why did you decided to come to this country?"

Buchanan wasn't expecting the question. He knew he would have to lie convincingly. He didn't want to have to lie to Bauer, he had taken a liking to the quietly authoritative Projects Manager, but how could he tell the truth? For all he knew he might at that moment be a fugitive from Irish justice. What should he say to him, that he was an arsonist, that he set a warehouse on fire in Dublin; that his came to the US to hide out?

"Oh I always wanted to come to the US. There's no work in Ireland anymore, what with the economy and all. Lucky for me I was working for Mr. Keller and he helped me on my way."

"What kind of work were you doing for Mr. Keller?"

"I was in sales . . ."

"Oh," said Bauer, listening more closely, "what kind of merchandise did you sell?"

"Computers, software . . ."

"Do you know anything about wood, cabinets, chairs?"

"Sir, I couldn't tell the difference between types of wood. Or trees for that matter. The only tree I know on sight is a chestnut tree, because it has chestnuts on it."

Bauer was unable to suppress a smile. This was one of the reasons he liked the guy, he thought, he seemed to have ready quips and an inherent sense of humor.

"Tell me," he said, "what kind of a learner are you? The feeling about you here in the Group is well, Mr. Keller is a partner in the business and wants a position found for you. The fact is no one in the executive offices wants to take on an untrained newcomer. Every department is pushed to the limit. Carlisle's competitors are flooding the market place with the cheapest unsealed white pine they can find. I don't know where people's taste has gone. They buy a chair or a table and judge it by how it looks, not caring that it could fall apart in six months." He stopped and looked at Buchanan for a few moments. He picked up an open letter from his desk and read through it. "This letter is from your old boss in Ireland, Mr. Keller. How did you like working in sales?"

"I loved that job."

"Can you tell me why?"

"I like to travel Sir, new challenges, new people."

Bauer went to the wide office window overlooking the joinery shop and asked Buchanan to join him. The workshop was a hive of activity. Wood workers were busy at every available bench. When an employee passed by carrying a chair Bauer rapped on the window. He went to the door, opened it and had a few words with the employee, Cesar, who handed him the chair. He introduced the smiling Mexican to Buchanan. After he left, he placed the chair in front of him.

"This," he said emphatically, "is what we call the Prix d'Or of the Carlisle collection. It's a period-piece, a reproduction of a French Louis XV salon chair. It's made from Rosewood, one of the most superior hardwoods. Cesar made that. Look at the intricate work, he's one of the finest carvers in the country. See the motifs, the filigree of the petals? Cesar has been with Carlisle furniture for over 18 years, a lot of the men are here since they were teenagers."

When they were seated again Bauer continued.

"Ok, let me explain how our sales department works. Right now Carlisle has four salesmen allocated to four different States around the country. You've already met Tim Scofield, the sales director. I'm in charge of the factory floor so Tim co-ordinates with me a lot about the status of his salesmen, their sales, territory, problems etc. Here's what I have in mind, a proposal I want you to consider. Tim has agreed that you'll be working directly for me initially. I'll give you a three month trial period on the road. If that doesn't pan out, I'll find something for you here in the factory. I'm putting myself out on a limb for you but I believe with a little luck and your undoubted enthusiasm it should work out fine. Carlisle will provide you with a car and expenses."

"Oh, er, what will I be selling . . . ?"

"That," Bauer pointed to the Rosewood chair, "it's part of a range of 15th century French furniture. Your clients will be very upmarket; hotels and boardrooms, that kind of thing. If you accept the job I'm offering you I will expect you to report to me here every morning for the next three weeks at 9:00 AM sharp. I'll put a second desk in here. You will familiarize yourself with hardwoods and softwoods and the furniture designs Carlisle specializes in. As you can see," he indicated the bookshelves behind him, "I've a wide variety of books on the subject. Feel free to borrow books and bring them back to your hotel. Spend some time out there on the factory floor; just stick a white coat on you so they'll know you're part of the team. You'll find the guys at the benches glad to help you. They're craftsmen and the best at what they do and like to show off their skills. Learn as much as you can because when you leave here you'll be completely on your own. Hopefully you'll find out there's more than just chestnut trees in a forest." They both smiled and relaxed back in their chairs. "How do you feel about all of that?"

"Sir, I look at it as a great opportunity. I'm so excited I don't know what to say."

"Ok, well, first things first. I'll have someone from Human Resources show you how to get a driving license. I take it you have a valid Irish driving license?"

"Yes Sir, I do."

"Good. Right now I've got some projects that I need to check up on. Find your way up to Human Resources and fill out the required forms to become an employee of Carlisle. I'll phone them so you'll be expected. That should take up the rest of your day. We have a canteen, get some lunch. I'll see you back here tomorrow at 9:00 AM sharp.

Three weeks later Buchanan sat in Bauer's office. Outside on the street, the company car he was driving was parked and ready to go. It was 10:00 AM on Monday morning. He could hardly keep still with restless energy coursing through his veins. He wanted to be on the move to the exotic faraway places he had been transfixed with and drawn to all his life. There were moments when he couldn't believe his luck. Here he was with a new car at his disposal about to traipse around the US of A with all expenses paid. He had already provided Bauer with an itinerary of the proposed route he was taking. He had spent some time in planning and in researching the background of likely clients. He had studied trees and wood and grains until the early hours of the morning and being young and fit, was unfazed by any deprivation of sleep. Bauer was very impressed with the knowledge Buchanan had accumulated in three weeks of cramming. He could converse authoratively on the Prix d'Or range of Carlisle period-pieces. At the time for his departure Bauer walked Buchanan out to his car, shook hands with him and stood on the sidewalk as the car sped away. As he returned to his office Bauer mused on the chance he had taken in placing so much trust in someone he hadn't even known up to three weeks ago. But the young Irishman had convinced him he had star quality by his intelligence, wit and jocular humor. He was a bright spark alright; it was up to him now to bring home the bacon to Carlisle.

Sean Buchanan released the handbrake of the car and drove out of Manhattan. The car was packed with samples of Carlisle merchandise. Bauer Bauer had given him freedom to choose his own route. He had painstakingly mapped out a clockwise course around the US, starting by going south through the great southern states skirting the eastern seaboard, west to the Pacific Ocean, north to the Canadian border and returning back east to New York City. Buchanan was beside himself with excitement at the prospect of setting out on what he considered the adventure of a lifetime. He had to convince himself that this was a job of work; that he would get paid to do this. He had an itinerary, maps and a list of potential clients given to him by Bauer Bauer.

Out on the road an irrepressible force drove him ever onward. Like a great wind filling a sail, his exuberance steered his course; against a backdrop of breathtaking wonders of geography and color. In planning the marathon jaunt around the US, Buchanan decided, in a moment of inspiration to make contact with diverse institutions where legions of Irish Diasporas had settled en-bloc along the route he was taking. Irish emigrants had established a lasting influence in societies into which they had quickly assimilated; in law, in religion and police forces. Considering his youth and lack of familiarity with the vast territory he was about to cover, Buchanan showed great maturity and resolve in the strategy he planned. It could be said he was a little audacious as he began telephoning such dignitaries as

JOHN FLANAGAN

Chiefs of Police and catholic Bishops in the capital city of
each State he passed through.

Much later in time, when Buchanan's stateside odyssey
was revisited, it was said it was his uniqueness, his panache
and flat Dublin accent that was like a magnet to the
ensconced custodians of Irish culture. They welcomed the
voluble young salesman with open arms. High ranking civil
officials, clergy and business leaders of Irish decent urged
him to stay in *their* State, *their* Capital.

By the time he arrived in Birmingham, Alabama
his journey was proving momentous and profitable; far
exceeding his expectations. For the Irish expatriates who
had settled successfully in the US, he was like a fresh breath
of spring. Rank and file police officers vied with each other
to invite him to their homes, especially if they had an
eligible daughter waiting in the wings. He quickly learned
how, with profuse apologies, to extricate himself from any
romantic entanglements. Of the many Irish emigrants,
estranged from but still emotionally attached to Ireland,
their delight in meeting him was deeply felt. He had decided
that he would be returning to Ireland, but at what point he
did not know. The treated him like an envoy; they wanted
him to chart their progress, to tell their loved ones at home
that through toil and effort, they had done very well for
themselves in the New World, and their hearts were forever
at home. He filled his notebook with names and addresses
of friends and relations in Ireland and promised to visit
them all.

Near Tucson, Arizona, along his chartered route to the
southwest, he had to pull the car off the road to just sit and
stare at the vistas ahead. He was staggered by the ineffable,
wondrous beauty of the pink, orange, ochre and crimson
landscape ahead. Above him, massive banks of startling

white clouds floated serenely between the purple sage of the plains and the azure blue limitless sky.

Police Chief Daniel Murtagh in San Diego, California, typified the many high ranking officials of Irish background Buchanan would meet. Through Chief Murtagh he met local clergy, invariably of Irish decent. In every mile of his circuitous journey around America, it was the Irish connection who eagerly paved the way. A network of contacts was established for him in every major city through which he passed. The welcoming hands of civil and religious leaders reached out, glad for the opportunity to be united in helping one of their own. Without realizing it, Buchanan was tapping into emotional well-springs of centuries-old Irish traditions of charity and benevolence to lost pilgrims, far from home; forced by circumstances to sever ties to all they held dear, dragged from the clutches of loved ones they would never see again. Buchanan was a catalyst for all that. The joy in greeting him and assisting him, overcame the sadness of his eventual leave-taking.

By the time Buchanan reached Boston, Massachusetts, his last port of call, he had been on the road for three months. During that time he had achieved legendary status within the Carlisle Furniture Company. In the long history of the company, no salesman had come close to the avalanche of work orders that landed on Bauer Bauer's desk. They had been forced to sublet the work to cope with the demand for every Carlisle line. Bauer Bauer, his immediate boss and mentor who was taciturn and phlegmatic by nature, was heady with delight as the work orders came pouring in. In the beginning he had to withstand some blistering criticism from fellow board members when he gave a job and a company car to an untried emigrant just "off the boat". The same men were now effulgent in their gratitude and praise. Buchanan booked into the InterContinental Hotel on Atlantic Avenue in Boston. He was no longer counting pennies when it came to lodgings and gourmet food. He filled out his daily logbook and thought with some satisfaction how successful it had all been, and he wasn't quite finished yet. He had timed his arrival in the city to coincide with the Boston Police Annual Dinner and Dance. Next to the 17th of March Saint Patrick's Day Parade, the police Dinner and Dance drew every civil and religious figure of note in the state of Massachusetts. Buchanan sat at the table of Police Commissioner Myles Garvey and Monsignor Martin Twamley, along with silent, watchful men of Irish extraction who exuded charisma and power by their mere presence. They were the watchdogs of Boston's financial health and wealth. The night proved to be a resounding success for Buchanan who received, in an envelope slipped across the table to him, orders for $20,000 worth of Carlisle's Prix D'Or line of furniture. He gasped when he read the envelope's contents and looked up to see the smiles of his benefactors about the table. One of the silent men picked up a glass and raised it.

"To Sean," he said, in what Buchanan believed was a Wexford accent, "a toast, keep the green flag flying, Sean." Everyone raised a glass to him. He was left emotional and speechless.

By the end of the night he found himself gravitating towards a group of fellow Dubliners, drinking around a table. They were newly arrived in Boston, and as he found out when he sat down and joined them, most were undocumented; that is to say, in the country illegally. He was delighted to be regaled with news from home. While he soberly nursed a glass of white wine; a habit he got into while on the road as a travelling salesman, those around the table were pie-eyed from overindulgence. They were boisterous and loud; not listening, unless they weren't talking. Introductions were made, names were exchanged and summarily forgotten. By and large they were envious and curious about Buchanan having seen him dine at the VIP table, plus the cut of his clothes. As he was also from Dublin and of their age, they felt they had a divine right to know what he was "up to". The noisy banter got around to sport and the Irish economy. As the night drew on Buchanan was enjoying the idle, animated chatter. He was not paying too much attention; his mind was on the following day when he would report back to his employer, Carlisle Furniture in Manhattan. Very suddenly, so quickly he thought he must be dreaming, or the drink had gone to his head. He looked at his wineglass, he had taken no more than a few sipfuls of wine. He believed he had heard the words 'burning warehouse' in the excited babble around the table. His face froze as he reached over and put his hand on the shoulder of the speaker.

"I'm sorry, I've forgotten your name . . ."

"Oh hi, I'm Tony Leonard . . ."

"Tony, did I hear you say something about a warehouse?"

"Yeh, that's right. The whole bloody building went up in flames; belonged to the Keller Group. My uncle lived in the housing estate close by, he was very lucky. It was one of the biggest fires ever at home . . ."

"Yeah?" said Buchanan nonchalantly, "I heard about it in the news, was anybody hurt?"

"Naw," butted in Mickey Finn, "nobody, not a scratch. A few firemen got sick with fumes, and a few old folk. They were taken to hospital but they were let go. Mind you, it was touch and go there for a while. The fire went on and on . . ."

"How did it start anyway?" Asked Buchanan.

"Dunno," said Leonard, "there was a lot of rumors flying around, some said it was a ready-up, you know? An insurance job." Finn took a deep gulp from his pint of Guinness, put the glass down and tapped the side of his nose with his finger. "That's right, a set-up. Buranyway, a fire Chief went on the news, said it was dicey wiring that caused the fire, overloaded circuits or whatnot. And that was that . . ."

As the festivities came to an end, Buchanan finished his glass of wine and bid adieu to the noisy Dublin revelers. As he was about to stand up and leave, a few of the party plied him with requests for help with their undocumented status. When he was not immediately forthcoming, a few became verbally abusive. He tried in vain to point out he had just been issued with his own Green Card and wasn't in a position to help anyone. Buchanan had a short, sharp temper and was on the verge of standing up and confronting the more vociferous of the party around the table, but he resisted the impulse. Most had too much drink taken, others had fallen mutely silent. Buchanan wanted to help them if he could. They were expatriates like him, lonely and cut off from home. He wanted to laugh, but couldn't at the anomaly of distraught, undocumented Irish emigrants, fearful of arrest, blatantly parading around under the very noses of law enforcement officials at the Boston Police annual Dinner and Dance. When tensions and tempers around the table abated, Buchanan made a conciliatory gesture of taking names and addresses. He said he couldn't promise anything but he would do his best to help. With that he got up and left. He walked the short distance back to his hotel. In his room he kicked off his shoes and stretched out on the bed. A great weight had been lifted from his shoulders. No one had been injured in any way by the fire he started in the warehouse in Dublin. In a strange surreal way his memory of it was dream-like. He remembered setting the timer in the janitor's utility room. He was sure he would spend the greater part of his life locked in a prison cell. Now all that fear and concern, while it still impacted his daily life, the danger to others was passed; the massive fire claimed no lives. With a huge sigh of relief he turned on his side and fell asleep.

Early the following morning he showered, breakfasted, and set out on the final leg of his journey; the 210 mile trip to Manhattan in New York City.

He drove along at a leisurely pace. He had no idea what faced him at Carlisle. Hans Bauer had asked him to arrive at company headquarters at a specific time. He made a couple of stops along the way, had coffee, read a newspaper and generally tried to savor the moment. He had done well and saw no reason why he should not have a job with Carlisle. He could not bring himself to think about tomorrow, he would face each day one at a time. The only thing he knew for certain was that at some point he would return home to Ireland. The past three months of empty hotel rooms, travelling alone, eating alone, had created an ache, tugging at him to go back. But he had to face the reality of the prison cell that could face him if he returned home. Edward Keller could prove he was the arsonist, a reluctant one, but an arsonist nevertheless who set the warehouse alight in north Dublin. He could do nothing, hopefully time itself might provide an answer.

When he finally arrived at Carlisle, the building seemed unusually quiet. He parked the car and went through the revolving doors to the lobby. The security guard asked him to be seated while he made a telephone call. He was leafing through a magazine when he looked up to see a smiling Bauer Bauer approach him with his hand held out. He was dressed in his white shop coat and carrying his usual clipboard. They shook hands cordially and sat down. After a brief chat during which Bauer welcomed him back to Carlisle, he stood up and asked Buchanan to go with him to the Convention Hall. As they moved along the corridor Buchanan looked sideways into the vacant offices.

"It's very quiet around here Mr. Bauer," observed Buchanan, "where is everybody?"

Bauer turned to him and smiled.

"Yes, it is very quiet around here. Well, you'll soon know why."

With that he pushed open the double doors of the Convention Hall. Buchanan was not expecting what happened next. The large Hall was packed with Carlisle employees. As the doors swung open a cheering ovation erupted, fixing him to the spot. The employees, from every section of the company, surged towards him, back-slapping and smiling. He was virtually surrounded by his well-wishing fellow workers. He could do nothing but shake his head, smile, and shake all the hands that were thrust at him. He raised a playful fist towards a beaming Bauer. A few of the Irish employees of Carlisle had obviously conspired in making banner that stretched across the back of the stage with the words, 'Cead Mille Failte Sean'. Across the stage long oblong tables were set up. The floor of the hall was set up with circular tables, filled with pastries and refreshments. The well-wishers found their way to the tables, sat down and availed of the tasty fare. The executives and board members of Carlisle took their places at the tables on the stage. Buchanan felt a tap on his shoulder and turned around to see Bauer motion for him to follow him to the stage. He was seated next to Tim Schofield, sales director of Carlisle. Bauer, who had been asked to MC the occasion, went to the podium and spoke into the microphone.

"Mr. Chairman, ladies and gentlemen, on your behalf I'd like to welcome back Sean after his three very successful months on the road. Well done Sean. We will now have some words from Carlisle chairman, Mr. Elmer Curtis."

The chairman left his seat and joined Bauer at the podium.

"Thank you, thank you, ladies and gentlemen," said Curtis as he took out some notes he had hastily written. He was in his fifties, austere, aloof. He seldom ventured out of his executive suite on the top floor of the Carlisle building. In his 23 years as an executive he had rarely been seen in the factory or at business functions to which regular employees were present. Elmer Curtis 3rd exemplified the unbreachable barriers of class and privilege and general workers in Carlisle's. He disdained to attend meetings with representatives other than management. It was an attitude endemic in his character, fostered in the rarefied atmosphere of Yale and the Clubs he frequented. His executive colleagues had urged him to speak, and there was great advantage to be gained by the example set by the newcomer Buchanan. It mortified him to heap acclaim on one of 'that class' but he was without option. He spoke into the microphone in his inane, vacuous monotone.

"It is my belief that the endeavors of Mr. Buchanan will bring new health and vitality to our company, in these trying times. There are some difficult times ahead, according to forecasts. Let us all be inspired by the example of Mr. Buchanan, we'll all strive to do better."

Curtis hung his head and closed his eyes for a moment. There, it was done, and he felt almost weak from the effort to inspire them. God, how he hated them, how he reviled the inchoate mass it was his fate to preside over. He opened his eyes as someone in the hall began clapping, and spontaneously everyone in the hall stood up to applaud. After some more words, and partaking of refreshments,

the employees found their way back to their work places.
Buchanan went with Bauer to his office where they sat and
had coffee.

The first decision Curtis made was to insist Buchanan be
made an assistant to sales director Scofield and be sent back
out on the road forthwith. He would brook no opposition.
He was adamant and threatened to demote any of his
executives who did not agree. The chairman gave full vent to
his considerable ego. Buchanan promised to be a goldmine,
if his three months on the road was anything to go by. He
wanted results. He didn't intend for his star earner to be
restricted to the confines of a joinery shop learning about
wood, which was what Bauer wanted; he wanted him back
on the road where he belonged, filling the coffers of Carlisle.
He snapped up the telephone and called Bauer.

Buchanan was at the window of his room in the Hampton
Inn Hotel, looking down on midtown Manhattan, in deep
thought. If the chairman had been a little more tactful, the
matter of where he was putting Buchanan might have been
settled more amicably. But Elmer Curtis 3rd never bothered
to find out what kind of a person his star employee was.
After long deliberation Buchanan decided to leave Carlisle
Furniture; as long as he was a Carlisle employee he would
be connected to Edward Keller in Ireland. While he stayed,
Keller was literally his boss, by virtue of his shareholding
in Carlisle. Once he made his decision to leave, Buchanan
confided his plans to Bauer. The projects manager expressed
his surprise and disappointment. He also kept silent until
Buchanan made the announcement himself. A few days later
Buchanan handed Tim Scofield his letter of resignation. It
caused a minor furor among the workforce who believed
Buchanan had helped the future prospects of the company
by his success on the road. Elmer Curtis 3rd raised his

eyebrows for a moment and shrugged his shoulders. He was not surprised at anything 'his kind' would do.

When the time came Buchanan left quietly and moved to a modest apartment in Guernsey Street in Brooklyn. He had laid his plans carefully. Before he took the apartment he scouted around the area to look for a job. He had obtained an excellent letter of reference from Bauer. The letter opened doors for Buchanan. He got a job as a sorter in a Post Office on Meserole Avenue in Brooklyn; and found a modest one-bedroom apartment, suited to his needs, on Guernsey Street, just around the corner from his work place. With the plan he had in mind, such an arrangement would save him the expense of buying an automobile. New York City's subway would take him anywhere he needed to go. Moment by moment he drew a clearer perspective of what he wanted to do. He stretched out on the bed in his new apartment and stared at the ceiling and considered his options. The US offered opportunity and reward, but it was not home and home was where he wanted to be. He missed his friends, he missed his mother. Buchanan had now arrived at a time and place where he felt a compulsion to redirect the course of his life. Circumventing every critical decision he had to make about his life, was the remorseless guilt he carried with him daily. The warehouse he had set ablaze in Dublin was an albatross, a weight that insinuated itself into his every waking moment. There were times when he could escape its odious presence and acquit himself gainfully, as he did when he had taken to the road as a salesman. It was his natural exuberance, his joy of life that enabled him to exorcise for a while that dark shadow from his life. Financially he was more solvent than at any time in his life. The generous commissions he earned on the sales of Carlisle merchandise gave him the independence to make decisions in his own interest. He had to face reality when he yearned for home. There was no work available in Dublin except perhaps the most mundane, at a minimum wage. His education was of the most rudimentary level. Coming from a small family on the verge of penury, he had left grammar school at the age of 14 years, and went to work as an errand boy in a solicitor's office. He reached out to the bedside table. He thumbed through the Brooklyn College brochure he had picked up at the college a week before. At the college he had enrolled for a night-study business course. From the moment his tuition began his life revolved around the college. After work at the Post Office each day he commuted to the college by bus, had a bite to eat, and studied until 9:00 P.M. He spent his week-ends studying on campus. Weeks and months passed by. In Brooklyn College he learned to curtail his exuberance of temperament and personality. There were several attractive girls taking the course and he regretted having to curtail his amorous inclinations. He was invited to join in social activities on campus, to which he politely declined. In time he came to be seen by classroom colleagues as pleasant enough but somewhat aloof, and he was left to his own devices. He was pragmatic with regard to engaging in the extra-curricular activities of the college, he simply didn't have the time; He was forced by a Spartan lifestyle to impose strict junctures of time limits regarding work and college commitments.

When he had finished reading his report in the Mansion House of the warehouse fire to the assembled audience and Press Corps, Fire Chief Ted Forbes exited the building with all possible haste. He picked up his car from nearby Saint Stephen's Green and drove onto the N 11 route going South. After Bray he turned right into the Wicklow foothills. He wound his up to a deserted car park adjacent to Powerscourt

House and gardens. Today the famous 18th century estate was closed to the public, making it was an ideal setting for a surreptitious rendezvous. He turned off the engine, pushed the seat back and tried without success to ease the raging turmoil of his mind.

His son Tim was foremost in his mind. He was hiding out in his boat on the river Shannon in Athlone, County Offally, in fear for his life. A gang owned Tim, body and soul and was chasing him down because of gambling debts he had run up in a Turf Club owned by Henno, their employer. Henno was an unreformed, convicted drug peddler, who in a moment of inspiration found a lucrative source of income by turning turtle on his friends and volunteered to become a police informer. He bought the Turf Club with reward money for informing; generously lodged to his account by a law enforcement officer. In essence Henno was a small-time hood, vicious and vengeful in collecting debts. Tim Forbes had racked up losses of 8,000 Euros in playing the horses and poker games over a two year period. Ted Forbes and his wife Eileen knew nothing of their son's dilemma until it too late. He was an ideal son, he was well liked and popular in his job where he was known as a talented engineer; he even talked to his parents about forming his own company. He drank moderately, smoked a little. There was nothing in his behavior that would remotely suggest he had become addicted to gambling. Henno, knowing Tim's background and ample income, allowed his credit to mount with his debts until it reached 8,000 Euros, at which time he demanded full payment. Tim was unable to raise the amount and was too ashamed to tell his parents. Henno had a gang of four reprobates who were his debt collectors. They began calling his place of work several times a day. They called his home where Mike and Eileen were upset by the coarseness

of their voices, giving them an inkling for the first time
that their son might be in some kind of trouble. Finally the
gang confronted Tim in the street, and threatened him and
his family unless the debt was paid immediately. At that
point Tim acquainted his parents with the details of what
had happened. He tried to express the shame and guilt he
felt and then fell into a state of apoplexy, a kind of numbed
stupor. His father took over the situation from that moment.
He waited a few days until Tim had recovered his strength.
Late one night he loaded his car with groceries and a strong
flashlight. He got Tim to hide under a blanket on the back
seat. He looked around the street where he lived, drove away
quickly and began the 130 kilometer drive to Athlone where
his motorboat was berthed.

Ted Forbes was in no position to come up quickly with
8,000 Euros to settle Tim's debt. Even with his fine house in
Cornelscourt to offer as collateral, the recent run on banks
had forced them to adopt a siege mentality and they would
not budge. At no time in his life had he seen the banks so
tight-fisted, so wary. One of the biggest disappointments
of his life was when his friend and golf partner Edward
Keller turned him down when he asked him for a loan of
the money. It wasn't so much the refusal that shocked and
surprised him; after all, with the Irish economy in tatters,
Keller must have his own dire issues to grapple with.
It was what happened later, after Keller refused him the
loan and then joined him later at the bar of the golf club
where they were members. He remembered so well how
upset, how aggrieved, the normally composed Keller was.
He had moved his bar stool closer to him and inclined his
head and whispered into his ear at the crowded bar. What
Keller imparted to him caused him to close his eyes briefly
in despair and disbelief. Keller spun a tale bordering on

the surreal; a preposterous criminal scheme involving the arson of his own property, to defraud an insurance company, to avoid bankruptcy and ruin. Finally, as if the Fire Chief was already a co-conspirator, Keller whispered about giving him 15,000 Euros to recover a timing device, and any other evidence that would suggest arson in the warehouse fire.

He stretched drowsily in the car. He had allowed himself, from tiredness, to fall into a restless sleep. Suddenly he was thrown into a state of alertness as the front passenger door was pulled open. Edward Keller had jumped hurriedly into the car. He was agitated and nervous, looking about him.

"It's too open around here. Drive up behind the house, find somewhere closed off to park."

Forbes drove towards Powerscourt House, turned right behind a long rectangular shed and parked out of sight. He reached down and searched under the driving seat. He brought up the broken timer used to set the warehouse fire. It was burned beyond recognition with the blackened wires attached. He handed it to Keller who looked at it for a few seconds. From an inside coat pocket he took a long thick envelope and handed it to Forbes. Forbes opened it, checked the contents and put it quickly into the glove compartment.

"It's all there," said Keller, "don't you want to count it?"

"I'll count it later," said Forbes, "right now we should get away from here. We better not be seen together."

He took Keller back to his car, and sped away fast. As he drove through the massive gates of Powerscourt demesne with 15,000 Euros, Forbes, a fastidious, careful man, was in the crux of a moral dilemma. Heretofore his deeds exemplified the cherished credos of his Catholic faith. He felt his rigorously held convictions were now compromised; he became a fraud the moment he retrieved the timing device from the fire scene, and issued a false report of the fire. His religious belief was the bedrock upon which he conducted his life's affairs. It filled him with confidence in dealing with the world at large, and the men under his command in particular. He shook his head in despair. The content of his character, his ethics and moral fiber came tumbling down like the Walls of Jericho, when put under enough pressure. It was a sickening fall from grace for the proud Fire Chief. 15,000 Euros! Of course he had to take the money, even as his conscience recoiled.

After he paid off his son's gambling debt, Tim Forbes pulled up stakes and went to Paris to begin life anew.

Life was not the same again for the Fire Chief when he reassumed his duties at the stationhouse. His brief sojourn into the nether world of criminal activity exacted a lasting personal toll on the life and times of Chief Forbes. His subordinates and friends noticed a puzzling behavioral change in his personality; a change that diminished his stature. He seemed lack-luster at best; his normally imposing authority gradually eroded as the days passed by. The militant spit and polish standards for the stationhouse and fire tenders deteriorated until the Chief became an object of derision for his men who gradually lost all fear and respect for him. His manner and indecision portrayed how much he had lost his way. The myriad of engaging expressions flitting across his face were but a masquerade to obscure the lost soul lingering within. Chief Forbes opted eventually to take early retirement. He spent most of his time alone on the golf links after he retired. His wife Rose was more than happy to have him home; it brought an end to the terror she felt every time he responded to an outbreak of fire.

Quite without warning, at the relatively young age of 53 years Edward Keller died of a heart attack. His death sent shock waves through the business sector of the city at a time when the faltering economy was beginning to see a run on the banks. The major part of his assets, holdings and portfolios of property was inherited by his son.

The death of Edward Keller made headline news. The funeral was attended by government and business leaders, dignitaries of the church and the many charities he had sponsored. Standing by his father's graveside Clive Keller lapsed into a quiet despair. As the graveside oration was read he made no attempt to suppress the flow of tears that fell from him. He closed his eyes and dwelled on how he had fallen so abysmally short of his father's expectations. No one among the packed congregation of mourners, with just one exception, would have believed business leader and philanthropist Edward Keller, left another, dark legacy behind him when he died. The exception was retired Fire Chief Ted Forbes. None present could have guessed at the feverish mind-set of Keller leading up to his premature death. His wife Rose said he had withdrawn within himself; he didn't want to see or talk to anyone, not even on the telephone. He slept badly and seemed to have an enormous weight on his shoulders. Up to his final moments, Keller was convinced his worst fears were about to unfold; about the warehouse fire, that either Fire Chief Ted Forbes, or Sean Buchanan, off in New York, would destroy his pristine reputation and legacy. His fears exacerbated the pressure on his damaged heart and hastened his demise.

After the funeral Clive Keller was too distressed and lacked the business savvy to take over the extensive network his father had founded. When he finally assumed control, it was at a time when the Irish economy was spinning out of control. Within a year of his death, his late father's corporate enterprises faced ruin: In an effort to postpone the inevitable doom, Clive Keller sold or liquidated company after company in an effort to remain solvent. The struggling Northstar Insurance Company was all he could finally salvage from the ashes of his father's empire.

Leonard Cobb dismounted from his horse after a brisk gallop over his vast property in Annamoe in County Wicklow. He kicked his boots off inside the door, asked the approaching servant to fix him a drink, and sat down in the living room. He picked up a letter delivered earlier and mused over it for the third time. It did no more than confirm his own suspicions, the probability, that the Wentworth Tech warehouse fire was the work of an arsonist. There was still no concrete proof. He slowly let the letter fall onto his lap. With anger building up inside it took an effort to prevent rising, heated emotions from displacing his calm state of mind. Drinking deeply from the glass the servant had laid before him, he relaxed the taut and jutted muscles of his face. It was two years since the time of the warehouse fire and his father's demise shortly after. He believed more than ever that the late Edward Keller was responsible for his father's death. He finished the drink and put the glass on the table beside him. His expression hardened again as he devised a strategy to exact revenge on Clive Keller, the present owner of Northstar, and bring the Company back to the Cobb family fold.

When Edward Keller purchased Wentworth Tech two years prior, he applied to the Cobb family owned Northstar Insurance Company to provide cover for his property. Several insurance companies had earlier refused him. The problem was the Wentworth Tech warehouse was filled to capacity with combustible material that made cover prohibitively expensive, but required by law. Northstar agreed to deal with Wentworth Tech as a last resort; like most insurance companies they were struggling in a failing economy. To limit risk, Northstar owner John Cobb, charged an exorbitant fee for the policy. It was at the time when Leonard Cobb, the chairman's son, was co-opted to the board of Northstar. He had recently graduated with honors from the Harvard Business School. Along the way he was tagged with the nickname wunderkind owing to the proclivity with which he maxed exams. When he became part of Northstar he was excited and happy; it was a family tradition. His grandfather Augustus Cobb founded the Northstar Insurance Company in the year 1918. The fortunes of Northstar gradually prospered in tandem with the integration of succeeding generations of the Cobb family into the life and times of the village of Annamoe in County Wicklow. From humble beginnings they grew in stature and social eminence within the village community. Indeed the family influence in the village became considerable over time. Augustus Cobb, a lover of horses, became a Master of Hounds. The annual hunt ball in the Cobb's manor house became famous over the years, drawing devotee expatriates from abroad, with sprinklings of Americans and Europeans. The family produced gifted progeny, including doctors, solicitors, politicians and sportsmen. In his time John Cobb took over as the hunt Master until an ailing heart forced him to pursue a less physical pastime. He ruled over his large family like a jovial elder statesman. They were keen spirited, unified siblings, exulting in a happy home life in the quiet pastoral setting in County Wicklow. Of his seven sons and daughters, all of whom he loved, it was known by all that his favorite was his youngest, Leonard Cobb.

Sean Buchanan graduated with a degree in business studies from Brooklyn College. He continued to be an employee of the US Postal Service and was promoted to Assistant Manager. By this time Buchanan had an agenda and was waiting for the propitious moment to make his next move; to return to Ireland. Another year passed and finally he prepared to make the voyage home. He handed in his notice to quit at the post office. When the day of his departure arrived he took a taxi to the JFK International Airport. The flight east across the Atlantic Ocean proved less stressful for Buchanan than the outward journey. He wondered wishfully if his accursed claustrophobia might be diminishing. He wondered if his four years in New York had altered who he really was. Time would do that, alter him regardless of circumstances. He felt older. He hoped whatever changes evolved in him would prove of enduring and deepening merit to his character and resolve. Why could he not perceive, with precise clarity, since it was his own mind and his own body that he was living in, who or what he was? At 28 years of age, he wondered from what well the essence, the fortitude of character sprung. Could the steadfastness of character that he aspired to, only be forged on the anvil of overcome adversity; the triumphing over the sea of troubles that constituted his life?

When the aircraft touched down in Dublin Airport at 9:00 AM the following morning, Buchanan made his way through customs and out to the taxi rank. He had to find the biggest taxi in the rank to accommodate his six suitcases and bag of golf clubs. A light rain began falling steadily as the taxi drove out of the airport. In the four years of his absence, he didn't notice too many changes as they wound their way out of the city to the western suburb of Drimnagh. He wasn't sure if he was mistaken but he thought he sensed a feeling of apathy, of resignation in the air. When he asked about the economy, the taxi driver went into an immediate diatribe about the Celtic Tiger and politicians driving the country to rack and ruin. He was still orating loudly when they reached the small council house in Mangerton Road, Drimnagh. Buchanan's mother, Paula, lived alone in the house. She was expecting him and was waiting for him at the front door. She was ecstatically happy to have her son home again. Buchanan settled into his old top front bedroom. He hung up his clothes and filled up the chest of drawers before going down and joining his mother in the sitting. She fussed over him as of old. She spent hours regaling him with all the news and gossip since his departure to the U.S. Later in the day as he stretched out on his bed he thought about bringing to a close his foremost concern: how to retrieve the incriminating tape that Edward Keller had of him breaking into the warehouse and stealing the computers. Before he could make any important decisions about his life or future, he must get back that tape. He could only guess as to where it might be. Since Keller senior had died, his son Clive now ran Northstar Insurance. He remembered Keller senior had the tape in a desk drawer; but that was in the old Wentworth Tech building. What had happened to the tape? Had Clive Keller seen it, how many others had he shown it to? He went to a sideboard, picked up a pack of cigarettes and lit one. It was a habit he picked up in Brooklyn to cope with the endless hours of study and endure the trauma of loneliness. He looked out on the wet grey drabness of Mangerton Road. The wind driven rain was heavier now and noisily pelted on the windows. He hadn't the faintest idea of how to unravel the problem of getting his hands on the tape. Its very existence made him a fugitive, it would just be a matter of time before he was arrested and put in jail. He must somehow, as much as the idea felt repugnant to him, find a way to inveigle himself into Clive Keller's good graces. He had never met Keller; the success of the plan that was forming in his mind was predicated on his own anonymity. From reading the

Irish Business Review and the newspapers, Buchanan had found out that the staff of Wentworth Tech had been made redundant when Keller bought control of Northstar, the running of which now fell to Clive Keller. There were no employees still around who would remember Buchanan had worked for Wentworth Tech. The biggest hurdle he had to overcome would be facing Clive Keller. How could he ask him to surrender the tape, if in fact he had it?

Over the following month Buchanan made it his business to find out as much as he could about the life and times of Clive Keller. He established that Keller was a member of the Kilternan Golf Club where he spent a lot of his time. The first order of business for Buchanan was to buy a car. He had been frugal with the money he had earned and saved in the U.S. He bought a two year old black Saab that was ideally suited to what he had in mind. In the second month of his homecoming he drove to the Grange Castle Golf Club. Dressed in a dark blue conservative suit and tie he walked through the foyer and asked to see the manager. He shook hands and introduced himself. He took from his wallet his Long Island golf membership card whereupon the manager invited him to his office. The manager was very impressed by the mien of Buchanan. He helped him fill out an application form and they spent some time chatting about New York. Without much ado he granted him membership of the club. Buchanan wrote out a cheque for the fee and left Golf Club with a sigh of relief.

Over the next two weeks Buchanan spent several days at the Kilternan Golf Club, honing his game. He chose times of the day when activity at the club was relatively quiet. He lingered in the lobby and club rooms, slowly perusing the photographs adorning the walls. His patience was rewarded when he stopped suddenly at a photograph of Clive Keller, with his name typed beneath. Buchanan inched closer when he saw the strong family resemblance in the facial features between Clive Keller and his deceased father. Now that he had located Keller, he had to face an inevitable confrontation with him. Only then would he know if Keller could identify him; if he had looked at the tape of the stolen computers.

On the following Friday night Buchanan stood before a mirror in his bedroom in Drimnagh. With meticulous care he tied the knot in his necktie. He reached out for the jacket of his grey double-breasted suit and put it on. He was satisfied with his reflection in the mirror; it was close enough to the impression he wanted to create. This was a big night for him. He would meet Clive Keller and could prove to be in dire circumstances as a result. He could end up being arrested; it all depended on how much Edward Keller had revealed about him to his son. He gave a wry smile at his reflection in the mirror; burglary and arson were hanging over his head like the Sword of Damocles.

Police Captain Noel Byrne Parked his car in Molesworth Street, Dublin. A light rain was falling as he mounted the flight of steps leading to the double-doored entrance of the Masonic Lodge. He was in plain clothes, with an overcoat and a fedora hat pulled well down. Even out of uniform he didn't like walking the streets of Dublin. It was with a sense of relief he inserted his key in the lock and pushed open the door. He hung up his hat and coat and climbed the carpeted staircase to the dining room. He walked with the assurance of familiarity through the lodge, having been a member of standing for the past 28 years. He sat at a table in the dining room, asked the waiter for a soft drink and sipped on it. He stood up as Leonard Cobb came to his table. They shook hands and sat down. The younger Cobb showed a marked respect and friendliness towards the police captain. He was a life-long friend of his father.

It was two years after the death of Edward Keller and the warehouse fire. Cobb was uncertain as to why Byrne had telephoned him and wanted to meet him. As Lodge members, their paths crossed often, sitting on various committees. After the warehouse fire, Byrne had commiserated with Cobb on the death of his father, knowing full well the young man held Edward Keller responsible for his father's death. Byrne led a quiet, some would say, monotonous life. He lived with his with his wife Emma in a comfortable, detached cottage in Clonee, five miles northeast of Dublin. He grew his own vegetables and had a small rose garden that occupied most of his spare time. It was no longer his habit to mix socially in the locality. He had done so before, but a few drunken thugs that he had earlier had bound over to the peace, confronted him in a shopping center. It was only his wife's coaxing that calmed him down. After that he resolved to stay away from the village. His friends, and his wife's, were Masons. His profession as a police captain was important to him. He was intensely proud of being a vanguard in societies moral and ethical crusade against crime. All important aspects of his life revolved around the Masonic Lodge. He made the ethics and principles enshrined in the Lodge's charter guidelines for his life. Among the many friends he had in the Lodge was the late John Cobb, his wife Ruth and their son Leonard.

Both men had solemn, thoughtful expressions as they sat across from each other at the table.

"Len," began Byrne, "I've got some things to say to you, and I don't rightly know where to begin. I'm at a stage in my life when I'm doing a lot of soul-searching. There are things on my mind that may, or may not have any bearing on reality."

"Whatever it is Mr. Byrne, I hope it's something I can help you with."

"I want you to cast your mind back a few years Len, back to that warehouse fire. Your father's company Northstar provided insurance cover. The whole debacle ruined his health . . ."

Cobb had gone very pale. His features became stern leaving his face cold and implacable.

"I did more than ruin his health Mr. Byrne, it killed him . . ."

"I know that Len, he was one of my best friends, as you know."

"What's all this about Mr. Byrne?"

"For the past few months I haven't been able to sleep well. I've been having crazy dreams . . ."

"The work of a Police Officer is very stress related, have you been to a doctor?"

"Oh sure, all he wants to do is put me on medication. I've never had to take a sleeping tablet in my life . . ."

Cobb looked closely at his friend. Byrne was 56 years old; a solid trusted friend. He was obviously disturbed about something, but so far he had no idea what he was talking about."

"You remember I was asked to investigate the fire by Garda Headquarters. That's what's been bothering me. How long ago was it?"

"It's been more than four years now. Eh . . , Mr. Byrne."

"Alright Len, I'm getting to it. Well, as you probably know I worked with Fire Chief Forbes. Something happened, it didn't seem important at the time . . ."

Captain Byrne proceeded to relate each detail of his and Forbes last day of investigating the fire scene in Wentworth Tech's warehouse. He told Cobb about the wiring Forbes had cut away from the fuse box; how he watched Forbes put the cut-away cable into his dungarees pocket.

"I don't know what I was thinking Len, Chief Forbes was a man I respected. I never liked him but he was a courageous fireman. When I saw him remove what I now believe was evidence of arson I, I was just dumbstruck. You see Len, just weeks before, that building had passed a safety inspection. In his press conference Chief Forbes said an old space heater had caused an electrical circuit to overload and ignite. I made it my business to talk to the janitor. He told me and I believed him; he said he never used the old heater because it wasn't working. He had been intending to throw it in the dumpster but he never got around to it."

"Mr. Byrne, can you hazard a guess about what he was doing with the wire-cutters?"

"Well, after we finished writing our reports, the following day I went back to the site on my own. I saw where he had cut away some wiring going down from the fuse box. Then he hacked away at the melted vinyl and pulled out something. It . . . , it had a shape to it. It was small and round, about the size of a tennis ball, according to the impression in the vinyl that covered it. There was something else . . . , there were fragments of glass embedded in the vinyl."

"Mr. Byrne, if only you had said something . . ."

"Say what Len, that I saw him put something in his pocket? He's a decorated, professional firefighter with decades of public service behind him. He has an unblemished record. Where's the evidence to accuse him of anything? He could sue me for defamation and that would be the end of my career. You can see that, can't you Len?"

"Yes, I suppose so."

"Len, don't despair. That's not to say I don't know in my gut that Chief Forbes was criminally irresponsible in his investigation and making a false report of the fire. The question is who had most to gain by saying the fire was accidental, and not arson?"

"Who else, Mr. Byrne? Edward Keller of course."

Clive Keller was sitting alone in the lounge of Kilternan Golf Club when a stranger came in and introduced himself. When Sean Buchanan expressed his condolence on the passing of his father, Keller invited him to join him in a drink. His cordial smile gave no indication that he knew Buchanan. Keller led him to the bar. Buchanan could feel his pulse pounding as he spoke with Keller. He stared at him, waiting, searching his face for the least sign that he had been recognized by the owner of Northstar Insurance. It took some time for Buchanan to re-gather his aplomb and breathe more freely. Whatever tangled or clogged path he may face tomorrow, tonight he had overcome the biggest hurdle. It was an incredible stroke of good fortune that Keller did not know who he was. After a few moments of idle banter, Buchanan, sipping a glass of white wine, said he had returned to Ireland from New York City, just a few days before. He was dressed in a grey tweed overcoat, dark grey suit, white shirt and blue silk tie. Keller was immediately taken by Buchanan's strong and assertive personality, his open, agreeable demeanor. When Keller invited him to dine with him in the club restaurant Buchanan smiled and nodded. As they waited to be served, Keller listened, intrigued by the detailed knowledge Buchanan had regarding his late father's business transactions, naming former CEO's and directors of now defunct companies. He was impressed by the concern Buchanan showed for his latest woes; the depressing results of Northstar in the marketplace. He was most surprised of all when Buchanan told him he had held a minor position in sales when his father bought Wentworth Tech. Normally staid and withdrawn in the presence of strangers, Keller, perhaps aided by a surfeit of strong wine, felt sufficiently uninhibited to ply Buchanan with endless questions. He felt there was something in Buchanan's character that inspired confidence and he wanted to know him. What was his background, Keller asked him, for whom did he work? What did he do in the way of work? Did he intend to return to New York? Buchanan told him he had held down a good job in the Carlisle Corporation, a furniture company in Manhattan in New York City. He also worked for the U.S. Postal Service. He felt he had a bright future with them but he had to quit and return to Ireland because of his mother's failing health. He was 28 years old, he had no siblings; there was no one else to care for her. He answered Keller's queries crisply and clearly, providing, verbally, names and dates of management positions he had held. Keller sat back in his chair, nodding agreeably. He admired what he saw as Buchanan's resilience in the face of his personal problems. He told him, if he wished, he would look to see if there was an opening for him in Northstar. Buchanan thanked him profusely. In the ensuing amiable repartee between them as the meal ended, Buchanan effected a subtle subservient demeanor that was not unappreciated by his host. When Keller emptied his wine glass and stood up, smiling graciously, Buchanan stood up with him. As they shook hands in parting, Keller, not so inebriated as to take a stranger at face value, or lack the savvy to put a measured rein on an impulsive philanthropic gesture, asked Buchanan to send him a copy of his curriculum vitae.

When Buchanan's CV arrived on his desk it showed he had a business degree from Brooklyn College and excellent job references. Keller read through it very carefully; these were trying times and he could not afford to hire irresponsibly. Buchanan had glowing references from the Carlisle Furniture Company in New York City; a company in which his father had a financial interest. They were sorry to lose him. He made a snap decision to hire Buchanan as a personal assistant. Buchanan was bright; he could do on-the-job training and learn the ins and outs of the insurance business. Further down the road, if he proved equal to the tasks assigned him he would give him a challenging role within the company. Feeling elated about hiring Buchanan he threw the pen down on the desk and reached for the telephone. He called the Managing Director of Northstar and told him of his decision to hire a personal assistant. The dumbfounded executive was shaking his head in disbelief as he put the receiver down slowly.

Northstar Insurance Company used the ground floor of a renovated five-storied Georgian tenement house on Dublin's Dawson Street. It had 14 employees down from a staff 0f 40 in its heyday when John Cobb was chairman of the company. They were the great old days, still fantasized about by the older hands. All that sense of bonhomie changed since Edward Keller took control of Northstar, and it passed on to his son Clive after his death.

Buchanan encountered some settling-in problems when he joined Northstar. No one could make sense of him being hired at all, considering the downturn in the crippled economy. The Managing Director saw him as a direct threat and it was as much as he could do to extend common civility to him. The older staff generally was critical of Buchanan despite his efforts to blend in and be cordial. He seemed to some to have an attitude of self-importance. The inquisition continued apace in Northstar's Friday night binges in The Bailey pub. Noreen, the long serving and long suffering secretary of Northstar since the days of John Cobbs presidency said that whatever the reason may be that Mr. Keller offered Mr. Buchanan a job, it couldn't be because they were old school chums; she was emphatic about that. When pressed, she laid her second cognac down on the bar, exulting in the limelight. She patted her hair.

"Mr. Buchanan," she said, "could not be deemed to be on a social parity with Mr. Keller, it takes more than a business suit to be a gentleman. Mr. Buchanan is in just too much of a hurry; he's got an agenda, believe you me."

An old timer in the group, well into his cups, passed the remark that Mr. Buchanan must be one of those new entrepreneurs. A giggle was raised when some wag said that the Irish for entrepreneur was chancer. Some were critical of, among other things, his general demeanor. Oh, he had a great smile and peppered his conversation with endless jokes some of which were deemed to be insensitive at best. There was something oddly secretive about him that couldn't be pinned down.

It was generally agreed that Keller and Buchanan were ill-matched as friends. It wasn't so much that the relationship lacked cohesion, which it did, but given the diametrically opposed character and personality traits of both men, merged in a business environment could only prove dysfunctional at best. Buchanan was taller than Keller; he had a confident personality that came with a short sharp temper that didn't endure fools well. It was a constant struggle to curb his natural inclination to cynicism. He had a commanding voice and with regards to observing social etiquette, was considered to be somewhat rough around the edges. It seemed that in befriending Buchanan and making him a personal assistant, Keller was seeking out the same assertive, self-confident traits that defined his father's character, qualities that made him feel secure, that equated with success. Clive Keller had an agreeable, very affable personality in social gatherings where there was a noticeable absence of angst and stress of any kind. In such a setting he could charm all and sundry with his wit and ready humor. Attending to business in Northstar board and shareholders meetings, where he was called to account for questionable decisions, was anathema to him.

Gratefully Buchanan was now always on his right at such gatherings, deflecting or absorbing blame; taking on his own shoulders reproaches directed at him. After a few months Buchanan became so adept at conducting meetings he had but to raise his voice an octave to quell any dissonance remotely aimed at Keller. He became indispensable to Keller's peace of mind. A few weeks later, he asked Buchanan to come to his office with the express intent of promoting his assistant. Buchanan sat across the desk from Keller and listened quietly as Keller sang his praises and offered to elevate his status within Northstar Insurance. When he had finished speaking Keller sat back in his seat and smiled paternally, waiting expectantly for gushing exhortations of gratitude and praise. He waited in vain. Buchanan stared back at him grimly, his mouth set in a resolute line. The prolonged silence unsettled Keller; he felt himself lapsing into a despondent mood. As they stared at each other across his desk, a certain uneasiness now cast a fleeting shadow across the face of Keller. Something, barely perceptible, had changed Buchanan's mood; the benign facial expression was gone, his face was a mask of grim truculence. The prolonged staring made Keller feel uneasy and challenged. He had spent his adult life avoiding confrontations of any kind; he despised that weak aspect in his character because it undermined his value to himself. He knew, that in order to avoid serious stress or anxiety he would ultimately concede to compromise.

Buchanan stood up from the desk and walked over to the ground floor rear window that looked out into a secluded, ill-kempt back garden. Keller felt he was dealing with a different person from the one he hired as a personal assistant. Buchanan mood seemed bitter and resolute as he turned around to face Keller.

"We need to talk Clive." He said

Looking at the man whom he had hired as his personal assistant, now addressing him with this brazen attitude, the reason and origin of which he knew nothing, he felt he was fast approaching one of those unsavory moments of his life, rife with stress and anxiety wherein he would be forced to capitulate, to concede, to compromise, to cave in to adversity. Buchanan had come back from the window and resumed his seat. The silence became a stifling chasm between the two men. He couldn't begin to guess what was going through Buchanan's mind. He had been more than generous with him, gave him a job, opportunities to advance in Northstar. Why this adversarial posturing?

"What's on your mind Sean?" he said.

"Well, I didn't want it to come to this. I appreciate your offer of promotion and all that. But the fact is, there are things I have to say that you are not going to like . . . I'm sorry, I truly am . . ."

"Whatever you want to say, let's have. I've always been honest with you and I don't appreciate this . . . , this skulduggery from you."

Buchanan became grim faced. He was unhurried, deliberate.

"What I'm about to tell you is completely my own fault, it's got nothing to do with you. You see, your father . . ."

Buchanan's voice trailed off until it sounded like an echo chamber inside Keller's head. What new challenges, what new stress was Buchanan about to assail him with? Would he recoil and take flight as was his traditional wont, in coping with stress and contention? Would his timorous and affable character induce him towards appeasement and compromise, yet again? Or would he for once find the gall to fight; to break the mold of his self-inflicted creed that made of him a consummate coward. He felt anger taking root within him and he fought to control it. He felt if he lost his temper he would lose his humanity, he'd be a traitor to his background, his upbringing. He had never, not for a single moment seen his favorite role model, his father, lose his temper. Before him sat a virtual stranger upon whom he had heaped abundant favors and who was becoming confrontational and he hadn't the least idea why. He sat erect in his chair. The voice of Buchanan was droning on. "I'm just sorry it had to be you . . ."

"Sean, I don't know if it's something I've said or done that's put you in this state of mind. I don't wish to pry into your personal affairs but, is your mother's health ok, is that what's bothering you?"

Buchanan flinched and stared at Keller. He looked disoriented for a moment before he recovered his composure.

"eh . . . , no, no. My mother's doing fine . . ."

"I'm glad to hear it . . ." Keller stood up from the desk. With his hands thrust into his trousers pockets he sat on the front edge of the desk looking down at Buchanan. "How long have you been working for me . . . ?"

"About three months."

"Any complaints about of any kind, about how I've been treating you so far, any of my staff giving you a hard time . . . ?"

Buchanan began to fidget uncomfortably in his chair. His expression softened significantly as he became subdued. His face flushed crimson.

"No, but you don't understand . . ."

"How the hell do you expect me to understand if you won't tell me. And what was that you just said about my father?"

Keller went slowly back to his desk. He sat down and leaned back in the upholstered armchair and waited.

"I've told you already," began Buchanan, in a more conciliatory tone, "that I worked for your father in Wentworth Tech. I worked as a salesman. I might as well come out and say it, I was a thief, and a compulsive liar at that time of my life. I don't know why I was that way, I just was. One night I broke into the warehouse and stole lot of computers. The security cameras caught me on tape. Your father waited for a few weeks to call me to his office. He played the tape of me doing the break-in. I listened to him in a state of shock while he made a proposition to me. He said I could avoid jail time if I did something for him."

Buchanan stood up, walked to the back window and looked out. As night was falling all he could see was the reflection of the office behind him in the window. He went back to his chair. Keller sat motionless, watching his every move.

"I have what is called chronic claustrophobia. It's an unreasonable fear of the dark and enclosed spaces. Like a prison cell for instance, it's difficult to explain if you don't have it."

"I'm sorry for your personal problems, but what's all this got to do with my father?"

"I'm coming to that. And when I tell you, unless you have something constructive to say I don't want to listen to any indignant denials, or arguments from you, because I know you won't believe what I'm going to tell you. All this happened when your father's business was going under. The Celtic Tiger was fizzling out, your father's debts were massive and the banking sector was collapsing. He couldn't borrow one penny, no matter where he looked. In me, your father found the means to escape ruin, to avoid the shame and disgrace of bankruptcy."

He was looking steadily at Keller. He hadn't flinched.

"Your father told me he'd have me locked up in a prison cell unless I set fire to his Wentworth Tech warehouse in Santry. He showed me the tape of the night I broke in and stole the computers. It was irrefutable evidence of my guilt. He didn't mince words, your father; he told me he had influential friends in the police and on the bench, meaning judges. That's when I realized just what kind of a man your father really was: You see, I had just told him about my claustrophobia, I thought, I hoped I might solicit . . . , well, some kind of compassion from him, and do you know what he said to me . . . ? He said he'd see to it that I'd spend the rest of my life in a padded cell unless I did what he wanted."

For a moment Keller looked as if he wanted to interrupt Buchanan. He shook his head slowly, as if in disbelief.

"Go on," he said.

"This company, Northstar Insurance, once belonged to a man by the name of John Cobb. Just like every other business of the time, Northstar under John Cobb was suffering from a down-spiraling economy. His company got a massive break, or so it seemed, when your father asked him to provide insurance cover for his new Wentworth Tech property and two-story warehouse. Because his own company was in trouble financially, John Cobb charged an exorbitant fee to insure Wentworth Tech for 200,000 Euros. Your father paid the fee. When he caught me stealing, I was delivered into his hands like a sacrificial lamb, and he made the most of it. With the threat of a prison cell hanging over me, I was his to command."

Buchanan suddenly stood up, clearly agitated. He ignored Keller who was sitting zombie-like, with his arms folded. He continued to talk as he walked about the office.

"Your father was in a hurry, and he was blunt. His bank was about to foreclose on existing loans, he was pressed for time. He wanted Wentworth Tech to go up in flames. He had every detail figured out. He took a timing devise from a wall safe and showed me how to use it. It was simplicity itself; all I had to do was press an on/off switch. He said he would connect the timer to a cable going into a fuse box in the warehouse. After that he planned to spend a week in Paris on company business. All I had to do was break into the warehouse again, and turn the timer on. This time, he assured me, the security cameras would be turned off."

He sat down. His breathing came in stifled gasps.

"For Chrisake," he said to Keller, "what manner of man was he, to think up something like that? And what bothered me most, apart from my phobias and such, was the small housing estate next to the warehouse. People could be incinerated if those houses got caught in the fire. When I said I wouldn't do it he said it was that or a padded cell. I couldn't get through to him. He was obsessed with getting his hands on that insurance cheque, nothing else mattered. Well, I set fire to the building and he got what he wanted; a big fat insurance cheque from Northstar. I read a report of the fire when I got to London. It was an act of God the wind was blowing away from the nearby houses. I hated myself for cringing like a coward and becoming an accomplice in his murderous scheme. Well, in the heel of the hunt, it all turned out to be a successful caper for your father."

Buchanan sat up and made a dramatic flourish with his arms, and gave a cynical smile as he looked at Keller.

"This company, Northstar, that you now own, was bought on the settlement of a fraudulent insurance claim, a claim that forced John Cobb into bankruptcy. Can't you see the delicious irony in all of it? Your father got 200,000 Euros from the insurance company for torching his own building, and ends up owning the insurance company. How lucky can you get?"

Keller looked as if he had given up on an inner fight, a turmoil within himself. His expression was one of resignation.

"There's something else . . ." said Buchanan.

"I don't want to hear anything more . . . , you've said enough."

"No, there's something else, I should say someone else. There had to be a third man to bring the whole fraud to a closure. I was in London, your father was in Paris. Someone had to cut away the timing device from the fuse box that would have proved arson was the cause of the fire. The investigating officer reported nothing untoward, which meant a false report was made out. The next question is, who was the third man?"

Keller ignored the question. He was struggling with the enormous impact of everything Buchanan had told him.

"I've got a question of my own." Said Keller.

"Oh . . . ,?

"And if I do ask you some questions, are you going to give me the runaround? Just tell me why I should ever again believe anything that comes out of your mouth?"

Buchanan seemed to be caught off guard by the sharp invective of from Buchanan.

"It wasn't by accident you walked into my golf club," said Keller, "and wormed your way into this company, was it?"

"To answer your question, no, it took a long time in the planning . . . , but I . . ."

"And the reason you gave me for coming home from New York, your mother's bad health, that was another lie, wasn't it? Well, congratulations, and for what it's worth, you really made a sap out of me." Keller smiled, a cynical, humorless smile, "you know, I thought you were the real McCoy. I thought together we were going to get this company moving. I believed with you on board we could get on top of this failed economy, beat the daylights out of our competitors and come out of this with flying colors."

"But I want that to happen, to work with you . . . ?

"Now enlighten me. What's the reason for this elaborate charade of yours, what are you after?"

Buchanan had lapsed into a brooding, thoughtful silence.

"Cat cut your tongue?" Said Keller, "you never struck me as a man lost for words . . ."

Buchanan aroused himself. His eyes were dull, disoriented. He blinked and tried to focus on Keller.

"I can't blame you for a moment, judging me as you do. You'd have to be me to understand. I was born with this affliction, and it affects every waking moment. I try to cope with life, with this hanging over me, this phobia. Every living organism fights for survival, for life. If I'm locked up in a small space, I'll turn into a vegetable; I'll become mentally incompetent, sooner or later. I tried to explain that to your father, but he just used it to his advantage. My being here is all about the tape your father had of me stealing the computers from his warehouse. I just want to get it and burn it so I can breathe freely again; think of a future again. I've saved some money, I'd give every cent I have to get that tape back and become a normal human being again."

"Well, I can't do a thing for you. I've never seen any tape such as you describe . . ."

"Oh, well then, all is lost . . ."

"My father did leave behind some old trunks and boxes. Mostly souvenirs of his travels. A lot of it is junk. Everything was stored away in the cellar of our home."

"Do you think you could search for it."

"Let me tell you something. I'm just as anxious as you are to find that tape and see it destroyed, but not for your sake. Whatever criminal wrongdoing my father may have done, for my mother's sake I want his reputation protected. She couldn't withstand the shock of having his legacy vilified. I'll search the basement; if the tape is there I will contact you. Now, there's something you better understand. From this moment you are no longer my business assistant. Send me a letter of resignation. Now would you please get out of my sight . . . ?"

Buchanan did not move for a few moments. He was about to say something to Keller but changed his mind. He walked thoughtfully, slowly out of the office.

Early on the following Saturday Clive Keller drove out to the high-elevated landscape of County Wicklow to the scenic village of Annamoe. He had telephoned Leonard Cobb to say he was coming to see him. A stunned silence ensued after which he impressed upon Cobb the serious portent of what he wanted to discuss. He finally pulled up at the well-preserved manor house and parked the car. He took out his briefcase, went to the house and pressed doorbell. As he was expected, the door was opened almost immediately by an elderly maid. She took his gloves and overcoat and led him to a drawing room, where he sat and waited. Some minutes passed during which he heard several voices which seemed to carry from an upstairs landing. One male voice was more vocal, louder than the rest. A door closed and the sounds became muffled. Behind him a French door that led into a back garden opened and into the room stepped a middle-aged, matronly woman, carring a basket with some gardening tools. Immediately behind her, wearing a floral patterned dress, a young woman carried a tray with potted plants. They had not at first noticed Keller who was sitting with his back to them on a high-backed sofa. He raised himself slightly off the sofa when he heard them entering the drawing room. From the moment he laid eyes on the younger woman Keller's mouth fell slightly ajar. She was about 24 years old and seemed to skip into the room. She had a radiant Hellenic beauty that made him catch his breath. Her shining black hair was thrown back over her shoulders. Her face was animated and smiling as if she had been indulging in jovial pleasantries. When Keller stood up and coughed to let his presence be known, they looked at him in surprise, and smiled cordially. The older woman approached him first.

"Good morning, who has left you alone like this? Whoever it was I'll give them a piece of my mind. Oh, excuse my manners. My name is Helen Cobb. I'm the mother of everyone around here. And oh, this is my youngest daughter, Siobhan."

Keller shook hands with both women. Siobhan stood by her mother's side and smiled at Keller. She was tall and elegant. It was as much as he could do to drag his eyes from Siobhan to look at her mother.

"My name is Clive Keller. I'm very pleased to meet you both."

For the most infinitesimal measure of time, Keller's name impacted Helen Cobb's aura of graciousness. A chimera, too fleeting to create an impression, departed the moment it crossed her brow. His name did not register with Siobhan, but she was looking at him curiously.

"Your face looks sort of familiar. Have we met . . . ?"

"No, no, I am certain we have not. Oh no, I assure you Miss, I would have remembered . . ."

Siobhan looked at her mother and they both smiled warmly as Helen Cobb turned to Keller.

"Tell me, which one in my family did you come to see."

"Mr. Leonard Cobb."

"Ah, Len, do you know each other?"

"No Ma'am, we have never met."

"Well, I apologize for my son's tardiness. I'll go get him . . ."

Helen left the room and closed the door behind her.

"I don't want to impose, really. I don't mind waiting . . ."

Keller involuntarily looked at Siobhan, regretted what he said instantly and began to blush.

"Forgive me . . . ," he said, "perhaps . . ."

At that moment the door was thrown open and Leonard Cobb entered the room. His face looked grim as he approached Keller. Siobhan ran towards him and linked her arm through his. She was acting demurely and with some interest towards Keller. When she looked at her brother's grim aspect, she stepped forward and stretched out her hand towards Keller.

"It's been really nice meeting you Mr. Keller. I still can't help feeling I've seen you before. I'll leave you two . . . , goodbye." She turned on her heels and exited the room.

Cobb brusquely pointed to two armchairs with a coffee table between. They were in close proximity when they sat down. Cobb's austere features had not altered since he entered the room."

"You invited yourself here, what is it you wanted to talk about?"

"I'm not going to waste your time or mine. I'll be direct in what I have to say."

"That would be appreciated."

"I've just got some information from what I consider a reliable source. First let me say I had no idea what happened to the Wentworth Tech warehouse fire. Now that I know it was arson, I understand why I was not told every sordid detail."

"Who did you get that information from?"

"That's none of your concern. And let me tell you, if you decide to call the police, even if it means going to prison, I will never reveal the source of my information. Go ahead and call the police if you have a mind to, I'll wait here until they come and arrest me."

"Well, now let me be blunt. I couldn't care less if you went to prison for 100 years; if you know the name of the arsonist, you're aiding and abetting a serious crime. You're protecting someone who made my father bankrupt, ruined his health and caused his death. You've got some gall, coming here. What do you want?"

"I want to make restitution . . ."

"What . . . ?"

"Restitution . . . Northstar Insurance was taken from your father by fraudulent means. I want to make amends for the sins of my father. I owe you a life; I can't give you your father's life back. I can give you back the property my father took from your family . . ."

Keller reached down and put his briefcase on the coffee table. He unsnapped the locks and took out two large manila envelopes. He placed them on the coffee table in front of Cobb, who now bore an expression of incredulity.

"I know nothing can compensate you and your family," said Keller, "for the loss of your father. I wish I could undo the tragedy your family has suffered. In those envelopes you will find deeds, titles and documents of ownership of

Northstar Insurance Company. You will honor me if you will accept Northstar as a partial reparation for the injustice caused to your family by my father. As you will see by the audits the company has achieved some degree of success in the marketplace, considering the weak economy. They're a good team in Northstar. I would hasten to recommend, if you so wish, that you retain the present staff. Some of the old staff have been with Northstar a long time. I've often heard them speak of your father in glowing terms. Oh, and there is a new employee, Sean Buchanan. He worked for a company in New York that your father had shareholdings in. He has excellent business acumen, I would recommend him without hesitation."

From the outset Cobb listened to Keller with the emotion of heightened anger clearly written across his face. As Keller continued, Cobb's expression gradually changed from incredulity to amazement.

"I'm not sure if I understand. What are you saying, do you want me to buy back Northstar?"

"I'm suggesting nothing of the kind; It's yours, lock stock and barrel. I want Northstar back to its rightful owner."

"But .. , but," said Cobb, "how much will it cost me? I'm not sure I could raise .. ?"

"It won't cost you one red cent ...."

"I don't understand .. , why are you doing this?"

"I'm doing it for my father .... , and my mother. He lost his way there for a while. He did things that were out of character. Personally, I think it was the pressure of business, it affected his mind and his judgment. If you knew him, as my mother and I knew him, I think you would understand."

He pointed to the manila folders.

"Everything you need is there. Have your solicitors draw up the necessary papers to transfer Northstar back to you.

The company will then return to where it belongs. It has, after all, been in your family for over 100 years."

Keller stood up and looked at his watch.

"Send those papers to me and I'll sign them right away. And now Mr. Cobb, I'll say goodbye. I . . . ?

Cobb jumped immediately to his feet. He grasped the envelopes close to his chest.

"No . . , no," said Cobb, "you can't leave like this. I'm not a person who excites easily, but this, this is simply unheard of . . . No, wait, I must tell my mother, she won't believe it, please, just give me a moment."

Cobb rushed from the room. Keller could hear him raising his voice, mustering his family for an impromptu meeting on the wide staircase. Absolute silence prevailed as he quietly regaled the proceedings with Keller, surrounded by his mother and siblings. Stifled gasps, an utterance of disbelief, shrieks of suppressed joy, loud acclimations all emanated from the family gathered on the staircase, listening to Leonard Cobb. As one, they rushed back into the drawing room, to stop and stare at a wide-eyed Clive Keller, standing still and holding his briefcase. Keller was overwhelmed. He was ushered to the large sofa where he was seated and plied with endless questions. Leonard Cobb put the envelopes on the table and went back to watch Keller. He saw the young business man who but moments before had been a sworn enemy, basking in a wealth of heartfelt veneration from his family. And rightly so, he thought, after such a magnanimous deed. His four sisters and three brothers, all accomplished and successful in their chosen careers, were not, by nature, easily impressed nor placated. The youngest sister, 24 year old Siobhan, in her last year at university, sitting next to Keller, was moved to tears by the enormity of what had transgressed. She had adored her late father and was very affected by his passing. When she looked at Keller, he too was moved by her emotional distress. Her mother, who was sitting on a chair in front of Keller, took her daughter's hand.

"Well, young man," she said loudly and cheerfully, "what must you think of us at all? We haven't even offered you a cup of tea, or would you prefer coffee?"

"Oh, I .., really, tea would be fine."

"We have a nice wine, unless it's too early."

"A glass of wine would be very nice. Thank you."

"Siobhan," said her mother, "come and help me fill up some glasses."

Siobhan dried her moist eyes and jumped up joyfully. She walked hand in hand with her mother to the kitchen. While they were gone Leonard Cobb and the eldest sibling of the family, Adam, placed chairs in a semi-circle in front of the sofa. Keller didn't seem to mind being the center of attention. His austere demeanor gradually relaxed as he began to interact cordially with everyone present. His eyes wandered to the kitchen from time to time.

"I've been a solicitor quite a while now Mr. Keller," said Adam Cobb, "I've never witnessed such a . . . , a grand gesture in my life. You've fair taken my breath away . . ."

"Oh, well, it was just doing the right thing . . ."

He was delighted to see Siobhan and her mother come back from the kitchen, laden with salvers of wine glasses. They filled the glasses with wine and handed them around. The mother, Helen stood up and raised her glass.

"I can't adequately express what's in my heart, Mr. Keller, but I know I speak for all my family when I tell you how happy you have made us this day. I'd like to propose a toast, for the health and happiness of Mr. Cobb. God bless you Sir."

All present, save for Keller, stood up and joined Helen in her toast. Siobhan reached for her handkerchief and dabbed her eyes, but she was smiling as her eyes filled with tears. When all were sitting again, Keller raised his glass.

"Thank you so much," He said, raising his glass, "a toast your family, one and all. It warms my heart to be among you. May I ask of everyone, Mr. Cobb sounds awful, if you could call me Clive."

His request was greeted with smiles of acquiescence.

"I hope you will forgive me," said Gladys, an architect by profession, "but I'm sure we are all concerned, but what will you do now, for work I mean . . . ?"

"I have some investments that are holding their own, quite adequate for my needs."

"But you could stay with Northstar surely," said Leonard, "as you say the company is trading well."

"Well Leonard, do you know I've really never felt business was in my blood. I tried, but that was just to please my father . . ."

"But you did so well, the results prove that . . . ," said Maureen, a well-known Actress.

"That was a matter of luck, really. I was fortunate enough to have a good team behind me."

"You are too modest, Clive," said Helen, "you were the motivator, the captain of the ship . . ."

"May I ask you," said Siobhan meekly, "did you discuss this transfer of Northstar with your wife?"

"Oh, no I'm not married . . ."

"What about your girlfriend?" Said Siobhan, "excuse me, I shouldn't . . ."

"No, I'm afraid I don't have much of a social life . . . I had a girlfriend but she couldn't cope with the hours I spent in the office . . ."

Siobhan sat back in her chair. A suggestion of a smile played about the corners of her lips. She tried to avoid the knowing looks of her siblings.

"I'll have to place where I've seen you, I just can't remember. But I don't get out very much either, I'm in Trinity all day, and studying all night . . ."

"Oh, you are in Trinity . . . ?" Asked Keller. "What are you studying?"

"I'm majoring in geology, did you go to Trinity?"

"They were the happiest days of my life."

"Really, what did you do . . . ?"

"I started business studies, but I hated every minute of it, so I did art, and discovered a whole new world . . ."

Siobhan made a sudden exclamation of surprise. She raised her hands to her cheeks as she stared at Keller.

"Ah, now I remember now . . . You were the impressionist painter that caused such a fuss. Yes, it comes back to me now. I went to one of your lectures. Do you still paint?"

"There has been just no time to paint, what with coping with the business, board meetings and that. But now, I will have the time; the more I think about painting again, the more excited I become."

Helen turned sideways and had a few moments conversation with Leonard, and then with Siobhan. They both nodded eagerly.

"Clive," said Helen, "I was just wondering if you live alone?"

"Oh no, I live with my mother in the family home in Foxrock. I was born there."

"Have you or your mother any engagements tonight?"

"My mother is very much like myself, we don't go out much. No, we don't have any plans for tonight . . ."

"Well then, why don't you and your mother join us here for dinner? We would be delighted to have you both."

"For dinner?" Said Keller with a fleeting glance at a smiling Siobhan, "why yes, my mother and I will be delighted."

Shortly afterwards Keller bid farewell to the Cobb family. When he arrived home he filled in his mother about the mornings events and the invitation to dinner. Rose Keller, in whom her son confided everything, was in total agreement with her son's decision to return Northstar Insurance to the Cobb family.

Sean Buchanan was alone and despondent in his small bedroom in the council house in Drimnagh, Dublin. It was early morning, three weeks after he had lost his job as Personal Assistant to Clive Keller. He was anxious and confused about what to do next. He was out of a job and didn't how to go about getting one. His primary concern, the source of all his distress; was to get the tape, the evidence that could send him to prison for a long time. He felt vulnerable, near to breaking point. It was 2:00 P:M in the afternoon, when he heard the doorbell ring. He went to the window, opened it and looked down to see a van driver handing a package to his mother. He quickly went downstairs, signed for the package and took it into the sitting room. His mother called out to say she was going to do some shopping. He heard the front door close behind her as he sat down in from of the fire. He feverishly ripped off the covering of the package and finally sat back in the armchair as in a trance. He held in his hands a black cassette tape. A small note with it contained a few words,

'As promised. It was locked in my father's safe. No one else has seen it.'

The package had no name or return address. He went to the television set, turned it on and pushed the tape into the cassette player. He sat back and watched himself break into the Wentworth Tech warehouse and steal the computers. He suddenly jumped up, extracted the tape from the player and threw into the fire. Picking up the poker, he raked the smoking plastic over the coals until the last vestige of the tape was reduced to ashes. When he sat back down he was emotionally spent. Having spent so many years fretting over the destructive potential of the tape, now that it was gone he felt almost weak.

Three days later a postman arrived again, this time with a certified letter. Buchanan signed for it, took it to his room and opened it apprehensively. The return address showed it came from Northstar Insurance. He took the letter out, read it wide-eyed and fell down on the side of the bed. Leonard Cobb wanted to interview him for the position of Director of Sales for Northstar Insurance.

Clive Keller entered the large foyer of the Gresham Hotel in O'Connell Street, Dublin. He waved to Alan Pembroke who had risen from his seat to greet him. They shook hands and sat down at a coffee table. Pembroke sat on the board of trustees in Trinity College. He was also an old friend of the late Edward Keller. He proved to be eagerly receptive to a letter Clive Keller sent to him just days before, to arrange their meeting. Keller, who had retired from business at so young an age, wanted to teach art in Trinity. He wanted to become a member of the faculty. Pembroke and his Trinity colleagues were excited at the prospect of having Keller with them again. He was well remembered for the way he stimulated a broad interest in art. He was an inspirational lecturer. His impressionist paintings garnered fame beyond the walls of Trinity. Pembroke confirmed Keller's appointment to the staff of the famous university. He would begin his classes on the following Monday. When they parted company, Keller went into the hotel dining room where he was shown a table. He sat down and ordered two glass of white wine, while he patiently waited for his paramour. He looked at his watch. Every moment would be an eternity until he beheld her. He was madly, divinely in love. Siobhan Cobb breezed through the foyer towards his table. She exuded grace and confidence as she took his hand and kissed him. A finger of her left hand was decorated with a diamond engagement ring. She picked up the waiting glass of wine. They raised their glasses to each other.

If happiness could be equated with wealth, Sean Buchanan, by his own admission, was among the wealthiest of men. He had a very successful career as the Sales Director for Northstar Insurance Company. We find our enterprising pilgrim in the pilot seat of a small Cessna 140 propeller driven aircraft, which he recently purchased. He is soaring alone in the clear blue skies over Newcastle airfield in County Wicklow. After six months of training, it's Buchanan's first time to pilot the aircraft solo. He maneuvered the Cessna down to the airstrip to make a perfect landing.

After parking the aircraft Buchanan got into his car and picked up the N50 motorway to Dublin. When he reached Drimnagh, a large moving van was parked outside his mother's house. Several men were loading the contents of the house into the van. His mother was at the door, looking a little lost. She had lived in the house for over 30 years, since the day she got married. Buchanan was born there. He knew the flood of memories of times past, would dwell on her mind. But it would pass. She had already seen the new house they would be moving to. It was in Greystones, where she used to take excursions to when she was a child. It was right beside the sea. Her son had hired live-in help, a retired nurse to help her with her health and chores around the house.

Dinah Buchanan was so proud to see her son come up in the world. She had guided and encouraged him through all the years of his life.

"Sean," she used to say to him, "study hard and one day you will see. You will be somebody."

Buchanan had a few words with the van driver. He settled his mother into the passenger seat of the car and began the drive to Greystones. Buchanan was moving on.

THE END